Worth the Fight

L.D. Davis

Prologue

Fool (noun)
1. a silly or stupid person; a person who lacks judgment or sense.
2. a professional jester, formerly kept by a person of royal or noble rank for amusement: the court fool.
3. a person who has been tricked or deceived into appearing or acting silly or stupid: to make a fool of someone.
4. an ardent enthusiast who cannot resist an opportunity to indulge an enthusiasm
5. a weak-minded or idiotic person.

I was every definition of the word. I was the man who lacked judgment or sense. I'd been kept by a person, apparently for her amusement. I'd been deceived into acting stupid—both by my keeper and myself. The enthusiasm I irresistibly indulged in was the said keeper.

To have endured all the above for several months, I was definitely an idiotic person.

I repeatedly gave her the benefit of doubt. She wasn't herself. The woman I loved and had loved for some time would not normally put either of us in such difficult circumstances. The woman I loved—the real one, not the imposter who'd taken her place—was strong in mind and soul. She had an abundance of confidence and knew she deserved respect, happiness, and monogamy. She would've never gotten involved with her boss, especially her boss who had a steady girlfriend, and she certainly wouldn't have lied to her doting boyfriend's face day after day.

The woman I loved wouldn't do any of that.

She wasn't the most innocent person, but she wasn't cruel. This woman—this other female who'd taken her place—was malicious and weak, and I was tired of her slowly breaking my heart.

When you know in your bones, right down to the cellular level, you're supposed to be with someone, it's hard to simply walk away. When you know beyond a shadow of a doubt someone is your soul mate, the one person in the universe you cannot be without, it's hard to just give her up, even if she crushes you under her foot while whispering sweet nothings onto your tongue. Every time I considered pulling away and leaving her, I felt physical and emotional pain that nearly crippled me.

So, I hung on.

For months.

But I couldn't hang on anymore.

I'd just have to suffer and find a way to deal with the agony. The longer I'd stay, the more pain she'd inflict.

I knew she was on her way over. She was excited to go to the beach and have fun, pretending the other one wasn't waiting for her somewhere when the day came to an end. I hadn't spoken to her in a couple of days, other than a few short text messages. I needed time to make the necessary phone calls and convince my family, who'd come to love her, why they needed to let her go. I also needed every ounce of strength I could muster to do what I deemed necessary. I couldn't risk her weakening me with her kisses, her touches, her smiles, or incredible sex.

The heavy creak of the front door and then the soft pads of feet heading toward the bedroom alerted me to her arrival. I shifted slightly where I stood. My movement, as quiet as it was, must have notified her of my presence. I heard her light footsteps pause and then change direction. As soon as she saw me, her smiling, beautiful—*so beautiful*—face began to change. She was the other half of my existence. Surely she could feel something bad was about to go down.

"Lena's not doing as well as we'd hoped." My quiet words broke through the still air in the room. At least I didn't have to make anything up. I didn't have to stoop to her level and lie. My sister was very sick. The thought nearly choked me, and I had to resist the urge to walk across the room and find comfort in her arms.

"I'm sorry." Sincerity glistened in her eyes, and it seemed as though she wanted to approach me, but she hesitated. I was glad. If she touched me, I might've changed my mind.

"I'm going to leave sooner than I planned."

"How soon?" Her voice became unusually high and her eyes widened.

"Next week." I stood stiffly, trying to ignore everything about her that would typically drive me crazy. Like the way her teeth sank into her plump lip. "By the end of next week."

Emmy took a step back as if my tone alone was frightening. Good. She should've been afraid.

Adding another nail to her coffin, I said, "I've decided I don't want you to come with me."

I watched her delicate throat bob and constrict as she struggled to swallow. The corners of her mouth twitched with an attempt to smile, but it came off as awkward and made her appear uneasy.

"I understand. You have a lot going on with your sister and family."

"This isn't about my family. It's about you. I don't want you." I uttered the words as coldly as I could manage, wanting her to *feel* their icy stabs of pain.

It worked. Her smile faded and she took another step back.

"I thought if I gave you some time, you'd make a decision." I tried to be firm, but my emotions were hard to keep down. They leaked into my words, seeped into my voice, and I couldn't keep them hidden. "I thought you'd stop stringing me along as a backup and really commit, but you haven't. You're still seeing Kyle."

Her eyes closed and she swayed slightly at the impact of my words. I should've cared that she looked like she was going to fall, but coldness trickled in, adding to my anger and hurt. I didn't know it was possible to feel indifference, anger, maligned, and unbearable grief simultaneously.

Until now.

She hung her head. Tears slipped down her cheeks. I wanted to slap them off her face, but I don't hit women. Ever. I'd rather die than hit her, but the desire didn't fade easily. She knew she was caught, the charade was over, but it didn't stop me from telling her the rest of my thoughts.

"I'm not sure which part bothers me the most: the fact you've been lying for months, or that you thought I was too stupid to see what was going on. I can't count the number of times you've lied about where you were or who you were with, or the times you climbed into my bed still reeking of him. How many times have I kissed you and your mind was with him? I've given you opportunity after opportunity to come clean, but you never did."

She continued to stare at the floor. She wasn't brave enough to even look at me, to see the man she fucking broke! She had the courage to spread her legs for that asshole and lie to my face, but she couldn't meet my stare. How Ironic.

I growled and stepped toward her. I spoke softly, my tone laced with unspeakable threats. "At least give me the courtesy of looking in my fucking face while I am talking."

Slowly, she raised her head and met my stare. Her shame was palpable, her eyes filled with self-degradation and regret, but it was too late. I didn't care if she detested herself. She deserved to loathe herself. Hell, she deserved my animosity, too, but despite my conflicting emotions, I couldn't make myself hate her.

"I looked like the biggest idiot at work, committing myself to the girl who was obviously fucking Kyle Sterling."

She gaped at me in surprise. Surely she wasn't that dense. I almost snorted. Had she taken her mouth off his dick long enough to look around, she wouldn't have been so shocked.

"Everyone knows, Emmy," I told her. "Despite your sneaking around, people still know. You both think everyone else is too dumb to figure it out."

She shook her head in disbelief, which infuriated me. Fire raced through my veins. This was the biggest response I'd gotten out of her, and it was because everyone else knew she was a slut, not because I, alone, knew she was.

"Don't you fucking shake your head." A fierce growl erupted from my chest as I pointed in her face.

She backed away from me with fear blazing bright in her eyes, but I didn't care. I wanted her to be afraid. I pushed forward until I had her backed against a wall.

"You're more upset everyone else knows than you are about *me* knowing!"

She jerked her head in reflex at the decibel of my voice when I yelled, and hit her head on the wall. On any other day, I would've immediately felt bad and made sure she was okay, but this wasn't any other day. I hoped she hurt her head, though I knew it would never compare to my own pain.

"No, that's not true," she protested and wiped at her tears.

It only fueled my fire. "Like I can believe anything you say now!"

"I'm so sorry," she sobbed.

"Maybe you are, but I don't forgive you. I can't even forgive myself for falling in love with you, knowing you were Kyle's whore." My voice was sharp, deep, and filled with abhorrence.

She turned to me with wide, teary eyes. She'd never witnessed me behave like this before—ever. I never had a reason to. Apparently, Emmy brought out the worst in me. She glanced away from me, toward the living room, as if she contemplated leaving. It's not possible for her to believe she could do the shit she did and just slither away.

I saw red—only red.

My anger and pain consumed me.

I roared as my fist moved on its own accord and slammed through the wall only a couple inches from her head. She screamed and winced, cowering as though she thought I'd hit her. I backed off. I wouldn't strike her, but the chances of me handling her too roughly were very high.

"Luke, your hand!" She reached for my fist, but I shifted away. I could barely feel the dull pain in my knuckles. The ache in my chest muted every physical discomfort in the rest of my body. The complete silence around us made it easier to hear the soft patter of blood dripping from the tips of my fingers and hitting the floor below.

"At least let me help you take care of your hand," she begged, cautiously reaching for me again.

I let her. I don't know why. I was beyond angry and not even sure I was in full control of my actions, but I allowed her to nurse my injured hand. I couldn't take my eyes off her. She was gorgeous, even crying and sad, but she was dangerous.

She ruined me.

I was completely decimated.

There would never be anyone else for me other than her, but she was already gone. She'd been gone for a long time. I just hadn't accepted it.

Her fingertips lightly flitted over my wrist, and I fought not to touch her.

"I didn't know how to let go of either one of you," she whispered.

I forced my voice to remain ice-cold. "Fortunately, I made that decision for you."

Tears erupted from her sorrow-filled eyes. She sobbed until she looked like she'd collapse. I hated her for crying. I loved her for crying. I fucking hated the conflicting emotions.

She released my injured hand and began to turn away from me. I wasn't in control of my actions; otherwise, I would've stopped her. My traitorous desires made me crush her body to mine and kiss her with every emotion running though me. It went against every ounce of angst she made me feel. It hurt me to kiss her—I knew I'd never do it again.

I forced myself to stop. I held her chin in my hands and wiped away her tears with my thumbs. Her face blurred before me as my own pain overflowed and spilled down my face.

"Listen to me." My voice broke with the strain of my words. "I don't ever want to see you after today. Don't call me, don't text me, don't email me. Whatever relationship you were building with my family, it's done. They've already cut you off at my request."

God. This was it. This was the end. It was over. I was over.

I'd die without her.

I would die *with* her.

"I love you, Emmy, but you fucking broke my heart. I know I'm partly to blame, I know, but…" I stared at her hard. I wanted her to know how much I meant my next words.

I wanted her to feel pain as I felt it.

"I hope Kyle Sterling rips your heart out of your chest and makes you choke on it."

Chapter One

My cell phone was wedged between my shoulder and my ear while I listened to the woman on the other end bitch about my lack of commitment. I juggled my briefcase and my duffel bag as I unlocked the door to my apartment before kicking it open. I dropped the bag on the floor by the door after it closed behind me and set my briefcase down with more care.

"Claire, I told you in the beginning I wasn't looking for anything serious." A wave of exhaustion hit me when I pulled open the fridge to get a much needed beer. "I was very clear about it, and you said you were fine with it."

I should've known better than to believe she'd be okay for more than a few weeks. Claire wasn't a casual-sex kind of girl—she was a settle-down-and-get-married-and-have-kids kind of girl. I knew that very well. I had dated her for a year before moving to Philly many years ago, but she'd been adamant she could handle a casual relationship.

"I thought you just needed some time to deal with whatever the hell you had going on in your head," she whined. "I thought you'd come around."

I took a pull on my beer and rolled my eyes at this bullshit. I didn't realize she was so stupid. "Have I ever been anything but straight forward with you, Claire? Have I ever said one thing and meant another in all the years you've known me?"

She paused for a moment before answering. "No, but...but you were never...brokenhearted before. The circumstances are different."

I closed my eyes for a moment. The last thing I wanted to talk about was the state of my heart.

"Yes," I reluctantly agreed. "The circumstances are different, but that doesn't change my direct approach."

"I turned down other guys for you, Luke!"

I suppressed a frustrated groan as I dropped down onto the couch. "You could've ended our agreement at any time if you wanted to be with someone else. Listen, Claire, I don't mean to hurt you. I really don't. The last thing I want to do is hurt anyone, but..."

"But what?" she snapped. "But you want to sleep with other women? Is that it, Luke?"

"Not at all." I glanced at the pile of mail on my coffee table, remembering my sister Lena told me I had a letter delivered by courier yesterday. "I don't sleep with more than one woman at a time, Claire. You know me better than that, but I don't want a relationship, either."

She said something in response, but I didn't really hear her. The envelope on top of the pile caught my eye. I wasn't sure if my brain registered it correctly until I picked it up and held it only inches from my face.

Emmy sent me a letter.

I was disappointed how my heart rate suddenly increased, and further disappointed at how my hands itched to open the envelope, but a large part of me wasn't sure if it was something I wanted to unveil. After months of trying to push any memory of her out of my head—only to be repeatedly reminded of her when I saw her mother—I had at least gotten to the point where she wasn't the first thing on my mind when I woke up and the last thing on my mind when I went to sleep. I'd finally gotten to the point where my pain was dulled, and more often than not, forgotten. I was able to go days without thinking of her more than once or twice a day, opposed to the constant torture of hearing her voice in my head and smelling her skin in the weeks and months after I broke up with her.

"Are you listening to me?" she whined again. I realized at that moment how much Claire whined, which was a lot. Even during sex, she did this weird sniveling thing she probably thought was sexy, but it really wasn't. Not even a little.

"I gotta go," I said, distracted. "I'll call you soon."

I didn't give her an opportunity to respond before ending the call and dropping my phone on the couch beside me. I stared at the envelope, weighing it in my hands. After all this time, I had no idea what she could've possibly had to say to me.

"Only one way to find out." I exhaled and began to slowly peel open the mail. I pulled out the folded paper inside. I could burn it or push it into the garbage disposal and not worry about whatever Emmy had to say. I could put it back in the envelope, reseal it, and send it back without looking at it. I was tempted to do any one of those things. I had finally started to move on, and I didn't want to find myself stuck on someone who didn't deserve my time or my thoughts, but I knew I had to open it, even though I had a gut feeling it was about to change my life.

I unfolded the letter and began to read.

Dear Luke,

I have rewritten this letter a dozen times already, but I feel there is no smooth way to lead up to what I have to say, so here it is: You are the father of a five month old, beautiful baby boy. His name is Lucas, in honor of his father, and he was born May 18th.

I didn't tell you because I know you hate me, and my biggest fear is that you will hate my son, too. Maybe that fear is unreasonable, but I have had a very hard time getting past it.

I am in Chicago for a day or so, at the Fairmont, room 317. If you would like to meet your son, I will be here all day today.
I am sorry for keeping this from you, and I am sorry for forcing my mother to keep this from you. Please don't be angry with her. It is my fault entirely.

Sincerely,
Emmy

The paper fluttered to the floor as I stared at nothing with my mouth hanging wide open.

This had to have been a joke. It couldn't have possibly been true. Even Emmy wasn't that cruel to keep a child away from me, and her mother was the bluntest person I knew. Surely, she would've fallen over herself to tell me about my son—if I really even had one.

And then I realized something. Samantha didn't go out of her way to spend as much time with me as she did with my sisters. I didn't think anything about it because they were all women, and women tend to cluster together, but she could've been avoiding me. It's possible those looks of pity weren't for her daughter destroying my heart, or that my sister was near death, but because she knew a big, earth-shattering secret.

"Shit!" I jumped off the couch and dashed for the door. I took a detour into the small kitchen for my keys and then ran out into the hall.

I rocketed out of the parking garage and onto the street, just barely missing oncoming traffic. I hated driving in the city and usually took public transportation, but I was anxious to get to the Fairmont. My mind raced all the way there, and I couldn't keep hold of any one thought before another rushed forward to take its place. It wasn't until I dashed into the lobby a little while later another thought occurred to me, halting me in my tracks and knocking the breath out of me.

Lucas might not have been my kid at all. He could've very well been Kyle Sterling's.

"Can I help you, sir?" the woman in guest services asked me.

It took me a few seconds, but I was able to tell her why I was there before I started toward the bank of elevators.

"Miss Grayne stepped out," she called after me. "Can I have your name?"

I stopped and took a few steps back until I stood in front of her again. "Luke Kessler." I was curious as to why she needed my name.

She smiled at me. "Yes, I was expecting you yesterday. Miss Grayne and the baby went out a little while ago. Maybe you can wait for her in the lobby." She gestured toward the fancy furniture behind me.

I nodded and wordlessly walked away from her. There was nothing to say. One thing was confirmed: there definitely was a baby. The question was whether or not he was mine. This was definitely something Emmy wouldn't drag me into if Lucas wasn't my kid, but the possibility still existed that he may not have been. I wouldn't know. But I had to wonder what I'd do about it if he was. I was so confused and jolted.

Suddenly feeling like an ass for showing up to meet my son for the first time empty handed, I got up and marched to the gift shop. There were little shirts with Chicago scrolled across them, but I didn't know what size the kid was. There were little sippy cups and a few other baby items, but I didn't like any of it. I wasn't going to give my kid some cheesy souvenir shop gift—*if* he was my kid.

I told the woman at guest services I would be back shortly. I rushed out of the hotel and used my cell phone to find a store to buy Lucas a gift. Once inside the baby store, I felt overwhelmed by all the possibilities. There were so many items, things I'd never seen before or heard of. Emmy and Sam probably made sure Lucas had everything he could've ever needed, so I walked away from the gadgets and headed toward an aisle of toys.

As I searched through the options, I pondered what I liked as a kid. Hell, he was five months old. He probably liked anything that tasted halfway decent when it went into his mouth. I picked up a little stuffed whale. It reminded me of a vacation my family took to Sea World when I was little. My parents were hard-working, lower-middle-class people. Trips to Sea World and the like were few and far between—if ever. It hit me then how hard it must've been for them to afford that trip. I don't know how they'd continued to feed us and keep a roof over our heads the months preceding and following. But my parents wanted to make sure we actually went somewhere and did something. They tried to give us a little more than what their parents were able to provide to them.

If the baby was indeed my kid, I wanted to be able to give him more than what my parents gave me, too.

I took the whale to the checkout line. Lucas or Emmy may not understand the significance of the whale, but I would. Besides, it was a sensible gift to give my son who I was just meeting for the first time, though nothing else about the situation was sensible.

I returned to the Fairmont and sat back down in the chair I'd been in earlier. I had an unobstructed view of the entrance. I didn't take my eyes off it. I'm not even sure I blinked. There's no telling how long I stared before I saw first a stroller full of bags roll inside, and then the waves of brown hair stuck to her face from the October wind. I watched as she pushed the strands off her smooth cheek and smiled at the blond hair, blue-eyed infant in her arm before continuing to push the stroller with her spare hand.

Even from where I seemed to be stuck in the chair, I could see Lucas was my son.

Somehow I pushed myself up and moved across the lobby until I stood in their path. As soon as our eyes met, I felt immeasurable emotion from anger to fear and remarkably, love. For half a moment, I wanted nothing more than to take Em and our son into my arms and make everything the way it should've always been.

But then I remembered she fucking broke my heart.

I inhaled sharply as that old knife twisted in my chest, and then I turned my attention to my child.

My son.

I stared in awe at the replica of my own startling blue eyes, gazing back at me in wonder. I fought back emotions as I offered him my finger before remembering I had touched all kinds of gross things since leaving my apartment, and I didn't want my fingers in his mouth.

"You didn't come," Emmy blurted out.

I felt bad for her for a minute. It must have been torture for her as she waited for me to respond. She must've thought I didn't want Lucas, and I couldn't imagine how that must've felt.

"Yeah, I'm sorry," I said. "I was out of town. My sister just happened to be in my apartment dropping off some things I left in her basement when the letter came. I didn't read it until this morning when I got in."

I looked at her, hoping she believed me.

"I understand." She shifted the baby from one arm to another. "Can I hold him?"

"Of course."

Carefully, she passed him to me. Again, I had to fight back emotions as I regarded this perfect baby boy I helped create. I had a great relationship with all my nieces and nephews, and at one point

17

in my life, I had wanted children, but after what I went through with Emmy, I hadn't considered it again. However, only moments after meeting Lucas, I knew I'd never be the same. I was grateful to hold my son.

****

I stayed with them all day that day. I played with Lucas, I talked to him, I held him, I changed him, and I only released him long enough for him to get fed. I should've turned away when I saw how uncomfortable she was breastfeeding him in front of me, but it wasn't about her. It was about our child. Everything about him was perfect, and I couldn't take my eyes off him, even though he was suckling on his exposed mother.

I'd only been with him a short time, but I couldn't imagine just leaving and having to deal with child custody agreements and the distance that would surely be between us when Emmy went back to wherever the hell she came from. Moreover, if she was with Kyle, I'd have to fight to make sure Lucas knew who his real father was. The idea I would have to go up against Kyle again for someone else I loved infuriated me. I let him win last time, because Emmy stopped being worth the trouble when she allowed the situation to continue, but I refused to let him win my son.

As the day wore on, I grew angrier with Em for keeping my child from me. It stirred the pot of negativity I'd been carrying around for her. When Lucas took a nap, I threw myself into my work, virtually ignoring her so I wouldn't snap—and I was very close. I had never in my life hit a woman, but the urge to put my hands around her throat and squeeze was pretty damn overwhelming. My sense of right and wrong, and the fact our child was sleeping a few feet away, were the only thing that saved her from my wrath that day. I couldn't even look at her, but I chanced one glance and immediately regretted it.

Besides the fact she looked like a scared, trapped, and wounded animal, Emmy was breathtaking. Her hair had grown significantly and the extra pounds she'd put on during her pregnancy gave her curves she'd never had before. Her skin seemed softer, and I desperately wanted to touch her to find out. Instead, I made some ridiculous comment about her hair growing out, and the sound of the baby waking from his nap stopped me from saying anything further.

I went back to virtually ignoring her until Lucas went to bed for the night. Still seething mad, I turned to her to confront her, but I bit my tongue when I saw the sullen frown on her face. She was actually pouting. I scratched my head, trying to figure this out, but then I realized I'd completely monopolized Lucas, and Em didn't get much time with him herself. I couldn't blame her. He was a remarkable kid.

Reflexively, my hand lifted as if to pat her knee, or something else equally comforting, but I remembered who she was and what she'd done and kept my hands to myself when I spoke. "I'm sorry. I totally took over today"

"I'm not used to sharing him." Her gaze fell to her hands in her lap. She hadn't made eye contact since I first saw them in the lobby earlier in the day.

"I'm going to go pick up some dinner." Forcing myself to ignore her, I moved toward the door. "We'll talk when I get back."

"Hold on," she said and hurried into the bedroom. She returned a moment later and held out a room key to me. "You can let yourself back in. I'm going to take a shower."

When I took the key card from her, my fingers grazed hers. I was pissed off at the tremors of electricity that shot up my fingers and through my arm. It irritated me she still had that effect on me after all she had done.

I quickly pulled away and rushed out of the door.

By the time I returned with the food later, the sun had set. I stood by a window watching the headlights on the cars in city below as people went on with their evening activities, completely oblivious to the abrupt changes in my life.

I had a son. I was someone's father. I wondered if that fact would ever cease to be amazing and shocking.

There was nothing but white noise on the baby monitor, which meant Lucas was probably still asleep. Emmy had told me he'd sleep for several hours, if not through the night, but I wanted to see him again.

As I approached the semi-closed bedroom door, I could hear the shower still running in the master bath. I quietly went inside toward the crib, but my eyes drifted to the bathroom door, which was also slightly ajar. The scent of her favorite strawberry shampoo wafted out on a few billows of steam.

Maybe I shouldn't have been in the room. Maybe I should've waited for her in the living room, but she could take off in the morning and I'd never see my child again. I wanted to soak up every second I could get with him, even if he was asleep.

I leaned over the crib and watched as his little mouth made suckling motions. I couldn't believe I'd missed not only the first five months of his life, but every minute of the pregnancy. I missed sonograms, measurements, and most of all, his birth. I would've given anything to have been there when he was born. The fact Emmy denied me all of that made me want to snatch my son out of his crib and take him from her so she'd know how it felt, but I pushed those irrational thoughts away and thanked god I still had a chance—albeit, late. I looked at his little fingers attached to his little hands, and the wisps of blond hair across his forehead. His tiny chest rose and fell easily and his soft snores made me smile.

The bathroom door opened and I heard Emmy's sharp intake of breath when she saw me. I'd been so absorbed in Lucas I hadn't heard the shower stop.

"Sorry." I glanced over at her, taking note she was wrapped in a towel. I looked back at the crib. "I'm just...amazed. He's perfect."

"Yes, he is," she agreed softly.

I turned to her again. Her wet hair clung to her bare shoulders. The towel didn't hide her curves or the swells of her full breasts. If things were as they should've been, I would've relieved her of her towel and made love to her damp body.

But things weren't as they should have been.

Emmy cheated on me for months after I had given her my heart. Even after I told her I hoped Kyle broke her heart and made her choke on it, if she would've dropped everything and everyone and came after me in Chicago, I would've given in and taken her back.

But she didn't.

And that crushed me, too.

Then she hid her pregnancy from me, probably had plans to raise my son with that dick Kyle. She hid Lucas's birth, and for five months of his life, denied him his father. I never did anything to deserve such disgusting treatment. I did nothing but love her and then let her go so she could be with that asshole, yet she punished me relentlessly. My heart broke all over again as I stared at her in that towel. This time, however, the pain was so much deeper because my absence from my son's life was also heartbreaking.

I did what I needed to so I wouldn't do anything I'd regret with Lucas in the room. I turned away from this woman, the only woman in the world who still held the power to break me.

Chapter Two

Emmy squeezed herself into the corner of the couch, trying to shrink away from my harsh words. The couch appeared to morph into something that was about to eat—no, consume—her. I'd been downright cruel, and she didn't defend herself, not even a little bit—defeat was etched into her features. The Emmy I left behind in New Jersey wouldn't have let me verbally abuse her, whether she was in the wrong or not. This woman just sat there and took it. I never believed in attacking someone unwilling to fight for themselves, so I changed course.

"You do love Lucas, though," I said, pulling my anger in. "You're a good mother, I'll give you that."

She nodded, but didn't meet my eyes. It was obvious in the way she stared at the wall across the room that she was unwilling to look at me, but I couldn't take my eyes off her. My range of emotions waffled between anger and hurt, but pieces of me felt sorrow for her. This couldn't have been easy, even if she put herself in this precarious position in the first place by withholding such pertinent information. If I didn't hate and love her equally at the moment, I would've tried to soothe her, but then, I didn't really think she deserved sympathy.

I moved on.

"Anyway. I have to put the past behind me, for Lucas's sake. I want to be part of his life. I just started my own firm, so I'm not really in a position to do too much traveling right now. I don't know anything about your situation." I paused, unsure if I really wanted to know the answer to the question I was about to ask. I needed to know how much I'd have to fight to get her and Lucas where I needed them. "Do you have a job to get back to in Philly? Or anyone waiting?"

Her olive green eyes widened, the golden brown flecks becoming more prevalent as she finally met my gaze, shaking her head slowly. "I haven't been in Philly since January. My family packed up the house and sold it."

"You loved that house." I was surprised I hadn't heard about it before now. Another fact Samantha failed to reveal.

Emmy tried to shrug it off, but I could hear the pain in her voice when she spoke. "Whatever sentiment I had attached to that house was obliterated."

I had no clue what the hell happened in that house after I left. My first instinct was Kyle Sterling did something shitty. I couldn't shake the idea from my head, but I didn't want to ask. It wasn't the time, and honestly, I wasn't sure how I'd react. Instead, I asked the next obvious question.

"You say your family packed up—where were you?"

"The French countryside."

I was baffled at the French countryside's appeal. No one does that. No one just picks up and moves to the French countryside for the hell of it. She made it seem like she'd just gone to the beach for a few weeks or something.

"Is that where you live?"

"Oh, no. I've been stateside since the month before Lucas was born. I'm not really tied down anywhere."

I carefully worded my next question. "No boyfriends or anything?"

Her eyes slid away, and her body shifted slightly, as if she were uncomfortable. "If you're wondering about Kyle Sterling, I haven't seen him since I left Philly."

"I was curious, but it wasn't just about him," I said, though it really was mostly about him. I had to know if there was some other man in my son's life.

"I'm completely single." Her dismal tone matched the complete emptiness in her eyes, the soft sag of her shoulders, and the pathetic way she slumped almost inward.

Despite her reaction, I was relieved. I was able to breathe a little easier, but then I had to finish telling her my thoughts and plans on how this would work.

I ran my hand over my head and said, "I've been thinking about this most of the day."

Her eyes flitted over me curiously. "Thinking about what?"

"I want you and Lucas to move in with me."

Emmy froze. I knew I was asking her to change her whole life, but she owed me this. In the very least, I deserved to be near my son.

"It'll be good for Lucas to have his parents raising him together, at least at first. It gives him the best of both worlds. Developmentally speaking, he'll do well to have us both there at once. We'll both be able to participate in the everyday little things parents get to experience with a child. I don't want to miss *anything*," I said doggedly, even though my voice trembled on that last word. My hands balled into fists as I waited for her response. I needed her to give me this.

She responded with a small, skeptical voice. "What if you start seeing someone?"

I noted how she didn't ask the question of herself.

"I'm not seeing anyone, not really." There was no need to bring up Claire. "That's a bridge we'll have to cross when we get to it."

Emmy scrunched her nose up for a brief second. It was an analogy she hated, one I'd forgotten about until now.

"You won't have to worry about anything. I'll take care of the bills, buying the diapers and provide whatever you and Lucas may need."

"That won't be an issue. I can take care of me and Lucas," she quickly responded.

"Then take care of yourself if you insist, but I want to take care of my son."

She eased out a long breath. Anxiously, I waited for her to speak again, which took a couple of agonizing minutes.

"How big is your apartment? Lucas needs a crib and some other things."

"It's small, but you and Lucas can have my room. I'll take the couch. We can look for a bigger place later." I took a breath to keep myself from getting my hopes up too soon. "Does this mean you'll do it?"

Very slowly, she nodded. I released a sigh of relief and actually found myself smiling at her. She tried to smile back, but failed. Instead, she just looked plain scared.

****

I walked into my sister's house, unannounced without knocking. It was almost midnight, but I knew I'd find Lena in the kitchen sipping on a cup of hot cocoa. Even when she was at her sickest, she didn't deviate from this nightly ritual. She waited until all the kids and Chuck were in bed, or otherwise occupied, and made her cocoa the old fashioned way in a pot on the stove with real milk. She didn't care about the calories or the sugar. It was her way of unwinding, and it was one of few things she gave herself. Rarely did I interrupt this ritual, but these were special circumstances.

"Hello, little brother," she said from the kitchen table. She didn't look at all surprised to see me as she pushed a second steaming mug in my direction. "I was expecting you. Take a seat."

I hesitated before sitting down. I wasn't sure if she had expected me because she saw the letter I received, or if she knew about my son before me. My sisters and Emmy's mom, Samantha, were very close. I'd hated it at first, when she had pushed herself into my family after her daughter had broken my heart, but she and her husband, Fred Sr., were such a big support system for my family. I'm not sure what any of us would've done without Sam's big mouth and need to nurture.

I sat down across from Lena and looked into her blue eyes. Her eyes and my sister Lorraine's eyes weren't as shockingly blue as my own, but they were close. Hers were a little duller after battling breast cancer, but they were still alive, and they still seeped into my mind and soul like no one else's in the world.

Five years my senior, Lena had never treated me like a pesky little brother as most older siblings did. She'd been my best friend growing up, the person I could rely on to play with me when I'd had no one else, help me with my homework when my parents were working, and bandage my knees after I'd fallen off my bike. She'd attended all my sporting events, drove me and my friends around when she'd gotten her license, and she'd given great advice when girls became a factor. When I'd broken it off with Emmy, she hadn't offered her opinion on the matter, even though she and the rest of the family had adored her. I knew she'd wanted me to give Em another chance, but she never pushed the issue. She had simply been there for me, even though she had been in the middle of the fight of her life.

"He's beautiful, isn't he?" she asked quietly as she observed me.

I dropped my attention to my cocoa. It caused me great pain to know Lena knew about Lucas before me. "You've seen him before?"

"Just in pictures. I was giving Emmy the benefit of doubt. I knew she'd eventually come around and tell you on her own."

"You should have told me just the same," I said bitterly.

"I was afraid if anyone else told you but her, you'd overreact, and then she'd overreact and possibly run. Everything could've turned into one big pile of shit if things had happened that way, but they're not now. Right?"

"Right," I admitted grudgingly, knowing that she was correct, but it still didn't feel good to be the last to know. "Does Mom know? Lorraine?"

"No. Only Chuck and I do."

She sipped on her hot chocolate, and followed her lead. I was relieved to know my entire family had not been keeping the big secret from me.

"I asked Emmy to move in with me," I admitted after a few quiet moments.

"Did she say yes?"

I scowled. "Yes. If I could keep Lucas without her, I would, but I'm not that cruel."

"She did what she thought was best, Luke."

"Then her thought process is obviously flawed, Lena."

"I understand you're hurt and angry, but you're going to have to deal with it. You have to show your son how to treat women, even if it's the woman who broke his heart."

I let out a long breath and nodded in agreement. "I understand."

She studied me for a few quiet moments. Softly, she asked, "How do you feel?"

I narrowed my eyes at her. "What do you mean how do I feel? I'm angry and I'm hurt. I missed five months of my son's life—that's if you don't include the nine months he was in the womb. I feel this huge gaping hole inside of me I didn't have before. I know I shouldn't really feel this way today, but missing that chunk of Lucas's life is killing me."

She pushed out of her chair and walked the few steps to me. I immediately wrapped my arms around my sister's waist. I was shocked and ashamed when I felt the tears slipping past my closed eyelids.

"I didn't even have time to get my shit together," I sobbed. "She didn't even give me the time she had during the pregnancy to come to grips with being a parent. I have no fucking idea how to be someone's dad, Lena!"

My sister didn't try to hush me, and she didn't tell me everything would be okay. I always appreciated how she wasn't a bull-shitter.

"No kid comes with a manual, Luke." Her chest rumbled with a small laugh. "Whether you had nine months or nine years, you'll be trying to figure out whether or not you're doing the right thing for your kids for the rest of your life. We're all grown up and Mom still questions some of her decisions. You just have to do the best you can do, put your best foot forward and always put Lucas before yourself, before his mother, before anyone else in the world."

"I don't know how to do that and deal with Emmy, too. I fucking hate her, and I fucking love her. Being so close to her breaks my damn heart all over again. I'm so damn angry."

"You'll find a way to deal with it. You need to try to prepare for Lucas's homecoming."

I nodded in agreement. Lena stepped away, and I stood up, wiping at my eyes.

"Thank you."

"I didn't say anything profound." Her grin crinkled the corners of her tired eyes. "In fact, I wasn't very helpful at all."

"You were here for me…as always. I appreciate that."

"I always will be. Listen, why don't you bring them over for dinner tomorrow? I'll break the news to Mom and Lorraine, and we'll have a nice welcome party for your baby."

"Okay." I nodded. "That sounds like a good plan."

"Excellent!" She clasped her hands together with too much enthusiasm for this time of night. "I get to meet my nephew."

I shook my head with a small chuckle. "I better go. I have a lot to do. Thanks for the cocoa."

She hugged me. "No problem, little brother."

I left Lena's with a clear head and a determination I lacked deep down when I'd asked Emmy to move in with me. I sucked up my girly tears and drove back to my apartment, eager to make it a home for Lucas.

Chapter Three

I stayed up more than half the night looking for the best and safest baby items. I wasn't about to let my son sleep in some subpar crib on flammable sheets in clothing that would leave him itchy and red. I didn't care how much it'd cost me, though I may have snickered at the expensive top-of-the-line items my sister Lorraine had bought for her kids in the past. No kid needed a Gucci diaper bag. But there I was, entertaining the idea of buying an upscale version for my own child.

After a couple hours sleep, I pushed myself off my couch where I had crashed, and started the coffee pot in the kitchen. I had to clean and baby proof the apartment. I wasn't a pig or anything, but when you're used to being a single guy living alone without anyone to answer to, you kind of don't care much if you leave a few—or a lot—of dirty dishes in the sink and on the counters, or if the milk and eggs in your fridge predate the discovery of fire. You tend not to care that you have piles of dirty laundry on your floor or that some of it smells like sweat and ass. Though Lena was awesome, she was not the kind of big sister to come into my house and clean it. She had dropped off some of the crap I'd left in her basement before I got my apartment and left the mess as it was.

I put my coffee in a travel mug so it wouldn't spill and took it with me as I went room to room cleaning. I pushed all my dirty clothes into bags and called a laundry service to come take care of it. I wasn't opposed to doing my own, but I had too much to do in preparation for Lucas and Emmy. When the apartment looked pretty decent and actually smelled clean, I took a quick shower and got ready to pick them up.

Claire called on my way out. She had called me several times yesterday, but I had ignored her calls. She'd been the least of my worries and the furthest thing from my mind after I'd found out about Lucas. I mentally prepared myself for the blasting I knew I was going to get, and answered.

"What the hell?" she whined. "You cut me off yesterday and ignored my calls and texts. I get you don't want to be my boyfriend, but even for a friend that's a pretty shitty thing to do."

"I know," I agreed. "I apologize but something very important came up."

"What was so important you couldn't send me a text that said 'hey, I apologize, but something very important came up'?"

As an attorney, I was often put on the spot and had to think quickly, but now, I stumbled over my words. I didn't know how Claire would react, but after half a minute of silence, I realized it didn't matter. She wasn't my girlfriend, and Lucas would always come first, but I wasn't a complete asshole.

I checked my watch. I could spare a half hour before meeting Emmy, but not much more.

"Can you meet me at the coffee shop around the corner from your office?" I asked her.

"Sure, I guess. When?"

"I'll be there in ten or fifteen minutes."

"Okay," she said warily. "Must be something pretty heavy if you need to meet me in a public place."

I didn't respond. I told her I'd see her in a few and hung up.

I found Claire in the café a little while later, seated at a small table all the way in the back. Our relationship was casual; I hardly owed her a big explanation, but I had known her since I was thirteen years old, dated her for a year many years ago, and remained friends with her thereafter. I wasn't the nicest guy, but I wasn't a dirt bag, either.

"Hey," I said, taking the seat across from her.

"Hey." She eyed me with caution.

Her short blond hair was pulled back in a small ponytail at the base of her neck. Her dark blue eyes raked over me as they always did, assessing me. She was thin with sharp cheekbones and virtually had no curves on her body, but she was pretty nonetheless. She could've been a European supermodel. Too bad her looks weren't enough to entice me into a serious relationship.

"So, what's up?" She waited to speak until after I asked the waitress for a water. I drank nearly the whole pot of coffee while cleaning the house. I didn't need to be any more wired than I already was.

"Emmy sent me a letter," I started.

She shrugged. "So?"

Of course she would just shrug. She knew I had come home from the east coast with a broken heart, but she didn't know the specifics, and I never felt the need to relay them to her—even now.

"So..." I hesitated, and then decided to just be blunt. "So, she was apparently pregnant when I left and now I have a five-month-old son I didn't know about until yesterday morning."

Her eyes opened wide, and her slender fingers gripped her coffee cup so tightly I thought it would shatter in her hand. "What?"

"Yeah, that's about the reaction I had, too." It took everything in me to force the smallest smile upon my lips.

"That's nonsense! How do you even know that kid is yours? This is probably just a ploy to get you back. Is she stupid? Doesn't she know DNA will prove she's lying?"

I had questioned Lucas's paternity myself, and I was not at all happy with Emmy, but hearing Claire call the mother of my child stupid bothered me.

"Don't call her stupid. Don't ever be disrespectful to her. Ever."

It seemed as though my quiet anger unsettled Claire. She shrunk into her seat and dropped her gaze to her coffee. "I'm sorry, but...you must've had the same thoughts."

"I did," I admitted. "But then I went to see them, and he looks just like me, Claire. There's no mistaking who his father is. Besides, Emmy would never be that cruel or desperate."

She sat there in silence for a moment, her eyes searching mine.

"So, what are you going to do?" she asked quietly. "Are you going to be with her again?"

"No." I shook my head, even though she had her attention on her mug and couldn't see me. "But I asked her to move in with me so I can be a part of Lucas's life without all the crap that comes along with shared custody. She and Lucas will take my room and I'll take the couch."

"Oh." She put a hand to her lips as she thought about the situation. "That's a lot of changes in one day."

"I agree."

"And...you think this is going to work? You two aren't going to fight living under the same roof?"

I didn't think Emmy was capable of battling anything or anyone. By all appearances, all her fighting spirit was gone. "No, it will be awkward and maybe even a little tense, but I don't think we'll have any problems."

"Do you think…" She swallowed hard and turned her nervous attention to me. "Do you think you guys will…get back together…like ever?"

I thought about my broken heart and the time I'd missed with Lucas, and frowned.

"No," I said flatly.

"What about you and me? Can I still see you?" She forced her mouth into a smile, but she could not erase the worry lines around her eyes.

I shifted in my seat. "I'll need some time to adjust, Claire. I can't make any promises."

She nodded and looked away from me. I checked my watch and knew I had to go.

"I have to get going. I have to meet Emmy and Lucas." I reached over and touched her hand, making her look at me with shiny eyes. "We're still friends, Claire."

Her face softened just a little. "Of course we are. Good luck with everything. Keep me posted. Send me some pictures."

I stood up, kissed the top of her head, and left her sitting there. Even though I knew I had done the right thing, I felt like an asshole.

****

After one trip back to my apartment to drop off the belongings Emmy and Lucas had brought with them to Chicago, we went back out to buy everything Lucas would need. As I carried him in my arms and zipped around the enormous baby store, Em followed quietly behind, only speaking if I spoke to her first. I was fine with that. I didn't want to be her damn friend, but I didn't have to be a dickfuck about it, either. Silence was our common friend. She didn't say anything when I told her about going to Lena's, but she looked terrified. I wasn't her friend, as I said, but it wasn't necessary for her to be so frightened.

"They're going to be fine. No one is going to be nasty. They're not like that," I'd said, knowing she was afraid of facing my family after her Keep-Lucas-away stunt.

The old Emmy would've said something funny at this point while trying to express her anxiety, but this woman—otherwise known as Lucas's Mom—just absently wrung her hands together, swallowed hard, and stared at the floor.

True to my word, when we went to dinner, my family embraced her as if she had done no wrong. They treated her like she belonged and harbored no hard feelings toward her whatsoever. My family is great like that. Me, not so much. I talked around her, over her, and through her, pretending she wasn't really there unless it was necessary. I didn't do it on purpose, not really, but there was a barrier between us that wasn't there even after I broke up with her. The obstruction was there because of her actions, and I didn't want to try to break through it. I was fine working around it and limiting our communication.

The old Emmy wouldn't have taken this shit from me, but Lucas's Mom cowered in her seat. When she jumped up suddenly, excusing herself in a low murmur, Lena, Lorraine, and my mother all set their evil female eyes on me.

"This is hard enough for her," Lena hissed. "You don't need to be such an…" She considered all the kids who were around before continuing. "Asshole," she silently mouthed.

"You're going to push her away and she'll take the baby with her, stupid," Lorraine added and punched me in the arm.

I observed my mother's disapproving eyes and immediately turned away. She didn't raise me to be an asshole to women, but I couldn't help the anger I felt inside toward Lucas's Mom.

Lena got up from the table after giving me a final look of warning and left to go after her. When they returned a few minutes later, Lena immediately brought out the apple pie my mom had made for the occasion. Once my son's mother had a larger than reasonable slice of pie on her plate with a side of ice cream, she managed to even smile a little.

I rolled my eyes and said nothing.

If only pie could be the fix-all to my problems.

Chapter Four

I really thought I'd struggle falling into the role of being someone's dad without any kind of real preparation, but I found myself settled in the position with ease. Admittedly, Lucas's Mom was a large part of the transition. She wordlessly began routines that gave me plenty of quality time with my son while allowing me to take on some of the responsibilities involved—bath times, feedings, doctor's appointments, and more. Every minute with my son counted. Every second was an attempt to make up for all the previously missed moments. The truth was, I could never make up for any of those missed memories, but I damn well tried.

My new roommate stayed out of my way, but took care of me at the same time. She cooked, she cleaned, washed my damn underwear, and left reminders on the fridge. I always thanked her, but unless the kid was involved, we really didn't speak. At one point in her life, she would've had way too damn much to say, but not now, and neither did I.

At night, after the baby went to bed, I'd sit down on my bed-slash-couch and either work or just chill. Lucas's Mom would shut herself in the bedroom. I didn't know what she did in there. Okay, sometimes I wondered what she was doing, but I never cared enough to go find out or ask.

Though I enjoyed my new life as a dad, I started feeling a little restless. I felt trapped in my own home with *her* taking up the other half of my apartment. Having company over was just awkward—not because she was awkward, but because of the situation. One night, I felt like the walls were closing in on me. Lucas was in bed and his mother was in the kitchen cleaning up. The sound of running water, the soft scrubbing noise as she cleaned the baby bottles, and her occasional sniffle or clearing of the throat were driving me crazy. I jumped from the couch, grabbed my keys, and without looking at her, I announced I was going back to the office to work.

I didn't lie. I did go back to the office for a little bit, but instead of going directly back to the apartment afterward, I found myself parking my car near Claire's. I stood outside her building for a few minutes, debating whether or not I really wanted to go up there. I didn't show up for a booty call, but I just wanted a change in environment for a little while. Somewhere that wasn't home and wasn't work, somewhere rather neutral where I could just have a couple of beers and bullshit. I had friends I could've turned to, but so many of them still didn't know my circumstances, and I wasn't in the mood to explain that the woman living with me who—was also the mother of my child, was just that—the mother of my child and nothing more to me.

After too much time thinking about it, I went inside, waved to the doorman, and made my way up to Claire's apartment. She opened the door wrapped in a robe, her hair still wet from the shower. She looked surprised to see me but immediately stood aside to let me in.

"Never expected to see you at my door again," she said as I moved past her and headed to her kitchen for a beer.

"Yeah, me either," I admitted as I opened the fridge.

"Not that I'm complaining or anything."

I opened two beers and handed her one. I took in her damp breasts pressing against the silk fabric of her robe. They weren't very impressive, but from a guy's perspective, boobs are boobs, and Claire's were wet and her nipples were hard.

"Something catch your eye?" She arched an eyebrow invitingly.

I immediately glanced away and headed to her living room. I didn't pop in to fuck her. It suddenly felt strange to think about having sex with someone else when I realized I was someone's dad. Not that I wanted to have sex with my son's mother, because I sort of didn't like her anymore, but it felt strange to think of having sex with Claire anyway.

I settled down in an armchair, instead of the couch where bad things could've happened. Claire sat down on the couch, but made no effort to hold her robe closed. It hung open enough to show the swells of her breasts, the smooth skin leading to her exposed belly button, and just a trace of curly blond hair peeking out between her crossed legs.

"How are you and your happy little family?" The hint of sarcasm in her voice wasn't missed.

"My son is incredible," I said and tipped the bottle to my lips.

Some of her bitterness dissolved. "I guess you like being a dad."

"I do. Dirty diapers, puke, teething—all of it." A hearty laugh erupted from my tight chest, as if it'd been hibernating there for weeks. "I can tell he's going to be a handful when he starts walking and talking. He has a bit of an attitude already."

"Do you have any pictures?" She seemed genuinely interested, but I suddenly felt a little guilty for sitting in her living room and throwing my son in her face. She had wanted children a long time ago when we were dating, and back then, I couldn't be bothered with even entertaining the idea. I also knew I had hurt her, if only a little bit, when I stopped seeing her after I found out about Lucas, but she held her hand out and looked at me expectantly. With a sigh, I pulled my phone out of my pocket and brought up my photos before passing it over.

She gasped softly as one hand touched her chest. "Oh, he's adorable. He does look just like you, Luke. Gosh."

She examined picture after picture, asking questions and listening to my comments about each one. She laughed and smiled or clicked her tongue. Though I knew it probably bothered her inside, she didn't outwardly show it, which was a big step for Claire who was really good at wearing her emotions on her sleeve. I appreciated her genuine interest, and I had begun to relax, but then she reached the one picture of Lucas and his mother together. So quickly I almost missed it, I saw an expression of bitterness cross her features and disappear before I could open my mouth to address it. She handed my phone back to me then.

"He's a beautiful baby."

As if she'd just realized her robe was hanging open, her fingers made quick work of pulling it together to cover her bare skin as she looked at my shoes instead of my eyes.

"He is," I agreed with a faint smile.

"You seem happy."

I knew this statement had a double meaning. I had to be careful how I answered it so I wouldn't give her the wrong impression. "Lucas makes me very happy. I wish the circumstances were different, but it is what it is. I just make the best of it and push myself to be the best parent I can be."

She nodded, but it seemed to be an automatic response. There was a vacant look in her eyes, as if her focus was somewhere else. I wasn't sure she'd actually heard me.

Sounding as distant as she appeared, she asked, "Are you and Emmy trying to work things out?"

Clearly, she hadn't heard me.

"No." I leaned forward and rested my elbows on my legs. "I mean, we communicate as much as necessary, but we're not getting back together if that's what you mean. We're roommates who happen to share a child."

Claire finally met my eyes. "So…you're single?"

"Yes, I'm still single." My eyes raked over her body.

She was still sexy in her own way, but nothing like Em.

Though Claire probably hadn't noticed, I froze at the thought that had just fallen into my mind. Lucas's Mom was the last person I wanted to think about like that. I couldn't understand why my brain had gone to her. I wasn't blind, and I was still a man after all, so of course I had taken notice of her body over the weeks, but it didn't mean anything. Her beauty meant no more to me than that of a stranger.

"Why'd you come here?" Claire's skepticism shone bright in her eyes.

"I needed a break from the monotony that has become my life. Every night after Lucas goes to bed, I sit in the living room and work. His mother stays in the other room, but it doesn't really ease the obvious tension in the apartment. It takes a lot of energy to actively avoid someone within the same few square feet. Sometimes I need to unwind and I can't do it there."

Claire quietly considered my words. I wasn't sure what she was going to do with them. There was no doubt I was basically using her—I'd cut her off, and then dropped in unannounced only a few short weeks later because I needed to be somewhere other than home.

I have asshole tendencies at times, I'll admit that, but I try not to purposely hurt people. So, I stood up and walked my empty bottle into the kitchen to throw it in the recycling bin. When I returned to the living room, Claire's face was no longer creased with deep thought, but I didn't give her a chance to speak up.

"I'm going to go." I nodded at the door. "I shouldn't have come here. I shouldn't use you like that."

Claire got to her feet, forgetting about her robe as it fell open all the way, leaving nothing to the imagination.

"You're not using me," she said hurriedly. "We grew up together, Luke. We're friends if nothing else. If you need to stop by so you're not suffocating in your own home, I'm okay with that."

I ran a hand through my hair and let out a long breath. "Claire, honestly, I'm concerned you may not be able to follow that permanent line between friendship and romance. I'm still not ready for a relationship, especially right now, and I don't want to lead you to believe if you just wait around, it'll happen, because I can't promise that."

Her face fell a little, but then a corner of her mouth pulled up into a small smile while she shrugged one delicate shoulder. "We'll just have to be friends then."

My eyes fell back to her naked body.

"With benefits," she added and swept the robe back to put a hand on her slender hip.

I continued to stare at her body. "Is that a good idea?" Her posture shifted slightly under my increasingly intense gaze. "I think we can have a mutual understanding here."

"This needs to be entirely stress free," I warned as I moved toward her. "Friendship with benefits and nothing more."

"Friendship with benefits and nothing more," she parroted with a firm nod as she watched me advance.

"It doesn't mean I don't care about you." I gently placed my hand on her waist. She inhaled sharply as I pulled her against my body. "But I can't be anything more than your friend—with benefits. Do you understand?"

She nodded wordlessly. I pressed my lips against her jugular and inhaled the scent of her skin. She smelled like soap and something fruity. It wasn't a bad smell, but it didn't drive me nuts and perk up my cock as much as the aroma in my home, brought on by my son's mother. I tried not to notice, but it was impossible not to catch her lingering scent while living in the same small apartment with her. I hated what that fragrance did to me, making my physical response go against my mental and emotional reactions.

I needed to get her the hell out of my head.

I stripped Claire out of her robe and swept her into my arms, making her yelp in surprise. I carried her into her room and kicked the door shut behind me, anxious to forget about the woman who had the ability to fester in my heart and soul and destroy both over and over without mercy.

Chapter Five

I walked into the shit hole that was my office and was greeted by the receptionist from hell. With her brightly colored hair in an updo that reminded me of both a beehive and a bird's nest, pierced face and heavy makeup, she didn't make the few clients who came through the door feel very confident in my abilities or the abilities of my partner and the other attorneys working for us.

"Hey," Kacey said while chomping on a large wad of gum.

Kacey was the niece of my partner, Steve Keane. She definitely wasn't our first choice, but she was willing to accept the low pay that came with the job until we were able to take off, though I wasn't sure when that would happen. Not much of the necessary equipment was hooked up and there didn't seem to be any organization anywhere. Files sat in boxes on desks and the floor. The waiting area for clients looked frightening, and the whole place appeared dingy and unclean.

Hell, it *was* dingy and unclean.

"Hey." I walked past the gum muncher to my office.

I found a space on my desk to put down my cup of coffee and sat down.

Starting my own firm was something I had wanted since before I even finished law school, but I knew I needed experience and had to build a name for myself first. My first job out of college was with a small, piece of shit law firm in a bad neighborhood in Chicago. We primarily worked for low income families or petty-crime criminals, and we got paid virtually nothing. The work was rewarding and vastly philanthropic, but I had rent to pay, and I needed to be able to buy my own groceries so I didn't have to show up at my mom's or one of my sisters' for dinner every night. I took a position at another firm after a year and a half. It had a steady flow of paying clients and I didn't have to watch for flying bullets going in and out of work, but after two years there, I felt stagnant. I was ready to break away from my family, ready to get out of Chicago and do more with my life. So, I took a position with Sterling Corporation in Philly, and was soon traveling around the country to put out legal fires. My pay had tripled, I had succeeded in breaking away from my family, and it was there, in that building, I first met Lucas's mother.

The first time I'd seen her was on my very first day at work. I had immediately taken stock of her curves wrapped in her designer business suit, the soft shades of carmine and hints of blonds in her chocolate brown hair, and greenish-brown eyes that shined with amusement and mischief. She'd been beautiful, but it was those damn eyes that had gotten me, that had made me choose to stand beside her instead of the pretty redhead on the other side of the crowded elevator. She'd smelled good, like cherries, vanilla, and fresh air. I'd taken deep breaths as quietly as possible so no one would know I'd been on the verge of grabbing her and running my nose all over her body until I'd gotten my fill of her scent that had made me uncomfortably aroused.

Before the elevator could begin its ascent, too many people pushed their way in. We were literally wedged into the corner together. I kept my briefcase in front of me so she wouldn't feel my erection pressing against her thigh.

"Every morning I feel like I'm getting to third base with entirely too many of you," she announced loudly to the crowded elevator. It was funny, though she wore an all-business expression on her face—except for her eyes, of course.

I stared down at her, amused by her completely inappropriate declaration. A few people chuckled and agreed with her, while a couple of people up front apologized.

"Hello, I'm Luke," I said to her a moment later.

One eyebrow shot up as she openly assessed me.

"I just thought you should at least know my name if we're already at third base," I whispered in her ear.

I didn't know how she'd react. She could've told me to fuck off or slapped me across the face or even acknowledge me any further than the eyeballing I got from her.

Without wiping away her stoic expression, she opened her pretty mouth and said, "Well, Luke, you just took the fun out of being at third base anonymously."

Rumbling laughter started low in my belly and traveled up until my lips parted with a deep chuckle. "Well, since I don't know your name, there's still some anonymity."

"Oh, so I have all the power." Her painted lips curved with the smallest trace of a smile.

"I didn't say that," I quickly corrected her. "But I'm okay with allowing you to believe that."

The elevator stopped on my floor. A few people spilled out and I followed after them while winking at the nameless beauty at the back of the elevator.

I had no idea then who she was, and if it weren't for her smartass comment to everyone on the elevator, I may have just pegged her for a pretty face and kept moving. The fact she didn't hit me after I introduced myself, but made another wisecracking statement, left me thinking about her the rest of the day. I didn't see her again that day or the next, but on Wednesday, I settled down for lunch with a coworker in the small café next to the Sterling building, and before I could even dig my fork into my salad, a tray clunked down on the end of the table. I glanced up and found Miss Smartass herself standing there, looking from me to Ted.

"Are one of you guys going to move over, or were you hoping for some lap action?" she asked, turning to me with a challenging gleam in her eyes.

Before Ted could react, I quickly moved my tray over and scooted my ass to the seat by the window. She sat down and smiled at me.

"I thought for sure you would've preferred me to sit in your lap, Luke. We get to third base together on our first meeting and not even so much as a phone call from you after."

I laughed. I liked this woman more and more—every damn time she opened her pretty mouth.

"I apologize, but you see, it's hard to call you if I don't even have a name in which to stalk you by."

"Her name's written in men's bathrooms across the city," Ted said casually.

"Right next to your mother's." She snatched a fry off his plate and turned those sexy, mischievous eyes on me. "I thought we agreed there's more excitement in at least partial anonymity."

"Fine. Don't complain when I don't call."

"A good stalker would go out of his way to find out who I am." She had the nerve to put her fingers in my salad and pluck out a slice of cucumber. She pushed it into her mouth and looked at me defiantly, as if she dared me to say anything about her food-stealing ways.

"Or I could just go into the men's room and check out the walls and take a few guesses."

Any other woman would've slapped me or chewed me out. This woman, however, grinned and said, "Now I'm curious. I wonder if there really is shit written about me on the bathroom wall."

"I wrote some of it myself," Ted said with a shrug.

"Ted and I went out on a date once." She directed her comment to me, though she stared across the table at Ted. "I wouldn't give him head, so now he's a little bitter."

Ted's fork stabbed at the fries on his plate as he scowled. "When you take a woman out to the most expensive steakhouse in the city, the least a guy can get is some head."

She smiled widely at him before returning her attention back to me. "I ordered the most expensive meal on the menu and the most expensive wine. After dinner, I got him all revved up. You know, I had my fingers in his hair…" She ran her hand through my hair to demonstrate what she meant, all while looking into my eyes. "I trailed my fingertips over his strong jawline and down to his tight chest muscles…" Her hands mimicked her story and traveled over my chin and on to my sternum, where I was sure she could feel my heart trying to break free under her touch. I sat there, kind of mesmerized, as she took my tie into her hand and tugged lightly until our faces were only a few inches apart. "And I got this close to him, licked my lips, and ran my hand up his thigh." When her hand traveled up my leg, I prayed she wouldn't go any further and realize how hard she made me. At the same time, I prayed that she *would* go further and realize how hard she made me.

"And then she told me to fuck off," Ted added sourly, breaking the spell this woman had over me.

Her lips curled into a naughty smile, but she didn't immediately release me.

"He's right. I told him to fuck off. Ted has been running the steak and BJ game on women for too long. When he did that shit with my cousin Mayson, and she didn't go for the blow job, he said some very awful things to and about her. He didn't know she was my cousin when he was telling the story in the elevator one morning.

43

The best part is…" She let her head fall back and released a genuine, amused laugh.

"She recorded the whole damn thing," Ted said with a growl. "It was like an episode of fucking *Cheaters*. She invited half the women in the building to watch it."

She released my tie, sat back in her chair, and looked at Ted with a satisfied grin stretched across her lips. He didn't appear as angry as a guy in his position should've been. He regarded her with something resembling respect.

"Wow." I exhaled when I realized what my lungs were for. Breathing. "Remind me to never cross you…err…whatever your name is."

She picked up her cheeseburger that was almost as big as her head and winked at me.

"Emmy," she said.

Emmy.

It was a name that had changed my life.

****

I sat in my office chair, daydreaming about the past instead of focusing on the tangled web of shit on my desk. Those days didn't mean anything to me anymore, yet there was an ache in my chest as my mind flashed to her smiles and sassy mouth.

Ignoring the painful thumping of my heart against my sternum, I let out a long sigh and threw myself into my work. I had to be in court right after lunch. I didn't have time to focus on my personal problems.

I moved a few things around on my desk so I'd have some space to work and tried not to lose my temper at the mess. Granted, most of the mess was my own, but it was only because the office was in such piss-poor shape. No one seemed to have the time to make it all come together in the beginning, and now we had more clients than we did time or resources. I knew I'd have to crack down on Kacey and our paralegal, Craig, to start actually doing their jobs, but Kacey was kind of scary and I was worried she'd have a temper tantrum and leave, which would not help matters. Craig was the only paralegal we had and he was already stretched in too many directions in my firm, getting paid much less than he deserved or what he could make in another office. It was important I appreciated they both showed up to work every day and not push them, but something had to give.

After a stressful afternoon in court, I couldn't wait to get home and unwind with Lucas. No matter how busy my schedule was or how many nights I needed to work late, I always went home to see Lucas first. I never missed a bedtime, even if it meant I had to work later into the night. I never could've imagined the attachment I have with my son. In those first few moments of meeting him, I was unable to fathom how much his existence meant to me. My history with his mother was heartbreaking, and there was a time in my life I wished I'd never known her, but then I wouldn't have my son. He was the only reason I had to be thankful for ever knowing that woman.

Usually, when I walked through the door in the evenings after work, a homely scent wafted out from the kitchen where Lucas's Mom was elbow deep in cooking a good meal. There were some things I could give her credit for, like being an excellent mother. The first thing I wanted to do when she moved in was find fault in her parenting skills, but even matched up against my own mom and my sisters, the woman was phenomenal.

Some of the other things I gave her credit for may seem sexist, but it isn't my fault she rocked at them. She could iron the hell out of a pair of slacks and my dress shirts were always wrinkle free, hung up, and in order. The apartment was never more than a few minutes from pristine and always smelled the way I imagined homes in those ads for cleaning products would. The girl had cooking skills that could bring a man to his knees. It almost did the first few nights, but stubbornly, I hadn't wanted to give her the pleasure of knowing she'd done something well.

Yeah, I'm an asshole sometimes.

After my rough day, I secretly looked forward to a home-cooked meal and spending time with the best kid in the world, but there were no homely smells coming from the kitchen. In fact, there was nothing coming from the kitchen but silence, and I immediately figured out why when I saw the pair dozing on the couch. I put my briefcase down by the door and shrugged out of my coat before walking into the small living area. Emmy was on her back, knocked the hell out with Lucas sleeping on her chest. I knew she was sick just by looking at her. Her nose was red, her cheeks were rosy, and she sounded congested as she lightly snored. There was a box of Kleenex on the floor beside the couch and several discarded tissues nearby.

Careful not to touch her too much, I took Lucas from her arms so I could put him to bed. She sat up, startled by the loss. When she saw me, a wave of relief rolled across her face and she fell back on the couch with exhaustion. I carried Lucas into the bedroom and put him in his crib. I stayed with him for a few minutes, just enjoying watching him sleep. When I came out of the room, I found his mom picking up her dirty tissues.

"I'm sorry I didn't cook dinner tonight," she said, breathing through her mouth.

"It's okay. Don't worry about it." I loosened my tie and collapsed on the now vacant couch.

"I can make you something." She continued to keep busy by picking up Lucas's toys.

"I'm fine, but thank you."

I just wanted her to leave me the hell alone. It wasn't a requirement for her to make my meals. The fact she did was appreciated, but I didn't want her under the impression this was some kind of amicable arrangement. I was tired and grumpy, and I just wanted her to go in the other room like normal when Lucas was in bed, even if it was a little earlier than usual. For a few damn minutes, I just wanted my own apartment back, but since I couldn't have that, I had to settle for her slithering into the bedroom.

"Are you sure I can't make you anything?" she asked after carrying a couple of dishes into the kitchen. "It's not a problem."

"I said no! My god, it's not like you're my wife, Emmy." Even to my ears that sounded harsher than she deserved for just trying to be nice, but I wasn't about to apologize for it.

She stood in front of the bedroom door for a moment, her face frozen with consternation after my outburst. "Okay then…" Her tone was soft yet wounded.

She closed herself in the bedroom and I congratulated myself on being a giant dick.

****

The chilly autumn began to drift into the short days and long nights of winter. I still saw Claire once or twice every couple weeks, but that had begun to not be enough for her. I was extremely busy in my busted office, and if I wasn't there, I was with Lucas.

Not much had changed between his mother and me. She moved about the apartment like a scared stray, skittering out of my way when I came anywhere near her, always with her eyes cast down. The only time I saw her animated was when she was with Lucas or when her mother came into town for the holidays, though with the latter, it was more of an aggravation rather than an animation. She barely left the apartment, unless it was dinner every other Sunday with my family, trips to the grocery store or other errands; however, when Sam came into town, Lucas's mom found any excuse to get away. I swear she made up shit to do. I was pretty sure I'd never seen the woman touch gelatin, but one day when her mom was over, she had to run to the store for some.

She hadn't come back for three hours.

My rough days at work grew rougher. While the office was slowly coming together, it still looked and operated rather unprofessionally. The few resources we had weren't being properly utilized. We still had to turn away clients, and Kacey was as scary as before—and not the good kind of scary. We had to do something and fast before everything fell apart completely.

"Hey, buddy," I said to Lucas one evening as I dropped my suitcase by the door and threw my jacket over the back of a chair at the table. I swept him out of his pack and play and planted a manly kiss on his forehead. "How was your day, little man?"

I did what I did almost every evening when I got in from work. I put Lucas in his high chair and spoiled him with a jar of banana custard. His mother always had him fed before I got in, but I always felt he was entitled to a little dessert. I could tell by the look on her face she disapproved, but she never vocalized her objection.

"This stuff is gross," I said to the kid when we were nearly finished the jar. "I don't know how you eat it."

He scrunched up his little nose and grinned at me as if to say, "Good! More for me!"

When he was finished, his mother brought my dinner out to me along with a glass of homemade sweet tea, another thing she was really good at making. I thanked her, but that was the end of our conversation. She never sat down to eat with me and I never asked her to. I wasn't sure when and where she finally ate her own meal, but I guess I didn't really care. I appreciated what she was doing, being useful, but it didn't change anything. Even if her damn lasagna almost made me cry with joy.

As usual, she swept the baby away for a bath while I ate my dinner. I was done with my meal and watching the evening news by the time Lucas was bathed and ready for bed. Without acknowledging words to his mother, I did my usual and put him to bed after reading a short story.

As a family—if you want to call it that—we'd easily fallen into a regular routine without much discussion on the matter. Even the mutual silent treatment had become routine, especially after that night when Lucas's Mom was sick.

After he was asleep, I came out of the room and settled down on the couch with my briefcase and turned on *Family Guy* while she busied herself in the kitchen cleaning up dinner and putting away the leftovers. Another recent development was that she'd begun packing a lunch for me to take to work, I supposed in an effort to get rid of the leftovers.

She probably would've made an excellent wife if she wasn't a cheating, lying, deceiving bitch.

She exited the kitchen sometime later, turning the light off behind her. "I'm going grocery shopping," she said meekly as she hung near the bedroom door with her hands folded in front of her.

Despite the obvious personality changes in her I didn't necessarily care about, I was still a little stunned by her submissive behavior. Maybe to any other man, this would've been a turn on. In fact, sometimes the unbidden desire to see her submissively on her knees as she orally pleased me came into my head, but then the knowledge she was obviously a very scarred person always shattered that notion. Regardless of what she was to me, no person with such obvious demons should ever be put in that position. It just seemed…wrong.

"How much do you need?" I reached into my back pocket for my wallet.

I insisted on paying for all the groceries and household items we needed on a regular basis, even the things she needed. I was well aware she could pay for her own shampoo and body wash and feminine products, but if nothing else, she was still Lucas's mother. She was living in my home and caring for my son. It was my responsibility to see her needs were met. She was permitted to spend her own money on makeup or clothes for herself or similar luxuries if she wanted to, but I didn't want her paying for anything else. I had to come up with a better system than making her come to me every time she wanted to go to the store. All this extra communicating rubbed me the wrong way and only served to put me in a pissy mood.

She kept her attention on the floor. She still hadn't met my eyes after all of these weeks of cohabitating. Not that it really mattered. "I'm not sure."

I took my ATM card out and got up to hand it to her. "I am going to add you to my account so you can have your own card. Then you won't have to wait for me every time you need to go to the store."

She stepped forward and removed the card from my fingertips carefully, as if she was trying not to touch me. "That won't be necessary."

"It is necessary," I snapped.

"I'll just have to plan better. Then I can give you a heads up instead of springing it on you as I'm about to walk out the door."

I was exasperated, and even though I didn't care to see her eyes, I was annoyed she kept her gaze lowered like a damn slave. "*Or*, I give you your own card."

"Okay," she conceded. "Whatever's easiest for you."

She turned away from me and I went back to my place on the couch.

I could think of a million things that would make this life "easier" for us all, but that would require a time machine, and as far as I knew, the world was sold out of those.

Chapter Six

I felt the condom break just as my orgasm began. What fucking luck.

I pulled out of the writhing blonde with a curse and finished on her pretty blue bedspread under us, even though I knew I hadn't really pulled out in time.

I cursed like a trucker who used to be a sailor raised by a trucker and sailor as I made my way to the bathroom to take off the remaining pieces of the useless rubber.

"It's no big deal," Claire said behind me in the bedroom. "I'll go to the pharmacy in the morning and get that Plan B."

"That's not a guaranteed preventive, Claire."

"Nothing is guaranteed."

I laughed without humor. "How about abstinence?"

"Well...yeah, but you don't have any intentions of abstaining."

I turned around and walked back into the bedroom without answering her. I started picking my clothes up off the floor and putting them on.

She laughed uncertainly. "You're not seriously considering ending this with me."

"I don't know. All I know for certain is I don't need this shit right now."

"I told you I'll take care of it." She got up from the bed in a huff.

"Yeah? What if that doesn't work?"

She glared at me from the bathroom doorway. "Then I'll take care of it."

I stared at her, astonished by what her words implied. "I can't even believe you're suggesting that!"

Her anger flared. "If I were Emmy, we wouldn't even be having this conversation. You'd probably be glad to knock her up again."

My jaw tightened with silent fury as I pointed a finger at her. "Don't. Go. There."

As quickly as her anger had come, it dissolved. She released a deep breath and held out her hands, placating. "I'm sorry. I didn't mean that. I promise this isn't a problem, okay? I'll go to the pharmacy tonight if you want. Chances are the timing is all wrong anyway."

I ran a hand through my hair and let out a frustrated sigh. This thing with Claire had its high points, but more recently, I began to realize it wasn't really the arrangement I wanted, especially with her. Despite our agreement to keep our relationship as friendly as possible, she was still clingy and jealous, often calling me during my time with Lucas or trying to get me to meet her more frequently. Apart from all that, my workload was threatening to crush me and my associates. Whatever time I had left at the end of each day or during the weekends when I wasn't tied up with work was reserved for my child and my family.

"Luke." She said my name in a small voice.

"I can't do this anymore, Claire." I met her eyes. "It's not you, but I just…I just don't have time for this relationship right now."

Her words came out in a rush. "I won't push so hard. I'll take whatever time you can give me."

I shook my head. "Any extra time I have right now should go to my son." I sat down on the edge of the bed to put my sneakers on.

There was a pathetic note of desperation in her tone as she hovered in front of me. "What about time for yourself and your own needs?"

"Someday, hopefully under the right circumstances, you're going to have your own child. You'll put your own needs aside, and you won't regret it. I don't."

She looked horrified at such a prospect. It was almost funny. "That's like saying you don't regret giving me up."

"That isn't what I'm saying, Claire, but you look at it how you want to."

I knew she was about to cry and I didn't want to see that. I got off the bed, grabbed my wallet from the nightstand and turned away from her. I stopped in the doorway and spoke to her over my shoulder.

"I still care about you, but you want much more than I can give you. You should go find someone who's willing and able to give it to you."

She didn't follow me out and I was thankful.

I went straight home. I felt awful leaving her like that, but honestly, I was more worried about the broken condom. The last thing I needed was to have another baby—with another woman— when my relationship with Lucas's Mom was so damn broken. I felt like my whole life was turning into an episode of Maury.

In the living room, I stripped out of my jacket, sneakers, jeans, and sweater. I left everything in a heap on the floor by the coffee table and fell wearily onto the couch. I usually slept on an inflatable mattress, but I didn't feel like going through the motions of moving furniture out of the way, blowing it up, and covering it with a sheet. I really missed my bed. I was sure if I asked Lucas's Mom to switch for a few nights a week, she would meekly agree, but I didn't want to ask her for anything.

At the precipice of falling to sleep, I heard a muffled cry from the bedroom. In dad mode, I automatically got up off the couch. There was no regulation on who got up with Lucas on what nights, but since *she* slept in the same room with him, she almost always got to him first. Sometimes I went in and took over. She never argued, just simply went back to bed.

I pushed the door open just after another cry. I walked over to the crib, but was surprised to find him fast asleep and completely still. I scratched my head like a cartoon character. I must've been more freaked out by the condom thing than I originally though.

Movement on the bed behind me caught my attention. Just as a noise resembling a sob resounded in the otherwise quiet room, I realized it was never Lucas crying. It was her.

I don't know why this floored me. It literally made me immobile as I watched her hands shoot up as if blocking a blow.

"Please stop," she said in such a heartbreaking, pathetic, soul-crushing voice it knocked the breath out of me. "Stop it!"

It sounded as if she was trying to scream out her words of distress, but it was faint in reality. She turned to her side and curled into a ball as little sobs escaped her lips.

"My baby," she mewed. "You're going to hurt my baby."

It hit me then. Full force. I knew Kyle was somehow responsible for the emotional scars that Lucas's Mom—Emmy— tried to keep hidden, but now I believed whatever he had done was far more sinister than just being a douche bag. Whatever it was he did, he did it to my son, too.

****

The next day was off to a bad start. I'd sat up all night thinking about Emmy and her nightmares. I didn't know if I should confront her or leave it alone. If it was only her, I probably would've minded my own business, but Lucas was definitely involved, and he *was* my business. I just didn't know if what had happened to Em was when he was in or out of the womb.

By the time I fell asleep, the sun had begun to light up the morning sky. I was shaken awake by Emmy an hour after I should've been up and ready to walk out the door. I jumped off the couch, crashing into her. She stumbled back, but I grabbed her waist to steady her. That was the first I'd touched her in a long time. If I had a moment to comprehend anything, I would've thought about how surprisingly refreshing it was to feel her curves and not Claire's bony body. I released her as I murmured an apology and darted out of the room to get ready for work.

I showered in record time and almost shouted with relief when I saw Emmy had picked out a suit and tie for me and laid it out on the bed. Hell, she even put out a pair of boxers and socks.

I dressed quickly and dashed out into the living room. Emmy was holding a smiling Lucas in one arm and had my coat draped over the other while she held my briefcase. Again, perfect wife material, if she wasn't who she was…

I took the coat and briefcase with appreciation and leaned in to kiss Lucas goodbye. As I pulled away, I got a whiff of Emmy's scent and was shocked at how sad I suddenly felt.

"Just a second," she said and turned to the dining room table. She handed me a reusable shopping bag before shifting Lucas to her other arm. "Breakfast and lunch."

I held the bag and looked at it, feeling slow and stupid. She'd given me lunch before, and on weekends, she made me breakfast, but something about this was…touching.

"It's just an egg and bacon sandwich." She shrugged. "But I figured you don't have time to stop. I think I heard you tell someone on the phone you had to be in court rather early today."

I roused myself. "Yes. Thanks."

53

I turned away and rushed out the door before I did something ridiculous, like smile.

When I walked into the office, I was once again reminded of what shit shape it was in. Kacey sat at her desk texting on her phone. I usually ignored this, but I was moody.

"Put the phone away and do something useful," I snapped at her as I passed by her desk.

"We had to send away another client this morning," Craig sang, following me into my office.

I liked Craig. He was young, just barely out of high school, but he was a hard worker and took the pressure of working in our screwed-up environment well. He was a fast talker, though. Spoke a mile a minute, especially when he felt said pressure.

"We've got to get this office in order, Luke. This place is turning into an absolute nightmare when it should be effin' amazing. We shouldn't have to turn clients away just because we're completely unorganized. What's Kacey for? Isn't she supposed to be part of that organization process? And for shit's sake, the reception area out there looks like the greeting room to the gates to hell, and Kacey looks like a gargoyle guarding it. Who am I kidding? The reception room to the gates of hell are probably fucking fabulous. I keep looking at it and expecting to see Michael Keaton all dressed up as Beetle Juice and that guy with the shrunken head and the lady cut in half."

I stopped staring at Craig with an open mouth after every one of his rants a long time ago, but sometimes, it was the only reaction I could muster. This was one of those times.

"I wish I could do more, but I can't. I'm only one person working for four attorneys in a piece of crap law firm. No offense."

I couldn't be mad at him for speaking the truth. "None taken," I murmured as I searched for a file I needed for court. "Listen, money is extremely tight right now. I can't hire anyone else just yet."

"Then make that woman out there do her job," Craig demanded as he handed me the very file I was looking for.

"I'll try, but I don't want to push her out the door. No one else will work for what I'm paying her."

He headed to the door. "Maybe if you were paying her more money she would care a little more. Just saying."

The moment he stepped out of my office, Kacey pounced on him, yelling at him about not minding his own business; the usual pleasantries between the two young employees. A moment later, as I walked back through the reception area, I snapped at the pair to stop arguing and get back to work. That's all I needed was for one of my current clients to walk in and find a morning brawl.

Court wasn't much better. I lost good ground on what I thought was a very strong case in my client's favor. I should've been prepared for what the opposing counsel had up their sleeve, but admittedly, I was distracted by many things—Claire and the busted condom fiasco, Emmy and her nightmares and wondering how my son was involved, the state of the office and wondering how the hell we were going to stay afloat if I had to keep turning people away, and the fact my current clients weren't exactly rolling in the dough.

Later that night after Lucas was in bed, I sat on the couch and looked toward the kitchen where Emmy was cleaning. I couldn't see her, but I could hear the hum of the dishwasher, the water running in the sink, and occasionally, I'd hear a light cough or a sigh. I never cared to know what was going on in her head before, but now I was dying to get between her ears and find out the things she knew, to live through what she did when I wasn't there.

I was pissed Lucas was possibly hurt. The rage ran deep, contending with my dark emotions regarding the time I missed of his life because of Emmy's foolish decisions. I was angry for my son, but I'd be the biggest douche bag in Chicago if I wasn't also angry for his mother. Regardless of what she did to me, if Kyle Sterling physically hurt her, I wanted to personally break every bone in his smug body. I had wanted him to hurt her, I really did, but not with his hands. I had only wanted her to feel the same emotional pain I'd felt. I never wanted her to suffer any physical abuse, and admittedly, I was still a douche bag for wanting her to suffer at all.

Emmy stepped out of the kitchen, wiping her wet hands on her jeans as she took a look around the living room and dining area to make sure everything was tidy. She didn't once look at me or say anything before disappearing into the room for the night. Up until this point, this was our version of normal, and I was okay with normal. But this time, it didn't sit well with me and it made me uneasy.

So, I did what any grown ass man would do in my position. I went to my big sister's for some hot chocolate and a dose of harsh, cold reality.

On my way to Lena's, I dialed Claire at her office. She always worked late on Tuesdays. I wanted to make sure she was okay, but I especially wanted to ensure she went to the pharmacy like she said she would, but the call went to voicemail. It was possible she was busy or even in a late meeting, so I didn't call back. I had to trust she did what she said she would and not put us in a potentially dire situation.

I let myself into Lena's like I did the night after I met Lucas for the first time. This time, she wasn't expecting me, but when I stepped into the kitchen, she didn't seem surprised to see me. Immediately, she pulled another mug out of the cabinet.

"I'm glad you stopped by," she said as she poured me a cup of hot cocoa.

I gladly took the steaming mug from her. "Me too."

"Do you want some cookies?"

I looked at her with suspicion. "I came here to get some things off my mind, but bringing out the cookies means you have something of your own to say."

She grinned as she produced a container of cookies. "I can't offer my little brother a fresh, homemade cookie?"

"Now I'm just plain scared." I frowned, but eagerly removed the plastic lid and took a few of the treats.

Lena sat down across from me and didn't waste any time making me earn my treats. "You're an asshole," she said conversationally. "Do you know what an epic asshole you are?"

I said nothing, because I knew she was about to tell me what an epic asshole I was.

"You invite that woman and her baby into your home—to make it their own—but it's not a home. It's a tomb. With baby stuff. I know you were angry and hurt about what Emmy did, Luke, but you have to move past it, or let Emmy take Lucas and move out."

"Am I supposed to just forget what she did, Lena? Is that what you're suggesting?" I asked quietly, trying not to snap at her.

"Actually, yes. That's exactly what I'm saying, Luke. You're treating her like shit."

"I am *not* treating her like shit."

"Yes, you are! You completely ignore her, as if she isn't even worth the breath your words would use."

"Maybe she's not," I muttered, knowing how cruel I sounded.

"See? Epic. Asshole." She took a bite of a cookie and sipped her hot chocolate.

"What do you want me to do, Lena? Treat her like a fucking queen?"

She pointed at me as she swallowed. "That's exactly what you should be doing. Emmy is the mother of your son—you don't even pretend to talk to her even when you're surrounded by family. The only time you talk to her is if you guys need to talk about Lucas, and even then, you rather talk at her and not to her."

"Should I sit down with her every night over a cup of fucking hot chocolate and ask her how her day was?"

"It wouldn't kill you if you did. Can you not see she's suffering?"

I shifted uncomfortably. I tried not to see it, but of course I did.

"Luke, I think Emmy is very depressed."

I threw my hands up, irritated. "Oh, so now you're a psychiatrist."

"No, you asshole. I have a pair of eyes that work just fine, as do you. You can't miss the misery that woman is carrying around with her, but you choose to ignore it."

"I'm not the one who damaged her. It was the other way around."

"Everything is all about you, isn't it?"

I knew she was getting angry when she pushed away her mug and threw down her cookie. I also knew I'd be in a fair amount of trouble and at risk of getting my ass kicked if her hot chocolate was no longer hot when she got back to it.

"I understand you're still angry, but she's beating herself up enough, Luke. She probably thinks she deserves the way you're treating her, but she doesn't. Emmy is an excellent mother to Lucas and she's right here with the rest of us helping take care of Mom. Need I remind you of your clean apartment and hot dinners every night? She doesn't deserve to be treated as terribly as you're treating her. Stop punishing her. It's not like you to be cruel, but you're going above and beyond to be nasty."

I sighed as I focused on picking at my cookie. "I'm not sure I can just stop being hurt by what she did."

"You may never stop being hurt by what she did. But you won't even try. You need to really look at her and try to make it work better than it is now, because this isn't good for Lucas, either."

I knew she was right. No matter how stubborn I was being about it, I knew Lena was absolutely right, but I didn't know how to change it. I didn't know how to just suddenly open up casual dialogue with someone I disliked so hard for so long—someone I loved so hard but hurt me fifty times harder. That's why I was in Lena's kitchen, though. I don't know why I fought her when the very reason I showed up was to get advice on how to begin to repair my relationship with Emmy.

"She has nightmares," I said softly as I stared at the cookie crumbs on the table. "I don't know how long they've been going on, but last night I heard her and…"

I crushed the remaining cookies in my hand.

"What happened to her?" Lena asked gently. "Something happened. I can see it in her eyes."

Both of my hands closed into tight fists. "I think he hurt her. It's possible he hurt Lucas, too."

Her eyes widened. "The other guy?"

I nodded. She was quiet for a long time before she spoke again. "But…if he would've hurt Lucas, surely she would've said something."

I chuckled bitterly. "She didn't even tell us about Lucas until he was five months old, Lena."

"I know, but that's different. I think Sam would've spoken up."

"Maybe." I was doubtful. "Maybe Sam doesn't know."

She leaned back in her seat and tapped her fingers on her mug. "Emmy's not going to open up to you right now. It's going to take some time, and you're going to have to be nicer."

Lena was right. I felt a sense of resolve I hadn't felt since Emmy and Lucas moved in, but I still had my doubts. "I guess we should at least be able to have a conversation that doesn't involve groceries or the baby. But I don't want you to expect too much out of this."

"I only expect for you to be the kind-hearted soul I know you are. Maybe you can get her out of the house more, too. She doesn't get out much at all."

I snorted. "I should hire her in the office."

I was only joking, but Lena said, "Why not? Isn't that her thing?"

I looked at my sister. "I'm not sure if she's ready to go back to work, and we don't have a babysitter."

"You won't know until you ask her, and god knows you could use some help getting the firm in order."

I leaned forward, feeling a little optimistic about the idea. "What about Lucas?"

"I'll watch him."

"Okay." I nodded slowly. "I'll ask her."

Just like that, I got the answer I needed. I now knew how to begin the healing process with Emmy. I didn't set my hopes very high, but at least I now had a starting point.

Chapter Seven

Emmy moved around the kitchen preparing dinner, lost in her own thoughts. When I walked in holding Lucas, she only acknowledged me with a glance, as if I'd get whatever I needed and get the hell out. But when I moved closer to her, she looked up, a little startled.

I offered her a small, friendly smile. She drew back a little bit, probably not even realizing it. She wasn't accustomed to my smiles being directed at her. "I need a huge favor."

Her eyes focused on a point below my eyes, her brow furrowed.

"My office is a mess," I admitted, my smile widening a bit. "It's so disorganized and we're incredibly busy. My receptionist...well, she's just a receptionist. I need someone to come in and get us organized and on track."

Her gaze met mine for the first time in months, and her mouth hung open in genuine surprise. "You're asking me?"

"Yes, I am. You're a very good office manager. I wish I had thought to ask you sooner."

She hesitated, eyeing me with some suspicion. Finally, she turned her attention back to the stove. "I can try," she answered softly. "When?"

I adjusted Lucas in my arms. "Tomorrow."

She glanced at me and her son. "What about Lucas?"

"Lena will watch him."

I could tell she was conflicted. She probably had no intentions of going back to work anytime soon and leaving our son in the care of someone else. She bit her bottom lip as she thought about it. I'd forgotten how sexy I used to think it was when she pulled that lip between her teeth.

Slow down, I told myself. I had to remember my intentions were to get help in my office while opening a casual dialogue within our home, not to rekindle any kind of flame.

"I'll do it," Emmy said finally.

"Thank you so much." I realized I sounded like I was gushing a little bit. "I know you'll be a big, big help."

The confidence she once had in herself and abilities seemed to be missing along with the rest of the elements that had made her the Emmy of the past. "I hope so."

"You will be. I know it. Hey, at least this gets you out of the house for a little while. Maybe this will be good for you. You haven't been yourself." That was the understatement of the century. This woman, who'd been slinking around my apartment all of these months, was someone else entirely.

"I haven't been myself in two years," she said softly, still refusing to meet my eyes.

I took a deep breath. In order to move forward, we'd have to acknowledge some faults—both of us. I didn't want the conversation to get too deep after so much non-communicating, but I couldn't walk away from her words, especially since they made my chest ache a little bit.

I took a reflexive step toward her. "Look, I know I haven't made things any easier. I guess I didn't realize how bad things have been here until Lena brought it to my attention."

Finally, her eyes met mine again. I was shocked at how gratifying that was, but Emmy only looked at me for an explanation.

"She said it was like a tomb in here, that unless we're talking to or about Lucas, we don't speak. She said that even when we're at family functions, I barely acknowledge you."

I felt like the epic asshole I was for acknowledging it out loud. Lucas had been quiet throughout the conversation thus far, as if he'd somehow known this needed to be done, but now he'd gone back to babbling and vying for my attention. I gladly gave it to him, because I honestly felt a little nervous about what she'd do with the information I gave her. She'd either agree with my sister and put me in my place like the old Emmy would have done, or she'd just quietly accept and forgive. I kind of wanted her to tell me I'd been an asshole.

"What else did Lena say?"

I definitely had not intended to go down this road, but we were talking, and I started it, so I needed to answer her questions before she shut down again.

"She said she thinks you're depressed and you believe you deserve how I treat you…and that you're still beating yourself up. I guess I didn't stop to think about it before today, or I just looked the other way, but I suppose she's right...on all accounts. I argued with her at first, but she got really pushy, as only a big sister can do."

She didn't answer, and that was like an answer in itself. It was as if she conceded to what I said, as if she was just too damn broken and didn't care if we knew it.

I watched her for a moment while she began to clean up some of the mess she made cooking. I should've backed off and focused on bringing her up to speed with all she needed to know about the firm, but I couldn't stop myself from pushing the current topic.

"I'm really looking at you for the first time since the day I met Lucas. Em, you just seem hollow. Like everything that makes you who you are is missing."

"Who am I really?" she asked, focusing on her chore. "The woman who steals another woman's man? Am I the woman who cheats a good man out of everything he deserves? Or am I the woman who lets herself be used and abused? Maybe I'm the woman who keeps a child from his loving father. That's who I am, Luke. You're not missing anything great."

I did not expect to hear anything like this from her. I wasn't sure exactly what I expected, but it wasn't this self-loathing bullshit. She really was still beating herself up over what happened between us. I couldn't blame her when I was cold and hostile to her every damn day. And I'm not certain I'd heard her right, but I thought I heard her say she was abused. If I had not heard her nightmare, I may have overlooked that sentence entirely, but now it only further confirmed Kyle Sterling had hurt her.

I didn't trust myself to speak, but I couldn't close my mouth. I felt Lucas's slobbery hands on my face but I didn't care.

"Don't look so surprised." The hint of sourness in her voice was the bit of emotion I'd seen from her in a long time. "You said yourself you were wrong about who I am."

Fuck. I knew when I first spoke those words they were cruel, but now I knew she'd hung on to them, which fueled her self-hatred. I tried to find the words now to take back the hateful ones, or to at least take away their effect, but I only managed to sputter out meaningless jabber.

She took Lucas from my arms and turned away.

"I'll put him down for bed," she said. "Enjoy your dinner."

The bedroom door closed. I stood rooted to the kitchen floor for a moment before marching over to the door with the intentions of bursting into the room and forcing her to continue with the conversation. But I knew I could end up pushing her too far, causing her to shut down completely, and I didn't want that. I hadn't intended for our conversation to be a heavy one, but now that it had happened, I wanted more. I wanted to know what went on inside her head. Everything she'd done to me suddenly didn't matter anymore. What mattered now was I wanted the old Emmy back—not as my girlfriend, but as my friend. Not for my sake, but for hers...and for Lucas's. If I couldn't get her to climb out of this dark hole and back into the light, Lucas would never have any idea just how incredible his mother really was. He'd know a different person altogether, and that made me sad for him.

And maybe a little for myself, too.

****

I watched Emmy's face as she left Lucas with Lena the next morning. I could tell she struggled with it, but she sucked it up and quickly walked away. I understood how hard it must've been—she was never separated from Lucas for more than a couple of hours at a time, and now she had to leave him for an entire day. I also had a feeling she tended to use Lucas as a barrier between her and everyone else, and now she had nothing but her own skin.

To get her mind off Lucas on the drive to the office, I gave her as much information as I could about the firm and its needs. She listened intently and asked questions, but I don't think anything could've prepared her for the reality of the mess.

She stood in the middle of the main room turning in a slow circle with her eyes wide and her mouth unhinged. I was embarrassed. Emmy was an administrative beast. It was like having a dirty kitchen and bad food at a restaurant and having Robert Irvine come in, but I knew Emmy could be much scarier than the star chef. At least the old Emmy was. I was worried I'd only get the new, quiet, docile Emmy when I really needed Emmy the beast, but she didn't let me down.

My associates and I watched with amazement as some of the woman I used to know reared her awesomely scary head and laid

63

into Kacey after she walked in the door with her I'm-Just-Here-To-Get-Paid-For-Taking-Up-Space attitude. My partner, Steve, seemed equally impressed, and one of the other attorneys announced his newfound love for her.

I wanted to watch Emmy in action for a while longer, even though this was only a little bit of the old her. I was intrigued and even happy to see her emerge, but I had work to do. So I left her to what she does best and went into my office. I didn't see her again until I was on my way out for court. I was just blown over by all the work she'd accomplished in only a couple of hours, and I was even further impressed Kacey was actually working.

Emmy had pulled her hair back into a ponytail and rolled the sleeves of her blouse up to her elbows. The first few buttons were unbuttoned, giving me the smallest glimpse of ample cleavage. I had seen her breasts plenty of times since she moved in with Lucas, but seeing her with a kid attached to her wasn't even a little bit attractive, whereas seeing her clothed but sporting a little bit of cleavage was hot.

"This looks great," I said with a big grin on my face as I observed all the work she had done.

She blew out a hard breath. "We still have a very long way to go. Your files are a mess. I have Kacey fixing some of it, but it's going to take a while."

I nodded and watched her as she bit her lip and glanced around the office. She murmured what sounded like a list of things to do, more to herself than to me.

It brought a smile to my face to see a little bit of the woman I'd once known. "I have to be in court in a little while, but I'll be back to get you around five."

"No." She gave me a dismissive wave. "Just get Lucas and go home. I'll be fine getting back."

I wanted to object. I didn't want her overdoing it on her first day, but before I could speak, Craig and Lanna, my fourth lawyer in the firm, noisily entered the office, garnering our attention with their obnoxious bickering. It was their typical way of communicating with each other, but I didn't want Emmy to be put off by it, especially since it was often entertaining. I made quick introductions. Craig was so happy I'd brought in help that he embraced her.

I wanted to tell Em to leave at five, but when she turned her head to look at the client reception area she'd set up, I just barely saw the tiniest curve of a smile on her mouth. She was in her element and it had been a very long time since she was able to find something satisfying outside of Lucas. I couldn't squash that.

"Don't work too late," I advised.

She nodded reflexively, barely sparing me a glance before she tackled another task, whispering to herself.

I wanted to hug her with gratitude as Craig had done, but I thought better of it and forced myself to walk away.

****

When Emmy came home from work that night, she looked exhausted, but accomplished. She hugged and kissed Lucas for so long, I worried she may not want to leave him again, but then I realized we never discussed how long she'd be working for me. Maybe I'd bring it up over the uneaten dinner from last night I'd set on the table for us. Truthfully, I needed her for more than just a day. I knew if anyone could get us on track at the firm, it was Emmy, and I was still angry with myself for not seeing past my own rage and pain to ask her sooner. I really needed her, and I knew just how to sweeten the deal.

"My mom made you another apple pie," I said to her as she practically mauled our son with affection. "She said it's a gift for returning to work."

She frowned. "If I didn't know any better, I'd say your mother wants me to stay fat."

Fat? My eyes traveled over her heavy breasts, curvy hips, and luscious ass.

I held back my smile. "You're not fat, but if you don't want the pie, I'll gladly take it off your hands."

She poked me in the chest. "Touch my pie and I'll break your fingers. Lucas, say night-night to Daddy."

My heart beat a little harder at her words. Emmy usually only announced she was putting Lucas to bed before taking him from me, and she never referred to me as "Daddy," at least never within my earshot. The ice between us began to chip away faster than I could've hoped for. My regrets for not attempting to mend our relationship sooner were strong.

Emmy went into the bedroom to put Lucas to bed. I worried she would stay there after he was asleep and not come out for dinner. I didn't want to revert back to nights of tense silence. Now that I'd had a dose of the old Emmy, I wanted more. I wasn't sure how much more I wanted, though. I was still hurt by our past, but I was willing to move past it enough for us to at least be friends, and we weren't going to be able to be friends if she hid out in another room every night.

I walked over to the bedroom door, intending to drag her out—by her hair if necessary—and make her sit and eat dinner with me. I eased open the door quietly, not wanting to disturb Lucas if he wasn't yet asleep, but before I had the door open more than a few inches, I saw her.

Emmy stood near the bathroom door, pulling her slacks down over her thighs. The pants dropped to the floor a second later, leaving her clad in a pair of green cotton panties and her white blouse. I should've turned away and went back to the dining room, but I was frozen in place as she began to unbutton the blouse. She peeled it off and let it fall to the pile on the floor at her feet. A moment later, the matching green bra was off, but when she started to pull off her panties, I somehow made myself walk silently away.

I practically threw myself into the kitchen to start cleaning up imaginary messes. I tried to ignore the erection in my lounge pants and prayed Emmy wouldn't see it when she came back out. I had to get my head together. There was no denying Emmy was attractive, and even when my dislike for her was at its peak, I couldn't ignore that fact, but I had to put things in perspective. Anything beyond friendship for the two of us would be disastrous. Even a roll in the hay would be unacceptable—enjoyable, but unacceptable. The fact of the matter was: her cheating and withholding Lucas from me were injustices that would prevent me from ever being anything other than her friend.

I reheated dinner and had just set it down on the table when Emmy came out of the bedroom dressed in flannel pajamas. I was relieved I didn't have to drag her out by her hair.

She lingered near the table, obviously hesitant to sit down with me, as she looked at the two plates with her lip between her teeth. I understood what gave her pause. The only time we sat at the table together was when we were with other people, never alone.

I gestured at her chair as I opened a beer for her. She nodded, as if I had just given her permission, and sat down.

"Are you ready to quit yet?" I asked her, hoping she wouldn't say she was done after one day.

"I was ready to quit when I walked in the door."

I winced. "Sorry. There just hasn't been time to set up."

I knew by the way her shoulders squared and by the small crease in her forehead she was going into business mode. "Kacey and Craig both could've been helping with that."

"Maybe so, but in Craig's defense, he's one paralegal working for four attorneys."

She nodded once. "Fair enough. I think Kacey worked more today than the total time she's been with you."

"I guess Steve and I should've handled her better," I admitted. "I think she thought this would be a free ride because Steve's her uncle."

"You can't afford freeloaders. I think she'll work out, though. I need to ask you if it's okay for me to hire a cleaning company to come in and clean three nights a week."

"I can't afford it." I hoped my professional poker face hid how much it bothered me I couldn't afford to hire more help. I prided myself in taking care of my employees and my family, but truth be told, money was tight. I didn't really want Emmy to know how tight, especially since I'd vowed to take care of Lucas.

She was silent for a moment before quietly responding. "I can. I'll pay for it."

She couldn't be serious.

"No, I can't let you do that."

She spoke as if I hadn't just answered her in the negative, as if I hadn't spoken at all. "And I want to hire a few more people. You need at least one more paralegal."

I spoke slowly and clearly. I knew she was neither dimwitted or hard of hearing, but I needed to get my point across. "There's no money for that."

One shoulder rose and fell casually. "There's my money."

I shook my head adamantly. "No. I won't do that."

Hell no. I was the man of this household, and there was no way I'd let the mother of my child support us.

"Let's be frank," Emmy said before forking some pasta into her mouth. I waited patiently for her to finish chewing and continue with her thought. "If your firm doesn't get its shit together, you're going to drown. Chicago is full of other small firms who already have their shit together, and that's where the clients will go. I can even help you bring in upscale clientele, but you have to be a class act first."

I didn't want her to know how bad off I was. Accepting her money was a huge matter of pride for me, but she was right. I strongly believed Em knew what she was talking about. Her expertise had been proven in the past at Sterling Corp., and proven once again in my office in just one day. But my firm needed more than a small loan, more than what I thought she might have, and definitely more than I'd be willing to accept from her.

"I know your family is well off, but do you personally have that kind of money? I doubt it."

One of her eyebrows rose in challenge. "You don't know that. We've never discussed my finances before."

I spread my hands wide. "So, let's discuss them."

She glanced down at the bracelet on her wrist. I'd seen her wear it before, but it always seemed like it weighed her down. She'd fidget with it often, frowning and sighing. Before I moved back to Chicago, I'd never seen the bracelet before. I imagined Kyle had given it to her, and that bothered me more than I admitted.

"I am a trust-fund baby," she began, glancing warily at me. "I've been getting an 'allowance' dumped into an account every four months since I was eighteen. My parents paid for my education, my car, and all my needs until I got out of college. I've always worked and saved most of what I earned. My family doesn't flaunt their wealth, and unless you looked a little deeper, you probably didn't know we not only have our one 'plantation' in Louisiana, but several spread out in other states. Your cotton undershirt probably originated on one of my family's farms. My father is highly invested in oil and a couple other resources. The bar I love so much? It's mine. I own it, and it does well."

The shock I felt would've knocked me on my ass if I wasn't already sitting down. I didn't go to that bar very often with Emmy, but I knew she spent a lot of time there. It irked me a little she had failed to tell me she owned the place. I dated her for about eight months, and we were friends for a few years prior to that. I couldn't fathom why it was such a big fucking secret she owned the bar. I wanted to ask her, but she wasn't finished telling me about her apparent significant personal wealth.

"When Donya was modeling, she paid me to handle her finances. Then other models paid me to handle their finances. When I first started working at Sterling, I bought stock as soon as I could. I sold it soon after I left, and they were doing extremely well."

She paused and looked at me as if she wasn't sure she wanted to continue. I was pretty sure there wasn't much more she could tell me that could further shock me.

I was wrong.

"I also left with…with compensation,"

"Like a severance package?" I was still trying to recover from everything else she had just told me.

"Something like that." She paused before taking a deep breath and rushing her next words. "Walter Sterling paid me to go away."

I wasn't sure I heard her correctly. I thought she said Walter Sterling paid her to go away, but that would be a bribe. Emmy obviously didn't need a bribe, nor was the Emmy I knew that morally corrupt to accept one, but when she looked at me for a reaction, I realized she had really said what I thought I heard her say.

"Are you fucking serious?" I exploded. "You took a bribe?"

"Yep." I could tell that there was more she wasn't telling me. "I was going to return it, but after…after what happened before I left Jersey, I decided to keep it. I haven't touched any of it."

"What happened?" I leaned forward.

Whatever Kyle did to her had to be something significant if Walter Sterling felt it necessary to bribe her.

She gently shook her head, closing me off from that part of herself. I was disappointed, but I didn't want to push her, even though I felt kind of angry with her for taking money, for hiding the bar—hiding her wealth from me.

"I don't want to talk about that. My point is, I want to help you, and I'm perfectly capable of doing it. You should let me."

Fuck.

My brain was in overload with all I'd just learned. As much as I wanted to focus on the secrets that had been withheld, there would be time for that later. I had to seriously consider her offer. It seemed even more important to me now to be the one to support my son, and even Emmy to some degree—whether she needed it or not.

Yes, it was about my pride, but I always believed men should be the primary support for their families, and regardless of Emmy's large bank account, I didn't want to be upstaged. If I took a loan, which was already chipping away at my dignity, I could get the firm to the level it needed to be to succeed. I could then pay her back and continue to support her and Lucas.

"A loan," I forced myself to say. "Everything you spend I pay back…with interest."

"No interest."

I was unwilling to yield on this. "*With* interest."

"One percent."

One percent was like peeing in the ocean and she knew it. "Eight percent."

"Two and a half.".

"Seven and a half."

"Four."

Her stubbornness drove me fucking crazy.

"Six and three quarters," I insisted, trying not to lose my patience.

"Five percent is the highest I'll allow," she said with finality. "You're being ridiculous."

"You're being too generous."

Her eyes moved over my face. "I feel like I owe you something."

After the way I'd treated her for the past few months, I couldn't believe she actually felt like she owed me anything.

"You gave me a kid, Em. You don't owe me anything."

"What if he grows up and turns out to be a loser?"

I tried not to laugh, because I knew she was rather serious.

"Then I may insist on some compensation. Until then, you don't owe me anything. So I'll accept a capped loan, with five and a half percent interest."

"Capped? I don't know how much I'll have to spend in your crappy office." I loved that she didn't feel any need to be polite about the state of my office.

"Then I suggest you set a budget, Miss Grayne."

"Fine." She stood up and collected our plates. I followed her into the kitchen, pulled a beer out of the fridge, and leaned against the counter as she started to load the dishes into the dishwasher.

Her response had come too easily, making me eye her with distrust. "You agreed to that too fast."

"No, a budget is fine." She began to wipe down the counters and stove before getting a beer. Something was up; she gave in far too easily.

"So, what kind of budget did you have in mind?" I prodded.

"Oh, I don't know. Not much."

"I don't believe you. How much is not much?"

"Well..." she began slowly. "You need more staff, more equipment and furniture, advertising, and money just to function for your clients."

She was pussyfooting around, as if I would forget all about it and she'd get to spend as much as she pleased. "How much, Em?"

She shrugged. "I guess...one and a half million."

I choked on my beer while she stood there and watched me with mild amusement. If I didn't have to address this million-dollar shit, I would've done something else to amuse her. It'd been too long since I saw a genuine sign of amusement out of her. "*One and a half million dollars?*"

"I can do two or three," she said in a high voice, trying to stop her lips from curling at the corners. Now she was fucking with me, but if I let it go, she would seriously try to spend two or three million dollars. No one in this day and age just had a few million lying around. Except, of course, my baby's mama.

"I thought maybe a hundred grand, at most two fifty. Not over a million!"

She threw up a hand. "I said I can do two or three!"

"You're crazy. Two fifty, and no more."

"What's wrong with one mil?" She asked the question in the same way she would ask, "What's wrong with candy?"

"Did you ever consider the possibility I won't be able to pay that back?"

71

"You will," she insisted gently.

"You're insane." I frowned. Borrowing money from a bank was one thing, but borrowing this kind of money from Emmy, despite her financial situation, made me uneasy.

"I really want to do this, Luke."

"It's a lot of money, Emmy."

She shrugged and proceeded to stare me down. I stared back, trying to look as formidable as possible under the circumstances, but her pretty green and golden brown specked eyes burned into my own and straight through my head. Shamefully, I looked away first.

"Okay," I said grudgingly.

She failed at biting back a triumphant smile. "Okay."

Sulking, I gave the pie a glance. "Can we have pie now?"

"Of course."

Then it happened. She gave me a full-blown smile that made the shame I felt in taking her money well worth the price.

Chapter Eight

Emmy and I had a great second work day together. We accomplished a mountain of tasks, and everyone seemed to be on board with her game plan, even Kacey. We ate lunch at my desk, and though we worked throughout the meal and didn't discuss anything personal, it was nice. The heavy tension surrounding us only days ago was gone. We even ate dinner together again—takeout pizza, wings, soda, and leftover pie for dessert. Em was on the quiet side, but the line of communication between us was wide open, and we chatted with an easiness I hadn't realized I'd been missing.

After Lucas was asleep and the kitchen was clean, however, she silently began to slither into the bedroom without so much as a glance at me on the couch. It pissed me off a little bit, because things had been going very well.

"Hey," I said to her just before she stepped inside the bedroom.

She paused and looked at me with some apprehension. I guess I didn't blame her. I knew she wasn't quite used to our sudden burst of comradery. It'd take some time for her to trust that I wouldn't revert back to being a complete and utter assfuck. Now that I had her attention, I had no idea how to keep it. I contemplated making up some fake task for her to help me with.

But lying never got us anywhere before.

I gave her a teasing wink as I stood up. "You don't have to crawl back into your cave just because the boy is asleep."

"Oh..." She looked taken aback, but at least she met my eyes.

Then her gaze dropped and she focused at the floor between us.

Damn.

I took a few cautious steps toward her. She lifted her eyes from the floor and watched me warily. It hurt a little bit to see her eyes guarded, as if she had reverted back to that docile, wounded animal. In the office, she'd been in beast mode, ordering everyone about and making grown men quake.

I held my hands up, to surrender and to placate as I closed the distance between us.

"We've had a rough few months. "It's mostly my fault, and I'm sorry. I just…I think we can be friends, and I think Lucas needs to see that. I don't want to teach my son how to be a cold bastard like I was to you. Even if we're not together, he should see we're at least a team as far as he's concerned, not two separate entities who don't communicate. I don't want that for him, and I don't want him to grow up believing his relationships have to be just as dysfunctional."

"I…" she started, but then bit her lip.

"What is it?" I asked softly.

Her eyes glistened. Surprised, I inched closer. It seemed as though she was about to cry.

She blinked up at the ceiling, definitely blinking back tears. "The heels I wore the past couple of days were my pre-pregnancy heels. My feet are too fat for them still and I have blisters all over my heels. I was about to go in the bathroom and soak them. And maybe cry a little." She sniffled. It was pathetically cute.

I really shouldn't have laughed, but I couldn't stop myself. I threw my head back and laughed harder than I had in months, maybe longer than that. It felt really good to laugh so genuinely hard, and with Emmy.

"I'm sorry," I said through my final chuckles as she glared daggers at me. "The things women do to look hot in a pair of heels."

A blush rose in her cheeks, but she didn't respond.

"Okay, go soak your sore feet. Wear flats tomorrow."

She let out an aggravated sigh. "I don't own any flats."

"Take some time off in the morning to go shoe shopping."

"There's too much to do."

"I'm your boss," I reminded her. "I command you to go shopping for sensible shoes to be worn in the office."

An eyebrow raised and a hand went to her hip. "You're not my boss."

"You work for me. That makes me your boss."

"I work *with* you. I'm doing you an enormous favor by making your pretend office into a real one, and I don't get paid, Mr. Kessler. Therefore, I do not work for you and you are not my boss."

She was right. Furthermore, she *was* my benefactor. So technically, it was I who worked for her. She kind of owned me.

But pushing her buttons to make more of that snarky girl I used to know ease out of her dead shell was fun. "If you don't do as I tell you, I'll fire you."

"Fire me and your piece of crap office will eventually get flushed," she challenged.

"Is that the best you got? Crap and flushed? You reason like an eight-year-old."

Flustered, she blurted out, "Your mom!"

She disappeared into the bedroom while I went back to the couch, laughing at her.

About an hour later, Emmy sat her ass down on the other end of the sofa and propped her feet up on the coffee table with a small sigh.

"What are you watching?"

"One of those international real estate shows. This one's in Paris."

She threw me a curious glance. "I didn't know you cared about these kinds of shows."

"I usually don't. This one's in France, though. It made me think of your time there. Where were you in France?"

"Not too far from Burgundy."

I didn't know the difference between Burgundy and any other French town. "I guess that means nothing to me since I've never been to France."

"It's a little more than three hours outside Paris," she explained.

"Did you like it out there?" I tilted my head to look at her.

She looked at me for a moment before answering. "I guess so. The area surrounding the home I was staying in was…pretty."

"Who were you staying with?" I felt like an ass for not knowing any of this sooner.

"Helene and Marcus—they're friends of Donya's." She gave a small smile. "They were very kind."

"Did you enjoy your time with them?"

Her smile faded into a frown and she turned away from me. Her eyes focused on the flat screen in front of us. "I wouldn't say that."

I never asked why she'd gone to the French countryside. I'd been too angry and bitter to ask about it before. I had been curious deep down, but too stubborn to talk to her.

"Why did you go?"

She didn't look away from the television, and she was so quiet for so long I wasn't sure if she actually heard me. Then I saw her chest rise and fall heavier than it should have, and with her damp hair pulled back into a ponytail, I was able to see the pulse racing in the sensitive flesh below her ear.

"I had to get away," she said just above a whisper. "I needed to be somewhere…unfamiliar."

I felt an uncomfortable weight in my chest. It began to dawn on me why she sprinted across the sea.

"What did you have to get away from, Emmy?" I should've asked from *whom* she had to get away from.

She let out a heavy, weary sigh. "From life. I had to get away from life." She got up from the couch. "I'm more tired than I thought I was. See you in the morning."

She disappeared into the bedroom again. I sat on the couch and stared at the door, surprised by the anger that had reignited inside me. Emmy had kept so much away from me and she was doing it again. She thought by shutting herself in that damn room she could just cut me off and not tell me anything. I had the right to know what had happened, who or what chased her pregnant ass all the way to the fucking French countryside where she spent I don't even know how long with strangers, without her family and friends.

I pushed my hand through my hair and sighed with frustration. I kept telling myself this was about Lucas—what his life was like in utero—but honestly, it was about Emmy, too. I wasn't over what she did, not by a long shot, and though my change in heart toward her was rather sudden, it was genuine. I cared to know whatever her struggles were, but I was pissed off she'd chosen to run away to another country instead of humbling herself and coming to me for help.

She really thought I'd turn her away if something terrible had happened.

I hope Kyle Sterling breaks your heart and makes you choke on it.

The words bounced around in my head and answered my question. Yes, she probably did think I'd turn her away, even if something terrible had happened. Even though I knew Kyle Sterling was probably somewhere in the equation to blame, I had to accept the fact my own words may have impacted Emmy's decisions thereafter. I had to accept the fact I may be just as much at fault as anyone else.

Chapter Nine

After that night when she told me she had to escape life, Emmy stopped closing herself off in the bedroom. But her smiles were small and sedated, and laughter was nonexistent. Sometimes, she'd say something incredibly smartass and I'd get my hopes up the old Emmy was finally coming through, but her eyes always gave her away. There was something completely broken inside her.

It held her back.

It held her down.

And consistently snuffed out whatever contentment she managed to find.

There were times when it seemed this broken thing was on the mend, but it would snap her back into the dark in a second, unexpectedly.

I gave Emmy a lot of credit though; she kept trying. She focused hard on putting my firm together. She focused even harder on being a good mom, and even when it looked like she just wanted to suffer alone, she made an effort to be social. Whereas in the past, she participated in family functions out of obligation, she went out of her way to draw closer to my sisters and mother. It had to be very hard for her to put herself out there while struggling to breathe on the inside.

The nightmares didn't fade. Sometimes I'd stand in the dark doorway and just listen. They were all very similar. Someone was attacking her, and though the dialogue would sometimes change, the ending was always the same. It didn't take long to hear the name I'd suspected. When she begged Kyle to stop hitting her, I had to hold my breath to keep myself from vomiting. I never wanted her to know I heard her nightmares. I knew it would just make her regress, but that first night when she cried for Kyle to stop, I sat on the edge of the bed and stroked her hair until she quieted. Whether or not she knew I was there, I don't know.

I didn't ask. And she didn't tell.

Late one night after listening to another one of Em's nightmares, I slipped out of the apartment and drove over to Claire's. It was well past that seventy-two-hour deadline, by weeks, but I had to make sure she'd done what she said she would. On my way over, I worried maybe she didn't do the backup birth control, and thought about what that could mean for me, for Lucas, and even for Emmy.

I didn't warn her I was on my way over. I wasn't sure if she had anyone over, or if she'd even let me in, but she was alone and reluctantly opened her door for me.

"Why aren't you home with your son?" she asked dryly with her arms folded across her midsection.

I refused to go any farther than a few feet into her apartment. "I needed to follow up on something with you."

"If you're here to find out whether or not I went to the pharmacy…" She took a deep breath. "I didn't."

My eyes must've almost fallen out of my head. I opened my mouth to speak, but she cut me off.

"Don't worry, Luke. I got my period."

I let out a ragged breath I didn't realize I'd been holding. My anger quickly came to a boil. "Why didn't you go to the pharmacy and take the Plan B, Claire? Why would you even fuck with that?"

"Not that you would care," she sneered. "But I was in a car accident the following morning." She ripped her robe open and my eyes were immediately drawn to the fading bruise across her chest from a seatbelt. "Keeping your child out of my belly was the last thing on my mind."

"Shit," I whispered and pushed my hand through my hair as I stared at the bruising. "I'm sorry."

"I don't care if you're sorry." Her voice broke over the words as she pulled her robe together again.

"Claire." I moved to touch her arm, but she held up her hand.

"Just leave. Go. You got what you needed, as usual. Now go home to your family."

I was such a fucking jerk. She was right—our whole relationship had always been about me and what I needed. If I had been a decent guy, I would've left her alone so she could find someone to give her what she needed. Now that I knew we wouldn't be sharing a child, I could finally do that.

Saying sorry again wouldn't have made any difference. I gave her an apologetic look instead and let myself out. I went back home and was surprised to find Emmy awake and moving around in the kitchen.

I tossed my keys on the counter. "Hey."

She responded groggily, blinking away the sleep, and her voice hoarse. "Hey. Working late?"

"Yes," I lied. "Are you okay?"

"Yes," she lied as well, and took a sip of hot drink. "Would you like some hot tea?"

I watched her, studied her face for many unanswered questions. "Yes."

A few minutes later, we both stood in the kitchen sipping the warm liquid. We didn't speak, but I found comfort in her presence and hoped she found some in mine.

****

Vivian Deluca was my arch enemy. She had been my arch enemy since I ran up against her in court in my first year as an attorney. Only a couple of years older than me, she already had a strong foothold in one of Chicago's biggest, most reputable law firms. She ate guys like me for breakfast with her bare hands and dabbed away our tears that clung to her lips with high quality linen napkins.

What made matters worse, was Viv was sex in a suit. With smooth, edible-looking skin the color of mocha, she looked like she was a descendent of gods and goddesses. Her dark hair was always pulled into a fierce bun or a tight braid that trailed down between her shoulder blades, and she had a body that appeared both well exercised and well fed. She had a slim waistline, but generous hips and an ass that made even my mouth water.

Her suits always perfectly outlined her well-endowed chest and long, shapely legs, but she was a professional through and through. There was always only just barely a glimpse of cleavage, and her modest skirts never went higher than a couple inches above her knees. Her eyes, the color of honey, were shrewd and calculating. I'm sure many a man glimpsed the depths of both heaven and hell in them.

Vivian Deluca had the strongest personality I'd ever encountered. She was a bully in high heels. She didn't bullshit and she didn't play nice. Her sweet smile fooled only the foolish, and there were a lot of foolish people in Chicago.

She had been absent on the legal scene for over a year now. She'd won a huge case against the workers of a huge multibillion-dollar company and then went on sabbatical. There were a lot of whispers around town. Some people said a huge scandal broke out between her and one of the partners. Some suspected her evil deeds finally caught up to her and someone took her out, and then there were rumors she had a nervous breakdown. I didn't know which one to believe. I was disappointed she was gone, because she was great competition in court and I loved the look on her face the three times she lost to me.

Two weeks before Lucas's first birthday, Vivian Deluca suddenly reappeared on the scene. I'd met one of my clients at a pub close to the office. The client had to leave because of an emergency at home. I was just about to settle the bill when she slid onto the bar stool beside me. I didn't really look at her right away. The place was getting crowded and all the barstools would've soon been taken.

"Luke Kessler." Her familiar voice caught my attention.

I snapped my head up and met her honey eyes. "Vivian Deluca. What an unpleasant surprise. I thought I was rid of you for good."

"Oh, I'll bet you did. You and every other attorney in town." She turned toward me, crossing one leg over another. She was close enough her crossed leg brushed against mine.

I leaned back to assess her as she caught the bartender's attention and ordered a drink. "So, where've you been? Visiting your vacation home in hell? Torturing small children? Drowning puppies?"

"Aww." She made a sympathetic sound with her tongue. "You really did miss me, didn't you, Luke?"

"As much as I'd miss having someone pluck my fingernails out with a pair of pliers," I said cheerfully.

Her full lips pulled back into a dazzling grin. "I love it when you talk torture."

"There are a lot of rumors floating around about you." I threw money down on the bar.

"Oh, I'm sure they're all quite interesting, but the truth is unfortunately very boring."

"And that is?"

81

The bartender put her drink in front of her. She picked it up and took a long sip while I waited for her to answer.

"My divorce was final a week before my last case." Her smile did not falter, and that was a little scary and impressive. "My children were having a difficult time. I needed to focus on my family. At least two of the rumors were somewhat true. Our home had become a hell and my children were tortured."

Sometimes I had to remember that evil bitches were human, with human feelings and human problems.

"I'm sorry." I meant it. I didn't like her, but I did feel bad for her children.

"Don't be sorry. I'm not. Everything's fine now." She took another long sip of her drink as she openly looked me over. "I heard you became someone's father."

I smiled at the thought of Lucas. "I did. He'll be one in a couple of weeks."

"I heard your child and his mother both live with you, but you aren't together. That must be a frustrating relationship."

My smile slipped as my defenses began to go back up. I had to be careful not to show any form of weakness around this woman. "It's a functional relationship."

She chuckled, which made my blood run a little cold. "Oh, let's not talk in circles, Luke. It must be a sexually frustrating relationship."

I stared at her for a moment before breaking out in a grin.

"You know, I did miss how straight forward you are." I checked my watch to make a show of my impending departure. "As much as I enjoyed this little reunion, I must be on my way."

"Going home to your functional family?" she asked condescendingly.

I got to my feet. I found myself standing entirely too close to her. "See you in court sometime, Vivian."

She looked me over in a way that she'd never done before. It was a different kind of hunger from what I was used to with her. "Or, you can see me before then."

I laughed rudely, almost in her striking face. "Hopefully not." I started to move away, but she slipped her hand into my jacket and placed her palm on my chest. I was shocked into immobility.

She presented her case as she would in court. "We're both single, responsible adults. We can have a no-strings-attached sexual relationship."

She rendered me speechless with her proposal. I never once thought about taking Vivian to bed, even after I was able to acknowledge the fact she was a knock out. I was okay with stepping away from my dominant side every now and then for a good time, but Vivian seemed like the type who'd want to run the show. Not only would she want to run the show, but she'd want me in submission.

I *don't* submit.

"While that sounds very exciting and all together terrifying, I'm going to decline the offer." I gingerly removed her hand from my chest as if it were an alien, blood-sucking species.

"I understand," she cooed with her sweet smile. "You don't think you will be able to satisfy me, and I understand. Really, I do. I can be quite intimidating."

"I'm not intimidated, Vivian. I just don't like you very much." I started to move away again, but her words stopped me.

"Then we can have a very *functional* relationship, Luke. You see, I don't much like you, either. Therefore, there'll be no chance of either of us developing any type of emotional attachment. It would just be good sex, and I can only speak for myself, but I mean *really* good sex."

Vivian always had a predatory gleam in her eyes, but now she was a different kind of hunter. It was rather hot and I couldn't deny it with my cock beginning to stir in my pants.

But I couldn't be with her because I hated her, and for the same reasons I couldn't be with Claire. My free time should've been spent with Lucas and focusing on keeping my newly found friendship with Emmy in good standing. I didn't have extra time for screwing around.

"I missed the first five months of my son's life. I missed the entire pregnancy, too. As you well know, I have a very full schedule, especially since I now have my own firm, which is still in it's infancy. Any extra time I have goes to my child. I don't have time, Vivian. Not even for 'good sex.'"

She wasn't at all put off by my little speech. Just like she is in court, she was relentless at getting what she wanted—that being me.

"Luke, I'm now a single mother of three and I just started back to work last week. I, too, am limited on time, but I'll be damned if I'm going to just lie down and die. I completely understand your time restraints, which is another reason why we can work out so well for each other. We can take what we can get when we can get it without whining or arguing. If I don't have time, you shrug your shoulders and wait until I do and vice versa."

She put her drink down on the bar and wrapped her fingers around my tie. She began to adjust it as she spoke. "Think about it, Luke. No bouts of jealousy, no cute little text messages throughout the day, and absolutely *no* commitment. We'll simply be mutually exclusive fuck buddies, but when one of us is ready to break it off, the other won't try to hang on. It'll simply be over."

I peered down into her eyes. I really didn't like Vivian Deluca. I respected her as an attorney, kind of, but I didn't necessarily like her. And I didn't have time for this, regardless of what she said, sleeping with her could interfere with both our jobs if we came head to head in court.

And there was Emmy...

I wasn't with Emmy, and even though I occasionally had some very intimate and even emotional thoughts about Em, I wasn't sure if we'd ever be able to be anything more than what we already were. The pain of what she did was still there in the background.

"And here I thought you had a pair of balls." Vivian sighed after I didn't respond.

She started to turn back around in her seat, but before I knew what I was doing, my hand was on her thigh. She looked up at me as if she just won a motion in court.

A half hour later, I was following Vivian into her townhouse. There were no offers for a drink or any casual conversation. I pushed her up against the wall as soon as the door was closed and pushed her skirt above her thighs as I planted my mouth on hers. I set the pace, letting her know no matter what happens in the courtroom, as far as our sexual relationship was concerned, I was the judge *and* jury.

I won't lie and say I didn't enjoy the sex, because I did. Vivian liked letting go of the reins in the bedroom, and I liked having control over her. But when it was all said and done and I was on my way home to Lucas and Emmy, guilt pulled me down. If circumstances were different, I would've been going back to Vivian for seconds and thirds, but regardless of how I tried to categorize my relationship with Emmy, I felt like I betrayed her. I didn't like how that felt, and I didn't know it at the time, but this would come back later to bite me in the ass.

Chapter Ten

Lucas put his little hands on Emmy's cheeks and pushed them together until she made a funny face, accompanied by a cute little squeal. Lucas released a billow of deep-bellied laughter only little kids can do, and then Emmy joined him. He did it again and again, entertaining himself, his mother, and those who watched them.

Emmy's laughter rang through my ears, dripped down into my heart, and spread throughout my body, making my fingers tingle and small currents of electricity dance up and down my spine. I hadn't heard more than a little chuckle from her in more than a year and a half. Even big, genuine grins were hard to come by from this haunted woman, but those didn't come close to this beautiful laughter. I didn't know I missed it until I heard it.

I watched, riveted as Lucas made Emmy laugh repeatedly until something else caught his attention. I wished I could've heard it a little bit longer, but my crazy kid was already toddling over to a toy another child abandoned moments before.

We were in a bookstore on a Friday morning, four months after Emmy started working with me at the firm. It was our first family outing since the day after Lucas entered my life. It wasn't planned that way, but Emmy had been taking Lucas to the bookstore once or twice a week since dropping her hours to part time, and I asked to tag along. I'd gone to get Emmy one of those frozen coffee drinks and stopped several feet outside the children's area to watch and listen to her laugh. Now that it was over, I stepped back in as if I hadn't just been the creepy guy staring from afar.

"Thank you," she said with a brief smile, as if she wasn't just laughing a moment before.

I winked and sat down beside her on a tiny chair to watch Lucas play with another little kid. Well…Emmy watched Lucas. I kind of watched Lucas, but every few seconds I'd look at her. Her hair was pulled back into a ponytail, but a few loose strands hung around her face. She had on tight jeans, a pair of brown high-heeled leather boots, a white T-shirt, and a leather jacket that matched her boots. She looked incredible, and she smelled so damn good I was tempted to run my nose over her skin and inhale until I had my fill of her mind-altering scent.

"I can't believe he's one." She sighed longingly.

I nodded. "It's been a long seven months."

Her shoulders slumped some, though she didn't look at me. I had an idea what was going through her head. She was probably thinking about all the time I'd lost with Lucas in the beginning. I know I was, but I didn't want her hanging on that.

"He grew so fast," I added quickly before she could start creeping back into herself. "And my nieces and nephews grew so fast. Can you believe CJ will be going into eighth grade?"

She smiled a little. "He thinks he's a grown ass man."

I laughed at my nephew and his idea of "swag."

"It's not just the kids who are growing. My firm is growing at a faster rate than I thought possible. You really did some miracle work, Em. In a matter of months, you turned my shit hole firm into a respectable place."

"Miracle work is an understatement of proportions too large to fathom," she teased with a gleam in her eyes.

I laughed. "I'm so very glad you are so humble about this."

"There are so many things I've screwed up on in life, but I'm an administrative goddess."

I chuckled as I watched her struggling not to grin. "I suppose you want me to bow down and kiss your boots?"

"No, but a crown made of paperclips would be awesome."

I laughed again. Even though she was so low key from the person she was capable of being, she made me laugh and smile, and often.

"Are you looking forward to Lucas's party?"

She let out a sigh of exasperation. "Is my mother still invited?"

"Of course she is."

"No, not so much then." She looked at me pointedly. "That party is out of control; you know that, right? You know you went overboard?"

"He's my first son," I argued. "And he's perfect. Of course I went overboard."

Lucas's party was going to be a big bash. We were having it at my sister Lorraine's, and pretty much everyone we knew was invited. Emmy just wanted to have something small. She said Lucas was so young, he wouldn't remember it ten years from now anyway, but I overruled her and went all out. I invited all her family from Louisiana, her best friend Donya, cousin Mayson, everyone who worked in the firm plus a few other friends and their families. Of course our entire Chicago family—including her brother Emmet and his wife and son who had just recently moved to the Windy City so Emmet could work in my firm.

"This party is so big we had to take off all today to prepare," she chastised. "By the way, I don't see how you're going to get too much done sitting here in the bookstore watching our son chew on baby books that already have god knows how many other babies' DNA on it."

I jumped up and snatched the book from Lucas's mouth. I didn't do anything funny, but he thought it was hilarious and giggled. I scooped him up into my arms and planted a kiss on his forehead. I couldn't get enough of this kid.

I reached my hand out to Em to assist her out of the chair. She looked at my hand as if it was a foreign object. I wiggled my fingers, insisting she take it. After a few more seconds, she relented and allowed me to pull her to her feet. There was no ignoring the charge of energy zapping between our enclosed hands. I just barely stopped myself from gasping. I know she felt it, too, because her eyes grew wide for a moment and then it was over. She pulled out of my grasp.

"Thanks," she mumbled and made herself busy by picking up her big pocketbook that doubled as a diaper bag.

"No problem," I managed to say.

We walked out of the store, quickly falling into conversation about all the things we needed to do for the party, but I didn't forget the feel of her hand in mine.

****

Fuck me.

Emmy stepped out of the bedroom and my jaw dropped. I quickly closed it while she was busy smoothing the green dress that stopped several inches above her knees. The neckline dipped just far enough to give a little peek at her cleavage, but it covered enough to be suitable for a child's party. The dress was snug, not grotesquely tight as some women tend to wear their clothing, but it complimented her curvy shape. She wore a pair of dark brown heels that gave her an extra four inches in height and beautifully displayed her bare legs. Her brown hair hung loose across her bare shoulders and down her back, and though her makeup was light, it was complimentary to her naturally smooth skin and gorgeous eyes.

I'd seen Em in all stages of undress in recent months, and I'd seen her wearing some very attractive outfits, but the way she looked for Lucas's party beat them all. She was breathtaking, just absolutely beautiful.

"Can you zip me up?" She turned her back to me.

"Of course."

I couldn't stop myself from checking out her ass just before I gripped the zipper between my fingers. Holy hell, I was literally inches from her bare back, only inches away from expertly unclasping her bra and peeling her out of this dress.

I zippered her quickly and stepped away before my erection poked her in the ass.

"There you are." I turned away before she could turn back around. I picked up the bags we needed to carry with us to Lorraine's in an effort to hide my erection, leaving Emmy to handle Lucas.

The first hour or so of the party, Emmy seemed a little withdrawn. I was sure I wasn't the only one who noticed. Too many of her smiles were forced, and she didn't seem to be having a good time, even though she was surrounded by people who loved her and Lucas. I knew it was her first really big gathering since before she took off for Europe, but I really wanted her to enjoy herself. Though there were a lot of kids running about and a lot of loud talking and laughter, and even though her mom was there, I expected Em to at least try to. It was a pity she looked so gorgeous but awkward at the same time.

I followed her to a corner of the room where there weren't too many people around.

"It's a great party," I said as we watched one of her nieces play with Lucas across the room.

"It is." She bit her lip.

"What's wrong, Em? Why are you unhappy?"

I thought for sure she'd close down on me, but she looked at me and sighed before taking a step closer so she could speak in a lower voice. Her scent wafted over me, adding to the visual I had before my eyes. I was tempted to pull her to me, but I kept my hands at my sides. We were just friends. My wicked thoughts about her lately were going to do nothing but cause trouble we didn't need.

"It's just…" she started and then sighed again. "Lucas isn't the first grandkid. In fact, he's nowhere near the first grandkid. None of my siblings had a huge party for any of their kids. I feel so…weird…guilty even for throwing this big bash for my kid—even though you're technically the one who threw it."

I opened my mouth to speak, to try to ease her mind somehow, but Samantha stepped in out of nowhere. I had no idea where in the hell she even came from.

"Well, nobody thought you'd ever have any children or settle down," she said. "That's why this is a big deal." She began to move away, but then she added, "I'm talking to both of you."

"I guess that's true," I said, feeling a little embarrassed. "My mom and sisters thought that about me at some point."

"I didn't know that." Emmy looked at me with curiosity. "You seem very much like the commitment type."

Oh shit, this was uncomfortable. I didn't want to discuss this with her. I never showed her that part of my life. She gave me a look that demanded I speak, but I was reluctant—too reluctant. To my surprise, Emmy reached out and pinched the hell out of me.

"Dammit!" I blurted out and took a step back from her before she could do it again. "I played the field…a lot. I had a different girl on my arm every other month."

"I didn't hear anything like that back in Philly," Em said with some suspicion. "You had two steady girlfriends over the years."

I gave her a sidelong look. "Correction. I had three steady girlfriends over the years. The first two were always on and off, not as steady as you think. And there were more before and between."

"Oh." She frowned.

If I had to guess at what was going through her mind at that moment, it had something to do with our past broken relationship. I knew she was hard on herself for hurting me, and I had been hard on her, too, but I didn't want her remorse anymore. I wanted to see her smile and to have a good time.

"The second woman, Vicky, she was basically just a distraction," I continued.

Her brows rose a little. "From what?"

I leaned toward her and spoke in a conspiring murmur. "From number three who didn't yet know she was going to be number three." I walked away from her, from my number three, the only one that had ever really mattered.

A little while later, I was still concerned about whether Emmy was going to be able to loosen up and just enjoy the day, and then I heard it. That beautiful sound that curled around my heart yesterday drifted across the room and made me stop in my tracks to look at the mouth it had come from. Emmy stood with Mayson and Donya, laughing, smiling, and talking animatedly. I had not seen this Emmy in so long, I had begun to wonder if she existed. When her eyes briefly met mine, she didn't withdraw her smile, though it was meant for her friends. She allowed me a full moment of that wondrous sight and it made my heart nearly leap out of my chest.

I returned the smile and looked away.

****

I woke up early the following morning to use the bathroom, but as usual, I checked on Lucas and Emmy while I was up. I planned to go back to sleep, but Lucas was standing up in his crib, looking at me expectantly. I knew there wasn't any chance for me to sleep any longer. Emmy was knocked out and snoring softly. Too many of her nights were spent in terror. I preferred for her to get some rest, so I plucked Lucas out of his crib and took him into the living room where he wouldn't disturb his mother.

"You want some breakfast, buddy?"

He patted the head of the stuffed whale I had given him seven months ago. "Eat?"

"Yeah, let's eat." I ruffled his blond hair.

He followed me into the kitchen, speaking in his own language. I pretended to understand and responded as I prepared a bowl of cereal for him. It was some toddler cereal Emmy found in the grocery store. I don't know why she just didn't give the kid Cheerios. Out of curiosity, I used Lucas's little spoon and tasted a spoonful of the cereal. I wish I could've seen my face when the taste hit me. It was disgusting, but as a real man, I chewed and swallowed that shit, mindful never to try it again.

After Lucas had his breakfast, I turned on the television, playing one of the many episodes of Sesame Street we had on the DVR. As he made camp on the floor to watch, I opened the door and grabbed my newspaper out of the hallway and settled on the couch. Lucas would talk to me every now and then and I would answer. This went on for quite a while before I looked up and caught Emmy staring at me. I couldn't help the grin that spread across my face.

"Good morning, number three."

She muttered something that sounded like a greeting and rushed into the kitchen. Lucas followed after his mother a moment later and I followed after him.

"Cup?" he asked Emmy.

He gazed up at her, and the way she looked back down at him with unconditional love made me smile.

"You want your cup?"

"Ya." He patted the whale's head. "Cup."

I got Lucas some juice in a sippy cup, but he didn't waste any time hanging about. He wandered back into the living room and seconds later shouted, "Emmo!"

"Elmo," Emmy and I said together.

Leaning her hip against the stove, she was so cute in her Penn State shorts and T-shirt, and her hair mussed from sleep. "You want some breakfast?"

"Sure. I could use some food. I tried Lucas's cereal, but it wasn't for me." I made the same face I think I made when I first tasted the cereal. To my delight, Emmy laughed.

"Oh my god, it's that sound again," I teased.

She rolled her eyes and tried to make a straight face as she turned away from me. She opened a cabinet door and stood on her toes in an attempt to reach a box of baking mix.

"What sound?" she asked as she stretched, grasping for the box with her fingertips. "Why do you put things way up on the third shelf where I can't reach?"

"Because it's funny watching you reach for it." I moved behind her, close enough to feel the heat of her body on mine. I felt her freeze, but she didn't say anything or try to move away. I reached for the box and slowly brought it down before her.

"Thanks." She snatched it from me and turned her face away, but not before I saw the redness that had settled in her cheeks.

That made me happy, to see I had made her blush, but then I remembered I didn't want to fuck this up. Bending her over the counter wasn't going to help anything. I moved away from her as she began to gather her ingredients.

"I'm going into the office after breakfast," I told her, standing near the entrance and out of her way. "I have to be in court first thing tomorrow morning and I want to make sure I'm well prepared."

"Okay." Her smile came automatically, and I had to wonder if she knew she was doing it. I don't know what exactly changed within her yesterday, but I rather liked it.

"You had a good day yesterday."

"Yes, I did. My mom only irritated me a little bit."

"About what?"

She glanced at me with one arched eyebrow. "What do you think?"

I knew, but I wanted to hear her say it. I overheard Sam grilling her about her sex life. Emmy had given very vague answers. I was pretty sure she wasn't having sex with anyone, I found myself curious to know.

"Hmm. I don't know. It can't be your hair or your clothes. You looked amazing yesterday."

Her face turned a brighter shade of red. Flashes of her skin turning this very shade at the height of her orgasm invaded my mind. With that floating around in my brain, I shouldn't have pressed on with the conversation, but now the burning need to know if anyone else was making her come overtook any common sense.

She thanked me for the compliment, but gave me no other hint. Not that I needed one.

"Hmm." I pretended to think hard on the matter, then I snapped my fingers. "Oh. Your sex life."

"Bingo." She rolled her eyes. "She thinks it's one of those use it or lose it things, which made me wonder about her and my dad and that's when I decided to have a drink."

"Yeah, no one wants to think of their parents getting it on. No one wants to know that their parents are having a quickie. Stuffing the old wrinkled salami. Having afternoon delight." I continued with every sexual innuendo I could think of while Emmy covered her ears and begged me to stop. Laughing, I finally gave up. "Okay, okay, I'm done."

"My god, that was horrible," she said, shaking her head.

I still had a chance to abandon the path I was about to follow, but I didn't. I tilted my head to study her. "Now I'm curious."

"About what?" Her eyes widened. "My parents? Gross!"

"No, dummy. About you."

"What about me?" She quickly looked away, giving me the impression she knew damn well what I was referring to.

"Are you, you know, on the verge of 'losing it' from not using it?"

The glare she shot at me fell a little short. Her lips were pursed and her eyebrows were down in angry slants, but she couldn't hold my gaze, and her throat moved every few seconds as she swallowed. She stumbled over half a dozen words before finally getting out a full sentence. "I don't have time!"

"There's always time." I tried to hide my grin. She wasn't having sex with anyone, or if she was, not often. I pretty much knew where she was at all times, but there were a few late trips to the grocery store, and a few days when Lucas was with Lena and Em wasn't at work. It was possible she found time to squeeze it in somewhere, no innuendo intended.

"I am either with Lucas or at the office. Like you have so much time on your hands for sex."

I poked my head out to check on Lucas. When I turned back, I saw Emmy's eyes on my chest and arms. Admittedly, it gave my dick a little bit of a jump to find her checking me out. I almost flexed just to be a showoff.

Without thinking first, I said, "I've made time." I instantly regretted it.

"When?" Emmy held a spatula in her hand as she cocked her pretty little head to one side.

Telling her when I made time for sex would make me look like such a dickweed. I had felt some guilt before, but now the guilt for the many nights I'd left Emmy and Lucas to be with Claire was like setting a bomb off in my gut.

I resisted the urge to glance away from her. "It doesn't matter when."

Her eyes narrowed. "Why not?"

"We don't need to discuss it anymore." I turned away from her in an attempt to cut off the conversation, but Emmy wasn't finished. She threw a big wooden spoon, nailing me in the back of the head.

"Luke, that's not fair! You started this conversation!"

"I know, but now I don't want to talk about it." I picked the spoon up.

"Why not?"

"Because..." I paused and released a breath. "My answers will make me look...dishonest." I rubbed the back of my head where she had hit me.

She stared at me for a long moment as if trying to figure me out. Suddenly, she pointed her spatula at me. For a second I thought she was about to slap me with it.

"Some of your late nights at the office were booty calls!"

Oh shit. Sometimes I wished she wasn't so damn smart.

Reluctantly, I answered. "Some, but not all."

"Oh my god!" She laughed, but it sounded off. It was as if she laughed and smiled with the barrel of a pistol leveled at her head. "And when was the last time you got some?"

"If I answer, you have to answer the same question," I said when I should've just answered her question and walked away.

Emmy looked away from me and concentrated on flipping pancakes. Her mouth had formed into a straight, tight line, and her body had stiffened some. She couldn't have possibly wanted to know about the last time I had sex. I felt trapped now. If I didn't answer, she'd lose a lot of trust in me. If I did answer, she wouldn't trust me at all. But I guess it was always better to go with the truth...

"Two weeks," I blurted at the exact same time Emmy said, "Don't answer."

I don't even think she realized it, but as my words slipped past hers and into her ears, she froze. Her hand froze in midair, with a pancake still on the spatula, waiting to be put back on the griddle. Her mouth was slightly ajar and her eyes unmoving. It went without saying that my admission had hurt Emmy. Well, she could hurt me right back, because I needed to know when she was last with someone. If it was as recent as my own experience, it'd definitely hurt me, and I would definitely deserve it.

"Now it's your turn."

I watched with patience as she stacked a plate high with pancakes and bit her lip, considering my question. I doubt she really had to think that hard about it, but she was just as reluctant as I was to speak about it. In my mind, that meant she felt just as guilty as I had, and she didn't want to admit out loud she'd lied about a destination as I'd done in the past, so some asshole could put his hands all over her.

Color rose in her cheeks again as she responded quietly. "Almost a year and a half."

I gaped at her. It's not at all what I expected to hear, and admittedly, I was glad, but I had a hard time believing someone as sexually carnal as Emmy went a full year and a half without sex.

"You're kidding me."

"Nope."

She wouldn't meet my eyes. I wanted her to look at me. I'd make her do it, but Lucas yelled from the other room. Emmy turned away, busy with some task at the counter. Reluctantly, I left her and went into the living room. Five minutes later, Em walked out of the kitchen carrying one plate loaded with pancakes and scrambled eggs and a tall glass of OJ. She still didn't look at me before heading toward the bedroom.

I glanced at the plate of food and up to her face, which revealed nothing. She had closed herself off from me. "Aren't you eating?"

She spoke to me over her shoulder but kept moving. "I want to take a shower before you leave."

The bedroom door closed and I stood there staring at it for several moments before finally walking away.

Lucas sat on my lap as I ate my breakfast, taking it upon himself to put his little hands in my eggs or to take a piece of pancake. We conversed as much as a father could converse with his one-year-old son, taking very little effort on my part and freeing up space in my mind to think about the conversation that just transpired.

Emmy hadn't had sex for over a year and a half—since she was pregnant with Lucas. Thinking about whom she had sex with while pregnant with my son made my stomach churn, but I quickly pushed that thought out of my head. It had been so long for her, and

I doubted she was holding back just because she was someone's mother now.

The Emmy I used to know was a sexual livewire. She emanated intense, tangible sensuality that not only wrapped sturdily around my manhood, but it boldly invaded my brain and spread like stimulated tendrils down my spine, into my chest, and spread throughout my body, limb to limb, from the hair follicles on my head down to the very tips of my toes. A current seemed to ripple through her whole body under my caresses, kisses, and when I invaded her body with my erection. She shared that energy with me, made it grow with in me until lights exploded in my eyes like a transformer blowing from a power surge against the dark night.

Regardless of where she was in her life, the one thing Emmy had always been sure of was her sexuality and how to use it. Her confidence in herself as an overall person wavered during those hard times, but her confidence in her sexuality had remained ever present and always positively charged. Any man who met *that* Emmy would be helpless if she wanted him.

But there hadn't been a man.

And this wasn't the same Emmy.

That thought made my chest hurt, made my eyes tingle. The Emmy I knew now had lost so much, I wondered if she'd ever be able to find all her pieces again.

Lucas began to doze off in my lap even while his fingers were still sticky with maple syrup. I carried him into the half bath and rinsed off his face and hands before taking him into the bedroom and tucking him in his crib. He sat up and grinned at me as he tried to fight off his sleepiness. He looked like me more than anyone, but the smile that sprinkled fairy dust on my heart and made me feel like I was flying was all his mother's.

"Dad-*ee*," he cooed.

"Lu-*cas*."

He snickered, grabbed the edge of his favorite blanket, and lay his head down next to the stuffed whale. His eyes closed only moments later, and I was thankful he went down so easily this time. Usually, he was a handful. Lucas was always afraid he'd miss something and fought sleep hard.

I went into the closet to get some clothes and a pair of my sneakers that were mixed in with Emmy's shoes. Some of my clothes were hanging in the closet by the front door, but some of my things remained in the bedroom closet, pressed tightly to Emmy's. Occasionally, when I wore some of the clothes out of this closet, Emmy's scent lingered faintly on the fabric. It used to make me mad and I'd change into something that wouldn't remind me of her. Now, as I slipped the shirt over my head, I pulled it up to my nose and inhaled deeply.

I sat down on the edge of the bed to pull my sneakers on. Emmy walked out in a towel just then. She wasn't embarrassed as she was in the beginning when we first started cohabitating, nor did she give any indication she knew how sexually inviting she was in that towel with her wet hair falling down her back. She just looked…shut down. I had a feeling during her long shower that she regressed some, pulled back into herself a little, to escape our earlier conversation. As uncomfortable and maybe hurt as she may have been, I wasn't about to let her crawl back under her rock.

"Lucas crashed," I told her. "Hopefully he'll sleep this afternoon, too."

"Okay." She turned her back to look through her chest of drawers.

I got up and started out of the room, but paused before speaking to her back. "I'm sorry."

She glanced over her shoulder at me. "For what?"

"I was really insensitive a little while ago."

"It's fine." She shrugged it off, but I couldn't do the same.

"No, it's not fine, Emmy. I was an ass, and I'm sorry."

She was silent for many long seconds before she turned to face me, holding her clothes in her hands. "Okay. Forgiven."

"Okay." I was reluctant to leave it at that. "I'll be back in a few hours, maybe around three."

"Take your time."

I walked out, but realized I should've clarified something first. I went back in the room with a rush of words. "I'm really going to the office to work. Nothing shady will be going on. I promise."

"Luke, you don't owe me any explanations."

"I do, and I'll just be honest about it next time. So there will be no question about it in your head."

Even as those words fell out of my mouth I realized my mistake. I insinuated I'd tell her the next time I'd have sex with someone. I wanted to take the words back, because that isn't what I meant at all.

"I don't want to know," she said quickly, sounding panicked. Her eyes were wide and her one hand holding up her towel was bone white from the fierce grip she had on the material.

Her reaction, while typical of this warped version of Emmy, was still surprising. I could only stare at her for a moment, watching the rapid rise and fall of her chest and the plea in her eyes. I finally managed to stumble out an apology. "I'm sorry."

She tried to smile, but failed. She took a deep breath and I saw her shoulders relax some. "Dude, stop apologizing and go to work already." She forced a laugh and tried to appear normal. "It's fine—I'm fine. Really."

"Okay." I was still reluctant to go. "I'll be home as soon as I'm done."

"Okay, okay." She tried to wave me away, to dismiss me, although I felt like she was dismissing more than my presence. I needed her to know I didn't brush her off so easily.

She seemed a little annoyed when I didn't move. "What now?"

"I don't want you to think that you're not…attractive or desirable."

"Oh my god, Luke! Can you just go?" Her face had turned a shade of pink and she had the most uncomfortable looking smile on her face.

"Because you are. You're probably hotter than ever before, but we just have so much…shit between us, and we're not really on the same page and…"

My stupid words again. No one would believe I was a successful attorney, what with my recent propensity to say the dumbest things. I basically just told her I'd have sex with her if things were different, and I suggested that even though we had come a long way since she began working for me at the firm, it was not far enough. My words could've very well shoved her back into her shell. It was almost like saying her progress over the past few months wasn't enough.

"You know what?" She threw her towel hand up in the air and quickly grabbed it again when it began to slip. "If it'll make you feel better, I'll go get laid tonight. I'm sure I can find a date. Then you won't feel so…weird, and you're being really, *really* weird."

If she could've taken a sledge hammer and hit me in the chest right then, it wouldn't have compared to the pressure I felt against my sternum. No matter what lines I tried to draw between us, the truth was I didn't want anyone else to have her. That truth hit me rather hard. I'd thought about it leisurely before, but now it was a thought that caused my skin to crawl and made me violent.

"Sorry. I'm leaving."

I left before I could say another stupid word.

Before I pulled out of the parking garage, on a whim, I dialed Vivian Deluca.

"If this is about the offer you sent on Wednesday, the answer is still no."

"I called on a personal matter, Vivian. But since you brought it up, you already know you're going to lose. It would cost your client far less money to just settle."

"You know me, Mr. Kessler," she purred. "I don't like to settle. What is it that you desire?"

"Well," I started, rubbing the back of my neck with discomfort. "I can't deny I had a very fulfilling evening with you a few weeks ago."

"Oh, I hear a 'but' coming." She snorted. "Let me guess. You want out of our agreement? You've fallen in love with some poor, clueless woman?"

That shook me. I was going to break it off with her out of respect to Emmy, but it was possible it was more than that. It was possible I was…in love.

I chose to ebb around that instead of answering Viv directly.

"Whatever my reasons are, they're my own."

"That's it, isn't it? You know I can smell a lie—even one of omission. It's part of what makes me so damn good at what I do and why I didn't hang around in a marriage with a philandering husband. Luke Kessler…" She exhaled and her voice lost some of its usual edge. "You soft-hearted fool. I had no idea you were such a pussy for love."

There was that word again. *Love.* I didn't know how to respond because I wasn't really sure myself where my mind and heart were. She continued talking, not requiring a response.

100

"Very well then. For the record, I did enjoy your unusually large appendage. You were well worth the time. I'll see you in court next month. If you delay for anything less than death, I'll walk into your office myself and kick your ass. Take this time to prepare to lose."

I laughed. "Don't count on it, Deluca."

Chapter Eleven

"Shit!" I cried out when Emmy woke me up and told me the time. I scrambled off the couch, saying, "I can't be late!"

She smacked my arm as I passed by her. "Don't curse in front of Lucas, dumbass!"

I wanted to argue how she just did that very thing. "Shit" couldn't be any worse than "dumbass." But I didn't have time to argue. I had a very big day in court, up against Vivian Deluca of all people.

I rushed into the master bath and started the shower. I was so frantic, I started to step into the shower wearing my boxers and T-shirt. I struggled out of the clothing and climbed into the shower without checking the temperature. I let out a string of curse words as water hotter than Hades hit my skin. I adjusted the temperature and grabbed the body wash Emmy bought for me. Just when I started to wash, the curtain pulled back slightly and a hand appeared in front of me holding a toothbrush with the toothpaste already on it. I grabbed the toothbrush and began the almost impossible task of washing myself with one hand while brushing my teeth.

I got out of the shower in record time and rushed into the bedroom with a towel around my waist, and once again, my clothes were laid out on the bed. Emmy knew it was an important day and chose my best suit—charcoal gray—and a blue shirt the same shade as my bright blue eyes. I dressed quickly only to discover I didn't have a tie, but Em breezed in with my most impressive one, also blue but with gray stripes. I expected her to just hand it to me, but she surprised me when she flipped my collar up and expertly began tying it.

"I packed your briefcase, too," she said as she worked.

"Thank you." I released a relieved breath. I had stayed up late into the night going over everything and fell asleep with the papers scattered across the coffee table. I didn't have to worry that Em put the paperwork in wrong or disorganized, because she always seemed to know just what to do and how to do it.

She smoothed the tie down my chest. "Get your shoes on and I'll meet you at the front door."

When I made it to the living room, I found Emmy by the door waiting, somehow managing to hold Lucas, a paper bag, my briefcase, keys, and phone. I was so very grateful for her. From the day she moved in with Lucas, regardless of how I treated her, Emmy always took care of me. I'd been the shifty one, but despite her hardships and the black cloud that seemed to linger over her head, she was as steady as a rock.

I thanked her as I gathered my breakfast, my briefcase, phone, and keys from her. I kissed Lucas goodbye as I did every morning. Even though I already thanked Emmy, it wasn't enough. My words would never be enough to show my appreciation or to even describe the feelings that steadily grew for her. I gave her the best I could give her at the time and kissed her cheek before I walked out the door.

****

I beat the skirt off Vivian Deluca after five days of battle. She was so damn angry, which only made the victory that much sweeter. I liked beating Vivian. She was a true shark, and sometimes, it was nice being the bigger, badder shark-eating shark. I spoke to my clients for a few minutes, promising to follow up with them in a few days before they left. Vivian's clients had gone as well, leaving only the two of us alone in the room.

"Congratulations," she said as she closed up her briefcase.

"You don't mean that." I was unable to hide my self-satisfied grin.

"I don't say things I do not mean, Mr. Kessler."

I held the swinging door open for her and she breezed through it.

"If you wouldn't have ended our arrangement, I would've fucked you until my anger abated."

"I'm sure that would've been interesting."

Her voice came out in a low purr. "Oh, I would've brought you to your knees."

I opened the door for her, still grinning. "I guess we'll never know."

"I suppose not. My office will be in touch."

She stalked off without another word, making people scatter out of her way.

What a woman.

Just not the woman for me.

I stopped to chat with the security guard for a moment, asking about his wife and kid. I felt pretty upbeat as I practically skipped down the steps of the courthouse. I had battled Vivian as if she was some medieval monster. I didn't come out unscathed, but I'd won. In addition to bringing down Goliath, I also had Emmy to thank for my high spirits. Every night she helped me prepare for the next day, and every morning she made sure I looked my best and had everything I needed. The best part was that kiss I'd been planting on her cheek for five days. Even though it wasn't reciprocated, it gave me hope.

Maybe I'd stop back at the office for only a few minutes and head home a little early. Maybe I'd call Emmy and tell her to get Lucas ready and take them out to dinner. We had gone out only a couple times since we started communicating again, and it was always with other family members. This time we could go out, just the three of us, as our own family.

I liked the sound of that. It made my smile widen.

I was high on life. Nothing would bring me down.

Except the sight of Claire standing outside my office, with a nice, round, couldn't-miss-it-from-the-moon pregnant belly.

Chapter Twelve

"I heard someone had a big win today!" Emmy said when I walked through the door at home.

I was down. Claire had dragged my high spirits down to Earth and kicked them through the mud, but Emmy looked so delighted. I shoved away any thoughts of Claire as best I could and forced myself to smile as I kissed Em's cheek for the second time that day.

"I made you a celebratory dinner."

Her smile penetrated my skin and spread throughout my body. Though Em had been offering up smiles more often lately, it was rare to see one derived from within her soul.

I picked Lucas up in the living room and followed her into the kitchen. I could smell the garlic mashed potatoes and the green beans that probably simmered with bacon and onions for a good while. She pulled steaks out of the broiler a moment after I walked in.

"I heard that Deluca woman is demonic," she said, casting a glance at me. "I'm glad you beat her."

"I'm glad, too.".

She turned around and closely regarded me. I averted my eyes and focused on Lucas. I asked him about his day and attempted one of our insanely cute but manly conversations. Emmy put the kibosh on that. She knew me well enough to know when I was avoiding her.

"What's wrong?" she demanded with a hand on her hip. "Why aren't you happy about your big win?"

I looked at her with feigned surprise. "I am happy."

"Something's bothering you."

She was one to talk about something bothering someone. She who has nightmares and keeps quiet about her apparently violent past.

"I'm tired. It was a rough battle." I managed a smile for her.

Her eyes flitted over me and then she gave a half shrug. "Okay. Well, I hope your dinner makes up for the war"

"It will—it does," I said meaningfully. "I'm going to go change."

She bit her lip as she stared at me, but she relented. "Okay."

I changed in slow motion, sometimes stopping with my hands frozen on my shirt as I unbuttoned it while my conversation with Claire bounced around unwanted in my head. I said no one could bring me down, but I'd been wrong.

Claire had brought me down.

To my knees.

I hadn't been able to take my eyes off her midsection when I'd found her in front of my office. I'd almost turned and ran, as if I'd be able to ignore the problem if the problem wasn't right in front of my face. Instead, I'd stood before her and stated the obvious. "You're pregnant."

Her response was bitter. "I think I know that now."

I sputtered as I stared at her round belly. "You said...but you...you said..."

"Do you want to have this conversation out here on the sidewalk or can we go inside?" She didn't wait for my answer. She marched over to the door of the firm and went inside. I lingered on the sidewalk for a few seconds before following her.

The staff and my attorneys tried not to stare as I walked by, following Claire who had made a hot beeline to my office, but I could feel their eyes on me anyway. Everyone knew Emmy. Most everyone loved Emmy, and those who didn't love her still respected her. They all also knew we weren't a couple, but no matter how you spun it, it still looked like a betrayal. I was bitterly thankful Emmy had gone down to part time and only came into the office a couple days a week, and today was one of her days off.

I stepped inside my office and closed the door behind me before taking a seat at my desk. Claire sat on the other side, looking at everything but me.

My shock was quickly fading away to be replaced by a growing anger. "You said you weren't pregnant."

She shook her head once. "I said I got my period."

"You lied to me."

"I didn't lie."

I picked up a pen on my desk and held it in a death grip. "You said something happened that didn't."

"It happened. I did get my period."

106

I threw the pen down, making it skip across my desk and land on the floor in front of her. "You're pregnant, Claire!"

"Thank you for again stating the obvious," she muttered.

"Will you fucking look at me?" I roared so loudly she jumped in her seat. I had no doubt my voice was heard throughout the office.

Claire slowly dragged her eyes to mine.

My words were clipped. "Explain it to me. Why are you sitting in my office? With a fetus. *Growing* inside of you."

She visibly shivered at my tone and flinched at the word "fetus."

"It wasn't a normal period. It was extremely light and only lasted a couple days. I was stressed out after the accident and just assumed it was because of stress."

"It took you five months to tell me," I growled. "Five months! Five and a half months!"

Her voice and gaze sharpened. "At least it's *before* the baby's born."

"Don't do that." I pointed at her. "Don't you even think about bringing her into this. Don't compare what you're doing to what Emmy did."

"I couldn't even begin to compare, because what she did is so much worse!"

"You can't compare because you're not her! You'll never be her. So, if you think this little scheme of showing up months later with a baby growing in your belly is going to somehow draw us closer, you're pathetically wrong."

She sat there staring at me with her mouth open. Tears pooled in her eyes but didn't spill out. She could cry all day; it wouldn't make me sympathetic. I know she didn't break the condom—at least I hoped she didn't sabotage it—and I had an equal part in making the baby—if it was indeed mine—but waiting to tell me was bullshit. It seemed very shady she would wait. Claire and I had known each other since grade school, and clearly, we didn't know each other well at all. I never thought she'd deceive me like this, and she must not have known I'd react so negatively.

"I guess the two of you are back together," she said with bitterness as she wiped away the tears that had escaped.

"We're not back together, but we *are* a family, not that it's any concern of yours."

"You love her?"

I had to make sure she understood no matter what happened with that baby growing inside her, there would never be anything between us again. She just completely obliterated any chance of us ever being friends. Up until I saw her pregnant belly, I still cared about her. But now, I didn't care at all. I lost any and all respect for Claire. She had no qualms doing to me what Emmy had done, knowing how hurt I'd been. She was willing to hurt me all over again for her own gain.

Unforgivable.

"I *never* stopped loving her. I will *always* love Emmy."

She looked down and silently wiped away more tears. After a moment, she took a deep, shaky breath, reached into her purse, and pulled out an envelope.

Though her eyes still glistened, she had straightened in her seat and her voice grew cool as she passed it to me. "I need your DNA."

I stared at her, shaking my head. "You seriously just served me for paternity testing? I guess this means you fucked around with other people while we were together."

She rolled her eyes. "Oh, give me a break. We weren't 'together.' You made it very clear we weren't. Don't look at me like that or speak to me like that. You and I were not in a committed relationship, so I saw other people."

My jaw clenched as I leaned toward her. "I don't really give a shit that you saw other people. I really don't. What I care about is you were obviously fucking other people without protection, putting me at risk, and anyone else I have been with."

Her eyes grew wide. "You dumped me because you didn't have time but slept with other people?"

"That isn't any of your business."

She took another deep breath. "Look. I saw other people but I only slept with one, and he's clean—I'm clean. Therefore, *you* are clean."

"I'll wait to find that out for myself from my own physician," I said stiffly. I tossed the legal demand for paternity testing on the desk. "I'll be there as requested. Now get out of my office."

She'd gazed at me uneasily. Her lips had parted, as if she'd been about to speak, but my hard stare had shut her down. Without another word, she'd slowly gotten to her feet and left my office.

It wasn't until I found out Claire was pregnant I understood my true, deep feelings for Emmy. I didn't really know what I wanted from her until then. If the baby was mine, I didn't know how Emmy would react. I thought of her taking Lucas and moving out, which would gut me. I wondered if the news would send her back into her shell. Or worse yet, if she'd take it as a reason to move on herself and start seeing someone else. I didn't want any of that, but I especially didn't want to see her with another guy. I didn't want to see her with anyone but me, but I couldn't begin to push forward until I knew whose baby Claire was carrying.

I finally finished changing my clothes and joined Em and Lucas at the dining room table. Buzzing about to get dinner on the table, she rambled on about her day with Lucas and their outing with Lorraine and her kids. I loved our evenings together as a family. I loved hearing about her day and listening to Lucas's babble. This was becoming our ritual and I didn't want to lose it. Claire could take this from me.

I hung on to every word she said. Watched her mouth as she spoke and smiled, and watched her interact with our son. This was only a small fraction of what I could have with her later.

Until I got the paternity results back, I'd hold on to every damn second I could get.

Chapter Thirteen

Emmy was having another nightmare.

I was in the living room, staring at some infomercial on the muted television. I couldn't sleep, I was so damn worried about the paternity test. I'd take care of any child that's mine, but I didn't want to resent my own flesh and blood if I lost Emmy in the process. I contemplated how I could still be a father to Claire's kid and keep Emmy and Lucas with me when I heard sobbing from the bedroom. I jumped up and rushed to her.

"Em?" I called softly as I approached the bed.

When she didn't respond but continued to sob, I knew she was still asleep. I sat down on the edge of the bed and gently shook her. She lashed out suddenly, landing a punch right on my jaw. It stung, but that's not why I stopped touching her. Clearly, she thought it was part of her attack. Hesitantly, I reached out and smoothed her hair out of her face. She flinched, but she didn't freak out again. I laid down beside her and continued to run my hand over her hair.

"Em, I'll never let him hurt you again," I whispered, though I knew she probably couldn't hear me, or if she did, she probably wouldn't remember. "You're going to be okay. I'll always take care of you and Lucas. I won't let anyone hurt you again. You're safe with me, Em. Always."

The sobbing had faded, though she still shuddered every few seconds, and a few tears still managed to push through the corners of her eyes. I continued to smooth her hair and murmur my vows until her breathing evened out and the nightmare passed. I stayed there with her for a long time. I knew I couldn't be there when she woke up; so after a while, I lightly pressed a lingering kiss on her forehead before forcing myself back to the living room.

****

"Sterling Corporation, Mayson Grayne speaking," Mayson answered in a bored tone.

"You should leave that evil place and come work for a real man," I said huskily into the phone.

"If you keep talking to me like that, I may comply. What's up?"

"Nothing. I just wanted to say hello and see how you're doing."

She was unconvinced. "Uh huh. Really, what's up?"

"Can't a guy call and check up on his friend?"

"Of course he can. But that's not why you're calling me, *friend*."

"Okay, okay," I conceded. "I actually have something serious to discuss with you."

She let out a soft sigh. "Spit it out, Kessler."

"I'm just going to get to the point. Did Kyle hit Emmy?"

I heard a sharp intake of breath on the line. "You think so, too?"

My heart rate picked up. "So, you think he did?"

"Well…" She hesitated. "After you moved away, Kyle took her to Miami for a long weekend. She came back with a cast on her arm. Apparently she broke her wrist."

"What? Really?" It was the first I'd heard of it.

"Yeah. She said she was wasted and fell down."

"But you didn't believe her?" There was a pressure building behind my ribcage.

There was no pause on Mayson's end. "Absolutely not. How much has Emmy told you about my past?"

I didn't see how Mayson's past was pertinent to the situation, but I remained patient. "Not a whole lot. She doesn't really bring up other people's demons. I know you had some rough years when you were younger."

"Rough is an understatement. In a nutshell, I was on drugs, I had an eating disorder, and I had a very bad relationship with a very abusive loser boyfriend. The whole I-fell-down-because-I-was-drunk bit had been used by me many times in the past. She should've been more creative with me."

I dragged a hand over my face. "So, you're convinced Kyle did it."

"I am, especially since from that point on she just seemed to get more and more depressed. Still, I may have allowed myself to be fooled by her fall-down story, but the very day that cast came off, Kyle gave her a bracelet. She claimed it was just a gift for her

111

recovery, but I'd bet my ass it was an 'I'm-sorry-I'm-an-asshole-and-broke-your-arm' gift. And I would catch her staring at the bracelet, not with admiration, but with…I don't know…bitterness…sadness."

I was suddenly nauseous. "The bracelet…is it…does it have leaves on it and diamonds?"

I heard a gasp. "She wears it? Oh my god! That's so…so…I don't know…fucked up!" Fucked up indeed. I hadn't seen her wear it in a while, but now it made me wonder if she'd worn it to feel closer to Kyle. I couldn't fathom why she'd want that if his violent act is what got her the bracelet in the first place.

I ran a hand through my hair as I considered this. "Do you think he hurt her more than that?"

"She had an occasional small bruise here and there." Mayson sighed. "Not enough for me to believe he was pushing her around, but it's possible. Emmy's the last person I'd think would let some dick repeatedly hit her, but the more I think about it, I believe that's why she took off New Year's Day."

"Is that when she left Jersey?"

"Yep. Packed up and left all of a sudden. I didn't know she was gone until Sam called me to tell me Emmy had been in an accident. She said Em was banged up really good. It all seemed very mysterious to me, but I had no proof either way. Kyle had also disappeared off the face of the earth. I later found out he was in rehab, had been there since New Year's Day. That was one big coincidence.

"It was like someone flicked a light switch, Luke. New Year's Eve she was, well, depressed, but still kicking, and then suddenly, she was a completely different person. She crawled under a rock and died. Honestly, if she wasn't pregnant with Lucas, I'm not sure if she would've lived through whatever happened."

"I want to know exactly what it is she did go through," I said with desperation.

"You and me both. I tried to stay out of her business, but maybe I should've done something. I wish I could have helped her."

I closed my eyes for a beat. "Me, too."

I called Sam next. She had the other half of the story. She'd be able to give me more details about Emmy's condition when she arrived in Louisiana. I didn't bother with the polite greetings. I loved

Sam, but sometimes, I still harbored some bad feelings toward her for holding out about Lucas, and I didn't always like the way she made Emmy feel.

"Sam, what happened when Emmy showed up on New Year's last year?" I asked as soon as she answered the phone.

She was silent for a moment. "Why are you asking?"

I gritted my teeth and pounded a fist on my desk. "Sam, you infiltrated yourself into my family at a time I wanted no reminders of Emmy. You withheld your knowledge about my son while sharing dinners with my family and sitting with my sister through chemo. I want to know about Emmy on that day, and you're going to tell me."

She huffed. "Get your panties out of a twist, Luke. Emmy called sometime after midnight and said she was taking an early flight down. She got here a couple days late, though. She was in a car accident with one of her friends. She looked terrible. That's no big secret. Why don't you ask her about it yourself?"

"Sam, she's having nightmares," I said roughly. "No less than twice a week, she has them."

She sounded doubtful. "About the car accident?"

"I don't think there was a car accident." If she really didn't suspect Emmy had been abused, I didn't want to be the one to break it to her.

"Why would she lie about a car accident, Luke? She sure as hell looked like she was in one. She was all bruised and banged up."

"Whose car was she in? If there was an accident that banged and bruised her up, there had to be a pretty decent wreck."

"She wasn't very specific. I was just glad she and Lucas were okay."

"You're the nosiest person I know," I pointed out. "You sure were lacking in questions that day."

"Don't you judge me, Luke Kessler," she snapped, her southern drawl more pronounced. "Emmy was already depressed. I didn't want to push her. You didn't see how she was back then. I'm still amazed she didn't take her own life."

I inhaled sharply at the thought.

I rubbed my forehead. "So, you never second guessed her story on the car accident."

"What the hell for?"

"Did you question her about her broken wrist?" I fired at her.

"What broken wrist? What the hell are you talking about? Emmy never broke her wrist."

Samantha was so clueless, and I should've known as much. If Mayson or Sam had any hard facts, Kyle probably wouldn't still be breathing. I knew in my gut he'd hurt Emmy, and Emmy had protected him by lying to her family and friends.

Even though I'd never physically harm Emmy—or any woman—I felt responsible for the trauma she endured. I practically pushed her into the situation and wished terrible things on her. I was just as much responsible as Kyle was. If I found out Lucas had been harmed as well, I would never, ever even attempt to find forgiveness.

"Emmy broke her wrist two years ago. Late September, early October."

Sam's voice pitched high. "She never said nothing. Why wouldn't she have told me that?"

"I don't know. How was Emmy's behavior after the accident?"

She seemed reluctant to let go of the broken wrist part of the conversation, but she sighed heavily and moved on. "Like I said, she was depressed. She stayed in her room. She stayed in bed. She didn't talk to anybody or do anything but lay there and sleep or stare at the damn walls. It was like she up and died—at least until she took off like a bat out of hell for France."

I trembled with anger. No one had helped her. They let her suffer alone. It seemed as though no one even bothered to ask questions. I wasn't there and it was clear as day to me she had been abused, yet somehow, everyone else overlooked it or ignored the signs.

"No one helped her." I slammed a palm down on my desk. "Why didn't anyone help her?"

"We couldn't help her if she didn't want to be helped," Samantha argued.

"Bullshit! You're the most overbearing woman I know, Sam. While it was still fresh, you should've made her tell you, and you should've helped her. Now she's had all this time to build up defense after defense. She'll never admit it now because she's spent so much time in denial."

"*Admit what*? What the fuck are you eluding to, Luke Kessler? And how the hell did my daughter break her wrist? You

114

seem to know so much. Why don't *you* answer some damn questions. *Now*."

I closed my eyes for a moment and took a few deep breaths. It wasn't my place to tell her. Emmy needed to tell her. Hell, Emmy needed to tell *me*.

"I thought mothers had spidey senses," I said tiredly.

"Emmy never broke her wrist," Sam said indignantly. "She would've told me. I don't know where you're hearing these things."

"Your spidey senses suck, Sam. Emmy broke her wrist right after I left Philly. She broke it while she was in Miami with Kyle. She told Mayson she fell down after drinking too much. Mayson suspects it's why Kyle gave her that bracelet she wears."

There was a moment of silence. When Sam spoke again, I could hear a trace of doubt in her voice. "Emmy drinks like a damn fish, Luke. It's very possible she fell down, and Kyle Sterling gave her that bracelet because she worked her ass off for that dick."

I ran my hand over my face again. Samantha Grayne was anything but a dense person. The fact she had repeatedly overlooked signs of Emmy's abuse but could smell whether or not the woman was on a dry spell was troublesome. She was in Em's face about everything else but this one thing that ultimately changed Emmy's life. I was disappointed and hurt on her behalf. I didn't even want to think of how many other traumatic experiences she had throughout life and didn't have her mother to depend on.

"You go ahead and continue to keep your head in the sand," I said dryly. "Don't tell her we spoke about this."

Sam's voice softened to almost a whisper. "You think I'm a bad mother."

"I think…" I chose my next words carefully. I was angry and hurting for Emmy, but I knew Sam loved her daughter, and I know what it's like to close your eyes to what's in front of you and imagine things are different than what they really are. I did it when I knew Emmy loved Kyle, and I did it again after Em moved in. "Sam, I think we all make mistakes, but…I'm not going to continue to pretend Emmy is fine. I'm not going to continue to be blind and deaf to the fact she's in pain. Something happened, Sam. I don't know what, but it wasn't any damn car accident."

Samantha's quiet defiance sounded more and more like denial and doubt. "What do you think happened, Luke? My daughter

115

was in an accident. She would've told me otherwise. We don't always see eye to eye—"

"Try *never*."

"—*but*," she stressed, letting me know she wasn't going to acknowledge what I said, "Emmy would've told me if something else happened. My mind won't even go there because it's just incomprehensible."

And that pretty much summed it up. Sam had her head in the sand. Fine. I didn't want her to handle it anyway. I needed to handle it.

But I had no idea how the hell I'd do that.

After hanging up with Sam, I checked my schedule for the day. My afternoon was virtually open—open enough for me to skip out of work for the rest of the day after lunch. I picked up the phone and called Emmy.

"Hey, want to do lunch today and then take Lucas to the park?"

After the conversations I'd just had with Mayson and Samantha, and worrying about the upcoming paternity testing, I needed to see her, to be close to her.

"You're going to cut out of work early? Play hooky like a bad boy?"

Hell. She almost sounded flirtatious. She almost sounded like old Emmy. It was enough to give me a semi. "It's not hooky if I own the business."

"Hooky is hooky. Yes, we'll meet you for lunch and for a play date. Lucas could use a day at the park."

"We all could use a day at the park," I muttered.

"You okay?"

I forced myself to smile, even though she couldn't see it. "Yeah, I'm good. Text me where you want to meet for lunch. We'll meet a little early so Lucas won't get too cranky."

There was a teasing element in her voice that made me smile for real. "Eleven thirty good for you, hooky?"

"It's not hooky!"

After rearranging some of my appointments and pushing some off on other associates, I escaped the office a few minutes before eleven thirty. The moment I spotted Emmy and Lucas in the restaurant, I started feeling better. Lucas was happy and smiling and

Emmy looked gorgeous in her long, pink, strapless summer dress. Anyone looking at us who didn't know us could've guessed we were a happy family enjoying an afternoon together.

I doubted anyone looked at Emmy and guessed she had some deep dark secrets and was emotionally damaged and sexually stalled. I doubted they looked at me and guessed I felt such deep shame and regret, and was absolutely terrified of losing Emmy and Lucas. I doubted they looked at Lucas and felt sorry for him because his parents were fucked up.

After lunch, we went to the park and chased Lucas around the toddler playground and across the green grass. It was sunny and warm, and every time I caught a glimpse of Emmy smiling or laughing with the sun at her back, making her shine like an angel, it stole my breath.

I loved her.

I really loved her.

I was a fool for denying myself those feelings for so long.

"Someone is tired," I said, as Lucas sat down on the walkway and demanded to be picked up.

Emmy put a hand over her mouth to stifle a fake yawn. "Yeah, I'm exhausted."

I gave her an artificial look of disgust and then picked Lucas up as I continued with the conversation we were in the middle of before Lucas demanded to be carried.

Smoothly, without any hesitation or proof of the apprehension I felt inside, I took Emmy's hand in mine and continued to walk. Her hand was stiff at first. She was distracted by it, even though she tried to speak naturally, but after only a few minutes, she relaxed.

I relaxed, too, but more than that, I hoped.

Chapter Fourteen

If I were on the Maury show, I would've zoomed around on the stage shouting, "I told you," while laughing and indulging in the roar of the crowd. Claire would've run off stage to that grungy-looking couch where so many other baby mamas have cried, and Maury would've gone back there and tried to soothe her while doing his best to squeeze another show out of her so they could find the father of her unborn child.

But I wasn't on Maury, and as far as I knew, Maury didn't do paternity testing before the baby was actually born. Half a show would be lost without an innocent child's face on the big screen so the mother could shout about how many of the features are the accused father's.

Instead of a victory dance, I took the document to the shredder and shredded the fucker.

I wanted to go home and hug my son and my wom—Emmy—but my schedule was pretty heavy, leaving me no wiggle room to leave early. I rarely worked late anymore. I took my work home with me and did it either at the coffee or dining room table. I wanted to spend as much time as possible with Lucas and Emmy. I even changed my schedule so at least one day a week, I only worked half a day to be with them. Em thought Lucas was my reason for the changes, and she was right, he was, but I don't think she realized she was the only other reason.

I hadn't asked her about News Year's Day yet. She still had nightmares, and I still snuck in and gave her comfort in her sleep. Shamefully, I sometimes welcomed the nightmares so I had an excuse to hold her. A couple of times I just barely made it out of the bed before she woke up completely. It killed me not to be able to lay there with her every night, but I had to be patient. I had to give her a chance to find herself again before I swept in and changed everything.

As long as my work schedule permitted it, I'd go with her and Lucas to New Jersey for Labor Day week. Emmy's cousin Tabitha, and their friend Leo, invited us to spend the week at Leo's house five blocks from the beach. If I was able to go, I'd talk to her then for sure. I wanted to take her down to the beach alone and tell her how I felt. If she rejected me, I'd at least have the option of walking into the ocean and drowning myself.

When I walked in the door that night, I tripped over one of Lucas's toys. Emmy rushed out of the kitchen, apologizing as she scooped up several playthings and threw them in a box that seemed to dominate the living room. I couldn't figure out how a one-year-old had accumulated so many damn toys.

I opened the closet to stash my umbrella and half a dozen other things fell out. I managed to stuff everything back in along with my umbrella, but I had a sneaky suspicion the door would burst open and vomit everything onto the floor.

My frustration began to mount a little while later as I tried to find something to change into. The closet and both dressers were stuffed with clothes, and what didn't fit was stacked in baskets around the bedroom. Emmy tried to keep things as organized as possible, but there was only so much she could do in the limited space.

After dinner, I tried to work at the dining room table, but the table was too small. Like everything else in the apartment. Frustrated and aggravated, I told Emmy we needed to move. I thought I heard some apprehension in her one-word answer, but a few of my papers fell off the table and I was too busy fuming to address it. Besides, it was possible there was no apprehension at all. I couldn't imagine what she'd possibly have to be apprehensive about. She didn't think we'd stay in this small apartment forever…did she?

"I'll call an agent tomorrow," I said.

"Can I get you something before I go to bed?" She lingered beside me. I wanted to reach out and pull her into my lap, bury my face in her hair, and kiss her neck to ease my frustration.

"No, I'm fine. If I need anything, I can get it. Thanks."

She started toward the bedroom but stopped halfway there.

"Luke, why don't you sleep in the bed tonight? You've been working your ass off and sleeping on a blow-up bed. It hardly seems fair."

I stared at her. She was inviting me into the bed? With her?

"Are you trying to seduce me, Miss Grayne?" I wriggled my eyebrows while praying she'd say yes.

She snickered and rolled her eyes. "I'm pretty sure my girly parts have withered up and turned to dust by now. I'm serious, though. Just come to bed when you're ready. I can come out here."

The little bit of hope she'd given me was quickly stolen away. I tried not to visually deflate.

I nodded slowly. "I'll think about it. Goodnight." I walked over to her and kissed her cheek as I did every night.

"Lata." She threw me the peace sign.

I smiled at her corniness and watched her until the bedroom door closed. I stood there for a long time staring at the door. I wanted to walk in, knowing she was in there changing out of her clothes, and grab her semi clad body and pull it to mine. I wanted to catch her off guard and take her mouth with mine. I wanted to lift her in my arms and lay her down on the bed and run my hand over her smooth skin while my tongue searched her mouth.

I walked to the door and put my hand on the knob. With my chest warm with anticipation, my lips burning to touch hers and my cock rising quickly in my pants, I found the strength of a thousand men to pull myself away. I palmed my forehead in frustration and made my feet carry me back to the dining room table.

I worked hard for the next several hours, trying not to think of Emmy laying there in bed, expecting me. I had to remind myself she was also expecting to get up and go sleep on the couch.

"Not happening," I muttered to myself as I started shoving files back into my briefcase. "She's going to sleep in that bed with me if I have to tie her down."

I walked through the apartment turning off lights before easing into the bedroom. The bed was lit up by the moonlight. Emmy lay illuminated beneath the covers like an offering from the gods.

I eased into the bed behind her. She immediately stirred and blinked her eyes open. I bit back my frustration. She slept like the dead when she had nightmares, never even knowing I was there. Now, the one time she'd actually invited me to my own bed, she decided to be a light sleeper.

"I'll go to the couch," she mumbled drowsily and started to move away, but I put a hand on her hip, restraining her. The hell if I'd just let her get up and go so easily. Never again.

"Does it bother you to sleep in the same bed with me?"

She peered over her shoulder at me and her mouth fell open. She stared at me for so long I wasn't sure if she heard me. A nervous tension eased into my chest as I began to believe maybe she was remembering all the nights I held her through her nightmares.

"What did you say?"

"Does it bother you to sleep in the same bed with me?"

"No. I thought it bothered you."

"Maybe in the beginning," I admitted. "But not for the reasons you think." Like even when I thought I hated her, she still had the ability to make my dick hard.

She settled back onto her pillow. "I didn't put much thought into it."

We lay there in silence for some time. Emmy seemed to be drifting back off to sleep, but I was wide awake. I wanted to settle in and pull her body to mine. I wanted to sleep with her in my arms without having to sneak out later, but I couldn't shut my mind off.

"I want to ask you something, and I want you to be straight with me."

She rolled over onto her back to give me her full attention. I smoothed my hand over her belly and propped myself up on my other hand.

"What is it?"

It was now or never.

"Did Kyle hit you?"

I heard her breath hitch, and even as the clouds began to block the light of the moon, I couldn't miss her wide eyes.

"Why are you asking me that?" she asked in a harsh whisper.

"You alluded to it months ago. You said something about being used and abused, and then when I asked you about your last day in Philly, you said you didn't want to talk about it."

I sensed the panic rising in her, heard the fight or flight element in her voice. "That doesn't mean anything."

Now that I opened that door, I'd have to push her a little. I needed to put a dent in one of the many walls she had carefully erected.

"Yeah, I knew you would react this way, so I talked to your mom and Mayson."

She muttered a curse and rolled out of bed and made a beeline for the living room. I was right on her ass. I'd make her hear me, make her talk to me.

"Mayson said you came back from a trip to Miami with a broken wrist, and the day after the cast was off, you were walking around with that fancy bracelet. You told her you fell while you were drunk, but she didn't believe you, and she especially didn't believe you after you started wearing the bracelet. She thought it was some kind of compensation from Kyle for breaking your wrist."

"Mayson is a crazy bitch. You can't believe anything she says," she stated so viciously she almost shocked me into silence. It was the biggest show of anger I'd seen from her since she moved in.

"That's cruel and wrong and you know it," I admonished her.

She kept walking away from me, but I stayed on her ass. I knew I'd have to stop soon before I pushed too far, but I couldn't just let it go like her family did. I couldn't just accept her words and put on my blinders. Wasn't gonna happen.

"Your mom said she didn't even know about the broken wrist until I asked her today. You gave her a different story about the bracelet. She also said you called her a little after midnight on New Year's and told her you were going to be there later in the day. You got there a day late, claiming you were in a car accident to explain away the fresh bruises on your face, on your arms, and even on your back."

The emotions forming on her face damn near broke my heart. She was horrified and terrified. Worse than that, she looked humiliated and guilty.

"He really fucked up your head, didn't he? You feel like you deserved everything he did to you."

She didn't answer. She stared at the floor and I stared at her. I wanted to take her in my arms and apologize, but I wasn't sure how she'd react. I pushed for enough already for the night.

"I'm sorry. I shouldn't press you like that. When you're ready to talk about it, I'll always be ready to listen."

I put my lips on her cheek, wanting so badly to touch her, but I again made myself walk away from her.

I went back into the bedroom, hoping and wishing she'd follow, but I knew she wouldn't. I laid there for a long time, praying I hadn't pushed too far. Every time I pictured the look on her face, my heart hurt for her. She thought she deserved whatever Kyle did to her—her lack of a response told me that much. Even in all my anger when we broke up and after I found out about Lucas, I would've never wished that kind of punishment onto her. I would've never wanted her to be physically hurt, nor blame herself. It wasn't until she failed to answer me I really understood how damaged Em was.

I couldn't give up.

I wouldn't give up.

****

I woke up and felt like shit. My head was pounding and I felt emotionally wrung the hell out from my confrontation with Emmy. There was no way I'd be able to sit in the office all day.

I went into the living room, not knowing what to expect. She wasn't dressed for work, but Lucas was dressed and she was packing up his diaper bag. She looked like she hadn't slept at all. She was pale and appeared even more emotionally drained than me.

"I'm not going in today. Can you drop him off at Lena's?"

"I'm not going in, either." I yawned. "I'll drop him off anyway."

I left with Lucas a little while later. My sister didn't waste any time telling me I looked like shit.

I yawned again. "Had a long night."

"Wanna talk about it?" She nodded toward the kitchen.

"No," I groaned. "I want to go back to bed."

"How's Em?"

"A mirror image of me." I wearily rubbed my head.

"Well, I guess that's progress." She kissed Lucas all over the face, making him giggle.

"You call both of us feeling like shit progress?"

"Don't curse in front of my nephew. And yes, I do. This means there isn't any more pussyfooting around. You guys are digging into the deep shit that needs to be dug into."

"Why do you and Emmy yell at me for cursing in front of Lucas and then curse in front him yourselves?"

"We push babies out of our *vaginas*, Luke," she said as if that answered everything.

I didn't feel like arguing. "I'll be back for him before dinner." I kissed Lucas and left before my sister pulled me into the kitchen for a talk.

When I got back to the apartment, I found Emmy in bed reading on the very Kindle I had given her as a gift so long ago. She used to sit in bed trying to read and failing because I was always trying to get into her panties. Most of the time I succeeded, unless the book was particularly good, then she shut me down. I wasn't going to try to get into her panties this time, but I did need something else from her.

I kicked my shoes off at the foot of the bed. "I have such a crazy headache. I feel like my head is going to explode."

I climbed into bed and put my head in her lap. I closed my eyes and waited. A moment later, I felt her hesitant fingers slide into my hair. When she began to stroke my aching head, I relaxed.

Later in the morning, after we had a couple of hours of sleep, we sat on the bed with the laptop open looking at houses. I had ordered some food and we were having a perfectly normal conversation about where to buy and how many rooms we'd need. I thought it was going very well. We sounded more like a couple than a couple of roommates—until Emmy fucked that up with one question.

"What are we going to do if, you know, you get married or something? I mean, it's something to think about if we're buying a house together."

I looked at her as if she'd just said the dumbest shit ever. We were sitting in bed together, looking at houses to share our son and our lives in, and she had to go and ask that question. Obviously, we were on two different pages.

"What happens if *you* get married?"

She laughed at herself. "I think my current state is as good as it's gonna get for me. I'm so not on the market."

"Why would you even say that?" I demanded. I didn't want her on the damn market—she was mine—but I didn't understand why she'd believe she had no chance at being in a relationship again while I was right in front of her.

"No one buys broken items." She reached in front of me to scroll through the houses.

"People buy broken cars and fix them up all the time."

124

"I'm not a broken hot rod. I'm more like a shattered vase. No one buys those."

I scowled. "Why are we talking about you like you're an inanimate object?"

She didn't even look at me as she ignored my question and tried to change the subject. "What about this house?"

I shoved her hand away and slammed the laptop shut. She looked taken aback, but sat there with her eyebrows raised.

"This is driving me crazy." I groused and got out of bed. "Sometimes I see that woman I knew so well, but as soon as she starts to come out, you push her back down into the dark."

"That's poetic." She'd said it sarcastically and with a fucking smirk, but as she began folding laundry, I saw her hands trembled.

I softened my voice and gave her a pleading look. "Why? Why are you so afraid to be her?"

She averted her eyes as she put an unordinary amount of focus into folding clothes. "Maybe you've forgotten, but that woman you knew so well screwed you over and broke your heart."

I felt little bands of patience snapping one by one.

"You know what? Honestly?" I snatched the clothes from her hands. "More often than you think, I do forget, and really, I may never forget entirely, but I have forgiven you. I forgive you entirely, no more animosity, but you can't forgive yourself."

"Luke, really! Why are you bombarding me with all this serious shit lately?"

"Because in order for us to move forward, we need to deal with that shit, Em! You need to deal with what Kyle did to you, and you need to deal with your feelings about yourself."

"I *am* dealing with it!"

"Hiding behind your kid and your job will only hold up for so long," I taunted.

She rolled her eyes and stormed out of the room.

I followed her, yelling. "Great idea! Run away! That's a great way of dealing with your problems."

I watched her pace anxiously back and forth and tried to rein in some of my anger and frustration before speaking again.

"So, you've made some mistakes. We've all made some mistakes."

"Yeah, your mistake was—how did you put it? Oh, yeah. You had this inflated idea of who I was and it's not my fault I didn't live up to your expectations."

She stood in the middle of the room, staring at the floor. Her chest rose and fell heavily. I couldn't miss the injury on her face and in her voice. I wished I could've taken back all the awful things I'd said to her, even if she half deserved some of them. Had I known then what I knew now, I wouldn't have made things any worse for her.

"I was hurting pretty bad," I said softly. "I wanted you to feel my pain. I apologize; I didn't really mean it. Had I known then how deeply damaged you really were, I would've behaved differently, and I should've anyway. I didn't treat you the way I should treat the mother of my child. I've really been trying to make it up to you and be a better man."

She looked up at me, surprised by my words. She didn't understand I'd been trying hard to win her over. I guess I hadn't tried hard enough.

I desperately wanted her to see the truth, to really feel it. "Em, I know you're broken, okay? But I need to know what broke you so I can fix you."

She stared at me with a dumbfounded expression. Clearly I hadn't tried hard enough, or she wouldn't again look so stupefied that I wanted to be part of her healing.

Her face changed in a matter of seconds. She looked worried and sad as she spoke in a small voice. "Why would you want to bother? Is it making me a bad mom?"

"You're an excellent mother. I want to because I love you, and it kills me to see you like this."

I watched her face after my confession. Utter confusion and shock.

"Oh."

Oh? *Oh?* I told her I loved her, and she said, "Oh."

The buzzer went off. I think we were both glad for the interruption. I went downstairs to get the food. On my way back up, I decided not to continue the conversation. Honestly, my fucking feelings were a little hurt. I'd waited a long time to tell her I loved her. Even more, I made it clear I wasn't going anywhere, I wanted her and I wanted to fix her and she said, "Oh."

We were both dysfunctional people. For the rest of the day, we avoided serious conversation, even though we were sitting on a mountain of serious topics to discuss. We both pretended as if our intense conversations hadn't happened. We watched television, ate food, joked around, talked about work, and acted as if we were both at ease when we each knew the other was not. We even slept in the same bed, but I stayed to one side and her to the other. We may as well have slept in two separate universes.

I woke up early, before Emmy and Lucas. I stood in the kitchen for a long time thinking over a cup of coffee with the radio playing softly in the background. I wasn't ready to give up on Emmy, but I didn't know if we were really getting anywhere. I needed to change my approach. Forcing her to talk about her pain only left us both frustrated and possibly a little more fractured than before.

By the time Lucas woke up, I had formed a plan. By the time Emmy got up, I was downright giddy about it. It was so simple I felt stupid for not thinking of it sooner.

"Are you playing hooky again?"

"Impossible. I'm co-owner of the firm. I can do whatever I want."

She smirked. "Humble."

"I want to take Lucas to the zoo today, but tonight, you and I are having a date night."

She frowned doubtfully. "Date night?"

So simple. We didn't need to have any uncomfortable conversations. We didn't need to talk about how damaged we were. No confrontations or yelling or frustration. I'd take her out, like I used to, just the two of us. A night on the town with some dinner, drinks, and whatever else the city had in store for us. Emmy hadn't had one of these nights in a very long time, probably since before Lucas was born. She needed this. I needed this. *We* needed this—together.

"Yep. I already asked Diana to babysit. I know I'm not Brad Pitt, but I think I make a pretty good date."

A small smile appeared on her face. "I guess."

"Oh my god, Lucas! Did you see that?" I exclaimed.

"Smartass," she muttered before walking into the kitchen.

"And don't think your cute ass is getting out of this," I called after her.

"Stop cursing!"

"You need to get out. You never do anything. You're a hermit. You're hermit lady. All you need are cats."

She appeared in the doorway. "Okay, I get it." She shook her head and rolled her eyes. "I'll go."

I pointed a finger. "No backing out."

"No backing out."

"Because I will pick you up and carry you out of here if I have to."

"I'd like to see you try." She snorted and went back into the kitchen.

****

When Emmy stepped out of the bedroom just before my cousin Diana arrived, Lucas and I both stopped what we were doing and stared.

"Ohhhhhh," Lucas cooed, staring at his mom.

"Wow," I said, unable to close my mouth.

Emmy rolled her eyes, like she couldn't believe she was as hot as she looked. She had on a black tank top with thin straps that was snug at her breasts and swayed loosely at her hips. The blue jean capris she had on were skin tight, and she wore them with a pair of fire engine red sandals with high heels and straps around her ankles. Her hair was loose and wavy, and whatever makeup she had on made the green in her eyes look like shiny specks of glitter.

"Where are we going?" she asked soon after we left the building.

I took her hand. "Let's just see where our feet take us."

She blinked at me. "You mean you didn't plan anything?"

"Nope."

"You suck a little at this dating thing."

I peered down at her suspiciously. "Was that a joke?"

"Nope."

We chatted about nothing of importance as we strolled through the city. Conversation came easily and Emmy smiled and laughed often. I should've been satisfied with that, but when she didn't think I was looking, I saw the tension lines around her mouth and sometimes caught glimpses in her eyes of what appeared to be anxiety.

"This is a hot date," Emmy said a little while later in a Barnes and Noble.

"I know you think so. The only thing missing are your sexy pink rubber gloves."

"Maybe we should go buy some. I mean, if that's what rocks your boat."

She was what rocked my boat. I had a visual in my mind of her answering the door at her house in Jersey, wearing a pair of short shorts with bleach stains, a holey T-shirt and those pink, rubber gloves. Catching her in such a casual state really had been a turn on. I was so glad she had to go upstairs that day and change so I could get my erection under control.

"Only if you promise to wear the gloves and nothing else."

She snickered and said, "Yeah, because my body is so rockin' after having a baby."

"I think your body is even more rockin' than before you had a baby," I responded seriously and openly looked her over.

She looked at me with some doubt. "I haven't lost any weight since the day Lucas was born."

"You're hot, I'm telling you."

"You think so now, but you haven't seen the stretch marks on my belly."

"I don't care about your stretch marks." I'd kiss every line on her stomach if she gave me the chance.

Emmy took a breath and changed gears.

"Are you flying to Jersey with me and Lucas for Labor Day?"

Though I had personally been invited, I wanted to know if Emmy wanted me there.

"Do you want me to?"

One of her shoulders rose and fell casually. "Yeah. Sure."

I frowned. It was like the "Oh" thing all over again. "Don't be so excited about it."

"I don't get excited about anything these days. Don't take it personally."

I was well aware nothing seemed to excite her, but a little bit of enthusiasm would've been nice.

She gave me a wide smile and batted her pretty eyes a couple times. "I would love for you to come."

"Right here in the book store?" I growled low in my throat and my mouth pulled up into a flirty smile. "I knew my badass girl was in there somewhere. I haven't done it in a public place since that one time in the bathroom at the diner."

Her face was red almost instantly. "Walking away now."

She left me alone with the two old women who appeared out of nowhere. I smirked and followed Emmy out of the store.

"Are you having a good time?" I asked as we walked to dinner.

Her smile was genuine, but the tension was still there. It was like she was waiting for the bottom to drop out from under her.

"I am. I haven't had a real date night since…well, since we were…together." She cleared her throat in a lame attempt to cover her discomfort.

"We should make this a ritual. We should have a date night at least once a month."

If she said "Oh" again, I'd have to pull a Lucas and sit down on the sidewalk and wait for someone to pick me up.

"You owe me a date on the boardwalk, buddy," she said, poking my arm.

Dozens of needle like pains pierced my chest. The day Emmy and I broke up, we were supposed to go to the boardwalk, get on some rides, play some mini golf, eat greasy, sugary, messy food, and frolic on the beach like a happy couple.

The Friday before our date, I'd been in the file room on my floor at Sterling Corp. The room had row after row of files. Sometimes, if someone was working quietly at the back of the room, you didn't even know they were there until they either spoke up or showed themselves. I'd been at the very back, not caring if anyone knew I was in there or not when I'd heard approaching voices.

"I don't understand," I heard Lynn, one of the clerks say as she entered the room. I didn't know who she was with, nor did I care until I heard my name. "She's fucking him right under Luke's nose. He's either extremely thick headed or he just doesn't care."

"It's not possible he doesn't know," I heard my own secretary, Tracy, say. "How can he not know? Everyone else knows. Carol saw Emmy and Mr. Sterling making out in a Walmart parking lot of all places, and other people have seen them out together from time to time. And Harriet, you know Harriet—Huge Ass Harriet?"

"Oh, yeah. She works up there with them, right?"

"Yeah. Huge Ass Harriet said their relationship may as well be broadcasted on national television. They fight out in the open in front of the staff sometimes, and sometimes Emmy comes out of his office with that just-fucked look. Then she comes up here and smiles at my boss, putting her lips on him and pretending everything is so perfect."

"There's no way he doesn't know," Lynn said. "She's pretty and I heard she's good at her job, but that can't be why he stays with her. I don't understand how he can stay with her knowing someone else is hitting it."

"Maybe he's in denial," Tracy said, hitting a little closer to the truth. "Maybe he really loves her and he's just hoping for the best."

"The best he's gonna get is a broken heart," Lynn said. "Ahh, here's the file Vince needed. I told him it was here. I swear this company needs to make people do a basic skills test before they're hired."

The door had closed. I'd been left alone to deal with my denial.

I blinked away the memory and refocused on the present. I didn't want to think about those days again. I just wanted to move forward, and the opportunity to do so was right in front of me.

"I'll take you wherever you want to go," I promised.

A little while later, we slid into a booth at the Hard Rock. We ate dinner at the Hard Rock in Atlantic City on our first date.

"Does this remind you of anything?" I asked her as I picked up my menu.

She hid her face behind her menu before speaking. "It reminds me of a lot of things."

I wanted to ask her if she remembered practically tearing my clothes off that night on my couch. I wanted to know if she remembered writhing under me and screaming my name. I wanted to know if she remembered how it felt to be so deeply, physically connected we became one fluid entity. I wanted to ask her if she loved me right away like I did her. If she knew I loved her the moment I saw her in her cleaning clothes and pink gloves.

The waitress appeared at our table before I could say anything to Emmy.

"Two Irish Car Bombs," I said before Emmy could speak up.

Emmy seemed a bit taken aback. "I was just going to get a cola."

"A cola?" I asked incredulously. "A *cola*? Since when did you drink girly drinks like…cola?" I said the word with disdain.

"Since I got pregnant and subsequently had a child to breastfeed."

"Your breasts…" I let my gaze settle on her chest for a moment. "…haven't been food for Lucas for months."

"Well, still…" she said, visibly uncomfortable with the conversation. "I'm a full-time mom and part-time miracle worker at Kessler, Keane and Associates. I'm also a full-time…whatever it is I am to you. Housekeeper and Organizer Extraordinaire."

"Emmy. You're more to me than a housekeeper and organizer."

She locked gazes with me, and I swear it looked like she held her breath.

"You're also a cook, a time keeper, a fancy ironer, and…" I laughed as she threw her menu at me.

Our drinks arrived and we gave the waitress our orders. I started on my drink while we chatted. Emmy often looked at hers but made no move to touch it. I had no idea what the hell she was afraid of. It was beyond obvious she needed it. She tried to act natural, but I could see her pulse racing in her jugular and her hands twisting and untwisting her napkin so tightly her knuckles were white.

"Drink up," I finally said once I finished my own drink.

She stared at hers. "This is going to hit me like a pile of rocks."

"It'll loosen you up a little."

She narrowed her gaze at me. "Are you calling me uptight?"

Uptight was an understatement, but I said nothing. We sat there staring each other down, wordlessly daring the other to look away first. I watched with alarm as I saw what only could've been described as panic take over in her eyes. She looked like she was suffocating as she began to tear her napkin to shreds.

I reached across the table and stilled her hand by taking it into mine. "Hey. Are you okay?"

It was obvious the action of taking her hand had only made things worse. I didn't understand it. I was boggled. I wondered if she secretly hated me...or if it was something else.

Suddenly, she pulled her hand out of mine and picked up her drink. She stared at it for a moment, as if she felt intimidated by it. After a deep breath, she put the glass to her lips and tilted her head back. I couldn't stop the grin from forming as she chugged the drink. The glass slammed down on the table as Emmy's face puckered—something I'd never seen her do before. With the alcohol still burning in her throat, she waved the waitress over and ordered two more drinks, plus shots of Hennessey.

I clapped my hands together, happy to see that my old Emmy showed up for dinner.

The drinks kept coming. Em seemed to have been making up for all the drinking she didn't do before. Her tongue loosened and the tension seemed to all but melt away from her body.

"Do you know what it's like to wash the underwear of the guy you have a baby with but you're not sleeping with?" she crooned after another countless shot.

"No, I don't know what that's like." I laughed. "I'm not that kind of guy."

She giggled. "Right. That makes sense."

"So, tell me what it's like. You don't like my underwear?"

"I love your underwear. I'm just amazed boxer briefs can contain that monster." She realized what she said and clapped a hand over her mouth as she laughed with wide eyes.

The "monster" twitched and challenged that assessment.

"You know you don't have to wash my underwear," I said to her after she stopped laughing.

She took another drink of her beer. "I know. Can I tell you a secret?"

"I wish you would," I muttered.

"I like taking care of you. It makes me feel useful and...I like the look on your face when you eat something I made. I like seeing you look dapper in the dress shirts I ironed. I like the way you smell when you come out of the shower using the body wash I selected for you. I like tying your ties and laying out your clothes. I liked getting your firm in order and watching you work." She gazed at her drink and bit on her bottom lip.

I stared at her in disbelief. She loved me. I heard it in her voice. I wasn't assuming she loved me just because she took care of me. She took care of me because she loved me. She didn't have to do any of it. She could've hired someone to come in and clean. She could've let my clothes pile up until I ran out of dirty underwear. She could've left me on my own for my meals and let me get to work late and look a damn mess.

But she didn't.

She loved me.

She laughed softly as she blinked back to the present. "I'll bet it was your full intention to get me drunk and make me say things I wouldn't normally say."

"Oh, baby, you didn't used to need alcohol to speak your mind," I reminded her.

Her smile faded some and she looked a little uncomfortable. She put a hand to her chest and took a few deep breaths, as if trying to ease some anxiety. It knocked me down just a little, to see she still felt anxious. She swallowed the rest of her drink. When she tried to get the waitress's attention again, I put her hand down.

"I think you've had quite enough, drunkard. Besides, I already paid the bill."

"You started this drunk fest!" She laughed and grabbed her purse and began to slide out of the booth.

When she stood up, she swayed and started to lose her footing. I caught her, put my arm around her waist, and led her out of the restaurant. I didn't mean for her to get this drunk. I hoped she wouldn't hate me in the morning.

As we stood on the sidewalk looking for a cab, Emmy wrapped her arms around my neck. I looked down at her with amusement and wonder.

"You're so good to me," she sang.

I chuckled. Even if she was angry in the morning, it was well worth it to have her arms around me and to feel her body pressing against mine, even if just for a moment. I kissed the top of her head and waved down a cab.

"What's with all the fucking little kisses lately?" she asked after we started moving. I had my arm around her waist still and her sweet smelling head rested on my shoulder. "I don't know if you're kissing me like I'm a pet or like a friend or like a lover. They're really conflicting kisses!"

I laughed. She was fucking adorable, looking up at me with a cute confused expression on her face. I couldn't hold back anymore. I wasn't sure what kind of asshole it made me to want to kiss a woman who was clearly inebriated, but in her intoxication, she was more like the woman I used to know than she had been in a very long time.

"I'm sorry," I said softly as I gazed down at her. "Let me clear that up for you."

I put my hand under her chin and tilted her head back. I had one second of indecision, but when she closed her eyes in anticipation, my decision was made. I gently pressed my lips to hers. When she responded easily by parting her lips, I took it as an invitation and slipped my tongue into her mouth. I groaned as I tasted her for the first time in nearly two years. Her tongue slid over mine in an attempt to participate. Her mouth was like heaven, soft, warm, and joyous. Her mouth was like hell, because once I was there, I'd willingly sell my soul to stay there.

Emmy locked her hands around my neck and climbed onto my lap. We both moaned as she grinded herself over my erection. I put my hands on her hips and lifted mine to grind into her harder. She pushed back and nipped at my tongue. She began to move faster on me, harder, and kissed me deeper as she seemed to search for some kind of release. I was more than willing to give it to her, right there in the back of the cab. I was willing to make her come, groaning in my mouth because I was unwilling to stop kissing her. I was ready tob push her over the top. I began to move my hand toward her breasts when the cabbie interrupted and ruined the moment.

"Hey," he called to us, forcing Emmy to pull away from me with wide, startled eyes. "Why don't you pay me and take your sexcapades to your bedroom?"

Emmy looked horrified as she threw open the door and scrambled off my lap. I wanted to grab her and not let her run away, but the cabbie again demanded to be paid.

"You could've driven around the block once or twice." I growled, handing him a twenty.

"I ain't no mobile Motel Six, buddy."

I got out of the cab without getting my change and hurried inside. Emmy had already taken an elevator upstairs. I waited for the next one with impatience. She looked horrified. Horrified! I didn't know what to think or how to feel. The one thing I did know is that I wanted to make sure she was okay.

When I finally got to the apartment, I watched her with unease. She was stiff in her movements and speech. I needed to drive Diana home, but I was tempted to just give her my car keys and let her drive herself home so I could go to Emmy. Instead, I ushered my younger cousin to the garage.

"Did you enjoy your date?" Diana asked in the car a little while later.

I answered absently. "Yes. It was fun."

She giggled. "I see that."

"What?" I looked over at her.

"You have lipstick smeared across your mouth."

I hastily wiped my mouth with the back of my hand. "Did Emmy say anything when she got upstairs?"

"Not really. I did most of the talking while she answered like a robot. Even if she did say something, I wouldn't repeat it. What goes on between the two of you is none of my business and…ew."

She punched the radio on. I pushed on the gas pedal a little harder, anxious to get back home.

Chapter Fifteen

The apartment was quiet when I got home. The bedroom door was closed. I assumed Emmy had gone to bed, but if she thought she'd get away from me by going to sleep, she was wrong.

I turned off the lights in the living room and kitchen and went into the dark bedroom. I took my jeans off and got into bed next to her. Her eyes were open. She silently stared up at the ceiling. I put my arm across her midsection and moved in close to her.

"Too much too soon?" I whispered.

She shrugged. Shook her head. Nodded, and then shrugged again. "No. Maybe. I don't know."

"Tell me what you're thinking."

At first I didn't think she'd tell me. I thought she'd push me away and close herself up tight, but to my surprise, she took a couple deep breaths and began to speak in whispers.

"I feel…anxious…all the time. My chest is so tight with stress and tension. It feels like there's a boa constrictor inside, squeezing me so I can't breathe. Different situations make it better or worse, but it's always there. Always. When I'm with Lucas it isn't bad. When I'm working…or eating Grace's apple pie it isn't bad. But other…things…things that should make me feel better…don't."

It clicked in my head almost immediately. "Like me. I don't make you feel better. That's why before you started drinking, even when you seemed to be having a good time, you looked anxious."

"The snake squeezed tighter," she confirmed.

This was much worse than the "Oh" incident. I was crushed. The last thing I wanted to do was bring Emmy any further pain, and without trying, that seemed to be all I was doing. When I confronted her about Kyle, I could've pushed her over the edge, completely blinded by her emotional stability.

"I didn't realize I make you feel worse." I tried to hide how much this hurt me. I started to roll away from her, but she put a hand on my arm.

"It would probably be a good feeling if my past wasn't my past," she said quickly and gave me a pleading look.

"I only know some of it." I wasn't about to start pushing her to talk about all that again. If she wanted to tell me on her own, I wouldn't stop her. "I know my part in it."

"I know, but I'm not ready to talk about that. One thing at a time. It was hard enough telling you what I just told you."

"Do you feel any better after getting it off your chest?"

Her voice tremored. "No. It made it worse." I thought she was going to cry. I didn't want to see her cry. I wanted her to feel better. I wanted to ease her tension and anxiety, not increase it.

"Let me help you release some of that tension," I whispered. I couldn't stop myself from pressing my nose against her neck. Her skin smelled so good. I put my hand on her hip and eased it down to her inner thigh. I needed her, and she needed me even though she didn't realize it. I lightly kissed her neck and murmured, "I won't continue unless you want me to."

She didn't speak, but a very soft, barely audible moan slipped past her lips. I'm not even sure she realized she did it.

"Do you want me to keep going?" I whispered against her ear.

Her breath hitched. "Yes."

I didn't give her an opportunity to finish the word. I crushed her mouth with mine and pushed my hand up the leg of her shorts.

"You're wet," I said against her lips. "How long have you wanted me?"

She tried to answer, but I claimed her mouth again and ran a finger over her panties and found her clit. I pressed and moved my finger in a circular motion. Emmy moaned into my mouth as her hips rose slightly off the bed. There were too many clothes between us and not enough skin. I broke free of our kiss and quickly pulled her shorts and panties off. I yanked her shirt off her and quickly removed mine. I wanted to take my boxers off, but I was sidetracked by her beautiful, full breasts.

I groaned as I closed my mouth over one hard nipple. Emmy cried out and grabbed the back of my head.

"Beautiful," I murmured before moving to the other breast.

I flicked the nipple with my tongue. I looked up into her face and watched as I bit down. She started to shriek and quickly clamped a hand over her mouth while throwing nervous glances at Lucas's bed. I eased the pain I caused her by licking her gently.

"I'm going to make you come all night," I promised her as I moved down her body. "You're going to beg me to stop." I nipped at her inner thigh. "But I'm not going to listen."

"You sound…mmm…very sure of yourself," she panted as I teased her with my fingers.

"I know your body, Emmy. I don't care how long it's been. I know your body, and your body will remember me."

I slipped two fingers inside her, slid them in deeply and held them there. Emmy writhed against my hand, desperate for movement.

"Ask me to fuck you with my fingers, Emmy. Ask me."

She moaned and bit her bottom lip as she gazed down at me. "Please. Please fuck me with your fingers, Luke."

"What if I say no?" I pulled my fingers out a little.

She whimpered. "Please. Luke, please?"

I rammed my fingers back in and she was quick about covering her mouth before crying out.

"You're so wet," I groaned as I begin to slide my fingers in and out of her hot tunnel. "I'm going to make you feel so good, baby."

Emmy's hips circled, grinding into my hand with every thrust of my fingers. I had no doubts of her sexual drought. My fingers were very snug.

"More," she groaned as she bit her bottom lip.

"Can you handle more?"

She moaned a positive response. I added a third and slid my fingers in deep and hard.

"Oh my god. I'm going to…unhhh…"

Her thighs clamped shut over my hand as her body raised off the bed. Her walls contracted, squeezing my fingers in a vice grip. The pad of my thumb found her clit and it was all she needed to fall over the precipice, trying not to scream my name as she came hard on my hand. As her body fell back to the mattress, I forced her legs apart and pulled my wet fingers out of her. I put my hands under her hips and elicited a small yelp out as I yanked her ass down to the edge of the bed and got on my knees. Eagerly, I pressed my tongue into her dripping cunt. The instant her nectar hit my taste buds, I groaned and my dick jumped happily. I missed Emmy's scent and the sweet taste of her body. I hadn't realized how much until my tongue was buried deep, trying to lick out every drop her body produced.

With another groan, I stroked my tongue through her folds to her clit. Emmy immediately tried to wriggle away, but I held on to her legs tightly.

"You're not going anywhere," I growled at her and yanked her a little closer. I flicked my tongue over her clit as she squirmed and moaned. I released one of her legs. "Behave and don't try to move away."

I covered the little bud with my lips and sucked at the same time I pushed my three fingers back inside her heat.

"Fuck!" she hissed.

Her fingers were in my hair pulling and twisting. She pressed on my head and then tried to push me away as she began to unravel. Press and push, press and push. She couldn't get enough of what I was doing to her, but it was too much.

I sucked harder as I used the tips of my fingers to massage her G-spot. Now she was just pushing, trying hard to wriggle away. I warned her.

I bit down on her clit and she fell to pieces, biting the pillow she was using to muffle her screams. I pulled my fingers out of her and made quick work sucking her juices off them as if I had just had my fingers in the most delectable dessert. Groaning again, I dipped my tongue once more and licked her until I was satisfied I had lapped up every drop of her orgasmic moisture. I quickly pulled off my boxer briefs and got on the bed. Emmy's arms were outstretched to welcome me as I settled carefully on top of her.

"Oh, fuck," I gasped.

We were skin to skin with my erection nestled against her warm and moist sex. Her breasts pressed against my chest, her arms wrapped around my torso and her legs wrapped around my waist. One of my hands dragged lazily up and down one side of her body, caressing her soft skin. I stroked her face with my other hand as I gazed into her eyes. My heart pounded hard in my chest, desperate to mold with her heart and become one.

I knew in that moment I could never be without Emmy again. I could never be with anyone else again, because no one else would ever matter as much to me as she did. The love I felt for her was nearly too much to contain, and the only reason I didn't say the words that were hanging on my tongue was because I didn't want her to have to think about that. I didn't want her mind to wonder about the implications, which I knew it would, because regardless of how much of the old Emmy was beneath me, she was still the new, contemplative, afraid-to-live-love-and-be-loved Emmy. I just wanted her to feel. Not think. Feel good. Not worry.

I kissed her, gently, sensually. I teased her tongue, daring her to play but then making her give chase. When she caught me, I pulled her tongue between my lips and sucked gently before giving it a little nip. Groaning with a small chuckle, Emmy bit back and then soothed with slow, luxurious strokes. She put a hand at the back of my head, deepening the kiss and turning it from playful to serious. She put everything she had into it, holding my head with both hands now as her tongue did things to my mouth that made my cock twitch and grow impossibly longer and thicker.

Emmy suddenly pulled away from my lips and looked at me with a very serious expression.

"You're not putting that thing inside me," she said and nipped my bottom lip. I groaned and grinded my cock against her. She groaned and pressed back. "I mean it."

"No, you don't mean it." I slid my cock along her pussy.

"You'll kill me."

"You'll die satisfied."

I kissed her to shut her up and positioned the tip of my cock at her entrance. It took every ounce of self-control I had not to push inside her.

"I'm practically a virgin."

"Then I'm practically your first." My tongue swept across her bottom lip.

"It won't fit."

"You'll adjust around me."

"What if I don't?" She looked up at me with both lust and apprehension.

"You will."

"What if I don't?"

I was tired of talking about it. I pushed gently, sliding in a couple of inches. Emmy's breath hitched and then she let it out in a low hiss between her teeth.

"You're so tight," I moaned and grazed her jawline with my teeth.

"Yeah, that's what I'm trying to tell you," she said, breathless.

I groaned and pressed in another couple of inches. Emmy moaned and bit her bottom lip.

"Baby, I need to be inside you. You need me inside you. You're going to take me all the way."

Hesitation, and then a small nod.

Slowly, I slid into her tight sex until I filled her completely. I held still for a moment, looking down into her face, etched in pain and pleasure as she came again. We were connected physically, but also on a much deeper level, so deep I couldn't even see where it ended. Maybe it didn't end. Maybe our connection went on forever. Emmy had nearly ruined me before, but now I was completely decimated.

She hadn't given herself over to me yet. I had her body, but I needed every part of her. She was mine, and I'd stake my claim by any means necessary.

I pulled out just as slowly as I had pushed in. I kissed her to muffle the screams that would come and thrust hard and deep. I swallowed her yelp and endured her fingernails digging into my shoulders. I didn't give her an opportunity to recover before I slammed into her again and again. I put my arms around her so I could hold her close as I thrust into her harder. Her nails drew blood, but her legs wrapped around me tighter as if she couldn't get me deep enough, even though I knew there was probably some amount of pain for her.

Her pussy held me tightly, wrapped around my manhood like a fleshy, warm, moist sheath. I wanted to stay inside her for all of eternity, but I felt my orgasm building quickly.

"More," Emmy groaned after pulling away from my lips. "More."

Without waiting for her to elaborate, I got up on my knees and immediately missed the closeness of her body. I raised her legs to my shoulders and leaned over her again, bracing myself on the headboard. I was so deep, which drove me fucking crazy—and it seemed to drive her fucking crazy as well. I had to clamp my own hand over her mouth as I began to drive into her wildly. She screamed into my hand and clawed at my chest.

"I'm going to come soon. You want to feel me coming hard inside you."

It wasn't a question. I wasn't asking for permission. I was going to mark her.

"But we're going to come together. You're going to have be quiet, sweetheart."

I took my hand off her mouth. She reached for a pillow, but I knocked it away.

"I want to see your face when you come—when I come inside you, Emmy."

She bit her lip and tried hard to keep her squeals and moans down. I braced myself on the headboard again and began to pound into her without restraint. She bit her knuckles as she tried not to scream.

"Oh shit. Come for me, Emmy. Come on...shit...come on my cock, baby."

I thrust into her so hard I pushed her up the bed several inches. She covered her mouth and screamed muffled words I didn't understand and then her eyes rolled back in her head. I had to bite my own lip as I began to unravel. I growled low in my throat as I began to come.

"Take it," I growled. "Take all of it."

I cursed quietly as I emptied myself into her. When I was sure I had given her every last drop, I let her legs fall limply back to the bed and stretched my body over hers. I put my arms around her again and kissed her deeply as I gently rocked into her. I was still hard and I wasn't ready to leave her warmth. I took her slowly, softer, stroking myself within her with care. I pulled away from her lips and kissed along her jawline and down to her neck as I put a hand in her hair. We didn't speak and we didn't get loud again, but we moaned as our bodies moved together, reaching for mutual satisfaction. No words were needed. As if on cue, when I again began to mark her as mine, she shuddered and gasped as she came with me.

I didn't immediately pull out. She looked up at me and smiled lazily.

"Your body remembered me." I kissed her nose.

"I don't think my body ever forgot you," she said sleepily.

"I'm going to make sure it never does." I murmured with my lips against her throat.

"Hmm?"

"Nothing." I gave her one last lingering kiss and rolled off her. I pulled her into my arms and kissed her hair. "How do you feel now?"

"Much, much better."

"Me too," I said, but she had already fallen asleep.

I ran my fingers over her belly. I felt a little guilty. A little cruel. A little bit like the bad guy. I purposely planted my seed.

And hoped it would grow.

Chapter Sixteen

"Your mommy is going to kill us," I said to Lucas.

"Emmo." He pointed to the television, as if to say, "Dude, shut the hell up. I'm trying to watch Elmo here."

We were sitting in the living room eating cereal right out of the box. There were a lot of Cheerios on the couch and on the floor, and not all of it was Lucas's mess. If Emmy came out and saw I'd let Lucas eat in front of the television and the mess we made together, she'd rip my head off.

I smiled as I thought about her lying in bed, sleeping sounder than I'd seen her sleep in a long time, completely naked with her just fucked hair. If Lucas was napping or not home, I would've gone in there and woken her up with a reminder of the night we shared.

My smile faded. She'd rip both of my heads off. I took no precautions, and in fact, went all primitive man on her and "marked" her. Twice. I may as well have peed on her. I even had the delusional thought if I impregnated her, she'd stay with me. I was so intoxicated by my physical connection with Emmy I'd obviously forgotten her last pregnancy didn't exactly send her running into my arms. It was an immature move. It was shady and wrong. I was no better than Claire.

But if she did get pregnant…

I looked down at Lucas and imagined a little girl who looked just like him. One thing was for sure, one day I wanted to have another baby, with Emmy. I'd do anything to keep her, but it couldn't be underhanded and sneaky, like trying to knock her up without her knowledge. I'd have to do it the old fashion way and work my ass off to prove to her we were meant to be.

My cell rang on the dining room table. I set the box of cereal in Lucas's lap and stood up, shaking off Cheerios in the process.

"Hey, Casey," I said to Emmy's sister-in-law. This Casey was unlike the Kacey in my office. This Casey was a sweet, smiling, southern woman without an ounce of whatever office Kacey had running through her veins that made her so scary.

"Hey, Luke. Listen, I know you took Lucas to the zoo yesterday, but we're taking Owen today and we thought maybe we

145

could take Lucas, too? We'll keep him all day so he and Owen will have time to play."

What a terrible father. All I could think of was getting Lucas to Emmet and Casey's so I could jump back into bed with Emmy.

"That sounds great, Case. I'll get him ready and bring him by. We'll return the favor, as usual."

She laughed. "Don't worry about it. I'll see you soon."

We hung up and I swooped into the living room to tear Lucas away from his sacred public programming.

****

My ego had just taken a double blow. First, when I came in with her favorite muffin from Panera, Emmy looked like she was about to kiss me. It wasn't my imagination. She had licked her lips and leaned in a little, but at the last second, she patted my arm instead. My hopes of not having an awkward after-sex-morning were blown away. Soon thereafter, she refused the check I offered in an effort to begin paying back some of the money I owed her. It was killing me to know I owed the mother of my child money, but she'd made some valid points that had me grudgingly pushing the check back into my wallet.

"I felt really good about paying you back." I pouted just a little bit.

"Aww," she crooned mockingly. "Do you want me to pat your arm?"

"Maybe later. I want to talk."

I wanted to be honest with Emmy. I wanted to tell her how I felt. I wanted to know if she felt the same way, too. I wanted to admit to her that I'd panicked inside last night, and made a foolish decision—twice.

There was so much to talk about.

She smiled nervously. "Oh boy. Can I at least have my coffee first?"

"Are you incapable of talking *with* a cup of coffee?"

"The damn stuff dribbles out of my mouth every time I try."

I grinned. "Maybe it's best to swallow rather than spit."

"Are we still talking about coffee?"

"You're successfully avoiding an inevitable conversation," I said, beginning to feel a little frustrated.

"You got me." She threw her hands up. "I'm so not ready for that conversation."

"I'm not going to let this one go."

"I know." She bit her bottom lip. "Maybe we can just postpone it."

I really believed she bit on her bottom lip on purpose. It wasn't a nervous bite. It was a come-hither-and-taste-these-lips kind of bite.

"I would need a damn good reason to postpone it." I stared at her lips. I already had a damn good reason to postpone it.

I put my hands on her ass and pulled her body to mine. I kissed her, expecting some resistance, but she kissed me back, hungrily. Her fingers laced behind my head and her tongue swept through my mouth as if only my mouth could quell her hunger.

I released the button and then the zipper on her shorts and pushed my hand into her panties. Emmy groaned and pushed herself against my hand as I worked a finger into her wet pussy. Suddenly, she threw her head back, moaning loudly as her orgasm hit her. In a hurry to be joined with her, I pulled her shorts and panties off and quickly removed her shirt. In five seconds, my pants and boxers hit the floor and I lifted Emmy up, about to slide into her.

It would've been a good time to ask about birth control, but after two successful internal finishes, the damage was done.

I rammed myself into her. She screamed like she couldn't scream last night as she held onto me for dear life while I pounded her into the counter.

"You're fucking. Killing. Me," she said each word with each thrust.

"Do you want me to stop?" I paused deep. She had to be sore from last night, after not having sex for so long and then having me bucking into her so hard.

"Are you crazy?" Her fingers gripped my ass and she pulled me deeper with a long groan. "If you stop I'll kill you."

"There's my girl," I growled and slammed into her.

Her hands were on the back of my head, her lips kissing me again. I held her up with one hand and palmed a breast. Her nipple was taut and grew harder when I pinched it between my fingers. Her sex contracted around my cock. I knew she was about to come again. I released her breast and reached down between us and thumbed her swollen clit. She began screaming my name, reflating my ego and sending a warm, fuzzy feeling straight to my chest.

With her body wrapped around mine, I turned to carry her to the bedroom, but I never kicked my pants away and tripped over them. We ended up on the floor in a tangle of limbs and discarded clothing, laughing and moaning. Soon the laughter was gone as I began to move once again. I moved at a slower pace, just savoring how her soft body felt under mine.

I traced my thumb over her lips and her tongue flicked out for a taste. I groaned and pushed in deep. I let my eyes take in her features—her cute nose, the delicate curves of her cheekbones, her gorgeous eyes, every freckle, and the scar in her hairline that was not there two years ago. I'd asked her about it once before but she blew me off, made it seem a trivial thing, but I knew it wasn't. I knew in my gut she'd gotten the scar from Kyle, along with so many others.

I'd never let him hurt her again, regardless of where we went from here, but I wanted to know where we were going. I loved her, but honestly, I wasn't sure if her reluctance was because of her personal demons or if she simply didn't want me. Or both.

Connected to her in the closest physical way possible, I confessed. "I really love you. Do you love me?"

She licked her gorgeous lips. "Always."

I needed to hear her say it. I went deeper and harder, desperately searching for what her heart really felt.

"Really?" I whispered.

Deeper, harder, searching for the answers within her.

She looked me in the eyes and stroked her fingers through my hair. "I love you."

She said it, and I loved hearing it, but there was something missing within the words. They weren't empty, but they weren't as full as my own.

I kissed her hard and slammed into her so hard she slid backward on the linoleum floor. I held her closer and slammed into her again as my fingers pressed into her skin.

I loved her so much. I wasted so much time trying not to, and now I wasn't sure if it was too late to have her. My heart was in her hands, and I had the unsettled feeling she either didn't know what to do with it or she would let it fall.

"You love me, but you don't want me," I concluded, unable to hide the unbelievable sadness I suddenly felt.

Emmy burst into tears and it killed me. I held her as tightly as I could hold her, only intending to comfort her. Her legs tightened around me and her hips ground into mine. She was crying almost to the point of hysteria, but her vaginal muscles gripped me again and I responded by thrusting deep. Her body shuddered violently as she began to come, sobbing my name and digging her fingers into my back. I fell apart, coming explosively as I had the most personal, raw experience of my life.

Breathless and heart sick, I wiped at Emmy's tears. "I didn't mean to make you cry."

She covered her face, trying to staunch the heavy flow of tears, but they kept coming. She sobbed as if whatever barrier had been holding back her pain all this time finally broke.

I got up and tried to console her. I had hammered her about Kyle Sterling and said some very cruel things to her over the past year, but she never cried. I didn't know how to feel. I definitely felt heartbroken for Emmy, but I wasn't sure if she was rejecting me or if she just didn't know what she wanted yet. If this was just a physical connection or if she wanted more. I needed to know.

My cell rang in my pants a couple of feet away, but I ignored it. It rang again and I ignored it again. I didn't want to let Emmy go. The least I could do after failing her before was hold her. When Emmy's phone rang a moment later, I became concerned Lucas could be hurt, or there was some other emergency. Reluctantly, I released her and went into the bedroom to get her phone.

"What?"

Lena's voice came down the line, frantic. "Mom's hurt."

My mouth grew dry. "What happened?"

"I'm not sure." My sister doesn't panic. My sister's like a rock. But I heard apprehension in her voice and that made me extremely nervous. "All I know is she's in the ER. I'm on my way now."

I asked her what hospital and told her Emmy and I would be there soon. I rushed out into the kitchen where Emmy was against the counter, still naked and crying.

"My mom was just rushed to the hospital."

Her eyes grew big, and just like that, the sobbing stopped. We rushed around the kitchen pulling on our clothes. I made a quick stop in the bathroom and then we were out the door.

"What happened?" Emmy asked in the elevator. Her voice continued to tremble, and every few seconds, a shuddering sigh would hit her, the aftermath of hard crying.

"I'm not sure yet." I pushed a hand through my hair. "Lena sounded really nervous."

Emmy let out a small gasp. "Lena never gets nervous."

"I know."

She slipped her hand into mine and didn't let go.

****

"I'm not dropping her off at some old folk's home," Lorraine snapped at Lena and me. "She's not a dog. We can't just leave her at the pound."

"The fact your mind even compares the two is disturbing," Lena said, shaking her head. "Fine, Lorraine. Why don't you let her come live with you?"

"I have a very full house as it is, Lena. You know I can't take Mom in. Why don't *you* take her in?"

"The same reason you can't, Lorraine."

"I think we should stop talking about Mom as if she doesn't have a brain left to think with on her own," I cut in.

"I'm not even sure if I trust your judgment, Luke," Lorraine said sourly. "You took off to the east coast without a thought about your aging parents."

"That was ten years ago, Lorraine," I snapped. "Kids grow up and move away. Get over it."

"This isn't about Luke," Lena said. "This is about Mom. The fact of the matter is Mom is getting older and we need to be sure she's safe." She shook her head and sighed as she checked the time on her phone. "Sam will be flying in in a few hours. We can talk to her and see what her thoughts are."

"Sam's coming in?" I asked, surprised. "Does Emmy know?"

Lena shrugged. "I don't know if she knows or not. I called her right after I called you."

I sighed and pulled my hand through my hair. "Don't get me wrong, Sam has been…very helpful over the past couple of years, but did you have to call her here? She's not our mom. Our mom is down the hall getting an MRI. Sam is Emmy's mom. You can't just steal her away when you feel like it."

"Steal her away?" Lorraine snorted. "She hates her mother."

"She doesn't hate her," I said quietly and looked over my shoulder.

Emmy stood on the other side of the room looking out the window. She hadn't moved. I'm not even sure if she blinked. She didn't seem to be focused on the here and now, but I wasn't comfortable whispering about her as if she wasn't in the same room.

"Their relationship is complicated. You're not making it any less complicated."

Lena was silent for a moment as she studied me. She looked across the room at Emmy for a few seconds before turning her narrowed eyes back to me. "I'll try to be more considerate."

Lorraine made an exasperated sound and stomped away.

Lena leaned in closely and whispered, "Don't fuck this up, Luke."

I stood there stunned. I'll never know how she was always able to figure out what the hell was going on in my life.

"You both have that just fucked look," she answered my silent question with a small smile. "I'm assuming you just fucked."

She raised an eyebrow at me when I didn't respond and walked out of the room. I stood there for a moment, silently staring at Emmy's form against the bright light blasting into the room through the window. Maybe I misinterpreted her crying. Maybe it wasn't because she didn't want me. Maybe I was being selfish and completely self-absorbed by believing it was just about me. Maybe it was about her. The conversation we'd had a couple days ago came to mind. She thought she was too broken to be salvaged. Maybe she was crying for the parts of herself she lost.

I walked across the room and joined her at the window.

"Are you okay? You've barely said two words since we left the apartment."

She blinked as if she was just waking up and looked around.

"I'm sorry." She turned around to face me. "Are *you* okay? How are you holding up?"

"I'm okay. I'm having a hard time accepting the fact my mom is getting old."

"It's funny. Your mom falls down the stairs accidentally, and I want to shove my mom down the stairs on purpose."

I tried to smile, but it faltered before failing altogether. Even though I was very concerned about my mom, Emmy and I needed to talk. I needed her to tell me how Kyle broke her. I needed to fix her, whether she'd have me or not.

"I said I'd wait until you were ready, but…"

"You want to know what is ultimately keeping us apart."

"*You* are ultimately keeping us apart, but I need to know why."

I pushed her hair out of her face and cupped her cheek in my hand. I started to withdraw, but she pressed on the back of my hand, holding it in place. Her eyes closed for a long moment and she exhaled slowly. When she opened her eyes, I was moved by what I saw there. She wanted me. I wasn't sure how much of me she wanted, but she did. When she wrapped her arms around me and stood on her toes to kiss me, I expected a little peck at best, but her tongue slid across my lips and I gasped lightly before opening up to her, returning her affection. Nothing else mattered in that moment. Where we were or why we were there didn't exist. Our past problems, our present problems, none of it had a place in our tiny bubble. The only thing that mattered was us, holding and comforting each other with a slow but passionate kiss.

Someone cleared their throat a couple of times, but we ignored it. The third time it was louder and more distinct. I knew without looking it was Lorraine. I reluctantly separated my lips from Emmy's and glared back at my sister.

She didn't even try to be modest about the big grin on her face. "Sorry to disturb you, but the doctor wants to talk to us."

With a sigh, I took Emmy's hand in my own and followed Lorraine out of the room.

"Oh, that's embarrassing," Emmy whispered.

"No less embarrassing than Lena's weird sense of what we were doing before we got here."

"What?"

I looked at her and nodded a confirmation.

"Oh my god, I'm so embarrassed." She covered her face with her free hand.

I stopped in the hallway about ten feet from where my sisters were standing and put my other hand on Emmy's neck.

"Don't be embarrassed. You didn't used to be embarrassed about these things."

"The circumstances are different," she whispered, throwing a nervous glance at my sisters.

"We were together before, Em. We made a baby together, and now we're raising him together."

"But there was a lot of shit in between."

"Yeah, there was. And eventually, we'll have to hash some of it out, but until then, don't be embarrassed. You love me, don't you, Em?"

She nodded, though her cheeks turned pink at the admission. I knew it was hard for her to say it.

"Luke," Lena called impatiently.

Ignoring my sister, I held Emmy's face in my hands.

"I love you. You love me, and we both love our son. That's all that matters right this minute. I don't give a shit what anyone else has to say about it. Okay?"

Fear and uncertainty blazed in her eyes, but she nodded anyway. "Okay."

I touched my lips to hers for a brief moment as Lena called after me again. I took her hand and led her down the hallway where my sisters and the doctor waited for us.

"I'll go sit with Grace while you guys talk," Emmy said and started to pull away, but I held fast to her hand.

"Don't be ridiculous," Lena said, rolling her eyes. She held onto Emmy's free hand.

I didn't miss the little smile on Emmy's face.

Chapter Seventeen

I sat on the couch watching as Emmy carried a load of laundry to the small washer and dryer unit next to the powder room. Focused on her work, she didn't seem to notice me staring at her.

After she put a load of laundry in, she moved to the kitchen. I could hear her putting things away and the faucet running. She was just doing what she did every night, but it irritated me a little. I wanted her to let the dishes sit in the damn sink and not care about a couple of crumbs on the counter.

"Em," I called to her.

"Be right there."

"No," I said firmly. "Now. Stop whatever you're doing and come here."

She didn't say anything, but I knew she probably stood there feeling indecisive. I didn't usually command her to do anything. I sometimes spoke firmly, and in the past, I was downright mean, but I rarely commanded.

"*Now.*"

A moment later, she appeared in the doorway with a dishtowel in her hands. She looked at me apprehensively. I gave her a look that said "get your ass over here now." She stepped back into the kitchen but only for a second and came out without the dishtowel. She stopped by the dining room table, crossing her arms and gearing herself up for a fight, but I didn't want to fight–or start one by trying to have needed discussions.

I crooked a finger at her, keeping my face passive. After another hesitation, she moved to sit down on the couch, but I quickly reached up and grabbed her arm. She let out a surprised yelp as I pulled her down into an awkward position on my lap. I took a moment to reposition her until she faced me, straddling my lap. She blew hair out of her eyes when she let out an exasperated sound as she stared at me. She was waiting for me to talk, but I wasn't talking.

I moved my hands up her thighs, slowly up her sides until they were touching her breasts. Without taking my eyes off hers, I swiped my thumbs across her covered mounds, searching for her nipples. Seconds later, I felt her response through her shirt as her peaks quickly hardened and pressed against the fabric. Her lips sensually fell open as her breath hitched. I continued to caress her with the pads of my thumbs while gazing into her eyes. She didn't dare look away as she began to lightly grind against me. When I began pinching her nipples, she winced at first, but maintained eye contact.

Grinding harder and faster, Emmy began to moan softly as I continued to squeeze her nipples. Her tongue licked erotically at her succulent lips. Her chest rose and fell at an accelerated pace and her fingers dug into my biceps. When she bit down hard on her bottom lip, I knew she was ready.

"Don't close your eyes when you come," I said in a harsh whisper.

And she was gone, gripping my arms as if she'd die if she let go, crying out my name and shaking violently with her hot, clothed pussy against my cock. But she didn't close her eyes and kept her focus on me.

"Good girl," I murmured and pulled her head down for a kiss.

When she pulled away a moment later, she looked in my eyes again while holding my face in her hands. She didn't speak, but she let her eyes convey the words she had a hard time saying with her mouth. She was scared, broken and sad, but only a blind man could miss the love burning in her eyes. Again, I pushed her hair out of her face.

"I love you, too," I whispered and kissed her again.

This time when she pulled away, she shimmied off my lap. She parted my legs and dropped to her knees while reaching for the fly on my jeans. With high anticipation, I helped her with my jeans and boxers until she was pulling them off and tossing them behind her.

"Let's see if I remember how to do this," Emmy teased, and holy hell did she tease. Her tongue flicked a glistening drop off the tip of my cock, making me groan and drop my head back. "Keep your eyes open."

Simpering, I was ready to make a sarcastic comment, but then the head of my cock slipped between her lips and her mouth slowly glided down my shaft. I cursed instead and fought the urge to throw my head back again and close my eyes. She took me in deep, passing her tonsils and easing down her throat. She swallowed hard, trying not to gag, but she kept going, trying to take in my full length. When she finally pulled back, she was gasping for air, but she had such a sexy, evil smile on her face, and she gave me another good lick before deep throating my cock again.

"Em." I groaned her name as I pulled her hair away from her face. "You look so fucking hot taking my cock into your mouth."

She released me again, but with a starving hunger, she started to suck me. Hard. Fast. One of her hands pumped my shaft as she sucked with fury. It felt so good I thought I could seriously cry. No other woman has ever been able to turn me on like Emmy, and none of them were able to drive me crazy with their mouths like she could.

I pumped my hips in time with her sucking, hitting the back of her throat with every thrust. She moaned around my cock and her eyes were glazed over with lust and hunger. I wanted to come in her mouth, and I was getting close to, but I wanted her on top of me, riding me.

"Em, stop or I'm going to come," I panted, but she kept going. In fact, she got more aggressive, sucking harder and with more fervor. I enjoyed it for a moment before grabbing the hair at the base of her skull and yanking her head away. Her mouth released my dick with a wet pop. "Take your clothes off. Now."

She pouted a little and I had to make a conscious effort not to laugh and let her continue. She quickly pulled her clothes off and I brought her to me. She climbed onto my lap and I positioned my cock at her entrance, but I sighed, knowing I couldn't go again without mentioning the obvious.

"Emmy, we need to discuss something."

"Now?" she asked in a high voice. She looked like she wanted to slap me.

"Yes, now," I moaned as I rubbed my cock along her slit. "Are we trying to make another baby?"

Her ruffled feathers settled down. "Oh."

"Yeah." I nodded, trailing my fingers over a breast. I couldn't stop touching her, even if it would have meant my death. "You're not on anything, right?"

"No." She shook her head slowly. "But since I had Lucas, I've paid close attention to my cycle. I'm positive I'm not ovulating."

"Are you sure?" I questioned, and again, positioned myself at her entrance.

She nodded.

"What if you miscalculated?"

She mirrored my thoughts from earlier in the day. "Even if I did, the damage is done."

My voice became whisper soft. "What if you get pregnant?"

Her tone matched my own. "I don't know. What if I do?"

I trailed my fingers down her cheek. "Then we'll have another beautiful baby."

"I'll bet you say that to all the girls," she teased as she rubbed herself against me.

I frowned. That was a little too close to home after what I'd just gone through with Claire.

"You're the only woman I've ever had sex with without a condom."

"Really?" She moaned as I again swiped my dick through her slit. "Why? Why me?"

I was frustrated in the way she pretended to be too dense to know she was the only woman ever worth the risk. I was further frustrated because her question made me believe there were more than just two of us she went bareback with.

"Do you really have to ask me that, Emmy?"

She stared at me with a stoic expression for what felt like forever before putting her hands on my face. She shook her head gently. "No. I don't, because I already know the answer."

She leaned in and kissed me while positioning herself over my cock. She pulled away after a moment and fixed her eyes on mine.

"This position is going to tear me in two," she said, but began to lower herself onto me anyway. She hissed as she slowly took me in.

"I'll put you back together," I promised.

She stopped about halfway, trying to get used to the feel of me, even though she just had me earlier in the day.

I had one hand on her neck and the other on her waist. "Do it."

She bit her lip and then dropped herself sharply onto my cock. She shouted an expletive, but didn't try to move away. I moved her slowly, trying to stretch her and acclimate her to my length and thickness. She began to relax after a moment and move on her own. Our eyes were locked once again.

"You're going to completely undo me," I groaned.

She didn't answer, but she put her hands on the back of the couch to brace herself. She eased up until just the tip of my cock was inside her, and then she slammed down on me. We both moaned as she circled her hips. Then she rose up again, just to slam right back down. After a moment, she was riding me hard and begging me to hold her closer. I wrapped my arms around her in a tight embrace as she rocked herself on my erection.

"Fuck." I felt my orgasm creeping up on me.

I didn't want to let her go. I didn't want this to end. We were connected on such a primal level. I felt like my body, mind, and soul were one with hers.

"Emmy..." I moaned her name. "Em." I couldn't say what I wanted to tell her, because I was groaning and growling and near shouting as I began to come, still holding her gaze. Emmy let a string of curse words loose as she came hard, pulling on my hair and riding me without any control.

When she finally began to slow down, she leaned in and kissed me softly, but her eyes were open and so were mine, and they were looking right into hers. Our eye contact finally broke when she tiredly rested her head on my shoulder. I lightly rubbed her back as we tried to catch our breaths. I could feel her heart pounding against me. Her skin was cool and sticky. The last thing I wanted was for her to peel herself away from me, but after a couple of minutes, she did, although she didn't go far. She lay down on the couch with her head in my lap. She was peering up at me, but this time, when I looked into her eyes, I hit a wall. She was already slipping away again.

"Maybe we should stop having sex. I'm being a girl about it. My feelings just grow stronger every time."

"Mine do too."

I shook my head. "Not enough."

"You don't know that."

"If it were enough, we wouldn't be having this conversation." Em knew me well enough to know I was beyond frustrated. While we had made considerable headway, I had a bitter feeling it would all be for nothing.

"I feel really fucked up inside," she confessed after a long silence. "I'm scarred and dysfunctional."

I glanced down at her, surprised she had chosen to actually say something real.

"Everyone is dysfunctional sometimes."

"No." She shook her head, frustrated. "I feel dysfunctional all the time. It's something that stays with me all day and all night, no matter what I'm doing. I always feel fucked up, and I feel like I can't be fixed. You want to fix me, but I feel like I'm a lost cause, and I don't want you to even bother trying."

The old Emmy was so confident about who she was and her self-worth. While she didn't lord it over anyone, she didn't take a back seat to anyone else or try dumb to herself down either She was powerful, confident, and unable to be broken. If something cracked in her façade, she fixed it. That woman would've never believed she was too fucked up to be saved.

"What did Kyle do to you to make you feel so low about yourself?" I growled.

She gave me an exasperated sigh and got up. She looked back at me with irritation and frustration.

"Luke, stop blaming Kyle! I did this to myself. I mean…he did a lot to contribute to it, but he didn't force me into anything. I made my own decisions. If this was all Kyle's fault, it would be easy to just throw all the blame where it belongs and move on, but it's not all his fault."

I got to my feet. "You're not a lost cause. Yes, you made bad decisions, but you're not doomed. I love you, Emmy, scars and all."

"Look," she said and hung her head low. Her shoulders slumped, too. "I'm afraid I'm going to fuck up again. I'm afraid I won't be able to ever give you what you deserve."

What I deserved was her, and I was about to tell her so, but her phone rang and she wasted no time going to answer it so she could abruptly end another conversation. I was ready to go snatch the phone from her and throw it away, but something in her voice made me pause.

"What do you mean it's on fire?" she shouted so loud I was worried she'd wake Lucas. "What happened? What do you mean you don't know?"

It took me a couple of minutes, but I was able to deduce Emmy's bar was on fire. I pulled on my boxers while she talked to Mayson. I handed her my T-shirt and her panties. She pulled them on as she fired off questions and apparently didn't get many answers.

"I'll be out there as soon as I can. I'll call you when I have a flight."

She ended the call with Mayson and ran her hand through her hair.

"Was anyone hurt?" I asked her, handing her a bottle of water.

"No. Lily got everyone out in time. Mayson said she's really upset."

I vaguely remembered the eccentric bartender. I had only met her a few times. Emmy didn't take me in there often, most likely because she didn't want everyone to know she was two-timing me.

I swallowed a bitter sip of water and pushed the idea out of my head, but it popped right back again. Emmy was going back to New Jersey. The odds of seeing Kyle again were high. I wasn't too worried about it when she was just going to the beach for a week, but now she'd be back on her old stomping grounds. Chances were Sterling would hear she was around and show up somewhere along the way. I had hopes she'd have enough sense to leave well enough alone and not get wrapped up in the man again, especially considering the possibilities of our relationship.

But not that deep down, I knew Kyle was Emmy's Achilles's Heel. She was drawn to him in the way an addict's needle is to their vein. She would think she could have just one taste, but before she knew it, she'd be completely lost to him and no one or anything else would much matter.

I knew this from my heart, and honestly, I understood it. Because Emmy…Emmy was my drug.

Chapter Eighteen

I had only begun to get used to sleeping with Emmy in my arms again. Now it was an adjustment to sleep alone in my bed and not hear Lucas's early morning babbling. They were going to be in New Jersey for at least two weeks, possibly longer. I wasn't sure if I could be without either of them for that long, despite how I left Emmy at the airport.

"I love you," I had told her, but she'd just stood there staring at me for what felt like forever before she'd returned the words in a stammer.

It was like pulling teeth to get her to say it to me. She had been about to go into what I deemed enemy territory—with my son no less. The least she could've done was humor me and push the words out of her mouth a little more smoothly. I told her not to worry about it and to have a nice trip. I walked away without looking back at her, because if I would've looked back, I would've begged her not to go.

I drove to the hospital after dropping Emmy and Lucas off at the airport. They weren't releasing my mom in the foreseeable future. The doctors had discovered she had a series of mini strokes and it was during one of these events she had fallen down the stairs. I hated she had been alone, even if only for a few minutes. Lena and Lorraine were still at odds at whether or not she should live on her own or where she should go. I honestly didn't want her alone, but I wanted her to make the decision for herself.

I only stayed at the hospital for a few minutes, long enough to see how Mom was feeling and to make sure there hadn't been any significant changes. I stopped off at the office on my way home to pick up some work and then went back to my horribly quiet apartment. I tried to focus on the upcoming week in court, but the silence was oppressive. I knew Emmy and Lucas weren't going to come barreling through the door at any moment. My life had changed after Lucas, but I wasn't aware how significant that change was until I was sitting in my living room, staring at his basket of toys in a corner of the living room. My life had been vastly empty without him, and admittedly, without Emmy, too. Though they were only supposed to be gone for a short few weeks, I felt loneliness and emptiness consuming me.

I was unsettled with her absence and with our relationship. I, of all people, knew sex didn't make a relationship solid, nor did the little baby talk we had. I wasn't even sure if we were in a relationship at all, or if Emmy was simply a horny ball of emotions as she struggled to break out of the darkness that still hung around her. I would like to think she wouldn't toy with me that way.

I snickered out loud. Sometimes I'm just fucking funny. Emmy toyed with me for months when she was running back and forth between me and Kyle. I had to believe she wouldn't repeat history. There was no way she'd break my heart again. No way.

****

Two days after her departure, Emmy called me early in the morning as I was on my way to court. I couldn't help but grin when I heard her voice.

"How are you guys?"

"We're great. We're getting ready to go to the shore for a few days."

"Oh, Lucas's first beach trip. I'm jealous I'm not there." I was going to miss another one of Lucas's firsts. It pinched at my chest a little bit, but I pushed past it. It wasn't anyone's fault this time.

"Sorry," she said sincerely. "Are you still going to come out here?"

"I don't know. Depends on your plans. You got there a week earlier than expected because of the bar, but are you still staying until after Labor Day?"

"I don't know. Depends on what I'm going to do with the rubble that used to be my bar."

I wish she'd just leave it and come back home, but she had to make those decisions on her own.

"Well, things are pretty busy here. I'm in court all this week. You let me know what you decide to do and I'll let you know if I can come."

"Okay." I could hear a hint of hopefulness in her voice, which made me hopeful, too. "You want to talk to Lucas?"

162

"Of course."

I only understood about half of what my son said, but he said it all with such conviction. I answered as if I knew exactly what he was talking about. He mentioned the plane, ice cream, and something about Elmo. I mean, there wasn't much else a one-year-old had to talk about.

"So, what else is up?" I asked Emmy after Lucas got bored talking to me. It was just a general question to keep her talking. Even though I had reached the courthouse, I wanted to keep her on the line for a little bit longer and use the sound of her voice to propel me through my day until I could speak to her again later that night.

"Well..." She hesitated. "I haven't...I mean, you and I haven't really talked since I got here and..." She let out a sound of exasperation. "You know I went to the bar right after I got off the plane."

"Right." I frowned. She was tripping over her words and she sounded a little wound up.

"When I got there, I was so absorbed in the wreckage I didn't notice him until he scared the shit out of me. I was holding this half empty bottle of vodka and I was about to drink it, because...well, because it's vodka. He said something behind me—I didn't even know he was there—and I dropped the bottle."

"Who was behind you, Emmy?" I asked slowly. I don't know why I bothered to ask. I already knew the answer. It took him all of five minutes to find her. I wondered if he could sniff her out like a hound dog.

"Kyle," she said and then blundered on, unaware she was talking herself into a hole. "We talked about the bar and he asked me if we could have lunch, and I said I'd have to think about it and then he left. Last night I was sitting in my hotel room. Lucas was asleep, everyone else was busy with their own lives, and I was curious. I called him. I don't know why—I mean, not really. But the moment he answered, Tabitha—of all people—showed up at my hotel door. I hung up with Kyle and Tabitha came in. You know, she finally told me why she's hated me all these years? And I understand now—I get it. I'll have to tell you about it another time. I'm just glad we made up. I called Kyle back. I just wanted to talk I guess, but he offered to bring me some food from the diner and just talk. I accepted, which was stupid, because I really wasn't ready to talk about what needed to be talked about I guess. You know how I am with talking."

Funny, because she was doing an awful lot of it at the moment.

"He came over with food like he said, but he also brought a bottle of vodka. He tried really hard to get me to drink that vodka, and I really, really needed it, but I didn't. We didn't talk about anything very important and then I showed him some pictures of Lucas, because Lucas was sleeping in the other room. I sat down next to him so I could explain some of the pictures and of course he tried to…kiss me…but I pushed him away. He left and then I just felt really stupid. I don't understand why I even asked him over. It was like my curiosity really got the best of me and I couldn't just leave well enough alone. But I won't call him again," she said firmly. "I didn't come here for him. I have to take care of this bar mess and hit the beach with Lucas and hopefully you'll join us."

I was fucking flabbergasted, and I couldn't ignore the pain tearing through my chest. My fists clenched at my sides and I closed my eyes because I literally saw red. I knew Kyle would seek her out, but then she invited him in—with my son a few feet away! I knew it in my bones Kyle had beaten Emmy. I couldn't believe she'd just invite him over for some damn diner food with Lucas sleeping in the next room. Furthermore, this was the man who ultimately broke us apart. No, I take that back. Emmy ultimately broke us apart, but he played a very significant part, and she just casually invited him in as if everything would play out perfectly, like they would just be able to forget about their torrid past.

I felt like Emmy and I had really come a long way since she first moved to Chicago. I really believed there had been a chance for us and she just totally obliterated it in the name of curiosity.

"Hello?" she tested after I'd been silent for too long.

"I'm here." I forced my eyes open. I still saw red. "I don't know what to say. I guess I'm fucking blown away."

"Nothing happened," she insisted. "I told you every detail."

"I don't doubt your honesty, Emmy. I doubt your decision making."

Because inviting Kyle Sterling over was a piss poor decision.

She was quiet, but I could almost hear her biting her bottom lip in distress. She had to have been extremely dense to not feel my anger and hurt through the phone line.

"Look. You made it pretty clear where we stand, so you do whatever you want, but you keep that asshole away from my son."

I ended the phone call with such fury I was surprised I didn't break the screen. I was tempted to send the phone flying across the cement, but it probably wouldn't have gone over too well in front of the security standing guard outside. I turned it off and shoved it in my pocket before storming into the courthouse.

****

The gavel slammed down, echoing throughout the courtroom as Judge Marsen yelled I was in contempt. I sure as hell was in contempt, standing in Vivian's face, screaming at her.

My day had gone from bad to worse. My open-shut case wasn't so open and shut, not with Vivian on the opposing counsel. I felt like she had pushed every button I had, including the ones Emmy had already pounded the hell out of. I was always a professional in court. Even when I found myself raising hell in my head as steam poured out of my ears, I never lost my cool like I did this time.

My arms were yanked behind me and silver was locked around my wrists as I continued to yell at Vivian. When I called her a heart eating bitch, even she lost what little composure she had left and whipped her hand across my face so hard I saw stars.

"Twenty-four hours in a jail cell should cool you down, Mr. Kessler," the judge said. "No bail. I don't want to see your face outside of that jailhouse until you have served a full twenty-four hours! Court is in recess until Thursday morning at nine a.m."

I was escorted via police cruiser to a holding cell generally used for city, state, or even federal officials who find themselves in a little bit of hot water. Judge Marsen was very generous, because she could've thrown me in with the general population.

"Dude," Officer Harris said, shaking his head after he locked me in.

"I know." I growled, pulling my fingers through my hair.

"Must be a woman."

My look of disdain was answer enough for him. I turned my back on him and walked the few feet to the back of the cell, looking for something to punch or kick.

"Look, I'm not an authority on the opposite sex or anything," Harris said. "But if she's got you this crazy, you need to fix it."

"Kind of hard to do locked in a cell."

"When you get out, go fix it."

I growled in frustration. "Can't."

"Can't? Or won't?"

"Did Oprah give you a show and stamp a Doctor title to your name, Harris?" I snapped at him.

He grinned. "Nah, man, but I have a wife, and I fought my ass off to get her."

I stood in the middle of the small cell looking at him with my hands fisted at my sides.

My tone was cynical. "Did you have to fight another man for her?"

"Brother, I had to fight off two exes and the general male population who even glanced in her direction."

The radio on his shoulder came to life and he had a brief conversation with someone.

"Gotta go." He pointed at me. "Fix that shit." A moment later he walked out of my view.

A little more than twenty-four hours later, I was rushing through my apartment packing an overnight bag. I hadn't even showered yet after sitting in the dirty cell all night, but the moment I was released, I only cared about getting home and getting my shit together. I called Lena as I stuffed the last of my items in the bag.

"Hey, jailbird," she said when she answered.

"How did you know?"

"Steve called me. What happened, Luke?"

"A lot," I said quickly. "But I'm just calling to check on Mom."

"She's fine. We didn't tell her you went to jail, though. She's being released today. For right now, she's going home and Sam is going to stay with her for a few days, but she wants to move into that assisted living place. Her mind is made up."

"I think that's best," I said in a rush. "Listen, I'm going out of town for…I don't know how long. Call me if you need anything."

"Where are you going?" She sounded alarmed. "What the hell is wrong with you?"

"I'm going to get my family and bring them back home where they belong."

"Umm?"

I sighed in exasperation. I didn't have time for this. "She spent a couple of hours with Kyle, out of 'curiosity.' I'm not letting him take my fucking family away."

"Luke," Lena said my name softly. "You can't go out there and drag her back here by her hair. You need to trust her."

"I *want* to trust her."

"How do you know she saw him?"

"What do you mean how do I know?" I groused. "She told me." I quickly rehashed what Emmy had told me.

"So...she could've said nothing. She could've let you find out on your own. Maybe she thought she was doing the right thing by telling you about it. Seems to me she's really trying to gain your trust."

I inhaled deeply and let it out slowly through my nose before I sat down on the edge of the bed.

"So what am I supposed to do, Lena? I don't want him around Lucas, and quite frankly, I don't want him around Emmy. I just want my family home."

"You're not going to get her back by caging her up, Luke. The whole time she's been out here she hasn't even gone to Louisiana. She hasn't gone anywhere, and you know Emmy's been all over the damn world. You can't make her come back here that way. It's only going to backfire."

"What if I ask her?"

"Then she's going to feel obligated and have the same result. You're going to have to trust her on this one, Luke. I know after the past it's hard for you to trust her where Kyle is concerned, but you have to let her work this out herself."

I drug a hand over my face. "What if she doesn't want to come back, Lena?"

"Honestly? I don't think that's going to happen. There's so much more to lose besides...well, besides you. Sorry, but that's true. I think she needs to get some closure and she'll be okay."

"What if you're wrong?" I asked tightly.

"I'm not wrong."

"What if you are?"

"But I'm not."

"Lena!" I roared. "This is fucking serious!"

"I know it is," she said soothingly. "And I am serious. I don't think I'm wrong, but in the event that I am, we'll worry about that then."

"So what the hell am I supposed to do until then?"

"Not get arrested for one," she muttered. "Go on with your life."

"Emmy and Lucas are my life. I can't just lie down and die and not fight for them."

"I'm not telling you not to fight, Luke," she said in exasperation. "I just want you to fight smarter."

Only because my sister rarely led me wrong did I not get on the next plane to Philly to drag Emmy back, but I wasn't sure how long my patience would hold out.

Chapter Nineteen

"Are you sorry for calling me a heart eating bitch?" Vivian asked me. Craig and I were walking into the courthouse Thursday morning when she walked up beside me as if she belonged with us.

I took a sip of my coffee. "Are you sorry for slapping me?"

She gave me a look of incredulity and laughed. "No."

"Then you are what you are." I tipped my cup toward her as if to toast to her heart eating bitchy ways.

"I'm going to take that as a compliment, Luke Kessler," she said and then snatched my coffee away from me. "Thanks for the coffee."

She walked ahead of me, drinking from my cup as if it were made just for her.

"Wow," Craig murmured, watching her walk away. "If I was straight, that could have given me a hard on. For a woman who eats other attorneys for breakfast, she's kind of hot."

I frowned. "She took my coffee."

"Forget your coffee. You better have a good apology for the judge, and you better put on your A game because Deluca looks ravenous."

I nodded in agreement and started to get my head together. My fight with Emmy was still fresh, but I needed to focus. With some effort, I was able to push her out of my mind and prepare myself for battle with Vivian.

"I hope you're in a better state of mind today, Mr. Kessler," Judge Marsen said half an hour later.

"I am. I apologize for my behavior, your Honor," I said sincerely, and then added, "Bad hair day."

A few snickers arose from the few people seated behind me, but the judge was not amused and neither was her bailiff.

I made it through the day without having another temper tantrum. I also made it through the day without checking my phone ten thousand times to see if Emmy called or texted. The only time she had called me since that phone call about Kyle was the night I was in jail. Even then, Lucas left a message for me on voicemail and she had said nothing. Maybe she was angry and hurt, too, not like she had any right to be.

Despite my original plan to drag her caveman-style back to Chicago, I was still too angry to talk to her. I talked to Lucas every evening for a couple of minutes, and Emmy made sure we Skyped every few days, and I was thankful for that. I didn't talk to her, but she was always there in the background holding Lucas. I couldn't get a read on how she was feeling or what she was thinking, and I had no idea what she was doing or who she was doing it with. Many times, I picked up my phone to call her. I wanted to hear her voice. I wanted to hear her reassure me she wasn't with Kyle. Hell, I wanted her to forget about the damn piece of shit bar and the beach and to come home.

But I always put my phone back down; stubbornness always won.

Fortunately, I was extremely busy at the firm with an upcoming mega case and I wasn't left with a lot of free time to harp on the whole situation. My staff and I were working late into every night, and the days I wasn't in court, I was up to my ears in paperwork, studying and researching and organizing to fortify my case. We had our biggest client yet. A win would not only bring millions to the firm, but create so many more opportunities to add to the ones Emmy had given us.

We were all feeling the pressure and stress. The holiday weekend was coming up and Steve and I wanted everyone to actually enjoy it and not work. The trial was set to start the Tuesday after Labor Day, so in the days leading up to the weekend, everyone was snippy. Emmy had finally decided to speak to me again and asked me about my Labor Day plans, but I was truly distracted by the work on my desk and gave her a simple one-word answer. A part of me was relieved she still wanted me, but another part was bitter and angry and stubborn. I should've said more, but I didn't. It really had less to do with her than with the unbelievable amount of work I had to do.

"If you're going to be like this again, I may as well not come back," she snapped. "Lucas and I can settle down somewhere else."

What. The. Fuck. Threatening to take my son away from me was the worst move she could've possibly made.

"I can't come out there, Emmy! I'm busy! Don't you understand that?"

She, of all people, should've understood. She had been at work the day I acquired the case, and she was there the day we got the court date. Maybe she had forgotten, but she should've known. There was nothing I wanted more than to spend my days on the beach with Lucas instead of waking up alone every morning wondering if she fucked Kyle yet.

"The only thing I understand is your bad attitude," she hissed and then hung up on me.

Cursing, I called her back but was immediately greeted by her voicemail. I put both hands in my hair and swallowed back a roar of exasperation. The past few weeks have felt like fucking junior high with Emmy. Instead of talking like the grown ass adults we were, we were playing childish games like Silent Treatment and Say Something Juvenile and Hang Up. I couldn't imagine what was next. It wouldn't surprise me if we started in on the Yo Momma insults.

It started deep in my gut and burst its way up and out of my mouth. I hadn't laughed in so long, truly laughed, and now I couldn't stop. I sat back in my chair laughing so hard my sides began to ache. Minutes later, when I was breathless and still snickering, I picked up the framed picture of Emmy and Lucas on my desk.

"Oh, you sure do make life interesting, Esmeralda Grayne." I chuckled as I ran my thumb over her smiling face.

All my anger and bitterness and distrust spilled out of me with my laughter. My epic temper tantrum was over.

My anger was gone, but Emmy was still pissed off. I didn't blame her. I'd been a royal jackass. I still got to speak to Lucas every day, and I spoke to Emmy briefly when she informed me she and Lucas would be going to Louisiana. That leg of her trip was unexpected, but it had been a long time since she'd been, and even as much as she disliked Sam, I imagined sometimes a girl just needed her mom. I also had a feeling she wanted a little bit more time to get her head together before returning to Chicago. I wasn't sure if she saw Kyle again or what it had done to her. I very much wanted to know, but I didn't ask. I let her do what she needed to do, even if it meant virtually ignoring me for a while longer.

More than a week after I put on my big boy pants, I was sitting in my office, preparing to meet a client. After all our prepping for trial, three days into it, the defendant wanted to settle, and their offer was more generous than we could've expected. Now I was back in my office, with a little less stress on my shoulders. The phone rang. I almost let it go to my voicemail, but changed my mind at the last second.

"Luke Kessler," I answered absently.

"We need a house, with a yard, so you can play catch with Lucas," Emmy said on the other line.

I smiled as my whole body relaxed at the sound of her voice. My chest felt so much lighter as relief washed over me.

"That's random."

"Sometimes I'm random."

"Sometimes?"

There was a brief silence and then a very quiet sigh.

"Are we still fighting?" she asked, sounding defeated.

"Depends," I said carefully. "Do I have to fight anyone for you?"

Her voice was small and quiet. "You would fight for me?"

"To the death."

I could almost hear her smiling.

I gave her my sincerest apologies. "I'm sorry I was being an ass."

"I'm sorry for giving you a reason to be an ass." Her apology was just as sincere.

"You don't have to apologize, Emmy. I've been trying to get you to open up to me for months, and I blew it the first time you said something I didn't like." Shame tingled up my spine as I thought about my behavior.

"Well, I didn't exactly make you feel secure in our relationship."

"If I'm insecure, it's my own fault. I trust you, one hundred percent," I said as Kacey stepped in and indicated my client had arrived. "Listen, I have to go. I have a client waiting for me. I'll call you tonight."

"Okay. I love you," she said, her voice high with hope.

My heart expanded and nearly choked me with emotion.

"I love you, too, babe."

Chapter Twenty

I was in bed with the phone pressed to my ear. I was sleepy, but I didn't want to stop talking to Emmy. I barely spoke to her for weeks, and the past few nights hearing her voice had fed my soul nutrients I didn't know were missing.

"When are you coming home?" I asked her as I stretched my arm across the bed.

She yawned. "You asked me that twice already tonight."

"Obviously, your answer wasn't satisfactory or I wouldn't be asking again."

"I'll be home in about a week." It was her third time saying it.

"That's a week too long," I murmured, but I understood. Emmy was making an effort to spend time with the family she always felt so separated from. I bugged her about coming home, but I understood why she wanted to stay.

"You've been gone too long," I said softly. "And I don't mean just physically."

She was quiet for a moment but I heard her soft sighing.

"It's been a long road back," she finally said. "I have to tell you something, Luke."

My eyes had been closed, but they opened and I rolled over onto my back and waited patiently.

"Before I left New Jersey, I went to see Kyle."

The last time she admitted something like this to me resulted in a very long, bitter standoff. This time I kept my emotions under control.

"Okay," I said tightly.

"I can't lie to you and tell you I don't care about him. I'll always care about him. I let him go. I don't know about him, but I gave myself the closure I needed. I don't know if I'll ever be...who I was before...the whole triangle debacle, but I feel like I'm ready to try now."

I wanted to ask her how she got her closure. If she kissed him. Pressed her body against his. If she found her closure in his bed. I didn't, though. I had to trust her. So I asked something less accusatory.

"How did he take it?"

"Resistant almost to the very end," she said, abstracted, as if her mind was back there with him. "But then, so was I. Whatever he had for me wasn't worth losing what I have now, and will have, with you. I just wanted you to know."

"Thank you for telling me. I don't want to talk about him anymore, at least not right now. Eventually, we will have to have a conversation, Emmy."

"Yeah, I know," she conceded. "What would you like to talk about?"

One corner of my mouth pulled up into a coy smile. "What are you wearing?"

She laughed. Her laughter edged away any thoughts of Kyle and what she could've done with him, and not too long after that, her soft moans over the phone washed away our bitter standoff altogether.

****

The evening news had just started. I was on the couch, willing the hours to pass faster so I could talk to Emmy again. I had spoken to her briefly earlier in the afternoon, but she was out somewhere and couldn't talk long. When I heard a key in the door, I assumed it was Lena. She showed up at random times to bring me home-cooked meals so I wouldn't be entirely dependent on Spam and take-out.

I heard little feet and before I could process what I thought I heard, Lucas appeared with his arms stretched out, squealing with joy. I knew how he felt because I was ready to squeal with joy.

"Hey, buddy! I'm so surprised to see you!"

I picked him up and squeezed him tighter than I probably should have as I kissed him until he pushed my face away. I rushed to the tiny foyer. Emmy was pulling shit through the door. I thought my heart was about to burst when I laid my eyes on her.

"Surprise," she said with a genuine but exhausted smile.

Jubilant, I couldn't stop grinning. "I *am* surprised. I wasn't expecting you guys for a few more days."

I maneuvered around a few bags on the floor to give Emmy a brief kiss. I wanted more. I wanted to kiss her until we both couldn't breathe and then take her to bed and kiss her some more before tearing her clothes off, but I had our son in my arms, and I wasn't ready to put him down for anything.

"We were homesick, weren't we Lucas?"

"Homethicks," Lucas repeated.

"I missed you so much," I said to him. "Don't ever leave your daddy again."

Emmy left the bags by the door and yawned as she moved into the living room.

"I'm so tired of driving. I think I'm still tired from the drive from Jersey to Louisiana, and that was days ago."

Lucas wiggled to get out of my arms. I put him down and he took off to go get reacquainted with his toys. I sat down on the couch, pulling Emmy down into my lap.

"I don't want you driving alone like that again." I felt like an idiot for not realizing until it was too late she had driven to Louisiana opposed to some kind of mass transit. The trip from Louisiana to Chicago was significantly less time, but even that made me feel uncomfortable.

"We had too much crap to cart around," she objected, but softened. "But I'll figure something else out next time. If there is a next time. I never want to do that much driving again. Like ever."

"No need to worry about that." I pulled her closer. "You're not leaving without me again. Like ever. You're never going to be out of my sight again."

She smiled up at me. "What about when you have to work?"

"I'll work from home."

"What if you have court?"

"I'll bring you with me and handcuff you to a chair."

She snickered. "What if I have to pee?"

"I've seen those parts of you before you know."

"What if I have to...you know..."

"Are you deaf? You will never. Ever. Be out of my sight again."

"I'm pretty sure there's some kind of law against restraining me."

"Baby. I'm a lawyer. I know my way around these things."

I kissed her before she could ask me any more what ifs. With my hand at the back of her head, I held her unyieldingly as I reacquainted myself with her mouth. It had been too long since I had tasted her, and I never intended to go more than a day without Emmy again. Wherever she needed or wanted to go, I would follow. I'd never survive another kind of separation from her or Lucas. They were my definition of home. They were where my heart was. Without them, I'm homeless, hopeless, and hardly worth breathing.

Lucas interrupted us before long, rightfully insisting he be the center of attention. I eased Emmy off my lap and chased the little man around the apartment. Soon, Em joined in and all three of us ran around the small space, laughing and playing, and probably driving the neighbors below us crazy. But they'd have to be patient this once, because life felt right again, and I wasn't about to let anyone diffuse that.

****

We were giddy, high off each other; laughing, groaning, moaning, and kissing. We had the most ridiculous conversation in the living room a little bit earlier, and it followed us into the bedroom as I stripped Emmy of her clothing.

"What if I put my favorite flavor of Jell-O on your lips so I could kiss it all off?" I murmured as I kissed along her jawline.

She giggled. "No, because I'll taste it, too."

Moaning softly, she arched her back as I pulled her shirt open and kissed her across her chest. I relieved her of the fabric completely and pulled the straps of her bra down her arms until she shrugged them off. Soon her breasts spilled free and her bra lay on the floor.

"What if I put some cherry flavored Jell-O on your nipples and licked it off?" I pulled a nipple into my mouth.

She inhaled sharply as her fingers entwined in my hair. Then she giggled again when I released her.

"You seem to have an obsession with gelatin."

"No, baby." I reached under her to unhook her bra. "You are my obsession, but I wouldn't mind pairing you with some of my favorite treats."

"You think a good rib eye is a treat." She laughed. "Are you going to insist on rubbing meat all over me next?"

I grinned up at her. "I have plenty of meat of my own to rub all over you, babe."

She laughed so loud I had to cover her mouth until she recovered so she wouldn't wake Lucas.

"You are so corny," she said afterward, and then sighed as my tongue traced a path down her belly and stopped just above her jeans.

I released the button on her jeans and pulled down the zipper. Emmy lifted her hips as I shimmied the pants and her panties over her hips and down her thighs. I quickly removed her last bit of clothing and tossed it behind me.

"Some grape gelatin sliding down here," I whispered as I ran a finger between her swollen lips.

"Maybe," she groaned. She pushed herself up on her elbows and looked down at me.

"Just maybe?"

I pushed a finger inside her and pulled it out wet with her juices and spread it across her sex before slipping it into my mouth.

I growled. "Then again, you are my favorite flavor."

I pushed her legs further apart and hastily pushed my tongue against her tight opening.

Emmy groaned and then chuckled. "I'm not Jell-O," she said and then inhaled sharply when I swept my tongue up to her clit.

"You're better than Jell-O," I said with my lips against her flesh. I sucked hard on her clit, making her cry out and thrust her hips up to grind her pussy in my face. "You're the sweetest of desserts..." I sucked her again and pushed two fingers into her core. "The heartiest of meals..." I bit gently on her clit.

Emmy let out a groan that started deep in her gut and came as she shuddered and trembled under my skillful tongue.

"I'm...ahhhh...not hearty." She panted. "Are you trying to call me fat? Oh fuck, right there." She moaned and moved her hips frantically as she reached for another oral orgasm.

Groaning, I lapped at the juices her orgasm had produced. She really did taste better than anything else on Earth.

"Phat? P-h-a-t?" I spelled out as I kissed her inner thighs. "Pretty hot and tempting? Yes, baby. You're super phat."

Emmy covered her mouth as she laughed. When she spoke, it was muffled by her hand. "You're so stupid!"

"Stupid?" I asked, as I kissed my way up her body. "Or *stupid*? Remember when stupid was good?"

Her laughter began to cut off her oxygen. When she finally took a breath, she begged me to shut up.

"There's only one way to shut me up," I said and laid a kiss on each breast before moving my lips to her throat.

She put her hands on my head and pulled my hair hard, forcing my face up to meet hers. Her kiss was deep and sensual. Her tongue slowly traced its way around my mouth with ease. As she kissed me, she worked on the button and zipper of my jeans and then pulled them down just below my ass. My erection sprung free, tapping her sex and making her wiggle and groan into my mouth.

I finally dared to break away from her perfect lips and quickly removed my pants and boxers before repositioning myself over of her. The head of my cock was at her entrance, but the look on her face made me pause. She looked like she was worried about something, but didn't want to say what by the way she was biting on her bottom lip. Then it hit me. I wasn't wearing a condom and I highly doubted while she was gone she went on any form of birth control.

I opened my mouth to speak, but she spoke before me.

"Are you really going to wear that shirt while you make love to me?" she asked, letting her eyes fall on the shirt I forgot I had on.

I looked down at my shirt and frowned. I could've taken the shirt off, but I hadn't realized it was so offensive.

"Stripes." She snorted, shaking her head. "You're so lucky I know what I'm getting under that hideous shirt."

I laughed now. More of our earlier conversation had followed us into the bedroom.

"Go ahead and laugh," she said primly. "I don't know if I'll be able to have an orgasm while running my hands up and down your horizontal lines."

"I bet I'll make you come at least three times, even with the horizontal lines on my person," I challenged.

"Psh." She rolled her eyes. "Don't be disappointed when I dry up and your dick gets chafed."

Positioning myself at her entrance once again, I said, "We'll see about that."

She opened her mouth to speak, but her words were lost when she swallowed back a scream after I pushed myself in balls deep with one hard thrust.

"I'm sorry, baby," I purred. "What were you saying?"

She opened her mouth to object, but I had already slid out and slammed back into her, cutting her off again and making her bury her face in my striped shirt. I circled my hips, grinding against her clit. Soon, she was biting my shoulder to muffle her cries as her body convulsed and her orgasm took over.

"That's one." I growled.

She looked up at me with vehemence. "Lucky shot, Kessler."

I laughed wickedly as I got up on my knees, and without warning, I grabbed Emmy and flipped her over like a rag doll. Then I was on top of her again, pushing myself into her from behind as I pinned her arms above her head with mine. My teeth sunk into the sensitive skin where her shoulder and neck met as I pounded into her. She pressed her face into the mattress to mute her cries and groans. With every thrust, she pushed her curvy ass up to meet me and take me deeper.

I cursed and growled dirty things into her ear as I slammed into her.

"This is my pussy, Emmy. Mine. If I tell you to come, you're going to come. Your body is mine—your tits..." I used one hand to reach under her and roughly squeeze a breast, making her shriek. My hand moved down to her ass where I gave it a firm whack. "This ass..." I reached under her and thumbed her clit. "And this pussy."

Emmy clawed at the sheets and bit into her own arm as she came. She tried to wriggle away from me, but I growled at her and pinned her with my body as I continued to fuck her hard with my fingers working on her clit.

"Too much!" she managed through gritted teeth.

"No, it's not," I hissed and then groaned in her ear. "And that's two."

I fit into her so perfectly. Everything about her right down to her inner walls was a perfect fit for me.

"You're fucking perfect." I groaned in her ear as she began to fall apart under me once again. "Three."

Before she could grasp she came three times, I rolled off her, onto my back, and forcefully pulled her on top of me until I sank into her again.

Her hair was tousled, her eyes were wide, and her flesh was pink. I groaned as I ran my fingers through her locks, over her cheeks and lips, down between her breasts, and over her tummy. Then I took hold of her hips and began to buck wildly into her, making her tits bounce and her mouth fall open and her head tilt back.

"How do you like my fucking striped shirt now?" I growled as I felt my orgasm rising.

She couldn't answer, because she was coming again. To my delight, she put her hands on her tits and started frantically squeezing and tugging at her nipples. I lost my composure, growling like an obscene animal as I thrust hard, coming deep inside her. I held onto her as she grinded on me, trying to take everything from me she possibly could, and I gave it, shattering apart as I did.

Emmy collapsed on my chest, holding on to me as if she would fall without my support. I wrapped my arms around her, listening to our ragged breaths and feeling our hearts pound together.

When we were breathing a little easier, I sat up long enough to finally pull the offending shirt off. I kissed the top of Emmy's head and stroked a hand down her back.

"Four," I whispered.

Emmy snickered and punched me in the arm, but otherwise, remained so quiet for so long, I thought she had fallen asleep. Eventually, she pulled herself off my body and disappeared into the bathroom. She came out a few minutes later and pulled on a shirt and a pair of shorts. She tossed me a pair of boxers, which I promptly put on. Even though we just did the dirty with our kid sleeping a few feet away, we didn't need to compound the awkwardness of that by being naked when he woke up, most likely before us.

Soon, Emmy and I were tangled together, contently drifting off to sleep.

"Luke?" she whispered softly.

"Hmm?" I murmured, too tired to open my eyes.

"Are you happy?"

I smiled lazily and gave her a squeeze. "Mmm hmm. The only thing that could possibly make me happier is making you my wife—and don't think you can get out of that, because you can't."

She was quiet again, and I was nearly asleep. In fact, my hearing had just begun to shut down, making her whisper barely audible. It didn't even register right away. It took a moment for her words to sink in and for me to react.

"I'm pregnant," she had whispered. "We made a baby."

Once the words really hit me, I bolted up so quickly I banged my head into Emmy's.

"Ow!" she cried, rubbing her head.

"We're having a baby?" I questioned loudly.

Emmy put her fingers to her lips to indicate I should keep it down as she shot a look over to Lucas's bed, but I didn't care.

"We're having a baby?" I repeated.

"Yes." She laughed quietly and then put her fingers on my lips next. "Yes, we are having a baby, but let's not wake up the one we already have."

I'd said nothing could make me happier, but I was wrong.

I embraced her and kissed her and repeatedly said, "We're having a baby!"

I gently pushed Emmy down on the bed and pulled her shorts down to her pelvic bone. I planted kiss after kiss where I suspected our child was growing.

"We're having a baby," I whispered as I lay my head on her belly.

Emmy ran her fingers through my hair and wiped away a few of her tears.

"Yeah," she said with a smile. "We're having a baby."

Chapter Twenty-One

Our family dinner was larger than usual. Lorraine's house was bursting at the seams with family and friends. Kids ran, crawled, cried, yelled, and played throughout the house. There was a happy and pleasant buzz of conversation and laughter and debates from all the adults, and various scents of various foods, cooked by random people, added to the warm atmosphere.

Many of the same people who were at Lucas's party were present, and a few others: Emmy's parents, Emmet and Casey, Donya and her baby, Mayson, Steve and his wife, Teresa, and most of the staff from KKA, my sisters and their families, and my mom. Tabitha couldn't make it due to her schedule, and Emmy's other siblings declined to attend for various reasons. That was fine. Besides Tabitha, everyone else that was important to Emmy was in attendance.

Our family dinners tended to fluctuate. On any given Sunday, random people showed up, or out of town visitors were invited. It wasn't surprising to see someone different walk through the door of whichever sister's house dinner was at. So, the amount of people at dinner this night didn't alert Emmy anything was different. Her best friend and cousin were already in town, as well as her parents.

She didn't question a thing.

Everyone was excited about Emmy's pregnancy. Many of the women cried. The men warned me about Em's impending hormonal mood swings and late night trips to the grocery store or fast food restaurant for ridiculous cravings.

It was a good night, and it'd only get better.

For dessert, there were many choices, but it went without saying Emmy had to have a slice of my mom's apple pie. I made her sit and relax at the dining room table while I went into the kitchen to get it for her. She was engrossed in conversation with Donya at her side and hardly noticed the large slice I put before her. She absently picked up her fork, even as the room fell uncharacteristically quiet. Before she dug into her pie, she looked around the table and asked why everyone was so quiet. She looked down at her slice of pie and gasped loudly.

Lying on the plate, beside the large slice of pie heaped with whipped cream, was a ring, gleaming in the light, diamonds sparkling.

By the time Emmy's eyes found me, I was already on one knee by her side. She covered her face as she laughed and cried simultaneously. I gently pulled her hands from her face and held them in mine. I knew we were surrounded by everyone we loved, but she was the only person in existence for me at that moment. I didn't hear the sniffles of women crying, the clicking of cameras, or hear the kids running around in the other rooms. I only saw Emmy's beautiful face and heard her shocked gasps as she cried softly.

I cleared my throat and began to speak.

"People like to tell those they love that they have their heart, but I can't say that because that wouldn't be true. You don't have my heart because you are my heart, and you are my lungs. Without you I am dark and hollow inside. Without you I can't breathe. Without you I don't have a reason to breathe. You light up the darkness, Em, and you fill in the hollowness. You give me sweet, refreshing breath. You are the oxygen my body can't ever be without. Emmy, you are…life, my life, and without you, I am dead. Please, don't ever leave me heartless, breathless, and lifeless again. Marry me, Emmy, and every day, I will give you more than my best. Every day, I will love you with my whole being. Every day, I will be your heart, your breath, and your life."

I reached up and wiped at the tears pouring out of her eyes. I used the sleeve of my shirt to wipe her nose, making her sputter out a small laugh.

"And finally…" I continued. "I promise I will never wear a striped shirt in your presence again, but I really like Jell-O. I think we can compromise with that one. So, please…marry me, Esmeralda Grayne."

She cried and laughed and made a weird hiccupping sound. It was so unattractive and so damn cute. After a moment, she calmed down enough to nod her head.

"Yes," she said. "I'll marry you, Luke Kessler."

I took the ring off the plate and slipped it on her finger, releasing a deep breath I didn't realize I was holding. Around us, our family and friends clapped and cheered, cried and laughed. Emmy grabbed my face in both hands and pressed her lips to mine. I put my hands in her hair and held her as we kissed deeply and without shame in front of our captive audience.

****

"I'm ready," Emmy said to me hours later as we lay in bed.

"For what?" I mumbled, already half asleep.

She had worn me out in the living room, completely manhandled me—only because I let her—after our return from Lorraine's house. Mayson had done us a big favor and took Lucas with her overnight. Without having to worry about putting him to bed, Emmy had attacked me before the door even closed.

"To talk," she said.

I opened one eye and looked at her. "About what?"

"About Kyle. You have every right to know what happened. I told the girls when I was in Jersey and I told my mom when I was in Louisiana."

"Why did you tell everyone but me?" I asked, not bothering to hide how aggravated that made me.

"You're...the hardest to tell," she whispered. "You're the last person... The things that happened to me are...humiliating, and up until the last time I saw Kyle, I felt such deep, debilitating shame."

"Baby," I said softly and shifted so I was leaning over her and cupping her face in my hand.

"And honestly, Luke?" she started with her forehead creased. "As much as I felt I deserved what happened to me, I was so afraid you would agree, because you hated me for what I did to you."

"I never hated you." I shook my head.

"You did." She nodded. "And that's okay. I understand. But even recently, when you wanted to know, I didn't want you to look at me...like *that*."

I touched my forehead to hers. "Tell me."

I felt her breath hit my face as she let out a long sigh.

"I want you to understand something before I start," she said earnestly. "Kyle was on drugs when he did the things he did to me. I'm not excusing his behavior, but the drugs changed him. He would've never hurt me if he was clean."

184

"Or he would," I argued, trying to bite back my anger. She was about to tell me how Kyle broke her, but she was defending him.

"Luke, I know him, okay? I know he wouldn't have hurt me."

"But he did," I spat out. "I don't care if you somehow convince me he was abducted by aliens and they programmed him to be an abusive asshole. I don't care what the reasons are behind his actions, Emmy. Facts are facts. If he was on trial for this, he would be convicted."

She was so quiet for so long, I thought she changed her mind about telling me.

"Tell me."

Her voice was extremely soft. "A few weeks after you left, I was really struggling. I hated myself for what I did to you. Kyle wanted to take me away for a long weekend. He said he wanted to spend some time with me before the busy season hit us full force, but I knew he was just trying to take my mind off you.

"We went to Miami. I chose Miami because, well, it's Miami, and Leo lives there. I thought we could have dinner with him, you know? Have dinner with a friend like a normal couple. Dinner was fine until Kyle realized Leo and I had a past."

This was news to me. I shook his hand at Lucas's birthday party, and friended him on Facebook for fuck's sake.

"What kind of a past?" I asked tightly, though I knew.

Emmy sounded a little irked by my question when she answered in short, snipped words. "We fucked, Luke. Three, maybe four times. Maybe it was three times and a blow job. Maybe it was two times and two blow jobs. I don't remember. I don't remember because I was a careless teenager."

I bit back any angry retorts I had and asked her to continue. I would have to get over the Leo thing. It happened too many years ago to be significant now, and at least he hadn't abused her.

"Anyway. When we got back to the hotel, Kyle was jealous and suspicious and argumentative, and I felt he had no right, considering the fucked-up situation we were in. When he went into the bathroom, I took off. I ended up at Leo's apartment, drunk off my ass. I was angry and bitter. I didn't go back to the hotel until morning—and no, I didn't sleep with Leo," she added hastily.

I felt some relief at that.

"When I got back to the hotel, Kyle had been up all night, and he was high. We argued and I said a lot of things I knew would get under his skin. I guess I pushed him pretty hard," she said, sounding mentally far away. "He pinned me to the bed. He was so angry. He squeezed my wrists so hard...he was extra strong and extra aggressive...he broke my wrist."

After speaking to Mayson about this, I already knew it had happened, but to hear Emmy say it was a different experience. I cringed and balled my hands into fists.

"And that's why he gave you that bracelet," I said, trying to breathe evenly and failing.

"You know about the bracelet?" She looked up at me with wide eyes.

"I had a feeling it was from Kyle. Just by the way you wore it, but Mayson confirmed it. I hated seeing it on your skin, Emmy, especially after I found out why you had it. You still wanted him after everything...I had a hard time understanding that. I still have a hard time understanding it."

"I didn't want him. If I wanted him, I would've gone to get him."

"Then why?" I pushed. "Were you feeling sentimental? Did you want him to break your damn wrist again?"

"No," she snapped and then sat up. "Maybe you're really not ready to hear this."

I took a deep breath and tried to calm myself down. I wasn't angry with Emmy. I was angry that she went through this shit. I was angry with Kyle. I was angry with myself for not being there for her when she needed me.

"I'm sorry. This is hard to hear." I reached up and put my hand in her hair. "I'm sorry. Lay back down."

Hesitantly, she shifted back into bed and I wrapped my arms around her.

"What happened to the bracelet?" I asked quietly.

"I gave it back to him the last time I saw him."

"Good." I was glad it wasn't in our home, like some kind of curse. "Tell me what happened on New Year's."

"I'll give you the short version of the night," she said and flung an arm over her eyes. "Drugs and alcohol don't mix, and Kyle

186

had had a lot of both. To this day, I'm not even sure how he managed to drive to my house without killing himself or someone else, because when he got there, he had already begun the transformation of becoming a monster. I think he must've taken something either just before he got to my house or before he came upstairs, because he changed so damn quickly. One moment he was somewhat coherent and the next he was…inhuman…"

She paused and took a deep breath and then breathed it out in a long shudder.

"He was too far gone in his drug and alcohol-induced rage. He had no more control over his actions than I did." She swallowed hard, moved her arm and peered up at me. "He attacked me— viciously," she whispered and then looked away. "In those few minutes, I was stripped of what little dignity and hope I had left. What wasn't broken before the first strike was destroyed after it."

I felt as if I'd been kicked in the chest. It ached so badly, I had to touch it to be sure it wasn't indeed bruised and broken. There was a roaring in my ears as my heart pumped extra hard to push my boiling blood through my body. I already knew it. I already knew Kyle had beaten Emmy, but again…to hear her confess it was unbearable. Hearing the pain and desolation in her voice was torture. I wasn't there for her. I was in Chicago trying so damn hard to forget about her, fucking other women and working my ass off. I had no idea she was suffering. I should've been able to feel it somehow.

I sat up and swung my legs over the side of the bed. I put my elbows on my knees and put my head in my hands. I felt Emmy sit up next to me, but she didn't touch me.

"How bad was it?" I asked her.

She hesitated. "You talked to my mom about how I looked…"

"I want to hear it from you, Emmy."

She shifted beside me. Out of the corner of my eye I could see her fidgeting with her engagement ring.

"You told your cousins and Donya," I said, losing my patience. "You told your mother. Tell me. We're getting married. We're having another baby. Tell *me*."

"I don't want those images seared into your brain. I don't want you to look at me and see me on that day."

I pressed my fists on my knees as I looked at her. I was barely able to control my sharp tone. "You have those images seared into your brain, Emmy. You have nightmares," I confessed. "You have them often and they're bad. If you can't forget that day, I can't either. Tell. Me. Now."

She took another deep breath and clasped her hands together as if she were about to give a lecture in class.

"I was slapped," she said, trying to sound very matter-of-fact, but there was a tremor in her voice. "Slapped to the floor. I was dragged to my feet by my hair and my head was smashed into the mirror of an antique vanity. When I ended up back on the floor, I curled into a ball to protect my unborn child as I got kicked, stomped, punched, and shoved. I didn't fight back, because fighting back would've been the same as signing a death warrant. I did, however, scream and beg for him to stop, even though I knew he couldn't hear me, he couldn't comprehend what I was saying because Kyle was gone. There was only this monster in Kyle's body. I got away by locking myself in the bathroom. Is that enough detail for you, Luke?" she asked, breathless.

I swallowed back a roar of distress and spoke with gritted teeth. "Was Lucas hurt?"

"No," she breathed out. "The doctor said he was unharmed."

"Obviously you didn't call the police," I spat out. "But why didn't any of the hospital staff? What did you tell them?"

"I didn't go to a hospital. Walter sent me to some under-the-radar doctor."

I stared, disbelieving. "You didn't even go see a real doctor?"

"As far as I know, he was a real doctor." She got to her feet and stood just out of my reach. "Are you satisfied now you have all the gritty, bloody details, Luke?"

I wanted to break something. I wanted to put my hand through a wall. I wanted break to Kyle Sterling and put *him* through a wall. I wanted to yell and I wanted to fucking cry.

I moved off the bed and reached for Emmy. I pulled her close, wrapped my arms around her waist and pressed my forehead to her belly.

"I'm sorry I wasn't there for you," I whispered to her. "I should've been there for you. This would've never happened if I hadn't left you."

"You had to leave." Her fingers began to sift through my hair. "I didn't deserve you and you didn't deserve what you got."

I looked up at her and said, "I came back for you."

Her fingers in my hair faltered for a moment as she looked down at me in confusion.

"What do you mean you came back for me?"

"I came back for you, Emmy."

She searched my face. "When?"

"It was a Friday, about a month after I left. I was going to take you back and I was going to do something I should've done long before and kick Kyle's ass. I looked for you at the office first, but when I found out you and Kyle were both gone on different errands, I drove to his place."

Her fingers stilled. "How did you know where Kyle lived?"

"When you're pretty sure your girl is fucking her boss, you make it a priority to know where he lives," I said bitterly.

I felt her inhale deeply, but she didn't say anything. I didn't expect her to.

"When I didn't find either of you at Kyle's, I drove to your house," I continued. "If you weren't home, I was going to get the hidden spare key and wait. I was about to get out of my car when I saw him pull into the driveway. Before I could really decide what to do, you came outside, carrying luggage."

I felt Emmy stiffen in my embrace. She was completely still.

"The day we went to Miami," she said flatly.

"Apparently so. I watched him kiss you…"

"And then I rested my head on his chest," she whispered, letting her hands drop to her sides.

"I couldn't make myself get out of the car after I saw that," I said softly, but then my tone hardened. "But if I had, Kyle wouldn't have broken your wrist. If I had gotten out of the car, chances are Kyle wouldn't have beaten you while you were pregnant with my son."

We were quiet again, staring at one another. I couldn't figure out what she was thinking and that bothered me immensely.

"Would you have left him and come back to me if I got out of the car that day, Emmy?" I asked after some hesitation. I wasn't sure I really wanted to know the answer.

She hesitated before answering. "I think no matter what answer I give you, it will only hurt you," she finally said.

I closed my eyes for a beat, unsure I really wanted to know.

"Tell me," I said once again as I opened my eyes and looked up at her.

She loosed a breath and rested her hands on my shoulders. "I don't know. That's the best answer I can give you. I don't know."

That wasn't even one of the two answers I was expecting, but she was right. It did hurt. She could've broken my heart all over again, or she could've appeased my heart, but then how would I have felt weeks later? Months later? Would I have trusted her or would I have been too bitter to even make a relationship work?

"I don't want to talk about this anymore." Emmy sighed. "Please."

"Okay, but if I ever see Kyle Sterling again…"

The threat—no, the promise—went unsaid, but very little imagination was necessary for her to understand the implication. It went without saying if I saw the man again, I'd try my best to kill him.

Chapter Twenty-Two

After intense hunting, Emmy and I found a house to buy. It was bigger than either of my sisters' homes, which meant we'd be hosting a lot of family dinners out of our large dining room, eat-in kitchen, and nook. Though there were only three and a quarter of us, we gladly took the five bedrooms the house offered. We never discussed how many children we wanted to have, but at least we had room to grow, because neither of us wanted to ever move again. It took a few weeks for us to get settled in. We had an amazing amount of stuff to move out of our small apartment, and we had to shop and wait for quite a bit of furniture to make our home comfortable.

Our wedding day was scheduled for four months after my proposal. We only invited about a hundred people—our families made up more than half that amount—choosing to keep it quaint. Emmy didn't care for large weddings. I didn't care how it happened, as long as it happened. Several times I insisted on eloping, but Emmy was adamantly against it.

"I'm putting on a gorgeous white dress and walking down the aisle with my family and closest friends gazing adoringly at me!" she had snapped at me the last time I made the suggestion. "Too many of my childhood dreams have been destroyed. This princess—and I *will* be a princess—is marrying her prince the proper way!"

I didn't argue with her. I didn't tell her there was nothing proper about a five month pregnant "princess" getting married in a white dress of all things. Her hormones made her a little batty. I stayed out of the firing zone as much as possible.

Early December. Life was good. I had won over the love of my life and she was going to marry me in two short months. We had an increasingly rambunctious son and another baby on the way. We had a beautiful, comfortable home we warmly shared with family and friends. My business was flourishing and all our demons of the past seemed to have been expelled. The thing about one's past, however, is that it doesn't always stay in the past. This is a lesson I would learn repeatedly over the next year of my life.

I was having a remarkable day. I had awoken with my morning wood in Emmy's beautiful mouth. While I was in the shower recovering from an incredible blowjob, my lovely bride-to-be made me a high energy breakfast with oatmeal, eggs, and fruit. My son was behaving, happy at the window watching the snow fall. Despite the weather, traffic wasn't too bad and I actually got to work early. I stopped in the new combination book and muffin shop next to the office and got two dozen muffins for the employees, and Iris, the shop's owner, had thrown in a few extra for free. By noon, I had a nice settlement offer on my desk for a case that was due in court the following week, and the business lunch I had went perfectly. I was ready to start singing Disney songs, because life was that great.

The phone in my office beeped from the front desk.

"Yes?" I said pleasantly to Kacey.

"Mr. Disgustingly Optimistic, you have a phone call on line two," she said dryly.

I didn't take offense. Kacey always spoke dryly, even when she was happy.

"Who is it?" There weren't too many people I avoided talking to, except maybe Vivian. But I only did that because it got her all rankled.

"Kyle Sterling."

There went my spectacular day. Just like that. Two damn words. One damn name. Gone was my high from my morning blow job, breakfast, well behaved kid, easy traffic, tasty muffins, generous settlement, and successful business meeting. I couldn't imagine why Kyle Sterling would be calling me. I hoped he was calling to tell me he was dying horrifically, but I knew there was no real chance in that.

"I'll take it," I said after a long hesitation.

"You don't sound too sure about that."

"I'm not," I admitted. "I'll take it anyway."

"Whatever."

Kacey disconnected and I sat there with the phone in my hand looking at the blinking light of line two, wondering what the hell Kyle wanted.

Shamefully, for a moment, I imagined he was calling to tell me he and Emmy reconnected and she was taking my son and going back to him. The thought only lasted a millisecond before I blasted it out of my head.

There was only one way to find out what the bastard wanted.

I pressed the button next to the blinking light.

"This is Luke."

****

The paperwork could've been done remotely. He knew that as well as I did, but he agreed to come to Chicago anyway. I was automatically suspicious about his easy willingness to come. I thought maybe there was an ulterior motive, like he'd try to see Emmy. I even had another moment of distrust for my fiancée, believing in the possibility she knew he was coming, and they had talked behind my back. But the moment passed, and I felt guilty for even considering it.

"Can I ask you for an enormous favor?" I asked Iris the day before the meeting.

I didn't know her well enough for her to do anything for me, but I felt it was worth a shot to ask. She was pleasant enough, but very straight forward. I wouldn't have to bullshit with her.

"An enormous favor?" she questioned with a raised eyebrow. "What kind of enormous favor can a muffin lady possibly do for an attorney?"

I laughed, despite the impending doom I felt. "You are much more than a muffin lady," I said.

She'd been wiping down the glass counter, but when I said that, she stopped, put a hand on her hip and said, "Oh, my. I have to hear this one."

"You are a generous muffin lady," I said, turning on my blue-eyed charm. "A pleasant muffin lady who is also a very accomplished pastry lady. Your buns make my toes curl." I leaned forward slightly. "They are the flakiest, tastiest, cinnamon buns in town."

She narrowed her eyes at me and just stood there for a moment before breaking out into a smile. "What do you want, Mr. Kessler?"

"I have a meeting with a client tomorrow morning," I spoke quietly. "I need a private place to meet him. I know the last tenant had a decent size office in the back. I was wondering if I could meet him here and use that space?"

"What's wrong with your office?" she didn't hesitate to ask.

I'd have to give her a little more information in order to convince her.

"Okay, listen," I said, sounding defeated. "This guy is very private. He's not comfortable meeting in my office, and he can't come after hours when everyone is gone because he has to fly back home immediately after our meeting. If you can't or don't want to do it, I understand, Iris. I can meet him somewhere else, but I thought this would be a good location."

She stared at me for a long moment. "You're not having some kind of homosexual affair are you?"

"Umm, no," I said, a little thrown by the question. "And if I were, I'd meet the man in question at a hotel, not in the back of a muffin book shop."

"You're not some underground drug lord, right? You don't want to use my muffin book shop to smuggle cocaine do you?"

"Do I look like a drug lord?"

"I don't know. Do you? I'm not sure what a drug lord looks like. Do they look like you?"

"I hope not. I promise, I'm not dealing drugs."

"You're not going to bully a juror back there, are you?"

Where the hell was she coming up with all of this stuff?

Amused, I shook my head. "I'm not bullying a juror."

"Will there be any illegal activity going on back there?"

I hesitated and then answered her honestly. "The man makes my blood boil. I can't promise I won't fuck him up while we're back there."

She gave a shrug. "Why didn't you just say so from the beginning? Yes, you can use the room. Just don't get blood on anything."

"You're my new best friend," I said with relief.

"I'm honored." She laughed. "Take your fiancée's muffin and get out of here."

Late the following morning, I walked into Iris's muffin book shop and found Kyle standing at the counter talking casually with her. When she saw me, she was suddenly interested in talking to one of the regulars on the other side of the room and left us standing at the counter. It took every bit of self-restraint I had to not slam his face into the glass display case. I hated this man more than I could've ever hated anything anywhere, ever.

"Follow me," I grunted to him and walked back to Iris's office.

I waited until I heard the door close behind us before I threw the envelope I was carrying onto Iris's desk. I turned around and surprised him with a right hook that sent him stumbling back several feet. He looked at me as he put a hand to his lip. His eyes flickered down to the blood on the back of his hand and the mother fucker snickered.

"Is that it?" he asked.

I punched him in the gut so hard he slammed against the door. I grabbed him by his coat, and slammed him into the wall hard enough to make his head roll back and hit it with a sickening thud.

"Fight back!" I yelled and swung him back against the door. "Fight back, you fucking piece of shit!" I slammed him up against the door again and again, but he didn't fight back. With a roar of anger, I lifted my fist, ready to knock him into the next decade, and he didn't even flinch.

"Don't pussy out now, Luke," Kyle growled out. "Hit me. What are you waiting for? An invitation? I invite you to hit me!"

"Fight back," I said again, breathless.

His next words should've signed his death warrant. He spoke slowly and clearly.

"She. Didn't. Fight. Back."

I roared again and threw him up against the wall once more. I wanted to beat the shit out of him, but unlike him, I refused to beat on someone who wouldn't retaliate. I refused to be like him. It didn't matter that Emmy had been a woman—a pregnant woman—and he was a man—the very man who'd beaten said pregnant woman. If Kyle had come here with the hopes I'd punish him for his fucked-up deeds, he'd be disappointed. If he believed getting the piss beaten out of him meant he'd somehow be redeemed, I wouldn't be the one to give him that atonement. Maybe he was fucking sorry, and maybe he wanted me to thrash him, but I was sure if guilt was eating him alive, it would do far more damage than anything I could dish out. I wanted him to live with that every second of his life and never feel like he had somehow made up for what he'd done to Emmy.

I dropped my hands and turned my back on him.

"Go ahead and fucking hit me!"

"Fuck you," I said over my shoulder as I picked up the envelope. I threw it to him. "You can fax it to my office when you're done."

He looked extremely disappointed, and then he just looked disgusted with me for not doing what he thought I should. I didn't give a shit.

I opened the door. "Get the fuck out of my city, and stay the hell away from my fiancée."

My words hit him just as hard as my fists, though the change in his expression and demeanor was small. His mouth opened slightly, his eyes widened only a fraction and he stood more stiffly. It quickly passed and he was back to wearing his self-righteous sneer.

As he passed by me out of the office, he muttered, "Fucking pussy."

I was tempted to punch him in the back of his head, but then I may not have stopped, and that's what he wanted. I wasn't going to give him what he wanted.

"Don't beat up your new girlfriend," I called after him.

He ignored me and kept walking right out of the shop. I hoped to god that would be the last time we ever had to deal with Kyle Sterling.

Chapter Twenty-Three

My beautiful bride was shining bright enough to light up the universe. I was damn near blinded by her perfection in her white wedding dress. Her dark hair was pulled up in an elegant style, leaving a few tendrils loose against her perfect skin. I had never seen her eyes shine so bright. I had never seen her smile look so…complete. As we danced to our wedding song, everyone else dissolved. Nothing else existed except her and me, and the sexy crooning of Babyface singing "Every Time I Close My Eyes." I sang along softly, never taking my attention off her teary eyes. I was lost in her and had no desire to find my way out. Ever.

It took years, broken hearts, and broken spirits before we could find our way to each other again. We traveled far and hard to reach our destination, but now that we were there, all the pain and doubts of the past suddenly seemed worth it. Life and its circumstances had helped us meld a bond that was unbreakable. We were invincible. There wasn't anything in the universe that could ever unbind us, and I'd die before I ever let that happen.

Every one of my heartbeats belonged to her.

Every breath was hers to take.

I was hers completely.

Chapter Twenty-Four

I grabbed Donya by the arm, pulling her away from my wife, and spun her onto the dance floor in one smooth move.

"Do you usually take women dancing against their will?" she asked, and then shrieked as I spun her around.

"Only the really pretty ones," I charmed, putting a hand on her waist.

She tried not to smile. "You're lucky you are kind of cute, Luke."

"Kind of?" I narrowed my eyes at her.

"Okay," she said in an exaggerated tone. "You're a sexy beast."

"That's better."

I dipped her low, making her laugh again. The song changed from "I Want You Back" by the Jackson 5 to "Dance With Me" by 112. Our playful dancing turned into a bit more of an adult affair. Donya got into the dance, not afraid to dance close to me with her best friend, my wife, only a few feet away watching on with amusement. She wrapped an arm around my neck and really got into it. I had a hand on her waist as I moved with her. I looked over at Emmy and wriggled my eyebrows. She shook her head, laughing.

When Marvin and Tammi started singing, I pulled Donya in for a semi-slow dance.

"You look really happy," she observed.

"I don't think it's possible to be any happier."

"Sweet." She nodded. "Cheesy and corny, but sweet. I've honestly never seen Em look so happy." She looked over at Emmy who was dancing with her dad.

"I really like you, Luke," Donya said, turning her attention back to me.

The song had changed again to "Try A Little Tenderness."

"In fact, I love you as much as a girl can love her best friend's husband without it being scandalous. But..."

"But?" I looked at her with both eyebrows raised.

"If you fuck this up beyond repair, I will kill you."

"I'd rather die than fuck this up beyond repair"

"We all say that," she said quietly. "We'd rather die than to hurt the ones we love, but we do. She did it to you. Hell, I've done it," she whispered the last sentence.

I frowned. I didn't want to know what she was talking about. I glanced at her husband, Jerry, standing in a circle of guys, probably talking about baseball since he's a professional player.

"It's my wedding day. I don't want to talk about that, Donya."

"I just want you to always be conscious of your actions, Luke," she said firmly and looked at me hard. "It's very easy to find yourself standing on the wrong side of the line without ever meaning to cross it."

We had stopped dancing and I hadn't even realized it until she kissed my cheek.

"Just remember what I said." She slipped out of my grasp and walked off the dance floor toward the exit. She threw a glance to her right, seemed to focus on something there for maybe two seconds before straightening her spine and continuing out of the banquet room.

Out of dumbstruck curiosity, I looked over to the right. I couldn't imagine who she was looking at, but when I saw an unexpected person look longingly at the exit, I blinked. By the time I opened my eyes again, it had passed.

I didn't want to know what the fuck that was about, and frankly, it wasn't any of my business.

I moved off the dance floor in search of Emmy and found her sitting at a table with her feet up on a chair and her hands on her round belly. I lifted her feet and sat down in the chair and then put her feet in my lap. As I rubbed her arch, she smiled contently at me and I smiled back. Lucas was at her side a moment later. I looked at the two and a half of them and felt so…grateful. There was no way in hell I'd ever find myself on the other side of that line Donya spoke about. No way in hell.

****

I kissed her ankle as I rolled her stocking off her foot. She was lying back on the massive bed in our honeymoon suite, caressing her belly and staring dreamily up at the ceiling.

"Was your wedding everything you hoped for?" I murmured as I stroked the bare skin of her leg.

She beamed and sighed happily. "It was perfect."

I reached under her wedding dress and started to slowly roll down her other stocking. She suddenly pushed up on her elbows and looked down at me kneeled between her legs.

"I've never seen you so energetic." She grinned. "I feel bad I couldn't dance with you that much. Stupid swollen feet."

"Marrying you was enough to power me up for a lifetime, baby," I planted a gentle kiss on her knee. "And we'll have a lifetime to dance together."

"I loved seeing my husband dirty dancing with my best friend," she said, trying to hide her amusement. "And my cousins. And my great aunt Edith."

"Hey, in my defense, it isn't very often a simple guy like me gets to dance with a super model."

"Retired super model," Emmy reminded me. "And you're anything but simple."

"Whatever." I shrugged. "I did stop Mayson from twerkin'." Just barely. "But my favorite was Edith. I had no idea that an eighty-three-year-old woman could drop it like that."

Emmy burst into laughter and fell back on the bed. I chuckled with her as I gently massaged her swollen feet.

"Come up here and kiss your wife," she commanded after her laughter had died down.

"Yes, ma'am." I climbed up on the bed beside her.

I rested one hand on her belly and used my other arm to balance myself over her. She dragged her fingers through my hair as she gazed up at me. I lowered my head until our lips were only just touching.

"I love you, Luke Kessler," she whispered against my lips.

"I love you, Emmy Kessler."

Her lips parted slightly, inviting me in. I took a moment to just breathe her in, to feel her hot breath across my lips. My tongue slowly swept across her bottom lip, tasting her.

"I love tasting your lips," I murmured before gently sucking her top lip into my mouth. Emmy moaned softly when I swept my tongue between her lips. Her tongue darted out of her mouth to meet mine, but I teased her and pulled back slightly. When she let out a frustrated groan, I chuckled against her lips and teased her again.

"Kiss me," she demanded, trying to pull my head closer.

"I *am* kissing you," I said, and pressed my lips quickly to hers.

She growled with frustration as she tried to follow my lips, but I continued to pull back until her head fell back to the bed. Now she was pouting, her bottom lip sticking out, showing her adorable frustration with me. I kissed her bottom lip and then the little indentation under her lip. I nibbled along her jawline and up to her ear. I gently bit her earlobe, making her release another soft moan. I found that sensitive place just below her ear on her neck and swirled my tongue on her skin. Emmy gasped as her fingers tightened in my hair.

I started to gently suck on her neck. Em began to breathe heavily and little breathy moans escaped her parted lips. I kissed my way back along her jawline until I found her mouth again. I crashed mine against hers with all the gentleness and teasing gone. My tongue battled with hers in an erotic challenge, but I kissed her more savagely, growling as I nipped and sucked at her tongue until she submitted. I took my hand off her belly and held her face as I took her mouth possessively, because she was my possession. Officially and forever.

I sat up, leaving Emmy gasping for air. I had to get her out of that dress. I helped her sit up and then get to her feet. I moved behind her and stared at the pearl buttons that trailed down her back.

"Are you fucking kidding me?" I growled in frustration as I started to release the buttons.

Emmy giggled. "Donya thought you should work for it."

"Donya's on my shit list," I muttered. "And I'm never dirty dancing with her again."

She giggled again and then said, "Hurry up."

"Don't make me tear this off you," I warned. I wasn't even half finished yet.

"Tear it," she said, trying to peer at me over her shoulder.

I looked up at her, unsure. "This is your wedding dress," I reminded her. "And I'm sure it cost more than I'd like to know."

"It did cost more than you'd like to know," she agreed and fortunately wasn't forthcoming with the amount. "But it's my wedding dress. I'm married now. It served its purpose. Now tear it off me."

Holy shit. My little sex goddess had been back for a long while, but she was definitely back with a vengeance.

I seized fabric in each hand and without second guessing her, I yanked it apart, hard. Pearly white buttons bounced onto the floor. Satin and lace split, the ripping noise oddly satisfying. I pulled the dress slowly down her legs. With my hands on her shapely hips, she put her hands on mine and stepped out of the remnants of the dress. I dropped my hands to her round, lace covered ass and squeezed. Emmy moaned and then let out a small yelp when I tore away the panties, too.

As I kicked the dress aside, Emmy's eyebrows rose.

"I said you could tear it off me, not kick it around."

"Quiet, you."

I hurried out of my own shirt as I gazed at her bare breasts, rounded belly, and the triangle of sparse hair between her legs. My wife was the most beautiful woman in the entire universe.

Struggling out of my pants, I kissed her supple mouth. Her hand slipped into my boxers and stroked my growing erection. I couldn't hold back the moan that was caught between her lips after leaving my mouth. When I finally got my pants and boxers off, I held on to the back of Emmy's head and deepened the kiss. After I found the will to release her lips, I gently pushed her down onto the mattress and made her lie back with her legs hanging off the high bed. I slipped my arms under her knees, positioned my cock at her entrance, but hesitated before pressing into her. It was our wedding night, and maybe I should've given her more before sliding into her.

"What's wrong?" she asked, looking up at me with concern.

"I should slow down," I said, trying hard not to surge forward.

"Baby, we'll have the rest of our lives to slow it down," she said gently. She locked her ankles around my back, but still I resisted.

"You deserve more," I said and started to back away.

"And you will give me more later," she said, wriggling her ass. "I want you just like this. Right now."

When I still hesitated, Emmy looked up at me and said in the most erotic tone I could have ever imagined "Fuck me, Luke. Fuck your wife."

I couldn't argue with my wife.

I plunged into her, fast and hard, until my balls were pressed against her luscious ass. Emmy cried out at the sudden invasion and clawed at the bedspread under her. It had been over a month since we decided not to have sex until our wedding night. Her walls were tight around my cock and I could feel her trying to relax to accommodate my size.

I pulled out slowly until I was almost completely withdrawn and then slid slowly back inside with a loud, guttural groan.

"Tell me how I feel inside you." I slowly eased in and out of her core.

"Enormous," she said and tried to snicker, but I slammed into her hard, and her little snicker turned into a cursed shout. "Shit!"

"Talk to me, baby." I groaned.

"I love your cock inside me. It feels so fucking good. Especially when you're...uhhh...deep, really deep. Go deeper, Luke," she commanded and then threw her head back with a moan when I did. She wiggled her hips toward me as if trying to feel me even deeper.

"Deeper?" I asked, even though I could feel the opening to her womb at the tip of my cock.

She nodded frantically. I tapped her leg twice to make her unlock her ankles from behind me. I pushed her legs back as far as I thought would be comfortable with her pregnant belly in the way, and pushed into her a little deeper. I looked down and watched my cock disappear into her hot core over and over again.

"Harder," Emmy pleaded.

I slammed into her hard, but not at my hardest. I was always concerned about hurting the baby, but Emmy looked up at me and bit her bottom lip.

"I said harder!"

"Em, I—"

"Harder dammit!" she shouted. "Use that big cock and fuck me harder!"

I was amused by her command, and extremely turned on. I wanted nothing more than to pound into her with all my might, making her take my cock all the way and watching her face as it stretched and battered her pussy.

"I don't want to hurt you or the baby."

"You're not going to hurt the baby. It's impossible for you to hurt her."

"What about you?" I knew her genitals were extra sensitive at this point in her pregnancy. It would be easy to hurt her instead of pleasuring her.

"I like when you hurt me with your monstrous cock." She growled and pushed her hips up to meet my shallow thrusts.

I stared at her blankly.

"Hurt me!" She roughly squeezed her own nipples between her fingers.

I was unable to deny either of us anymore. I yanked her ass to the very edge of the bed and slammed into her with all the force I could muster. I yelled out expletives as Emmy screamed. I hesitated for a moment to be sure it's what she really wanted.

"Do it," she gritted out through clenched teeth.

I began hammering her so hard it hurt my balls to smash up against her ass. I held her tightly to keep her from sliding back on the bed with each thrust. Emmy screamed incoherently and clawed at my arms as I fucked her fast and hard. I felt her pussy squeezing my cock as she came, but I didn't slow down to accommodate her orgasm. I kept going until I saw tears in her eyes.

"Don't stop!" she sobbed. "Don't stop!"

My orgasm hit me suddenly, without mercy. I shouted and growled as I began to come violently. Emmy convulsed and thrashed on the bed as her orgasm swam through her body.

My movements slowed and grew more gentle as I moved with my erection softening. I was overly sensitized, but I loved feeling her aftershocks. When I finally pulled out, Emmy shuddered and her legs closed on their own accord. I gave her a moment to recover before helping her get properly into the bed, under the blankets. I lay down beside her and kissed her gently.

"I love you," she murmured a little while later as she began to drift off to sleep in my arms.

"I love you, too, Emmy," I said and kissed the top of her head. "Always."

Chapter Twenty-Five

"I'm getting so fat," Emmy said, frowning down at her belly.

I rubbed her protruding belly affectionately. "Stop calling my daughter fat.

"I didn't call your daughter fat. I said *I'm* fat."

"You're not fat. You're pregnant and beautiful."

"I'm pregnant, beautiful, and fat," she said flatly. "And here I am in a muffin shop of all places, to feed my face."

"I think you're gorgeous," Iris said, passing a small box across the counter.

"That's something attractive people tell unattractive people to make them feel better about themselves." Emmy pouted, picking up the box.

Iris laughed but then narrowed her eyes on me like I did something wrong.

"What?" I asked, on the offensive.

"Take your wife home and make her feel like the beautiful woman she is."

"I did that already this morning—twice." I winked at them.

Both women rolled their eyes at me. I chuckled and dropped down to kiss Emmy's belly.

"See you later, baby girl," I said to my unborn daughter. I stood up and kissed Emmy in a completely public display of indecency. When I released her, she was breathless, but smiling. She glanced over at Iris and gave her an apologetic look, but Iris grinned at her and gave her a wink before turning away to handle some other business.

I put my hand on the back of Emmy's neck and planted a lingering kiss on her lips. "I'll see you tonight, baby. Be careful going home." I walked backward toward the door.

"Get out of here. You're going to be late to court."

"Why don't you sit down and I'll get you a cup of tea?" Iris said to Emmy as I walked out.

I threw one last glance back at my wife and Iris before rushing back to the office.

Emmy was seven months pregnant and we'd been married for a mere two months. We hadn't planned a honeymoon yet because of the pregnancy, but Em didn't seem to be in a hurry to take one. She never even mentioned where she'd like to go if she could. She'd been to so many places in the world, I had no idea where I could take her that would be different from the trips she's already taken, but one day, when our baby girl was old enough to leave behind, I'd take my wife on a real honeymoon.

"Fiji?" Iris had suggested one morning over a cup of coffee in her shop.

"She's been there already."

"Bora Bora?"

"Been there, been there."

"Cabo?"

"Three times."

"Australia? Africa? Virgin Islands? Japan?" Iris asked, her eyes widening with each shake of my head. "She's been to all those places?"

"And a few more." I'd sighed. "Her best friend used to travel a lot for work. Emmy often accompanied her, and some of the other places she'd gone to with her family or boyfriends."

"That's amazing," Iris had said, seemingly impressed. "But she hasn't been everywhere, and it's not really about where you take her, Luke. It's really about the time you get to spend with her there. I'm sure if you took her to any one of those places again, she would be delighted just to be there with you."

That made me feel better about the situation, though I still didn't have a clue as to where we'd go.

A month after we said our I Dos, Emmy's father, Fredrick, had a mild heart attack. Emmy had snapped at me after I delivered the news to her and tried to calm and reassure her with the words, "It was only a mild heart attack."

"A heart attack is a heart attack!" she had yelled. "That's like saying Lena only had a mild case of breast cancer!"

Point taken.

We flew down to Louisiana as a family. Emmy insisted she and Lucas would be okay going with Emmet and Casey, but I wasn't having any of that. They weren't traveling any further than the surrounding Chicago suburbs without me again, especially since she was very pregnant.

Em was laden with guilt for not spending enough time with her dad over the years. She'd worked so hard to avoid her mother, she had inadvertently avoided him as well. I understood how she felt. I had moved away from my family and rarely visited for many years. When my dad died, I was grief stricken and completely mulled over with guilt for not giving us the opportunity to have an adult father and son relationship. At least Em had an opportunity to make up that missing time with her dad. We stayed down south for a week and a half before I had to get back to work.

I couldn't be happier with my life. I didn't think we were untouchable, but after all the bullshit we'd gone through over the years—together and alone—I felt as if we could overcome anything. There wasn't anything in the world that could come between us. We were like the song said, solid as a rock.

****

Emmy stopped feeding me breakfast.

"I'm a gazillion months pregnant!" she had screamed at me one morning when I asked her what was for breakfast. "I don't want to get out of bed to make you breakfast—why don't you make me breakfast?"

She was trying to be crabby, but she hadn't expected me to actually go into the kitchen and make her eggs and toast and bring it to her in bed. She burst into tears. After I reassured her I wasn't angry and I didn't need her to make me breakfast, she finally looked at the tray of food and smiled through her tears.

"You're the best husband ever," she said and kissed me.

"I know," I agreed and kissed her back. "I have to go."

Lucas shuffled into the room, holding his stuffed whale, rubbing his sleepy eyes. He held up his arms and I obliged. I ruffled his hair and asked him if he slept well. He yawned in my face and nodded. I chuckled and kissed his head before putting him in bed with his mom.

"What are you going to eat?" Emmy asked, looking guilty.

"I'll get a cinnamon bun and some coffee at Iris's."

"Tell her I said hello, and thank her for the cookies she sent with you yesterday. Lucas loved them. Maybe we'll stop in later today."

"I will." I kissed her one final time, kissed her belly, and then kissed Lucas. "Have a good day, guys."

"Good day, Daddy," Lucas called after me, making me grin.

"Want to share some breakfast, Lucas?" I heard Emmy ask him before I headed downstairs.

When I walked into Iris's shop a little while later, I nodded at a couple of the regulars and made my way to the counter. I didn't see Iris around, but I figured she'd be out shortly. She rarely left the front unattended. She didn't have any kind of bells or anything on the door to let her know when someone entered. I had warned her that wasn't exactly safe, especially since she worked alone, but she seemed unconcerned.

I checked my watch. I had been standing there a good two minutes. I had a busy schedule ahead.

"Iris?" I called in the direction of the little hallway that led to her office, kitchen, and storage room.

"I'll be there in a second," she called back, and then I heard a distinctive grunt.

"You okay back there?" I asked, moving around the counter. I hesitated before going to the back. What if she was back there with a guy and that's what the grunt was? I definitely didn't want to walk in on that.

"Yeah," she called from one of the rooms. "I'm just trying to…gah! Trying to move something."

I walked back and checked first the kitchen area, but that was empty. I found her in the small storage room, on her knees trying to push an enormous box across the floor. I stood there for a moment, shaking my head.

"This is amusing," I said, leaning in the doorway and crossing my arms.

She threw me a murderous glance. "The damn dolly tipped and now I can't move these damn books."

I shook my head and stepped into the room. I offered her my hand. She looked at it.

"I promise you my hand is clean. Mostly." I waved it, indicating for her to take it.

Finally, she took my hand and stood up in her ridiculously tall shoes.

"Where do you want the box?" I asked her and effortlessly lifted it.

"What are you?" she asked, looking at me in awe. "A demigod? Kin to Hercules?"

I flexed a bicep. I couldn't resist. "Where do you want the box, woman? I need my cinnamon bun so I can get to work."

She pointed to a corner. "Over there, please, Hercules."

I put the box where she requested.

"Thank you, kind sir." She smiled and did a small curtsy. "Your cinnamon bun is on the house today."

"I'll take that as payment." I shrugged and followed her back out into the shop. There were more customers waiting, but she took me first. As she got my cinnamon bun and coffee, I told her what Emmy told me to tell her.

"I hope they come by." She smiled warmly. "But she needs to stay off her feet. Maybe I'll send some muffins home with you tonight. She loves the cranberry."

"I have to be in court this afternoon," I said. "Out of the city. I won't be back this way until you're closed."

"I'll be here late tonight prepping for the morning," she said, handing a regular their order. "I'll wait for you."

"Don't wait," I said, backing toward the door. "If you're not here, it's fine. I'll take her some tomorrow."

She nodded that she had heard me and focused on her customer. I walked out of the shop with my nose in my paper bag.

By the time I made it back to the office after court and wrapped up what I needed to do there, it was late. I usually didn't work after hours anymore if it could be helped, but sometimes it was necessary. I made sure Emmy was okay with frequent phone calls and often sent Lorraine's oldest daughter, Haley, over to check on her after school and help her out. Lorraine insisted I not pay my sixteen-year-old niece, but I always ignored this and paid her on the sly.

Iris's shop was closed as I'd expected. Most of the lights were off and the sign was flipped to closed. Subtle movement inside drew my attention. I moved a little closer to the window. In a dark corner, with her back to me, Iris was seated at a table. It was pretty dark inside, but there were some lights from the back rooms casting soft lighting into the main café area.

I was ready to walk away. She looked like she was just having a quiet moment at the end of a busy day. I wouldn't want anyone bothering me, but as I started to move away, I saw that she had bottle of alcohol at the table with her. Still, it wasn't my place or my business and I wanted to get home to my wife and son. Suddenly, she pushed herself up from the table and stumbled in those damn high heels. She caught herself, and held onto the table until she was able to balance herself. Then she grabbed the bottle and a coffee mug and slowly turned around to walk away from the table.

Again, I should have left, but honestly, I wanted to make sure she wasn't going to fall on her face and bleed out all over the floor. She took a few steps before she noticed me in the window. She smiled and said something I obviously couldn't hear because I was on the other side of the glass. I held up my hands, indicating I had no idea what the hell she just said. She rolled her eyes and walked unsteadily to the door. She set the bottle down on the counter behind her and unlocked the door, waving me inside.

I hesitated before crossing the threshold, but when she turned around to walk deeper into the shop, she stumbled again and started to fall. The coffee mug crashed to the floor, but I caught her around the waist before she could, too.

"Holy shit, Iris," I growled out and steered her to a chair. "Sit the hell down."

"I have to clean up," she mumbled and started to stand up, but I roughly pushed her back down.

"I'll get it. Where can I find a broom?"

She told me where to find it and I went to get it. I turned the lights on overhead and started sweeping up the mess.

"What are you doing drinking in here in the dark?"

"Should I drink in here in the light?" she asked dryly.

I glanced over at her, but didn't respond. I wanted her to answer my question. She could've seriously injured herself.

"Thanks for cleaning that up," dodging my question. "I appreciate it. I still have those muffins for Emmy if you want them." Carefully, she got to her feet again. She tried to stand still, but it was obvious she was pretty drunk.

"Do you need me to help you home?" I asked, though I really didn't want to. I really wanted to get my own ass home.

"I'll take a cab." She straightened her back. "I'll be fine. Thank you."

"Okay," I said slowly. After a moment, I returned the broom and dustpan to the closet I found them in. Iris had made her way behind the counter. She produced a box and pushed it toward me. I murmured thanks and picked it up.

"You go on home. I'll see you tomorrow, no doubt."

I looked her over. Something was off in her eyes. "Are you okay, Iris?"

She looked down at the floor. "I'll be good by morning."

I looked at my watch and sighed. "I'll make sure you get home okay."

She argued, but I had already grabbed her jacket, purse, and keys. I ushered her outside against her objections and locked the door. After dropping her keys in her purse and handing it to her, I walked her around the corner with my hand at her elbow to steady her and to catch her the few times she stumbled. I called Emmy soon after we got on the road.

"Hey," she said tiredly.

"Hey, babe. I'm driving Iris home and then I'll be on my way."

"Something happen to her car?"

"No. I'll explain when I see you. I just want to make sure she gets home safely."

"Okay, no problem. I'll wait up for you even though your son ran me into the ground today. I swear I'm going to tie him up one day."

"It's my duty to inform you I'd have to turn you in for that."

"Yeah, go for it," she said. "See you in a bit."

"I love you."

"Love you, too."

I ended the call and slipped the phone into my pocket.

"You're not going to really tell her, are you?" Iris asked.

I glanced over at her apprehensive expression. "Of course I'm going to tell her. Trust me. Emmy of all people will understand. That girl used to outdrink everyone."

"I'm already humiliated." She rested her forehead in her hand. "God. What will she think of me?"

I snorted. "Knowing my wife, she'll be jealous she didn't get to share a drink with you."

She sighed loudly, but no longer objected to me telling Emmy.

"Sorry I kept asking you questions. Your personal life isn't any of my business."

She didn't say anything for several minutes. I was content to let the silence sit between us.

"Sometimes, even when things are really good, darkness finds a way to sneak up on you," she finally said as she stared out the window.

"That can happen to any of us." It had happened to Emmy, and in a way, it had happened to me, too.

Iris laughed cynically, but said nothing. We were almost to her apartment, so I didn't feel the need to fill the silence with encouraging words. I really didn't know what to say anyway. I didn't know what her deal was, and not that I'm a heartless bastard, but Iris wasn't my problem.

I helped her out of the car and walked her to her door. I waited for her to unlock it and open it, and then backed away.

"Take those damn shoes off. See you tomorrow."

"Thank you, Luke," she said to my back.

"No problem," I called over my shoulder.

When I got home, I found Emmy in the kitchen reheating my dinner. I embraced her from behind and kissed her neck.

"You didn't have to do this," I said, taking the plate from her. "I could've reheated my own dinner."

"You had a long day, too." We sat down and I pulled her swollen feet into my lap before I began to eat.

"So, tell me about Iris," she said around a yawn.

I told her everything that had happened, starting with her telling me to drop by for muffins for Emmy. I didn't leave out any details, including my thoughts about how Iris wasn't my problem and I just wanted to get home to my own family.

Em frowned. "Poor Iris. Maybe she's just depressed? I mean as far as I know, she doesn't have anyone…not really. She has siblings and parents and all that, but she doesn't have any kids or boyfriends or a husband or anything."

"You know far more than I do. None of that ever comes up when I'm talking to her."

"After I give birth to your second spawn," she said, rubbing her belly, "maybe I'll offer to take her out for a night out on the town. We can get drunk and giggle about cute guys."

I raised my eyebrows at her.

"Okay, okay," she relented. "We won't get drunk."

"But you'll still giggle about cute guys?"

"Psh. Yeah."

"I'm going to knock that idea right out of your head as soon as I'm done eating my dinner," I promised.

She gave me a wicked grin. "I hope so, Mr. Kessler. I hope so."

"Oh, fuck it," I said pushing my plate away. I gently nudged her feet out of my lap and stood up. Emmy shrieked when I swept her into my arms and started for the stairs.

Chapter Twenty-Six

I cannot begin to describe the exhilaration I felt watching my daughter's birth. The love I felt for my wife expanded so vastly inside of me, I thought I'd combust into millions of pieces of heart-shaped confetti.

"I'm so glad you were here," Emmy sobbed as the doctors and nurses checked Kaitlyn's vitals and measurements moments after she was born. Emmy gripped my shirt fiercely. "I'm so sorry you missed this before."

"Hey, we're not going to talk about that," I said, pressing my forehead against hers. "You were amazing today. I'm so proud of you, and I'm so grateful for what you just did for us."

I wiped away her tears and kissed her gently on the lips. "I love you."

Emmy only cried harder when they put our daughter in her arms. "She's beautiful," she said through her tears.

"So are you," I said adoringly and pushed her hair out of her face before turning my gaze to my precious daughter.

"I'm never, ever, ever doing this," Mayson said from the corner she had squeezed herself into when Emmy started pushing.

I had managed to convince her to come out of the corner to meet Kaitlyn, but the moment the nurses tried to get the baby to latch on to Emmy's breast, Mayson was disgusted again.

"I'm never giving birth," she snarled to us as she hurried across the room to the door. "And the only lips that are touching my tits are a man's!" She stormed out of the room in a huff.

Later that night while Emmy slept, exhausted from twenty-two hours of labor, I held Kaitlyn in my arms and danced gently around the room, singing "Isn't She Lovely" by Stevie Wonder. I was so damn happy. It wasn't possible to be so happy, but I was. In a day or so, Emmy and I would be taking Kaitlyn home to Lucas, and our family would be complete.

I felt as if all my dreams had come true. I had the woman I always wanted, with beautiful children and a strong and supportive family. We had a nice home in a family friendly neighborhood and good friends. My career was higher than any of my expectations and continuously climbing. My sister was healthy and my mom seemed to have a bunch of years left in her. I couldn't have asked for anything more.

There was nothing more to be had.

Chapter Twenty-Seven

Iris and I never spoke about her drunken night at the shop again. Apparently, she and Emmy discussed it, but I didn't ask. I didn't even acknowledge the later times I saw her drinking. On the surface, things went back to normal as far as she was concerned.

When Kay Kay was a month old, Emmy brought her and Lucas to the firm to meet everyone. Even Kacey's dry ass had a smile for the beautiful baby, but when I caught her smiling, she scowled and looked away.

Emmy started meeting me once or twice a week at Iris's. She tried to get out without the kids for a little while, but sometimes they came with her. I was always glad to see my children, but when she came alone, her hands were free to hold on to me while I kissed her senseless. When the doctor cleared her six weeks after Kay Kay was born, she came directly to my office…and in my office…and on my desk…and in my chair…

Everything was perfect.

And just like that, everything fucking shattered…

That morning, I made love to my wife before leaving for work. I almost didn't go into work. I wanted to stay in bed with her all day, but she reminded me we had two small children who would interrupt our day of doing nasty things under the covers.

Before leaving, I ate breakfast with Lucas and read him a Dr. Seuss book. I fed Kaitlyn a bottle of breast milk and changed her diaper. After kissing Emmy and the kids goodbye, I told her I'd see her later in the evening and to be careful going to and from the doctor's office, because the weather was supposed to get bad. I suggested she ask Diana to come help her out and then I left. I called my mom using the Bluetooth in my car to see how she was doing, and hung up satisfied she was well.

In the office, everything was going so smoothly I felt I could sneak out for a little while and grab a cinnamon bun and a cup of coffee. I was a ball of energy when I walked into the shop and waved at the regulars. Iris and I exchanged our usual pleasantries as she bagged my cinnamon bun and poured my coffee.

"Do you have a minute?" she asked.

"Sure." I put my nose inside the bag. I loved the smell of a fresh baked cinnamon bun. "What's up?"

"I need help moving something in the back." She nodded toward the hallway.

"You really need to hire some hot young college guy to move stuff for you," I teased as I followed her to the back.

"Why do that when I can have a hot lawyer move things for me instead?"

"I don't look at Steve like that, but if you think he's hot, well, okay then."

She led me to her office and not the supply room, but I didn't think anything of it. I raised an eyebrow when she closed the door until it was only open a little bit.

"Actually," she said, rubbing her hands together and looking nervous. "I wanted to talk to you about something. I didn't want anyone else to overhear."

"Okay." I guessed she had a legal question. She probably had something going on, and I didn't blame her for not wanting her customers to overhear her problems.

"Okay," she breathed out before looking up at me. She took a step closer. I automatically retreated a step. I don't know why. I usually don't back down from anyone. Vivian intimidates people all the time by getting into their personal space and making them stumble until they're up against a wall, but it never worked on me. In my lifetime, a few guys have come at me, ready for a fight. Even if they were bigger than me, I always stood my ground.

But when Iris moved toward me, the hairs on my neck stood up. If I were a cat, my back would've been arched and I would've been hissing.

"I think there's something happening between us," she said, licking her lips nervously. "I think there is at least potential for something to happen between us, and to tell you the truth, I'm getting impatient. I'm ready to push it to the next level."

Say what?

My head fell to one side, tilting like a confused dog as I studied her.

"Wait. What?"

"I'm attracted to you, Luke, and I think you're attracted to me. I'm ready to move forward."

Did I fucking miss something? What. The. Hell.

"Iris," I said, shaking myself from a brief stunned silence. "You're friends with my wife. Emmy adores you. Have you been drinking this morning?"

That had to be the only explanation for the words falling out of her mouth.

"No, I haven't been drinking! I mean every word I just said. And I love Emmy. She's great, but that doesn't mean there isn't anything between us."

"Are you hearing what you're saying? You just told me my wife is great and then suggested there's something between us. My wife is more than great, Iris. My wife is fucking fantastic and there's nothing between you and me."

"Give me an opportunity here," she said, almost pleading. "I know you have to feel something, too. You're in here every day, we talk, we flirt, and you seem to really care about me."

I put my hands on my hips and looked up at the ceiling. She *was* fucking serious.

"Iris, I treat you like I treat every other woman who isn't my wife. You're blowing everything out of proportion."

She shook her head. "I don't think I am." She took another step toward me and I took another back.

"I can't." I looked at her more carefully and I swear her eyes were a little scary. I almost felt like she was about to pull a big ass knife out of her apron and go all Glenn Close on me. I chose my words delicately. "You're...you're a great woman, beautiful and intelligent, and sexy, but, I have my wife and two kids."

She inched forward and I inched back.

"I know. I love Emmy and the kids but I can't...I can't help the way I feel about you. I'm not asking you to leave them—just give me one night. One night, Luke. Or one day. I'll even close the shop for a day and we can go somewhere and just be together for one day."

I was beginning to feel sick to my stomach. I'd been going to her shop for months and just being a nice guy and had no idea she was building this crazy idea of us together in her wacked out mind. I just wanted to get the fuck out of there and go hold my wife.

"One day will turn into one more day, and one more day will turn into another day after that until it is out of control, Iris," I told her, and realized my choice of words could've done nothing but give her hope. I wasn't trying to give her any hope. "And this...this is madness. I would never do that to Emmy."

"I know you feel something for me, Luke. Don't you think about what we could be like together?"

"No, Iris, I don't think about it," I said, thoroughly disgusted. I never once considered any kind of relationship with her besides the one I thought we already had. I was perfectly happy with being friendly to the woman who made my favorite pastry and treated my wife and kids well.

"The fact you're still standing here, having this conversation, tells me you aren't as satisfied with your life at home as you pretend to be."

Okay, she was definitely delusional. I had no idea how I always ended up with delusional women. Even Emmy was delusional at one point, but Emmy is a fucking goddess and Emmy fixed her shit.

"I love my wife," I said simply. There was nothing else to say.

"I don't doubt you do, but if life with Emmy is so perfect, you wouldn't still be standing here considering this."

"I'm not..." I said, confused as to how my rejection had translated into consideration.

She stepped forward and I stepped back until I hit her desk. She put her hands on my arms. I should've moved away. I should've pushed her away. I wanted to, but she was obviously unstable. Though we never discussed that night I took her home, I had spotted her on a few other occasions drinking in the shop, both during and after hours. I didn't want to get involved again, and she was a grown ass woman. It wasn't my place or business, though I wondered if she wasn't having some issues. Sometimes she seemed like she was struggling to get through a day, but again, I didn't ask. It's not that I was heartless, but it just wasn't my place. If she wanted to discuss it with Emmy, then that would've been fine.

Now, with her standing there with her hands on me, I had the urge to slap some sense into her, but I don't hit women. Ever. I stood there, glaring at her.

"But you are," she said softly. "I have my hands on you and you're not pushing me away. I made a proposal and you didn't scurry away back to your wife. You're still here. We've been flirting with this for months, Luke. I'm tired of flirting. I'm forty-three years old and I'm over the flirting game. I know what I want, and I don't want to play games to get it. I don't know…maybe one day will lead to another day and another day after that, but if you think that will happen, then it means something. It means that maybe…maybe there's a chance for us. Don't you want to find out? Do you really want to be left wondering 'what if' when we can know for sure?"

Exasperated, I grimaced and pushed her hands off me. I opened my mouth to speak, and with animal reflexes, she was on me. She wrapped her arms around my neck and planted her lips on mine. I stood there for maybe one stunned second before peeling her off me and pushing her away. It felt like an eternity that her hands were on me, and my lips burned with shame for not blocking her before she could get that far, and for not reacting in a fraction of a second instead of the second it took. I was disgusted with her and even more so with myself for not walking the fuck out of the room the moment she opened her damn mouth.

I couldn't breathe. The ramifications of my lack of reaction ran through my head and knocked the breath out of me.

"No. I can't do this with you," I said, pushing her further away from me. "Oh my god." I was in a full blown panic now, bent over, ready to heave. My life was fucking perfect. I wasn't about to let Iris or anyone else ruin my family. "I can't. I won't," I said aloud to myself.

"Luke…" Iris put her hands together in a plea.

"No, Iris!" I roared. "Fuck." I put my hands in my hair, pulling hard in frustration and fear. I started pacing back and forth across the room. I couldn't believe I let this happen. I couldn't believe I just stood there, possibly fucking up everything. "Fuck fuck fuck. I can't believe I just did that. I can't believe I just did that."

"I know you're torn but—"

I said I never hit a woman, but Iris was pushing my limits. I got in her face so suddenly, she shrunk back as if I would hit her. "I'm not fucking torn. I'm a fucking idiot. I'm not coming back here—don't come to my office again, don't call me, and stay away from my family. If Emmy comes in here, you give her a fucking muffin or whatever it is she wants and stay away from her. I had to fight so hard to get her; I'm not going to throw my life with her away for you or anyone else."

A bell sounded from the front. It was the first time I realized she'd finally gotten one, but I didn't care about that damn bell.

"You stay the fuck away from me," I said with a brutal quietness that scared even me.

"I'm sorry," she murmured and began wiping away tears.

She turned away from me and opened the door, but she stopped at the threshold, staring at something I couldn't see. For a moment, I thought this was the part where she turned around and stabbed me with something. I stepped up behind her, hell bent on shoving her out of my way so I could get the hell away from her. I had told her to continue giving Emmy whatever she asked for, but I needed to tell Emmy what happened. If this had happened to Emmy with another guy, I would want to know. If she found out on her own, she may assume the worst on my part, and she may never forgive me.

I looked up, ready to push Iris out of my way and locked eyes with Emmy.

Chapter Twenty-Eight

Emmy ran away from me before I could even speak her name. I did shove Iris out of my way as I took off after my wife. I ran out onto the sidewalk, shouting for her as she ran down the street.

It started to rain hard. Before stepping into Iris's shop, I had been in such a euphoric mood, I hadn't even noticed the pregnant rain clouds.

"Emmy!" I screamed after her.

I felt like my whole damn life was running away. I had to catch up to her and explain. I was almost to her. Almost there, but she suddenly sprinted into the street. I watched in horror as she just narrowly missed getting hit by a car. I screamed her name again and again, and suddenly, she was being hit by someone's front fender. My heart lurched in my chest. Horror could not adequately describe what I felt as I watched her stumble from the impact. That car hit her pretty hard, but she didn't fall. She was so anxious to get away from me, she kept right on running. I also started darting around moving cars, playing a terrible game of Frogger, trying to reach her as I frantically called out her name. I had to make sure she was okay.

I ignored the horns honking and the people who dared to put their windows down in the rain to yell at me. When Emmy scrambled into the back of a cab, I chased after it and just landed my hands on the back of it before the light ahead changed and the car took off.

I ran back across the street and went right to my car, feeling lucky I had my keys in my pocket. My guess was she had parked and took the L. I decided to just meet her at home instead of trying to catch her at the station. Once I was inside the car, I started calling her repeatedly, getting her voicemail each time.

"Fuck!" I yelled, slamming my hands on the steering wheel.

I felt like my whole world was washing away with the rain. Emmy had run from me instead of punching Iris in the face and kicking me in the balls. I would've preferred that over her running away. I would've preferred for her to yell and scream and beat me than to run away. Running away signified defeat. Running away meant she had already given up on me before I even saw her there in that hallway. I had no idea how long she had been there, but even if she had been there from the very beginning, it was the end that would have done her in. The end where I didn't act fast enough to shove Iris off me before her lips could even touch mine.

My driving wasn't safe by any standards. I crept through red lights and stop signs, missing some altogether. I drove too fast for the weather and narrowly missed running off the road several times. When I sped into the driveway, I felt very little relief. I didn't see her car. It was possible she already parked in the garage and was waiting for me inside with a baseball bat, but what greeted me when I got inside was so much worse.

It was silence. And an obvious hasty retreat.

****

I held my tie in my hands as I called Donya again.

"No, I still haven't heard from her," she said when she answered. "Are you going to tell me what's wrong?"

"No," I said and hung up on her.

I stared down at the tie as I tried not to cry. I would rather hang myself with that fucking tie than to face a lifetime without Emmy.

It had been hours. Fucking hours. She wasn't answering my calls or text messages. She took the kids and left in a hurry, probably only moments before I got home. I called Sam and asked if she'd spoken to her but gave her no details. I didn't have time to give anyone information. I had to keep the line open in case Emmy called. I called Mayson and asked if she had heard from her, and got the same negative response.

Honestly, I was ready to call Kyle Sterling. I didn't want to believe she'd gone that far. To run back into his arms. If she did, it would've been my fault entirely, and I'd deserve nothing less than hanging myself with that damn tie.

My sisters heard nothing. The few friends Emmy had made over the year hadn't spoken to her, either. I tried calling Diana but only got her voicemail. It was as if Emmy and my kids were in the wind.

My kids...maybe I'd destroy their lives, too. They'd blame me later for having to grow up in a broken home and having to be shared between me and their mother. Fuck. I didn't deserve to be their father.

What if she was seriously hurt after getting hit by that car? What if she was dying somewhere while my kids sat by crying for their mother?

Like the weak man I apparently was, I cried again for the third or fourth time that day. I sat on the edge of the couch with my head in my hands, sobbing. I had fucking lost everything. If Emmy didn't come back, I wouldn't survive.

****

I had to find her. It was getting dark and she'd been gone for hours and hours. The irrational thoughts plagued my mind. I tortured myself with what ifs and wondered whether my family was safe and where the fuck they were.

I didn't know where to start, but I had to go look. I got up and just stepped into the foyer when the front door swung open. With wide eyes, I watched Emmy walk in, and my heart fucking shattered when she looked away from me. I wanted to pull her to me and apologize, but Lucas was there, needing attention. I was beyond grateful that he was even there for me to pick up in my arms. I told him I missed him and tried to control the quavering in my voice.

I looked at Emmy, hoping to god she wasn't just popping in to get the rest of her shit and leave again.

"I'll put him to bed and then we can talk?" I said to her, not hiding how much I was hoping she would agree.

She turned away from me without a word and carried Kaitlyn into the living room and said nothing. I had the awful feeling this woman I loved so much was going to leave me. She'd leave me for dead, because that's what I'd be without her.

"Emmy?" I called her name, trying not to break down with Lucas in my arms.

"Just put Lucas to bed," she said in a dead voice as she started to take Kaitlyn out of her car seat.

I stood there, staring at her back for a long moment. I was afraid to take my eyes off her again. I feared I'd come back down and she'd be gone again. And when I'd look for Lucas, he'd be missing, too.

I knew I was being irrational. I looked at Lucas and pushed myself to smile for his benefit and carried him to bed.

I read a book to Lucas even though he was exhausted. He had a long day on the lam. My usual fight to get him to sleep wasn't necessary, but I stayed there with him, reading even after he closed his eyes, until the book was finished. I had taken too many bedtimes for granted. I might not have this tomorrow or the day after.

Anxious to hold my daughter, I went to her room after Lucas was sound asleep. Emmy must've just finished feeding her, because she was still sitting in in the rocking chair with Kaitlyn, adjusting her shirt. Her face seemed so dead it killed a part of me.

I reached for my daughter. "Can I put her to bed?"

Emmy handed her over and stood up. Kaitlyn smiled up at me. At least one of my girls was happy to see me.

"Make sure she burps," Emmy said in a tone as dead as her expression. She walked out of the room without another word.

"Em, I'll be out in a little while and we'll talk, okay?" I called after her, sounding pitiful, but she didn't answer.

I sat in the vacated rocking chair and started to rock Kaitlyn while singing Stevie Wonder. I was just getting to know my daughter. Her mother couldn't take her away from me. As an attorney, I was well aware of my rights as a father, but with my busy schedule, I'd be stuck only able to see my kids on weekends and some holidays, and that wasn't what I signed up for. I wanted to be a full-time father, a full-time husband—I wanted my family as it was before Iris walked her muffin ass into our lives.

I didn't know what to say to Emmy, or if she'd even listen. She was really good at not listening all damn day. I could be a dick and trap her in the bedroom and make her listen, make her understand what really happened. I'd do whatever I needed to do to make her hear the whole story and pray she believed me.

I put a sleeping Kaitlyn in her crib and went to find Emmy. The bedroom was empty, but I heard the shower in our master bathroom. I stood outside the door for a moment of indecision. I felt like almost any decision I made would be the wrong one. There would be no right choice. So I stripped out of my clothes and pushed open the bathroom door.

When I stepped into the steamy shower behind her, she didn't try to move away. She just stood there, with her head down, letting the water pour over her. I needed to see she was okay after getting hit by a car. I gently touched her side and almost choked on the sob that pushed its way through my throat.

"Shit," I said and lightly traced my fingers over the discolored skin. "Shit." I tried to hold back my anguish. I grabbed her other hip and gently made her turn so I could get a better look at her injuries. Her entire right side was bruised and scraped. "Shit!"

I couldn't blame the driver for hitting her. I could only blame myself. I couldn't even blame Iris. The fault was all my own. Emmy could've been killed on that road. Hell, she could be dying while I stood there crying about it, bleeding inside. My actions could very well take a mother away from her children, a daughter from her mother, and a wife away from her undeserving husband.

I didn't feel like a man, standing there in the shower, crying harder than I had ever cried in my life. It would serve me right if, disgusted, she got out of the shower and walked away from me. But she didn't. Emmy wrapped her arms around me and held me. She caressed my hair and rubbed my back as I cried into her neck. I didn't even deserve to cry. If anyone should be crying, it should've been Emmy. She was betrayed and hurt, yet she was the one comforting me.

Even if Emmy forgave me, I wasn't sure I'd ever be able to forgive myself.

Chapter Twenty-Nine

The Patron stopped burning on the way down several shots later. Eventually, I couldn't even taste it. I understood how people got alcohol poisoning. After a certain point you don't even taste the shit anymore, and it's easy to keep drinking something you can't taste.

I sat in the dark kitchen in the still of the night, drinking alone. Emmy had gone to bed right after our shower. She didn't want to talk, and when I moved to put my arms around her, she stiffened under my touch before silently moving as close to the edge of the bed as she could get. I tried to lay there and just take my punishment—god, if this was even my punishment—but I couldn't stand to be lying in the same bed with her and unable to touch her. I got up after what seemed like ages of waiting to fall asleep and went into the kitchen to dig out the alcohol.

I wasn't a drinker by any means. I had a few beers after work sometimes, and I'd occasionally have some harder drinks when I went out, but I don't think I have ever consumed as much alcohol in one night as I did after the long day I had. I was drunk, beyond drunk, and a small part of my brain told me to stop drinking before I killed myself. I wasn't suicidal, but I simply didn't care.

Emmy had come home and slept in our bed after allowing me to blubber on her shoulder, but she didn't want me to touch her. I wasn't sure what that really meant for us. I didn't know what I'd wake to. Only twenty-four hours earlier, my future with Emmy and the kids was mostly clear. I had no doubts we would all be together, regardless of what attacks we may face as a family, but I had no idea I'd be the attacker. I had no idea what would happen when I woke up.

The overhead lights in the kitchen flickered on. I blinked against the harsh light and tried to focus on the person who had just invaded my darkness. Emmy glided across the room and stopped inches away from me. At least she looked like she glided. It could have been the alcohol misinterpreting her movements, or the woman really was some kind of goddess and goddesses had no reason to walk when they could float.

She picked up the bottle of Patron and studied it for a moment. She gave me a look I didn't understand and started to turn away—with my bottle. I put my hand on her arm in what I hoped was a firm hold.

"That's mine," I slurred. I felt myself swaying in the chair as I tried to focus on her face.

"Actually, it's mine," she said stiffly. She tried to pull away again, but I yanked her arm hard, making her stumble once toward me.

"Put the bottle down," I demanded.

"No," she said firmly and tried to pry my fingers off her arm. "It's two in the morning, Luke."

"I don't care what time it is." My eyes closed on their own accord for a brief moment.

"You've had enough to drink," she said sourly and snatched her arm away.

I opened my eyes and wished I hadn't. The room spun fiercely. I closed them again and rested my head in my hands.

"You don't get to sit in here, in the dark, drinking and feeling sorry for yourself," Emmy said a moment later.

"Where should I feel sorry for myself, Em? Huh? In our bed where you won't let me touch you?" I opened my eyes slowly and took a moment to let my vision adjust before looking over at where she leaned against the counter. "Should I go back in the shower and cry there? I cried on the couch today. In my car. In the driveway. In the fucking street after you got ran down by a car."

"I didn't get run down," she said quietly, biting her bottom lip and looking down at the floor.

"I thought you were dead somewhere!" I shouted, surprised to hear how angry I sounded. "I thought you were lying somewhere dead or dying with our kids looking on. I know you want to punish me, Emmy, but...fuck! Not like that!"

I picked up the salt and pepper shakers and napkin holders situated in the center of the table and hurled all of them one by one. Glass shattered and napkins floated through the air. Emmy looked at the mess for only a moment before her eyes flickered back to me. She said nothing as she stood there, nibbling on the tip of her thumb.

I pushed myself to my feet, knocking my chair back. I staggered as I just tried to find my footing, but my balance was fucked up.

"So, tell me, Em." I glared at her. "Where can I go feel sorry for myself and it not fucking offend you?"

She closed her eyes for a long beat before looking at me with resolution in her eyes.

"Do what you want." She started to walk away. I lunged for her, tripped over my own two feet, and just barely missed slamming my face on the marble countertop. Emmy stood a few feet away staring at me with a shocked expression. Shocked and, fuck me, scared.

"I wasn't going to hurt you!" I shouted it, because she had been ignoring me all day. I wanted to make sure she heard me. "I would never fucking do what he did to you!"

Her small hands curled into fists as she snarled at me. "No, you find other ways to hurt me."

"You wouldn't even let me explain!" I yelled and took a drunken step toward her. "You ran away and wouldn't let me tell you what happened!"

"I don't want to know what happened! I heard what I heard and I don't want to know anything more beyond that. I don't think I can bear it!"

I stared at her for a long time. She didn't want to hear it. It wasn't fair. I was wrong on so many levels, but it wasn't anything like she probably thought. And it wasn't fair because she didn't want to hear it.

"What the fuck do you want me to do then, Emmy?" I asked her. "I can't let you take my kids and leave me. I'll fucking die without you and without them."

"I'm not leaving," she said quickly.

I hung my head. I was relieved to hear her say that, but...but I couldn't...I couldn't formulate any more real thoughts. The room spun again and I had to hold on to the counter to keep from falling over. My stomach heaved and I found myself over the sink, violently puking up all the tequila I had drank. Even after my stomach had given up everything it had, which was only the alcohol, I continued to dry heave. I felt Emmy's hands on my back and I remembered feeling angry she was allowed to touch me but I wasn't allowed to touch her.

When my stomach stopped trying to escape my body, I felt so damn weak. I started to slide to the floor, but Emmy's arms were around me, supporting me. I draped an arm across her shoulders and allowed her to lead me to the stairs. Somehow, she got me upstairs and into our bathroom. She made me sit down on the toilet and I immediately slumped against the wall, with my eyes heavy and barely open. Emmy opened my mouth and brushed my teeth as if I was a little kid. She got me to sit up long enough to rinse and spit the water back into the cup. Then she took a damp cloth and wiped my face. She then helped me into our bed. With a long sigh, she sat down on the edge of the bed beside me, looking down at the floor and breathing hard as if she was about to cry. With the little bit of energy I had left, I touched her fingers with my own. After a moment of reluctance, she slipped her hand into mine. It was the only comfort I had before falling asleep.

****

I woke up in bed alone, thinking I was dying. My head had never hurt so badly in my entire life. Every muscle in my body ached and my stomach was in knots—literally and figuratively. I sat up slowly, remembering my drunken behavior from the night before, and groaned. On top of fucking up in general, I then pretty much forced Emmy into caring for my drunken ass after I yelled and cursed at her, as if I had any right.

I pushed myself out of bed and shuffled into the bathroom. I brushed my teeth and swallowed a handful of ibuprofen before making my way downstairs. I knew it was late. Obviously I wasn't going to work, but at the moment, I didn't even care enough to call the firm and let them know. There were bigger things to focus on.

I stepped into the kitchen just in time to see Lucas patting Emmy's injured side to get her attention. She cringed and gasped and quickly grabbed his hand to stop him.

"What is it, Lucas?" she said wearily.

"Mommy I yant wunch."

I glanced at the clock on the wall. It was a little after noon. The kid must've had an internal clock.

231

"I'll get your lunch, Lucas," I said, even though the idea of food made my stomach churn.

Emmy looked over her shoulder at me. I walked over and took Lucas's hand, but kept my eyes trained on Emmy's until I walked past her.

Kaitlyn was in her pack and play, kicking and gurgling at the mobile spinning slowly over her. While I fed Lucas and attempted to eat some toast myself, Emmy took Kaitlyn into the family room to feed her. I could see them from where I sat in the kitchen. I talked to Lucas, but I frequently looked at Emmy, trying to get a feel for what she was thinking or feeling, but got nothing.

After lunch, I took Lucas upstairs to lay him down for a nap. When I returned to the first floor, Kaitlyn was asleep in her pack and play. Emmy was at the counter, cutting vegetables.

"I called you out of work this morning," she said, not looking at me.

"Thanks." I stopped close to her.

"You should drink some Gatorade." She still wouldn't look at me.

"I will."

We were silent for a long time as she prepped for dinner and I stood there watching her. I still had no idea how she felt or what she thought about.

"Em," I started, but she held up a hand to stop me.

"We're moving on."

"But…" I started but didn't know exactly what to say. "Emmy, you won't even look at me."

"I'm slicing vegetables with a big, sharp knife." She forced a smile. "Do you want me to cut off my finger?"

"No." I hesitated before admitting my fear to her. "I'm scared to death you're going to leave, Emmy."

"I'm not leaving. I'm not leaving, so don't worry about that. You're still my husband. I still love you more than you probably deserve right now."

I watched her attentively. When she finished cutting the carrot, she put down the knife and finally looked at me. She smiled, but it was like a shadow of what her smiles used to be.

"Can you pass me the olive oil?" She gestured to the bottle near me. I passed it to her and touched her fingers as she took it from me, but she quickly pulled away and turned back to her dinner prep.

I tried to tell myself I had to just give it time. If she really just wanted to move on, I could be patient and wait for everything to fall back into place, but I had an awful feeling nothing would fall into the places they belonged. I imagined one of those learning toys with the different shapes outlined in a box, and the object was to match up the shaped blocks with the holes in the box. No matter how hard one tries, you cannot push the triangle shape into the circle hole and vice versa. I worried we would try too hard and just…well, break.

"How's your side?" I asked her. It was still a punch in a gut to picture her bruised side and how she got it.

"I'm sore, but it'll be fine," she said quickly, like she didn't really want to discuss it at all.

"Yeah, but how do you know you aren't seriously hurt?"

She shrugged. "I guess if I was, I'd know it by now. As soon as I get this in the oven, I need to run to the grocery store."

"I can go for you," I offered.

"No, I can go," she said too brightly as she pulled off her apron. She gave me another one of those shadowy smiles and left me alone in the kitchen.

I didn't think we should just go on as if nothing had happened, but Emmy seemed determined to do just that. I played along for her sake, but I was on edge, waiting for the other shoe to drop.

****

Emmy's hot mouth slid down my semi-hard cock. It responded by rapidly growing, lengthening and widening in her mouth. When her tongue swirled around the head of my dick, I moaned and pushed myself deeper into her mouth.

This was the best dream I'd had in a very long time. It was definitely the most realistic. I could distinctly feel the tip of my shaft hitting and passing her tonsils, the light grazing of her teeth, and her delicate fingers stroking me. When I reached down to put my fingers in her hair, the weight and silkiness of it felt real. My thumb slid over the small indented scar in her hairline. That detail, yet small in a physical sense, was a large detail for my brain to create and process and put in the exact spot that's on her head in reality.

I woke up, blinking down at Emmy sucking my cock, totally uninhibited. She had avoided touching me as much as possible for days. Smiling and laughing hollowly and pretending she was fine when it was clear she was not. When I left for work in the mornings, there was always tension at the corners of her mouth and eyes, and I couldn't blame her, because one day I went to work and when I came home, our lives were shattered by my actions—or inactions.

"Em." I gasped, putting both hands on either side of her head to stop her ministrations. "Stop. You don't have to—" I was cut off when she knocked my hands away and continued to suck me, wilder than before.

I dropped my head back on the pillow, lacking the power to make her stop. At least she was touching me. I thought I'd have to eventually beg her for sex, but here she was offering it up.

Emmy suctioned her lips, making her mouth tight around my erection as she bobbed her head, sliding my length in and out of her mouth with hot friction. I groaned and again thrust my hips up to meet her. She gave me one last good suck and then pulled me out of her mouth. She gripped me with both hands and started to lick the bulbous head like it was a lollypop in her favorite flavor.

"Emmm," I groaned as my dick twitched in her hands.

I looked down at her, but the room was dark. Unlike our apartment in the city, the moonlight was lacking. I could vaguely see her face, but I wanted to look her in the eyes. It wasn't something I had to have every time she gave me head, but I needed to see her eyes now. Though I physically enjoyed what she was doing to me, something felt off.

She released me and straddled me. She rubbed her moist slit along my shaft, priming me with her arousal. I reached up to put my hands on her hips, but she knocked my hands away again. She reached between our bodies and put the head of my cock at her entrance. There was no teasing, no hesitation before she dropped herself sharply, impaling her body on mine and then crying out. It didn't sound like a pleasurable cry. It sounded painful.

"Em," I said her name and put my hands on her hips, but again she slapped my hands away. "Emmy, are you okay?"

Ignoring my question, she began to move on top of me. There was nothing intimate about her rhythm, no give and take. She was all take, with a violent detachment that burned me deeply. She rode me hard, knocking my hands away every time I went to touch her, no matter where it was on her body. She grunted and sometimes groaned, but again it didn't sound pleasurable. It was angry and sorrowful and painful.

"Emmy," I said her name more firmly and gripped her hips to make her stop.

She tried to push my hands away from her, but I refused to let her go. She tried to move on top of me as she tried to bat my hands away, but I wouldn't let her budge. She let out a frustrated scream and slapped at my hands.

"We're not doing it like this," I almost yelled at her. If I couldn't touch her and if she couldn't stand to be touched by me, and if she was as mentally and emotionally detached as I believed she was, I didn't want to be inside her. It didn't seem right.

She stopped struggling, but I didn't release her. We were still physically connected as she sat atop me breathing heavily and trembling.

"Emmy, I can't make love to you when your heart isn't in it, and I sure as hell can't fuck you if your head isn't in it."

I expected something in reply, but she just sat there in silence as my cock began to soften.

I opened my mouth to speak again, but Kaitlyn's cries crackled over the baby monitor. It was a reflex to release Emmy at the sound of our baby crying, and she took advantage of it. She scrambled off me and hurried into the bathroom, probably to get her robe.

"I'll get her," I said, pulling my boxers back up. The bathroom door closed and I went to go take care of Kay Kay.

I fed Kaitlyn, changed her diaper, and rocked her back to sleep. By the time I got back into the bedroom, Emmy was on her side of the bed with her back to me. I moved over close to her and put my arm around her and tucked my chin into the space between her head and shoulder.

"Baby, are you okay?" I whispered.

She didn't answer me, but she very subtly rolled her shoulder, and I took the hint and backed the hell off. I lay in bed, wide awake for the rest of the night, staring at her back. In the morning, she'd pretend everything was okay again, and I'd play along.

****

"I told you not to come here anymore," I said to the woman sitting in the chair on the other side of my desk. "I don't even know why you sat your ass down in that chair, because you're going to walk out of my door in about five seconds."

"What if I came to apologize?" Iris asked.

"I don't care why you're here, Iris. I only care that you leave."

"It was a misunderstanding," she said.

"There was no misunderstanding," I said darkly. "You knew exactly what you were doing. Now get out."

She didn't get out of the chair. Even Claire knew when it was time to leave.

"I know how I must look...like some kind of a slut, but—"

"Even sluts don't do what you did, Iris." I growled. "Get. Out. Now. Don't stop to chat with my staff, just keep it moving. If your ass isn't walking out that door in the next ten seconds, I will embarrass the shit out of you as I throw you out."

"You wouldn't physically harm a woman." She snorted, but then her eyes grew wide when she realized I was counting out loud.

"Five. Six. Seven."

She got up and walked to the door, but then she stopped and turned around. She started to say how sorry she was again, but I stood up and started rounding the desk because I had reached ten. She scurried out of my office, but I went out to make sure that she left the building.

"Did you just scare the muffin lady away?" Kacey asked very quietly at my side as we watched Iris hurry down the sidewalk toward her shop.

"Yes," I answered simply.

"Good." She sniffed. "I don't like her."

"Me either, Kace," I said and went back into my office.

When I got home, Emmy was perky. She kissed me lightly on the lips after I spent a few minutes with the kids. She chattered

236

about dinner and her parents' upcoming visit. She smiled and pretended really well, but not well enough for me. At dinner, she only ate a small amount of food and rambled about the big lunch she had. She was lying through her teeth. Not that I could see the inside of her stomach, but I had been watching her like a hawk since the Iris incident only a week ago, and I knew she was skipping meals. I worried she was struggling hard inside, as hard inside as she was pretending on the outside. I worried about her health—mentally and physically. But I pretended right along with her as I always did, because I didn't know what else to do.

Later that night after I got Lucas to sleep, I ran downstairs to make sure the lights were off and the doors were locked. I grabbed a bottle of water and headed back upstairs. I opened the door just in time to see Emmy hurling something across the room. I heard glass shatter on the hardwood floor. I looked in that direction for a moment before looking back to Emmy. She looked at me briefly and then looked away. I put my water down on a bureau and began to walk over to where the object she had thrown was lying on the floor. I only got a couple of steps before I stepped on glass. I backed up, plucked the small shard out of my foot, and went downstairs for the broom and dustpan. While I was down there, I grabbed the sneakers I wore for yard work out of the laundry room and slipped them on.

When I got back upstairs, Emmy was still sitting on the bed, staring at her hands in her lap. I went to the source of the broken glass and tried not to make a sound even though my heart was screaming. It was our favorite wedding picture, framed in a heavy silver frame, but now glassless. I looked across the room at its vacated spot on the table on Emmy's side of the bed as if I couldn't believe it was the same picture. I kneeled there, plucking out what was left of the glass in the frame and then put it aside while I swept up the mess.

I wanted to comfort my wife, but I knew she wouldn't want comfort from me. I wanted to talk to her, but she'd just shut the conversation down. I wanted life to be normal, but we were in a seemingly endless cycle of pretend normalcy.

After disposing of the glass, I put the frame back on the table where it belonged. At least one thing about us should be where it belonged.

I looked down at her. I wanted to touch her, but I didn't think I could stand to watch her recoil from me again. Without a word, I grabbed my bottle of water and went downstairs.

Chapter Thirty

"You and Casey should come over for dinner," I told Emmet as we walked out of the office together one night.

"Absolutely not," he said, shaking his head. "We had enough of my mother this week. Nice try though."

"You guys only had her for three days," I complained. "We have her for five."

"Yeah, but we lived a little too close to her for a long time. You have only had to deal with her during visits. She's leaving tomorrow morning. You'll survive." He clapped a hand on my shoulder and then turned right while I continued straight across the street.

"Thanks a lot!" I shouted to my brother-in-law.

The truth was I could handle Sam better than her own family most of the time. I tended to ignore her crass comments and gently bumped her out when she tried to put her nose in our personal business. Usually, a visit from her wouldn't bother me, but Emmy and I were still pretending. Since Sam seemed to be a professional at seeing even the hidden things, we pretended extra hard in her presence. I knew Emmy wouldn't want to be hounded and I simply didn't want to snap on my mother-in-law, which was bound to happen if she nagged me about my marriage. I was thankful Emmy's dad had come along this time, too. Most of the time, Sam came alone, but since his heart attack, Fred had been traveling with his wife more often than not. At least when he was around, Sam didn't nag too much. Fred didn't like to hear Sam nag Emmy, and now Sam went out of her way not to upset her husband.

When I got home, I found the women and Kaitlyn in the kitchen. Through the French doors, I could see Fred and Lucas busy in the back yard. I didn't know what they were doing, but Lucas liked being outside and he loved being with his grandfather, so I didn't care if he did some of my work out there.

Emmy stood over Kaitlyn, cooing and talking to her. I swept the baby out of her seat, anxious to spend my time with her as I was every night.

"Hey, that's mine!" Emmy cried out.

It was show time. It was happy Emmy and Luke time. I leaned in to kiss her.

Our kisses without Sam around were always short and rather cold and chaste. Our kisses in front of Sam always gave the illusion they were more than what they were. I always kissed Emmy, but she never kissed me back. My tongue would seek entrance between her lips, but I was always denied. But she always ended the charade with a smile, as if she had enjoyed the whole thing. But this one was different.

Emmy's lips weren't rigid. They parted slightly, and I hesitantly pressed forward. When she didn't resist or bite my tongue, I felt hope tingling in my chest. When her tongue gently thrust forward to meet mine, the tingling changed to small bursts of hope. When I heard her sigh ever so slightly and felt her mouth relax, my small bursts of hope turned into an explosion of hope, radiating through my limbs.

The kiss was real. There was nothing fake about it, nothing pretended. If it weren't for the fact I was holding our daughter and my mother-in-law wasn't standing a mere three feet away, I would've explored her mouth for hours, relishing the realness of her kiss.

I found the strength of a hundred men to pull away from her lips.

"Hi, baby." I beamed at her. There was so much more implied in those words than a simple hello. I was saying hi to the woman who I thought had been lost to me. I was saying hi to the woman I knew before two weeks ago. I was saying hi to the real Emmy and not the pretend one I'd been living with.

I turned my attention back to our daughter and carried her into the family room, with my heart much lighter and my lips still burning.

Fred and Lucas joined us in the family room some time later. Fred held the baby while Lucas and I worked on coloring a picture of a Ninja Turtle. The news was on in the background and mouthwatering scents wafted in from the kitchen. Fred and I talked about the upcoming football season and the winding down baseball season. Sam poked her head in every now and then to see a news story. It felt like a normal day in a normal family, but Emmy was absent from the picture.

Later Sam told me to go upstairs and get Emmy for dinner. I dug my phone out of my pocket and started to text her.

"What are you doing?" Sam asked me. "Are you texting her?"

"Yes," I said absently as my fingers flew over the screen.

Suddenly my hands were empty. I blinked and looked at my phone in Sam's hand.

"I said to go upstairs and get Emmy for dinner. Not to text her," she spat.

I put my hands up in defeat. I didn't want to fight with her and delay eating the delicious food she had just made.

"Fine, okay," I said, backing away toward the kitchen stairs.

"And uh, no need to rush down." She sniffed as she put my phone on the counter.

"What is that supposed to mean?" I asked her and then thought better of it. "Never mind."

I jogged up the stairs. I assumed Emmy escaped from the kitchen so she wouldn't have to kill her mother. I found her in the bedroom on the bed, holding our wedding picture. I froze for a second, eyeing her warily. We had just shared an awesome kiss not that long ago. Was it just an anomaly?

"Hey," I said softly as I closed the door behind me.

"Hey," she said and tossed the frame onto the bed.

I had an uneasy feeling in the pit of my stomach. I felt like Emmy was slipping away from me again, that the kiss was only a short reprieve.

"You okay?"

"Great," she lied.

"Dinner's ready. Do you want me to bring it up to you so you don't have to deal with Sam?"

"No." She forced another one of those hollow smiles. "I'm not very hungry."

I couldn't pretend I hadn't noticed her eating habits as of late. It needed to be addressed. It wasn't just her I had to worry about, but she needed to eat right so she could produce enough milk for Kaitlyn.

"Em, you've been skipping meals like crazy lately." I decided to try a different approach. "Are you sick?"

"No. Just trying to lose a few pounds, and I haven't had much of an appetite."

I didn't necessarily disbelieve her. She hated the extra weight she put on after she had the baby. "You know I think you're beautiful no matter how many pounds you are, right?"

"Sure," she said, unconvinced, like I was lying.

I wasn't lying about that. But I was tired of lying about us— to her, to myself. I was tired of pretending. I was done with this pretending shit. I wanted my wife back all the damn way. I had been patient and waiting for things to shift back, but we seemed stagnant. I told her once I would fight for her to the death. Now it was time to fight, though the enemy I was fighting wasn't Kyle, it was us. I needed to know exactly how she felt and what she thought before I put on my armor.

"Em," I said her name with weariness. I was tired, very tired of our charade. I sat down on the bed beside her. "Just…just say what's on your mind."

"I have nothing to say. I said all I have to say. I'm not hungry and I'm trying to lose a few pounds."

"And you went to see a plastic surgeon," I said darkly.

That wasn't something she had told me about. I found out by accident only a few days ago. I answered her phone while she was in the shower, and it was a popular doctor in the area for cosmetic work. They called to confirm her follow up appointment. I canceled it.

"How do you know about that?" she asked quietly, and I told her.

"Why the hell are you seeing a plastic surgeon?"

"I need some work done. It's no big deal."

"You don't need any work done, and you were never into being plastic before. Why now?"

She stared up at the ceiling. "Just because. It's my decision, right?" She was trying to keep the conversation light, but I could hear the anxiety in her voice.

"It is your decision," I softly conceded. "But it's not like you."

"I guess we're all being someone we're not lately," she said and then bit her lip as if she hadn't meant to say it.

I hung my head, nearly blown over from her words, but tried to stay on topic.

"Em, I wouldn't change anything about you. I think every part of you is perfect. Will you please come downstairs and eat something? You love Sam's cooking."

"Maybe later." I knew she was lying as she sat there, palming her chest. I knew it ached, because so did mine. It ached so damn bad. There was no reason not to ask the obvious questions. There need not be any more holding back.

"Do you want to…separate? Do you want to leave me?" I swallowed hard after asking the questions. It wasn't something I was willing to grant her, but I needed to know where her mind was.

To my surprise, she looked at me with a stunned expression on her face. "I never said that."

"You act like it. You act happy when you're not, and I've tried everything to prove to you how sorry I am, how much I want you. What I did has not only devastated you but it's devastated me. I don't know what else to do."

"Luke, it's been two weeks," she said bitterly. "I would think you'd give me a little more time. It took you nearly two years for you to stop being angry about what I did to you."

"Emmy, I just don't want to find out six months from now that you can't get over it."

"I don't know what you want from me. I'm handling it the best way I know how."

"I just…I just want to know what you're thinking," I said. I knew I looked desperate, but I *was* desperate.

"You don't want to know what I'm thinking." She gave a humorless laugh.

"Dammit!" I snapped. "Emmy, I just told you that's what I want from you!"

She looked at me with slightly widened eyes, surprised at my outburst, but then she sat up and faced me.

"Okay. Here it is," she said. "Every morning you go into the office, I feel like I can't breathe. I put on a good show when you're leaving, but once you're out the door, I struggle to breathe, Luke, because I don't know—will today be the day you run into Iris? What will you say? What will she say? What will you do? Will today be the day she walks into the office despite what you told her? And will you let her in and close the door? What will happen behind that closed door? Will today be a day when you say you're working late but you're really with her?"

My eyes widened and my mouth fell open. Those were a lot of serious questions she asked herself every day. Her state of mind had become very clear, and I felt like an even bigger asshole than before, especially since Iris did come into my office and I hadn't told Emmy. I opened my mouth to speak, but she put her hand up and cut me off.

"Oh, I'm not finished yet," she said harshly. "I wonder how long you guys have been talking as more than friends. I wonder at what point you knew you were out of line and why you allowed it to continue. I think about how you told her she was beautiful and sexy while I'm walking around with baby vomit in my hair and my fat flabby ass. I wonder how many times you've kissed her before, if you've touched her, if you've made her come. I wonder what you think is wrong with me—what I'm lacking that would make you even turn your head to look at someone else. I wonder how you could do this after all the hell we had gone through to get to the happy place we were in—at least I thought it as a happy place. And…"

Her words gutted me. Her questions about my actions were understandable and expected, but when Emmy started questioning herself and the happiness we had, it was more than I could take. My eyes burned with unshed tears, but I had to fucking man up, and I needed to hear all of it.

"And what?" I asked her. "Finish."

"I've said enough," she said gently and looked at her hands in her lap.

"But you haven't said everything you're thinking," I said impatiently and gritted out, "Say it all."

I watched her delicate throat as she swallowed hard. After months of watching Emmy close herself off, I knew when she was trying to shut down. I wasn't having it. No more silent pain and anger. No more pretending. My emotions were heavy in my chest and pushed me slightly over the edge.

"Just fucking say it!" I yelled.

She flinched and looked at me with so many emotions spread across her face, I was unable to categorize exactly what she could've been feeling. I fully expected her to get up and walk away from me, but to my surprise, she got on her knees and wrapped her arms around me. I clutched her fiercely.

"I never touched her before that day, I swear," I said to her as I tried to keep it together. "I liked her but I didn't think anything of it until she said something on that day. There is nothing that you are lacking, Emmy. You're perfect."

"My mom thinks I have unattractive hair and I need to join a gym." She sniffed. Usually, Emmy didn't take her mom's critiques to heart. She was confident enough to not let it shake her, but I could hear in her voice she was questioning her appearance.

"Your mom is a crackpot," I told her and was rewarded with a real laugh. I pulled back and looked into her beautiful face. "Please don't get plastic surgery. When I say you're perfect, I mean it."

She looked me in the eyes, her own full of questions.

"Luke…did you kiss her or did she kiss you?" she asked after some reluctance.

"No, Em; she kissed me," I answered quickly and hoped it wasn't too quickly, indicating some kind of guilt.

The frown that formed on her face twisted my heart strings. "But you kissed her back."

"No, baby, I did not. I was so shocked I just stood there." I felt so ashamed admitting that. I felt like a lesser man for my inaction. "I can't believe I just stood there like that."

"But she said she was touching you. Was she?"

"A little bit," I admitted. "Mostly she kept touching my arms."

Emmy caressed my upper arms. Finally feeling her hands touching me so willingly was an incredible sensation. "Well…you do have yummy looking arms."

"But they're yours, not hers," I said softly.

"I think she gets that now," she said with a little bit of haughtiness. She climbed into my lap and rested her head on my shoulder. I felt megatons of weight lift off my chest. I finally felt like I could breathe again. Emmy was my source of breath, and for two weeks, I was near death.

I stroked her hair, inhaled her soft scent and let her body close to mine soothe my soul. "Have I told you I loved you lately?"

"No. You should sing it to me."

The last song at our wedding reception was "Lately" by Tyrese. I had held Emmy as close as we could get with an unborn Kaitlyn between us, dancing in a tight circle as I sang the song to her.

"You better sing that to me again," she had said with her lips pressed against mine. "And often."

And I did. All the way up to the day our world almost ended.

I sang to her now, running my fingers through her hair and caressing her body. I touched her face, her neck, her back, her arms, her legs, between her breasts. She didn't recoil. She didn't push me away. She accepted my touch as if she needed it as much as I needed to give it. She turned herself around and straddled me as I finished the song.

"I love you, too."

She kissed me. I pushed my hands under her shirt and caressed her bare back. Her hands roamed frantically over my body. She stopped abruptly, and before I could object, she started to unbutton my shirt. When that went too slowly for her, she let out an aggressive grunt and tore my shirt open. I was shocked and very turned on. This aggressiveness wasn't like the night I woke up with her sucking me. This wasn't anger. This was pure desire.

"Someone is a little eager," I teased and playfully pulled at her shirt.

"Just take my damn shirt off," she commanded and planted a kiss on my lips.

I chuckled and answered her demand. I removed her shirt and her bra and tossed them away.

"Did you lock the door when you came in?" Emmy asked with her lips on my jaw.

"Nope. Hopefully your mom will have enough sense to know what's going on up here."

"She probably knew it was going to happen before us."

"Mmm," I managed as her teeth nipped my neck. "You're probably right. She's the one who sent me up here. I started to just text you, but she gave me a hard time."

"Well, let's not disappoint her." She pressed her bare chest against mine.

"I can't wait for these to stop being a source of food," I said as I cupped one of her breasts. I missed pulling her nipples between my teeth and watching her wriggle from the sensation.

"If you don't want a source of food all over you, I suggest you make your hand migrate south."

I flipped her onto her back. She let out a little squeal I cut off with a kiss as I began to release the zipper of her jeans. I slipped my hand under her panties and flattened my palm against her clit. She moaned into my mouth and squirmed against my hand. I pushed a single digit inside her and eased it in and out, but this was going too slowly for me. I needed more. I pulled away from her warm mouth and quickly began removing her jeans and underwear.

"Someone's a little eager," Emmy mocked.

"Very," I said and quickly removed the rest of my clothes. Eager was an understatement.

Impatient, I pressed my body to hers, fitting my cock against her sex. I kissed her and rubbed the head of my cock against her clit. Emmy moaned into my mouth and pressed her hips up to meet my thrusts. My shaft slid through the length of her pussy, collecting her moisture.

"Shall I make you come like this?" I asked her, watching her face.

"Yesss," she moaned and then begged. "Please."

"You don't have to beg me, baby," I said to her as I rubbed against her harder and faster. Every time the head of my cock rubbed over her clit I groaned. She was growing wetter every second. "You're so moist, Em."

Emmy squirmed beneath me, moaning and licking her pretty lips. I knew she was getting close to coming and I planned to give her one hell of an orgasm. I kissed her, sucking in her escalating moans. Her orgasm began with a shrill sound out of her mouth as she turned her head away from my kiss to let it out. I slammed my cock into her, hard and fast. I groaned, but Emmy started to scream. I covered her mouth and watched her eyes roll back in her head and her face turn that sexy shade of pink. I held myself deep inside her as her orgasm began to fade. Hesitantly, I took my hand off her mouth. I needed to be deeper. I needed her to feel every inch of me. I looped my arm under her left leg and immediately felt myself slide farther in. Emmy tensed and her eyes grew large with alarm as she put her hands on me to stop me.

I understood. I'm not conceited, but I'm a very well-endowed man. Even after all this time, I sometimes hurt Emmy with my size, but it was always only at first. The pain always shifted to pleasure.

"I'm yours and you are mine. I'm going to have you all the way, and you're going to have me all the way."

"Too much," she managed even as I slid in another inch.

"I need to feel you, Emmy," I said and thrust into her hard and deep. She covered her mouth to muffle her own screams as she looked up at me with impossibly wide eyes.

I moaned and asked her, "You feel me?"

"How can I not?" she snapped.

I grinned down at her and pulled up her other leg. She looked very apprehensive, but I wasn't about to hold back. I pulled out until just the tip of my cock was in her slick entrance.

"Ready?"

"How can I possibly prepare to be invaded by your obscene freak of nature?" she shot at me and gripped the sheets in an effort to brace herself.

I was finished talking about it. I slammed my erection into her tight core until my balls were pressed against her. I groaned loudly as I felt her pussy contracting around my cock.

"You feel so fucking good," I told her. I pulled out and thrust into her again, harder than the last time. Emmy did nothing to hide her cries now. "You're so fucking perfect, Em."

I braced myself with my hands on the headboard and pounded into my perfect wife with wild abandon. I felt her walls clutching at my shaft. She was so wet I could hear the moisture as I slid in and out of her. I was hurting her, but I was giving her pleasure as well. Despite the pain etched across her face, she held onto my body, digging her nails into my skin.

I let go of the headboard and put my hands on her hips. Eliciting a yelp of surprise from Emmy, I rolled us over until I was on my back and she was on top of me.

"Oh my god!" she screamed. Her automatic response was to attempt to move away as the head of my cock hit and pressed on her cervix. I was much harder and longer than I was the night Emmy tried to angrily fuck me. The angle was different. I was deeper, much deeper. I held onto her hips and slowly rotated mine.

I looked up at her beautiful, flushed face. Her hair was stuck to her cheeks and neck. She looked wild and sexy.

"You're so beautiful, Emmy, so perfect," I groaned. I started to thrust while holding her in place. Emmy thrashed above me, clawed at my hands, and screamed my name again and again. I felt my orgasm rushing through me. I needed to come, mark her again as mine. I needed her to come on me, mark me again as hers.

"Come on my cock, baby! Shit, I'm going to come! You feel too damn…" I grunted and moaned. "…fucking…*perfect*!" I shouted as I began to come. Emmy burst into sobs as she came.

When she shuddered violently and collapsed on my chest, I held her tightly.

"I love you so much," I whispered to her. I felt her tears, hot on my skin. "You are my everything, Emmy."

Every emotion she tried to push away while we were pretending seemed to surface. She cried harder than I had ever seen her do before.

"I will do anything for you, baby," I whispered as I caressed her back and her hair. "You are perfect, so perfect…"

I held her for a very long time. I didn't try to hush her. She deserved to cry. I had hurt her so badly.

"Nothing and no one will ever come between us again," I told her, and meant it. I would protect and fight for our family always, at any cost.

****

We laid in bed for a long time after Emmy's breakdown. We talked quietly and caressed each other until we realized one of us would have to put the kids to bed.

Judging by the dark circles beneath Em's eyes, I knew she was exhausted, so I volunteered to take care of the kids so she could rest. I pulled on some clothes, kissed her tenderly on her pretty mouth, and went downstairs to tend to our munchkins.

Sam put her hands on her hips when I entered the family room. Lucas and Fred were picking up toy cars and building blocks and depositing them into a toy box in the corner while Kaitlyn snoozed in her baby seat.

"What are you doing down here?" she demanded. "Why aren't you upstairs still making up with your wife?"

"Sam," Fred groaned with exasperation. When she peered over at him, he shook his head disapprovingly before looking at me. "Sam and I would like to put the kids to bed, if you don't mind, Luke. It will probably be a while before we get to spend time with them again."

"Kiss your babies goodnight and get back to what you were doing," my mother-in-law said.

Fred's voice came out in a low warning. "Samantha."

I bid goodnight to Lucas with a hug he didn't want and a kiss he wiped off his forehead. Kay Kay slept on as I kissed her soft head. Fred and I exchanged a manly, wordless nod.

"Goodnight, Sam," I cooed and proceeded to kiss her face until she batted me away, giggling.

I jogged back up the stairs, eager to be back in bed with Emmy, only to find her gone. When I heard the water running in the bathroom, I disrobed and joined her in the shower. Then I joined *with* her in the shower, against the tiled wall, creating more steam than the hot water that beat down on our bodies. When we crawled into bed, we were both spent. The evening had been taxing, but so had the past couple of weeks.

I kissed her until she was nearly asleep. We both fell into a slumber shortly thereafter, tangled together in the middle of the bed.

In the middle of the night, I woke first. I kissed the top of her head and began to untangle myself from her. I didn't want to wake her up, but she stretched with a light moan and sat up as I pulled on a pair of lounge pants. She looked so cute as she tiredly rubbed at her bed head before rolling out of bed and getting dressed in a pair of her panties and one of my T-shirts. The shirt just covered her gorgeous ass. With her hand in mine, we silently crept down the kitchen stairs.

I hoisted her onto the island in the center of the kitchen, and kissed her gently and briefly before pulling away in search of leftovers. I tapped on the small radio on the counter and turned the volume down to a soft, but audible level. We listened to music as I prepared and heated a heaping plate of food for us. There were no words between us, but there were smiles and kisses until the timer went off on the microwave.

I carried the plate of food to the island after grabbing a bottle of water from the fridge. My fingers swept through the mound of mashed potatoes and I offered it to her. She met my eyes, opened her mouth, and sucked the potatoes off my fingers. We fed each other little bites of the late dinner with our hands, and with little kisses in between. Our voices were whisper soft as we chatted. Our laughter was quiet and breathy, and we touched each other constantly, as if we were afraid to stop.

When the plate was cleared, I didn't even care to move it before I lifted Emmy into my arms and pulled my pants down just enough for my erection to spring free. I pushed her panties aside and slid into her with her legs wrapped tightly around me.

We made love quietly, right there in the middle of the kitchen, and had fallen asleep again in our bed as the sun began its ascent.

Chapter Thirty-One

It was a beautiful Saturday. The heat wasn't oppressive and the sky was a perfect shade of blue with sparse white clouds. Everything seemed so much brighter after I got my wife back.

I took her parents to the airport with a smile on my face, and not just because I was getting rid of Sam and her big mouth. I even gave the woman a big hug that lifted her off her feet and kissed her cheek, ignoring her surprised outburst. I shook Fred's hand with enthusiasm. I hurried out of the terminal, anxious to get back home to my woman.

I plugged my iPod into the stereo for the trip home. I tapped the steering wheel to the upbeat 90s music as I sat in traffic. I sang out loud to the words I knew and whistled to the parts of the song I didn't know. I had a perpetual smile on my face, which only grew wider as I thought about the night I'd shared with Emmy.

The night had been magical. I was confident our day ahead would be just as magical. Our plans to take Lucas and Kay Kay to the park and then out to dinner after their naps weren't really remarkable plans, but we would be together, and that was all that mattered. Later, after the kids were in bed, Emmy and I planned to watch a movie and eat popcorn. It's the simple things in life that bring me happiness. My wife was happy and healthy and so were my children. Beyond that, everything else was a bonus.

When I got home from the airport, I noted Diana's car was parked at the curb, but Emmy's car was missing. I wondered where she had gone. She didn't mention she had anything to do.

I walked into the house and found Diana in the living room with the kids. She was on the floor playing cars with Lucas while holding Kaitlyn in one arm. She looked up at me with an "Uh-Oh" expression, but was quick to cover it.

"Where's Emmy?" I asked her after I took Kaitlyn from her.

She shrugged a shoulder as she got to her feet. "I don't know."

I narrowed my eyes at her until she threw her hands up. "I really don't know, cousin!"

"She didn't say anything?"

"Not really," she said evasively, gently kicking one of Lucas's cars with her flip flop.

"My car!" Lucas shouted and smacked at her toes.

"Sorry, kid." She headed toward the foyer. I followed in close pursuit.

"Diana," I said in warning. Something was up. I wasn't worried, really. I trusted Emmy, but I was beyond curious.

She blew out a breath, making her bangs flutter. "Look. All I know is she asked me yesterday if I could make it here at seven-thirty. She said I couldn't be any earlier than that and I couldn't be more than a few minutes late. When I got here she was rushing out the door telling me she'd be home before you. I was under the impression she didn't want you to know she was going anywhere."

"Huh." I didn't know what to think about it. There had been a few times in the past two-plus weeks where she insisted on running some kind of random errand or another, but I assumed it was to get away from me. Since we were good again, I didn't imagine that was the case, especially since she wanted to be home before me.

"Did she pay you?" I reached for my wallet.

"Yes, she paid me. I'm glad one of you got home early though. I have to go buy my books for school."

"Do you need book money?" I offered. My cousin Stacy, Diana's mother, didn't have a lot of money for basic needs, let alone to put her daughter through school. Emmy and I had been helping out wherever we could, including paying Di above and beyond for her babysitting services.

"Nope, I'm good," she said. "Thank you anyway."

She kissed my cheek and went out the door.

"If you need anything, let us know."

She walked backward toward her car, looking thoughtful. "Anything?"

I gestured for her to get on with it.

"I've never been able to go away for spring break," she said hopefully. Then she broke out into a grin and waved it off. "I'm kidding. You guys do enough already."

She waved as she opened her car door. I waved back, distracted by my thoughts. Diana was admittedly one of my favorite younger people in my family. She worked her ass off for everything she had, little as it was, since she was thirteen and took jobs

253

babysitting. Now she was putting herself through school and trying to help out her mom and younger siblings, too. She didn't easily take handouts, and I knew if I presented her with a trip to Cancun, she would decline. But if I took her with Emmy and I on our honeymoon to watch the kids… Hmm.

I was still thinking about it when Diana pulled away. I was about to close the door when I saw the woman who looked like she was on fire storming across the street from a car that had rolled up while I was talking to Di. She didn't just look like she was on fire because of her wild, red, wavy hair, but she had a hand on the round bump in her belly and I swear there was smoke coming out of her ears, but I couldn't ignore the pain that was stitched throughout her features.

She tried to force a smile as she approached. I smiled back. But even with all this damn smiling, I knew Emmy and I were about to run face first into another obstacle. I had a feeling I knew what was coming, but Emmy was clueless. She didn't know what I knew.

"Hello," the redhead said, her expression turning somber.

"Hello, Lily." Despite my better judgment, I stepped aside and let her in.

I led her into the kitchen and left Lucas to his cars in the family room. I watched Lily as her eyes wandered around our house.

"You have a beautiful home."

"Thank you." I shifted Kaitlyn in my arms.

"I live in a penthouse," she said conversationally. "I never thought I'd ever live in a penthouse." She looked at me with her steel-colored eyes. "Your home feels…like a home. Warm and fuzzy-like. My penthouse feels like a penthouse," she said dryly. "The 'home' part of my equation is currently absent."

I tilted my head with a million questions on my tongue, but I heard the front door open. I could almost sense Emmy's surprise. I couldn't see the door from where I was, but I knew by how long it took for it to close she was surprised to see Lily standing in our kitchen. Emmy appeared in the family room as she spoke briefly to Lucas and then she walked into the kitchen, looking both surprised and apprehensive.

It was an awkward few minutes as Emmy nervously chatted with Lily. We offered her something to drink and eat, trying to be hospitable and warm like we were to anyone who walked through our door.

Finally, after Emmy fetched a bottle of water for each of them, she asked Lily the big question that was hanging in the air. "So, what brings you to Chi-town?"

"Umm," Lily said, glancing at me. "I actually…" She looked at me again and seemed reluctant to speak, but then she sucked in a breath and finished. "I need to talk to you in private, Emmy."

I frowned as I looked at Lily. This had Kyle Sterling written all over it, and I wasn't sure if I wanted to drag his name into our marriage. I sure as hell didn't want Emmy dragged into Kyle's world again. I knew it had to be about Kyle. Emmy may have had an inkling that it was about Kyle, but she didn't know the details I knew. She didn't know that when Kyle initially contacted me about buying the bar property, he had told me he was buying it for Lily. I followed up with Mayson later and found out that the pair were definitely a couple, but Mayson and I agreed Emmy didn't need to know that bit of information.

"Oh," Emmy finally said. She looked at me and back to Lily. "We can talk upstairs?"

"No," I said, sighing. "I'll take the kids to Lena's for a while."

I didn't really want to leave, but I felt they'd be able to really talk without any distractions if the kids weren't there.

"Don't leave your house on my account," Lily said with genuine concern.

"It's fine," I told her, but I needed Emmy out of the room if only for a minute. "Baby, can you run upstairs and get Kaitlyn's diaper bag? And make sure Lucas goes to the bathroom. Once he starts playing over at Lena's, he doesn't stop, not even to pee."

Emmy got up. She looked at us like she knew something was up that we weren't telling her, but she continued on into the family room. I waited until after she was walking a whiney Lucas up the stairs before I spoke to Lily.

"Is the baby his?" I nodded at her belly. "Is it Kyle's?"

"Yes," she answered softly.

"Where is he? He did something, didn't he?" Of course he did something. If he didn't do anything, Lily wouldn't have been in my kitchen, knocked up and waiting to talk to Emmy alone.

"He's in London."

"What are you about to drag my wife into, Lily?"

"I'm not dragging her into anything. I have no one else to talk to about this, no one who understands him like Emmy does."

Though I knew it was probably true, I didn't like hearing it. I hated knowing Emmy was so intimately knowledgeable about Kyle.

"If he's gone, then maybe he actually did something right for a change," I said icily. "What happened to my wife could easily happen to you and your baby."

She was resolute. "I'm not going to argue with you about that, Luke. I don't believe he ever meant to hurt Emmy, and I sure as hell know he won't hurt me that way, but you have a right to feel how you want about it. I may even feel the same if I was in your shoes, but I don't want to hear it, do you understand? This is his child I am carrying." She gestured toward her belly. "Not someone else's. I can't just walk away. I need to know what Emmy thinks, what she would do if she had all the facts I have."

"That's what I'm worried about, Lily," I said darkly. I heard Emmy and Lucas descending the stairs behind me, but I asked a question I knew I wouldn't get an immediate answer to. "What will she do when she has all the facts?"

Emmy and Lucas stepped into the kitchen. I turned around and smiled at them as best I could. Now I was back to pretend smiles.

"Thanks, baby." I gave her a brief kiss as I took the diaper bag from her.

She looked at me as if she knew I was pretend smiling. "What's wrong?"

"Nothing." I took Lucas's hand in mine. "Let's get Kay Kay in her seat, buddy."

"I'll help you get them in the car."

"I got it, honey. Relax." When she looked at me with worried eyes, I gave her a reassuring smile, though I kind of needed someone to reassure me.

I got the kids packed up in the car a few minutes later and headed toward my sister's. I had a strong feeling our movie night with popcorn was canceled.

****

256

There comes a time in a man's life when he has to stop running to his sister's house for hot chocolate and cookies whenever life went awry. That time came for me when I got married. I didn't even talk to Lena after the Iris incident. I wanted to, because I was used to going to my sister with my problems, but I was a grown-ass man, and I had come to the realization that Lena never discussed her personal marital issues with me, and I wasn't naïve enough to believe she didn't have some of her own. My marriage was with Emmy, and no matter how wise I thought Lena was, in the end, it was just me and Emmy. Not me, Emmy, and Lena.

So, when I got to her house I didn't mention Lily. When she asked me why I was there, I told her Emmy was busy at the house and I wanted to get the kids out of her way. When she asked me how things were going, just a normal everyday question, I told her things were fine and didn't mention our recent issues at all. I was all about pretending again. Lena could see through me like streak-free glass on a sunny day, but she seemed to respect my lack of communion.

I tried not to think too much about what was happening at my home. Lily was determined to talk to Emmy and I worried she'd evoke memories and emotions Em had finally put to rest some time ago. We just eradicated the Iris ghost. We didn't need a Kyle ghost, too.

After an hour, the kids and I stopped at Emmet and Casey's. I didn't spend a lot of time with my brother-in-law outside of work, a problem I planned to rectify. He was a good guy, a great dad and husband, and a brilliant attorney. Outside of that, I didn't know too much about him. Before leaving, we made plans to get together for some drinks in the near future. He and Casey offered to keep Lucas for a little while since he had so much fun with Owen. I let him stay since our day was already ruined, and honestly, I didn't know what I would be going home to.

I was relieved not to see Lily's rental car on the street when I got home. I took Kaitlyn in the house, calling Emmy's name. When we got into the kitchen, I immediately noticed the bottle of tequila on the counter. There was a significant amount missing. I scowled as I slammed open the cabinet door, slammed the bottle back inside and slammed the door shut. There weren't any regulations in our home about Emmy's right to drink; I knew what I was getting when I married her, but the disappearance of the tequila this time was a strong indication of her distress.

I had a very bad feeling Kyle Sterling had just entered my marriage.

And where the hell was she? Her disappearance nagged at me. Did she just pick up and run off with Lily to handle the Kyle problem?

"She wouldn't," I muttered as I shifted Kay Kay in my arms and hurried up the stairs.

I found Emmy up there, pacing our bedroom, with the tip of her thumb in her mouth as she nervously chewed on it.

"You got into the tequila."

"Yeah, but there's milk in the fridge and freezer," Em said dismissively.

"Why don't we just get this conversation done and over with." I growled and sat down on the edge of the bed with Kaitlyn.

"Where's Lucas?" She paused in her pacing, looked at me, and then at the doorway.

"We stopped at Emmet's and he wanted to stay there. They were okay with it. They'll bring him home in a couple of hours."

"Okay." She went back to pacing without answering my question.

I had tried to be very patient since Lily walked through our front door, but my patience was slipping at an alarming rate.

"Emmy," I said her name in warning.

She stopped pacing and looked at me. Her eyes were brimming with unshed tears and she looked like she was afraid to actually speak her mind, but she did.

"I have to help them," she said.

"Help who? Kyle and Lily? No the fuck way, Emmy!" I exploded.

I felt the baby jump in my arms and saw Emmy start as well. I felt guilty for scaring Kaitlyn. I didn't want her to see me as some kind of monster, so I tried to speak in a more even and controlled tone.

"Let them take care of their own problems. You don't need to be dragged into that shit."

"I told her to fight for him," she said just above a whisper, looking at the floor deep in a troubled thought. "But he should fight for her, too."

"Well, I'm fighting for you, and I want you to stay out of it." I got up.

I didn't see how Emmy getting involved with their problems could've had a good outcome for anyone, especially us.

"You don't have to fight for me, you already have me," Emmy said, frustrated.

I had no idea why the hell she was frustrated with me. I wasn't the one talking nonsense. That was all her.

"If you wanted to help, you should've told Lily to stay the hell away from that bastard. She could get the shit beaten out of her, too," I pointed out.

"He won't do that to her." Emmy waved a hand, dismissing the prospect. This pissed me off even further. There was probably a time she thought he wouldn't do it to her, too.

"The hell he won't!"

Her jaw set stubbornly. "He won't do that to her."

"How the hell do you know, Emmy?"

Her eyes closed and her hands balled up into fists, like she was trying not to punch me. Me instead of him. "I know you can't understand this, I know you can't, Luke, but I know he will not hurt her like that."

"Even if you're right, it's none of your business," I said acidly and with finality. I gave her one last look of irritation and started out of the room. I was going to say over my shoulder, "And we're having our fucking movie night and our fucking popcorn," but she spoke first and stopped me in my tracks.

"It *is* my business."

I turned slowly. Patience. Gone. Emmy still loved Kyle Sterling. She had admitted before that she would always care about him, and I learned to live with that. But now she was all but shouting her undying love for him and it sickened me and stabbed me in the heart.

"Why, Em? Why is it your business what happens between Lily and Kyle?"

"Until he knows I've forgiven him, truly forgiven him, he will never forgive himself, and he will never go back to her."

I moved toward her. Her eyes looked worried, but she didn't shrink back. She held her ground, even though I looked as pissed off as I felt. I was holding it again, trying not to yell at her.

"You forgive him? You forgive that asshole for what he did to you and Lucas? For what he could've done?"

She closed her eyes for a moment. "Yes, I do, and I know you can't understand that, either."

Damn right I couldn't understand it. I couldn't fathom it. He had beaten her. He could've killed her. He could've killed Lucas. He fucking broke her. And she was going to stand there and tell me she forgave him. Caring for and loving someone sometimes can't be helped. The human heart works strangely that way. But forgiveness is an act of free will. You can choose to forgive or to not.

She chose to forgive.

"Are you trying to just get back at me for what happened with Iris?" I asked her softly. Was that it? Was she just trying to hurt me as I had hurt her?

"I'm not trying to get back at you for what happened with Iris, I promise," she said, holding her hands together in a plea. "But I can't pretend Lily didn't come here today."

"I can," I snapped.

"You're not that heartless, Luke! You're not. You can't pretend you didn't see her round belly and you can't pretend everything is going to be okay for her without Kyle. You don't know the things she's been through in the past. She needs him."

My eyes closed. She was right. I had no idea what Lily had been through in her life, but I couldn't dismiss the deep pain that seemed to be engrained in her eyes. She put on a tough act, but something or someone long before Kyle had scarred her. I thought about Emmy and her scars. I may not be able to understand it, but Lily obviously thought enough of Kyle to come all the way to Chicago, and maybe she thought he was the salve that could heal her. I disagreed. I believed he would eventually break her as he had broken Emmy, but both women seemed to see something I couldn't. Maybe because it wasn't there.

Lily was pregnant with Kyle's baby, and she looked like she needed him. I didn't know what had happened between them, and I still didn't think it was Emmy's place to get involved, but if the roles were reversed and I needed Emmy, and Kyle was the one who could give her to me, I would've jumped at the opportunity.

"What can you possibly do to help them?" I found myself saying.

We stared at one another for a long time. I had to brace myself, because Emmy was about to do something I didn't want her to do, but I couldn't lock her up and hold her back. I had to reach deep and trust that she would act rationally. I had to believe she loved our family and would do nothing to jeopardize it.

"I made a few phone calls and tracked Kyle down," Emmy said. "He's not in London like Lily thought. He's in Philly, but she doesn't know that yet."

"Okay," I said, feeling more and more uneasy.

She walked over to me and held out her hands for Kaitlyn, who had started to get a little cranky. I passed her the baby and ran downstairs for a bottle. When I returned, Emmy and Kaitlyn were on the bed. Handing Em the bottle, I sat down beside them and waited for the bombshell I knew she was about to drop.

"I'm going to Philly," she said quickly and then looked at me for my response.

I knew she wasn't going to Philly for a cheesesteak or to visit her old friends. She was going for Kyle. I wasn't surprised, not really, but it still hit me hard, and it showed.

Emmy reached for me and gently rubbed my cheek with the back of her fingers.

"I love you. You have to trust me."

"I trust you, Em," I said, my voice hoarse. "But it's very easy to find yourself standing on the wrong side of the line without ever meaning to cross it." This wasn't the first time Donya's words had slapped me or Emmy in the face.

One single tear escaped from her eye. "We are both painfully aware of that fact, Luke," she whispered. She turned her attention back to Kaitlyn and adjusted her hold on her while I sat there with my head hung and my regrets bouncing off the bedroom walls.

"I won't stay long," she said softly, running her hand lovingly over Kaitlyn's head. "Lily's baby needs her father, and...I think once Kyle gets over our past, he and Lily can be very happy together." She smiled, but the smile was sad. "I am two hundred percent sure he loves her far more than he has ever loved me."

She looked back at me. "You believed I was worth fixing, Luke. Even after I kept Lucas from you and broke your heart. You're a man of the law. You have represented criminals before. Did you believe they were worthy of being redeemed?"

This wasn't fair for her to use my work against me. I defended them with a personal detachment. They weren't the woman I loved or the man who had broken her.

"I believed under the care of the legal system they could be redeemed," I answered evasively.

She cocked her head to the side. "There is more to redemption than a stint behind bars and you know it," she said. "You know redemption is deeper than that. Redemption isn't serving your time without trouble. Redemption is coming to your senses and seeing clearly the people you have hurt and feeling deep regret and giving up anything and everything to take back what you have done. You point no fingers, you make no excuses, but you take on the entire weight of the pain you have caused, even if it means it will crush you. That's redemption," she finished sharply.

I hated Kyle Sterling, but my wife was…amazing. Her words penetrated me to the core. Not because I felt Kyle Sterling was worthy of redemption, but because I knew Emmy had spoken from experience, and she had been redeemed. I knew she was stronger than ever before and levelheaded, and she knew her heart. She would not stray.

But still…

"Is there anything I can say to make you change your mind?" I asked her.

"If you told me not to go, I wouldn't," she said carefully. "I respect you, Luke, but I'm hoping you won't do that."

And there it is. The final decision was left in my hands. Deciding what to do with it was another story.

Chapter Thirty-Two

Of course I let her go. I didn't have to like it, and though I trusted Emmy, I was on edge the moment she stepped through security at the airport and out of my reach. I had vowed to never let her go anywhere without me again, but there she was, walking away from me to go save Kyle Sterling from himself.

I went home to my kids. Diana was kind enough to show up in the morning so I could take Emmy to the airport. It was still fairly early when I returned. Lucas was asleep, but Kaitlyn was up and ready for the day to start, at least for a couple hours before she would be ready for one of many naps. I needed a nap myself. I must've looked as tired as I felt, because Diana told me to go to bed and said she'd stay with the kids a few more hours.

"I owe you big time," I said as I trudged up the stairs.

"You sure do."

I kicked my shoes off and fell into bed fully clothed. Emmy and I hardly slept at all during the night. After the kids were in bed, we sat up talking. She gave me a background story on Lily that left me cringing for the woman. She shouldn't have driven all the way out here by herself so far in her pregnancy considering her past history. She had apparently lost a baby around the same time many years ago. I hardly knew Lily and even tried to pretend her problems didn't matter, but like Emmy said, I wasn't that heartless.

When Emmy had started to tell me what she had learned about Kyle, I stopped her. I didn't want to know about his childhood and his mommy and daddy issues, and I didn't think it was my place to know. I understood why Lily felt the need to tell Emmy, but I didn't need to know. I did ask her why Kyle left Lily, however. That was unacceptable. I didn't expect him to stay with her if he didn't really want her, but he should've been around for his child. Period. When Emmy told me Kyle had sought out and then seen pictures and video of what he had done to her, and that it "undid" him, I was…shaken…into silence.

I always thought Kyle never really took full responsibility for his actions. I truly believed he was much more aware of what he was doing when he did it than he claimed. When he met me at the muffin shop and tried to get me to beat the shit out of him, I still didn't think he was taking full responsibility. I strongly believed he only tried to ease his conscience. I could argue he sought out the photos and video because he was a sadist, but even I wouldn't go so far as to make that claim. Despite how I felt about it, I really believed he loved Emmy, and even though he had hurt her, I couldn't see him wanting to sit down and relive the experience.

I'm not a professional psychiatric profiler. I could not say for sure that Kyle Sterling wasn't a crazy son of a bitch who got off on hurting women, but as far as I knew, before Emmy, he'd hurt no one and no one after her. I was forced to believe he truly did not remember very much about that night, that he really had been in a drug induced rage that blacked out any reasonableness. I was forced to believe he hadn't meant to break Emmy's wrist in Miami, and I had to believe he hadn't meant to beat her.

I am not a naturally ignorant man. I sometimes purposely blind myself to things I don't want to see and deafen my ears to words I don't want to hear, but that is willful ignorance. Though my education did not focus on drugs and the chemical reactions it causes in the brain and body, I know many drugs alter the mind so significantly a person can go from normal to monster in less than sixty seconds. Finally, I gave him a little bit of credit. He had not hurt Emmy on purpose, and I had to give him credit for seeking out the evidence of what he had done. I wasn't the one who had done the damage, but it made me want to vomit to even consider seeing that proof. I felt sickened in the past for causing emotional damage. I couldn't imagine how it must've felt for Kyle to know what he knew or see what he had seen. He must've feared he would do the same to Lily, and left to protect her and the baby.

With that said, I didn't then, and I do not now, forgive him. He still had choices before he ever laid a hand on Emmy. He could've chosen not to do drugs. He could've chosen rehab. There were probably more choices he could've made that I am unaware of. I had a better understanding of the circumstance, but I did not take away his accountability. His breaking of Emmy was not just physical, but emotional and mental and reached deep into her soul. He could've chosen to leave her alone before their relationship ever began, but then there were many choices I could've made, too, regarding Emmy…

But, as Emmy would say, it is what it is. We had each other and two perfect children. I wasn't sure if any altering in our past decisions would've led us to the current life we shared. If we had to go through all of it again to reach our pre-Iris days, I wouldn't change a thing.

I went to sleep with Emmy's soft scent on my pillow. I felt uneasy, but I trusted her. One hundred percent.

****

"There's a problem," Emmy said in a hushed tone.

I sucked in a large amount of air into my lungs as my uneasiness nearly exploded.

It was a little before noon in Chicago, nearly one there in Philly. I had stayed in bed until about ten. I woke up briefly when Emmy called to tell me she had landed and was on her way to Kyle's. I had to swallow the nervousness I felt about what she was about to do, but I didn't keep her on the phone to make her second guess herself. I forced myself to sleep again, though I kept waking up until I gave up. I had relieved Diana and was fixing lunch for Lucas while Kaitlyn napped when Emmy called.

When she said there was a problem, I almost dropped the knife I was holding to make Lucas a peanut butter sandwich. Had I done the wrong thing by letting her go? All kinds of unimaginable ideas rushed through my head.

"What's the problem?" I asked after some hesitation.

"Hold on," she murmured and I heard a muffled brief conversation and movement. The background noise changed, seemed a little bit louder, as if she had moved from inside to outside.

"Where are you?" I tried to concentrate on finishing the peanut butter sandwich.

"I'm at Lily's bar—or diner—pub—whatever, but she's missing, Luke." I heard her shuddering sigh. "I don't have a lot of time to talk. Vic took her. He just took her," she said and sounded close to panic, which made me panic. I had no idea who the hell Vic was or why he took Lily, but if it made Emmy panic, then I knew it was a serious situation.

"Emmy, what…" I didn't know what questions to ask. "Was she taken or did she just…leave?"

"Listen to me," she cried out. I heard her take a deep breath and then her words were hurried. "Vic used to work in my bar. He was obsessed with Lily. She stopped here for some reason this morning, but Vic had broken in and then he took her and I think I know where he took her. I think she's in labor, Luke. She grabbed her belly like she was in pain right before he took her. We're going to go find her. We're leaving in couple of minutes."

"You're not going anywhere!" I said much louder than I meant to. Kaitlyn startled awake and began crying and Lucas looked at me worriedly.

"I can't let him go alone. He won't behave reasonably and he'll kill Vic and then he'll go to prison and then my trip would've been for nothing."

"Let someone else go with him, Emmy," I said firmly. "You're walking into a dangerous situation. Let the police handle this."

"We're working on that, but it turns out that's more complicated than you would think," she said bitterly. "I'm going with him."

"I am telling you no," I said as I violently cut the sandwich up into four pieces.

There was a moment of silence on the other end. I poured Lucas a cup of milk and sat it in front of him at the table. I ruffled his hair and forced a smile for him so he would relax some. I picked Kaitlyn up in my arms and rocked her.

"I...I can't just walk away."

"You can get hurt!" My shouting didn't help to settle my kids. "If he ever really loved you, Emmy, he wouldn't let you go with him."

"He's already tried to stop me," she said irritably.

"Good! Finally, he's done something that makes sense!"

"Luke." Emmy said my name with a loud sigh. "I love you and I respect you, as I said last night, but I'm going."

"Dammit, Emmy! I would've been better off if you didn't call me and tell me you're willingly walking your ass into danger."

"Stop cursing in front of the kids," she said softly. "Kyle's coming. I have to go. Calm down. You're scaring the baby."

"Is there anything I can say to stop you?" I pleaded.

"No," she said sadly. "Not on this. Don't worry. I'll be fine. He won't let anything bad happen to me."

"He let something bad happen to her," I spat.

I heard a muffled conversation again and then Emmy said, "I love you. I'll call you soon."

"I love you, too," I said grudgingly. "If you get hurt or killed, there isn't anything in this world that will protect Kyle Sterling from me."

"I would expect no less," she said, and then the line went dead.

****

Before we moved into our house, I had a sound system installed. Whatever music I turned on in the living room could be heard throughout the house. Em and I liked to argue over what playlist to play. After many arguments and physical wrestling matches over whose iPod should be docked to the sound system, together we put together one long playlist full of songs we agreed upon. We named the playlist "LukeEm." I was listening to the playlist a few hours after she announced she was running head first into danger. I had Kaitlyn strapped to me in a baby harness as Lucas helped me move laundry out of the washer and into the dryer. He dropped more than a few pieces on the floor in the process, but he was having such a good time doing it, I didn't have the heart to stop him.

I was glad both kids were awake to keep me distracted. When they'd both been napping, I couldn't stop looking at my phone to see if Em had called or texted without me hearing it. I paced the entire first floor, worrying myself to the point of having chest pain. Eventually, I found things that needed to be done. I cleaned all three bathrooms and all the windows on the first floor. I started a load of laundry. I dusted and changed the sheets on our bed. By the time the second load of laundry was ready to go into the dryer, Lucas and Kaitlyn were both awake. Just in time, too, because I was on the brink of going crazy from my wandering thoughts and worries.

"Airs Mommy?" Lucas asked as we sat in the living room folding clothes

"Being a hero," I muttered.

267

Lucas scratched his head as he looked at me. He had no idea what the hell I was talking about.

"Mommy will be back soon, buddy," I said and kissed his forehead.

"Kay Kay pwetty," he said, looking at his sister. Quickly, he forgot about his mom, confident, no doubt, that she'd be home soon like I said.

"Yes, Kay Kay is pretty," I agreed and tickled my daughter.

After the laundry was folded, I put Kaitlyn in her stroller and made Lucas hold on to it as we took a short walk around the block. We stopped and talked to a couple of neighbors. I did my best to just enjoy the conversations, the nice day, the kids, and ignore the phone in my back pocket that wasn't ringing or dinging.

I grew more and more worried as time went on, but I was also angry. Emmy knew I was worried. She should've at least been sending me text messages so I knew she was okay, but I hadn't received anything. I wanted to give her the space and time she wanted and needed, but my patience was thin and I was sick of worrying about her. I was just about to call her and give her a hard time when my phone rang. It wasn't Emmy's number, but it was an unfamiliar Pennsylvania number.

My gut twisted in fear and my mouth went dry. Lucas was on the family room floor playing with his cars again and Kaitlyn was in her pack and play holding Lucas's stuffed whale. I tried not to imagine that the worst possible thing could've happened to their mother and that this was a phone call confirming it.

"Hello?" I answered cautiously.

"Hey," Emmy's voice floated over the line and I bent over with my head in my hand as I breathed a huge sigh of relief.

"I was so worried about you," I said, my voice tight with emotion.

"I'm so sorry." I heard the weariness in her voice. "My phone was in Kyle's car when we got there, but then I was locked in a police car and—"

"Wait wait wait." I interrupted. "Why were you in the back of a police car?"

"The police met us there. I tried to follow Kyle closer to the house, but he convinced an officer to lock me in the back of his police cruiser for my own safety," she said with disdain. "Then with all the commotion, they forgot about me for a while."

I was glad Kyle made that decision for her. If I knew Emmy at all, she didn't go easily into the back of that car.

"How's Lily? Is she okay?"

"Well, he didn't really hurt her I don't think, but she was in preterm labor like I suspected. Amazingly, the doctors were able to stop it, but she has to be on complete bed rest for the rest of her pregnancy."

I genuinely felt a measure of relief for Lily. "I'm glad she's okay. You'll have to tell me everything when you get home and not so rushed."

"I'd rather tell you now and just move on when I get home. I'm not ready to hang up with you yet. How are my babies?"

I blew out a relieved sigh and talked about the kids for a little while. Once Emmy was convinced the kids were okay and I managed to keep them alive, healthy, and happy in her absence, she told me the whole story about Vic and Lily, filling in the big gaps that she had left me with earlier in the day. We discussed the legal ramifications of Vic's options, and we both agreed the whole day had just been unreal.

"So, did you accomplish what you went there to do?" I asked carefully.

"I did. I had to throw a spatula at his head and attack him, but eventually he listened to me."

I wanted to chuckle, imagining Emmy jumping on Kyle with fury, but then I knew that meant she'd touched him. If he was like any other man, having an attractive woman who you happen to love attack you is very much a turn on. I could imagine Emmy's eyes flashing with anger before hurling herself onto him. I wondered if he just shrugged her off or if he tried to hold her arms in an effort to keep her from beating the crap out of him. I would have wanted to take advantage of her in that pinned position and figured he had too.

"I don't want to ask certain questions because in my heart I trust you," I said, sitting back on the couch with a sigh.

I heard a soft expel of breath on the other end of the line. "What do you want to know?"

Once upon a time I didn't ask the right questions. Once upon a time, Emmy didn't offer up any information. Hearts were broken.

Lives were altered. I trusted Emmy, but that didn't mean I had to be a fool.

"Did you cross any lines, Emmy?"

"Depends on what lines you're talking about, Luke. I held his hand while we talked and again in the car. He occasionally touched my hair. I hugged him and I cried with him."

Thinking about Kyle and his tainted tears touching her made my skin crawl, but I sucked back that comment and instead asked, "How do you feel?"

She expelled a soft breath and spoke just above a whisper. "I feel drained. And…a little sad. I can't deny that. But I'm sure Kyle and Lily are going to be great, better than great, and that's why I came here, right? They're each where they belong. Now I'm ready to go home, back to you and the kids, because that's where I belong. That's where I'm better than great."

A pressure in my heart eased. "Here is where you are perfect."

"I am only a reflection of my other half," she said, her voice trembling slightly.

I gripped the phone tightly. "Come home."

"I'll be there as soon as I can."

Chapter Thirty-Three

Emmy lied to me. She said she couldn't get a flight home before the morning, but as I walked through the house later that night turning off the lights, I heard a car door slam and the hum of an engine. I ignored it, believing it was one of my neighbors, because Emmy had sworn hours ago she couldn't get home before ten in the morning. I didn't know how I'd sleep without her in our bed. I was tired, but I didn't want to go lay in that bed alone. I'd see her in less than twelve hours, but that wasn't close enough. She wasn't close enough.

I turned off the lights in the kitchen and the family room. The darkness was interrupted by soft automatic lighting that fizzed to life only when darkness fell. Emmy hated total darkness. She said she's run into enough pieces of furniture to learn her lesson.

I walked down the short hallway toward the front door, choosing to take the front stairway to the second floor so I could double check the locks on the door on my way, when I heard a soft click as the deadbolt on the front door released. I stopped where I was, waiting to see who came through the door, knowing damn well no one should be coming through that door at nearly midnight. My sisters were not in the habit of dropping by after a certain time of night, and they'd call first. The only other person with a key besides Emmy and me was Sam, and I knew for a fact she was in Louisiana.

The door opened and Emmy stepped inside. I don't remember moving. I just remember feeling her weight in my arms as I slammed her against the door in a brutal kiss. She grunted from the force, but wrapped herself around my body, hands on the back of my head and legs locked around my waist. I crushed my body against hers, grinding my sudden erection into her as I devoured her lips and tongue.

I wrapped her pony tail around my hand and yanked her head to one side and tasted her neck with licks and bites as I growled with pleasure.

"You lied," I rumbled against her smooth skin. "You said you wouldn't be home until late morning."

I took her mouth again before she could respond. Using the door for leverage, I held her against it and palmed her breast through her blouse. Emmy moaned and her legs tightened around my waist as the friction between our clothed sex organs increased. Using her hair as a handle, I tilted her head up and kissed her delicate throat. When she spoke, her voice vibrated against my lips and I growled some more.

"After I left the hospital…ohhhhh…" Her fingers laced in my hair. "Kyle made quick work of chartering a plane for me." Groaning, she continued. "He thought I should be home with my husband after the long day I had. I wanted to surprise you."

I kissed her again, but only momentarily. I pulled away far enough to force her out of her jacket and pull her shirt over her head. I had no patience for her bra and tore it off.

"You should probably leave my boobs alone unless you want to get messy and weird kinky," Emmy said quickly as I palmed her bare breasts.

"I don't care about messy or kinky, baby," I groaned as I nipped at her shoulder. "I just want to touch and kiss you all over your perfect body."

I struggled briefly to release the button on her jeans. I nudged her to put her feet down on the floor and she complied. I dropped to my knees and started pulling her sneakers off.

"Umm," she said when I got the second shoe off and started yanking down her jeans and panties.

"What?" I wasn't really in the mood for talking.

"I've been in the same clothes for almost twenty-four hours. I kind of want to shower before you start licking things."

"Why take a shower now when you will need a shower when I'm finished with you?"

Her body trembled slightly from my words, and despite her protests, she compliantly stepped out of her bottoms. When I went to pull one of her legs onto my shoulder, she stopped me.

"Seriously, Luke." She laughed nervously. "I'm all sweaty and icky."

"Not yet you're not," I promised her.

Before she could say anything else I dragged my tongue from her entrance to her clit. Emmy shuddered and groaned and pressed her sex against my face. She tasted better than I ever remember her tasting. I dipped my tongue inside her and began to fuck her with it. She moved her hips in rhythm to my motions. Suddenly, she was

272

crying out my name and holding my head in place as she came. I groaned deeply as her juices spilled over my tongue.

She started to remove her leg from my shoulder, but I stopped her.

"I'm not finished with my late night snack yet," I murmured and found her clit with my tongue.

I flicked my tongue repeatedly over the little nub. Emmy's head was thrown back against the door as she simultaneously tried to wriggle away and pull harder on my head. Despite her warnings, I reached up with one hand and rolled one of her nipples between my fingers until she bucked against me and shouted obscenities.

I gave her a few good licks to get as much of her nectar as I could before I released her leg and stood up. I kissed her as I tugged on my lounge pants, making my erection spring free and land on her belly. My pants pooled at my feet where I promptly kicked them away.

"I need you," I said heavily. "Now."

I kissed her as I lifted her off the floor. Her legs wrapped around me once again and without any further teasing or testing, I thrust into her hard, slamming her back against the door. Emmy's fingernails dug into my shoulders as she gritted her teeth to keep from screaming. I groaned loudly as I desperately tried to wriggle myself deeper.

"I'm going to make you scream my name."

"Stop talking about it and do it." Emmy growled, tugging my bottom lip between her teeth.

I snarled and thrust into her so hard we both screamed. Never separating from her, I carried her into the formal living room and laid her down on the fancy couch. With her thighs spread wide, I looked at my cock buried in her. Her wet pussy gripped at my member. It looked obscene, my wide cock stretching her tight walls. I pulled out until I was barely inside her, looked into her eyes, and then slammed into her so hard her head hit the arm of the couch. My hands gripped her hips until I was buried deeply in her once again. Holding her tightly, I started riding her hard and deep, making her face twist into agonizing pleasure.

Soft yet firm, curvy, and lively, her warm body felt so perfect under my own. With every stroke, every kiss, and every touch, she responded, moaning, whimpering, and raising her hips to meet mine.

When she screamed my name as I knew she would, she fell apart under me, thrashing and writhing and sobbing.

I pulled out of her perfect pussy and straddled her chest with my throbbing cock at her lips.

"Suck your come off my cock, Emmy," I commanded.

She looked at me with fiery eyes and parted her lips. I licked my own as I slowly pushed into her mouth.

"Oh shit…" I groaned. "That's it, baby. Take it."

Her fingers gripped at my ass, pulling me deeper in. Her eyes were large and she struggled to breathe, but she pulled me farther still. I felt her gagging around my cock, but she didn't stop until— holy shit—she'd taken me to the hilt. If I had the right view, I'd probably be able to see her throat stuffed full of my dick.

Groaning and growling, I pulled out and pushed my way back in.

"Oh, Emmy," I panted out as I held my cock within her mouth.

When I pulled out again, she eagerly said, "Fuck my mouth. Fuck it hard and fast."

She didn't have to tell me twice.

I rammed my cock into her sweet little mouth until my balls were pressed hard against her chin. As I pulled out, Emmy gagged and her eyes teared. I started to pull away altogether, but she grabbed my ass again.

"I said to fuck my mouth!"

I shoved my dick back into her mouth and didn't stop. I did what she told me to do, listening to her grunts and the wet sounds my cock made in her wet mouth. I looked over my shoulder and saw one of Emmy's hands busy rubbing her clit. When she slipped a finger inside her cunt, I was ready to explode. As gorgeous and perfect as her mouth was, I didn't want to come down her throat. I wanted to come inside her pussy. I pulled out of her mouth with a loud slurping noise and a moment later, I slammed into her. We both shouted and growled incomprehensible things as we came together.

Exhausted, I collapsed on top of her and rested my head in the crook of her neck.

"A simple hello would've done just as well," Emmy teased, her voice hoarse.

"I had to show you how much I missed you."

"You missed me a whole lot."

"Yeah, and you better have missed me just as much." I nipped at her skin.

"Maybe I missed you more," she said, trailing her fingers over my back.

"I am a fine specimen," I said haughtily. "I can't blame you for missing me."

Emmy pinched me under my arm and I jumped.

"Shit that hurts!"

"Good!"

I could've pinched her back, but I gained much more pleasure from kissing her. And I did just that until we were both panting for air again.

Chapter Thirty-Four

The firm was exploding—we would soon need to move into a bigger office to accommodate our growth. Things had begun to get cramped. It was a complete one-eighty from what it was a year ago, and though we were all very good at our jobs, we had to give a significant amount of credit to Emmy for getting us rolling in the right direction. Only a couple of days after her return from Pennsylvania, I had to ask her to come in and work a few hours. We needed to stay organized and stay on track.

Emmy came in at ten that morning after leaving the kids with Lena. She had stopped at her new favorite bakery and picked up a few dozen gourmet cupcakes. She looked so pretty in her yellow blouse, white skirt, and black heels, laughing and smiling with a few of the girls in the office. I'd just stepped out to get a file, but I stopped to look at my beautiful, hot wife. She noticed me watching her and winked at me. The girls around her giggled, and I took that as a cue to go back to my office.

I was almost afraid to admit how happy I was—and I was disgustingly happy. Every time I seemed to acknowledge my happiness, something happened to challenge that claim. This time would be no different.

Emmy walked in carrying a cupcake and a cup of coffee for me. I hadn't asked her for the cupcake or the coffee, but being the most perfect wife ever, she had anticipated my wants and needs before I had to voice them.

"Thank you, beautiful," I said when she put the items down on my desk. She leaned over and gave me a brief kiss.

"You're very welcome, handsome."

"We have to start looking for a bigger office," I said, distracted as I looked over the papers in front of me.

"You may not have to look too far," Emmy said casually.

"Mmm," I murmured, not really thinking about what she said.

My phone buzzed on my desk.

"Yes?" I said to Kacey.

"Vivian Deluca is here," she said and sounded just as surprised as I felt. Vivian always preferred meeting on mutual grounds—at pubs and restaurants, not in my office, and never in her office. I didn't even think we had any cases in common at the moment, at least nothing that would warrant her showing up in my office.

"Let her in," I said.

Emmy stood beside me, looking at me curiously. "Who's here?"

"Vivian Deluca."

Her eyes widened. "*The* Vivian Deluca?"

I nodded. Before we had any further opportunity to ponder what the devil wanted, she walked into my office as if it was her own. That was Vivian. Her unrelenting confidence gave the impression she took over whatever room she entered.

She was smiling. A lot. I tried hard not to shift with discomfort in my chair. Her big, delighted smile was unnerving.

"Well, isn't this a surprise," I said coolly.

"And a delight?" she asked, cocking one eyebrow as she stood on the other side of my desk with one hand on her hip.

"Let's not get carried away with lies and misconceptions, Vivian. You must have a huge knife in that purse of yours."

"Why would you suggest such a thing, Luke?" She feigned shock.

"Because the only time you're this happy is when you've drawn blood. I'm assuming you're about to spill some of mine. Which vein would you prefer?" I offered up my wrists. When she snickered, I turned my head and offered her my jugular.

"Oh, Luke." She smirked. "Why don't you introduce me to your wife?" She looked at Emmy for the first time.

"Emmy Kessler, this is Vivian Deluca—AKA the beast, or the bitch. Whichever suits her for the day."

"Don't forget the heart eating bitch," Vivian chimed in with a wink.

I glowered at her as she reached across the desk to shake Emmy's hand.

"I am so delighted to finally meet you, Esmeralda Kessler," Viv said.

I turned my head to the side as the pair continued to shake hands. I'd never mentioned Emmy's full name. It hit me just as she passed Emmy an envelope.

"You've been served, Mrs. Kessler," Vivian said cheerfully.

"Uh," Emmy said, dumbfounded, holding the envelope as if it were a bomb.

"What the hell is this about, Vivian?" I demanded, snatching the envelope from Emmy's hand. "And since when do you personally serve anyone? Don't you consider yourself above such things? Don't you have minions to do this for you?"

"Usually." She chuckled and then sat down in a chair. "But this was just too good to pass up."

I unfolded the documents that were in the envelope.

"You really are a heart eating bitch, aren't you?" Emmy asked conversationally.

"Oh, sweetheart." She laughed. "You don't know the half of it."

"What is it?" Emmy asked me, leaning over my shoulder. "I don't know who would be taking me to court."

"Iris," I growled out and tossed the papers on the desk.

"Oh, shit," she muttered.

I stood up and faced my wife who had taken several steps back.

"So, why would Iris be taking me to court?" She always had been terrible at playing dumb.

Vivian laughed. "Luke, you didn't know? Honestly?"

"Shut up, Vivian," I said in a dangerous tone as I walked toward Emmy who shuffled away.

"Why is Iris taking me to court?" Emmy asked again as she moved away from me. I followed her patiently, unwilling to run around my office like a bunch of third graders with Vivian sitting in the middle instigating.

"Is that a cupcake from Carusos?" Vivian asked seriously. Out of the corner of my eye I saw her take my cupcake off my desk, along with my cup of coffee before settling back on the other side. "I adore a Carusos cupcake."

Emmy regarded Vivian with her eyebrows pulled down for a moment, but when she realized I was gaining on her, she scurried away.

"Apparently, you bought the building that houses her muffin book shop," I said to Emmy, as if she didn't already know. "Then you made a grand show of going into her shop to tell her you aren't renewing her month to month lease. She is claiming you harassed her and you're discriminating against her because of her age and because of her mental disease. Since her business was flourishing and she always paid her rent on time, it only makes your actions look less than honorable, and very possibly illegal!"

"I did nothing illegal," Emmy said stubbornly. And then she looked curious. "What mental disease? And how old is the bitch?"

"This cupcake is delicious," Vivian said as she chewed. "I tried one of Iris's muffins today. She makes one hell of a muffin."

"According to the paperwork, Iris is fifty-three," I told Emmy.

"Ew!" she cried, scrunching up her nose. "I heard her tell you she was forty-three."

"I guess she lied," I said dryly.

"What mental disease?" Emmy asked next.

"Bipolar disease," Vivian chirped in happily.

"I didn't know the Muffin Bitch was old," Emmy argued. "And I had no idea she was bipolar."

"She'll argue she told you. It will be her words against yours, the person who bought the building just to kick her out," Vivian said. "Damn, this cupcake is my favorite. Double chocolate?"

"You bought a building," I said in disbelief, shaking my head as I continued to follow her around the room. "Not just a little building, no. You bought a big ass corner building! Where did you get the money for that, Em? Hmm?"

"I used my own money," she snapped.

"Before we got married, we agreed you would not use your money except for maybe traveling back and forth to Louisiana. I don't remember saying it was okay to buy real estate!"

"It's my money!" she argued. "I should be able to buy the damn White House if I can afford to."

"Can you afford to?" Vivian asked curiously.

"No." Emmy shrugged. "But I can afford a hell of a lot. My money is just sitting in an account, growing. I'm not allowed to use it."

"Oh." Vivian laughed hard. "Luke, you're so damn honorable it's stifling"

"Shut up, Vivian." I growled. "As a matter of fact, get out, Vivian."

"I haven't finished my coffee yet. So, Emmy, this is off the record, but why exactly did you buy the building?"

"Don't answer that," I warned, but Emmy gave me a look of disdain.

"Iris almost destroyed my marriage," she said to Vivian, though she kept her eyes on me as we circled my desk and the chairs Vivian was seated in. "She threw herself onto Luke after she made such a big show to befriend me and my kids. I happened to walk in just before she kissed him."

"You're kidding me," Vivian said. "She failed to mention she had the hots for your husband."

"Luke and I have been through too much," Emmy said. I stopped moving and so did she. She eyed me warily. "It's taken us years to find our mutual happiness and Iris was all too willing to blow it up. She admitted to me she'd been lusting after him for months. I don't want that woman anywhere near my husband. Her stupid shop is too close for comfort."

"So, you bought it just so you could evict her?" I asked.

"Yes!"

"Oh, this is grand," Vivian said, getting to her feet. "Either way, Iris has a case."

Grudgingly, I nodded in agreement. Emmy looked irritated. She crossed her arms.

"I'm not backing down from this," she said to Vivian. "Besides, the building is a perfect location to move the firm into. So either way, that old muffin bitch has to go."

"Oh, I'm glad you're not backing down, Emmy." Vivian grinned. "I like a good fight, and I am guessing Luke is going to fight extra hard this time. Get all catty and show me his claws!" She growled and made a pawing motion in the air. I wanted to slap her, but I don't hit women.

"Get out," I told her sharply.

"Oh, I love it when you get bossy," Viv said, collecting her purse. She turned to Emmy and said, "I wish we could've met under better circumstances, Emmy. Honestly, I rather like you so far."

Emmy nodded as she regarded Vivian with deep thought. I didn't know what she was thinking. I imagined she thought about what a bitch Viv was and how fitting it was that she represented Iris.

Iris knew what she was doing by choosing my arch enemy as her lawyer. Well played.

"Did you sleep with my husband?" Emmy asked Vivian.

My jaw fell to the floor, but Vivian seemed unfazed.

"Yes," she said with a smile. "But that was a long time ago. Luke and I had a very nice no-strings-attached agreement, but he realized, very early on, that he was in love with you and broke it off so he could do the honorable thing. What gave it away?"

Emmy shrugged. "Woman's intuition. I feel like I should hate you, Vivian, but I rather like you also."

"Oh, come on!" I cried out. "You are forbidden to befriend her!"

Emmy looked at me dismissively and turned back to Vivian. "See you in court, Vivian."

"Oh, yes you will." She grinned. "But, Emmy, don't think because I like you I'll go easy on you."

"I'd expect nothing less from a heart eating bitch," Emmy said.

Vivian winked at me and walked out of my office. I looked at Emmy and resumed my pursuit of her. She began to move again, also.

"You are in so much trouble," I told her. "I can't believe you did that."

"I was only protecting what belongs to me," she said with a shrug. "I told Iris I would fight to the death rather than let someone destroy my family."

"Really."

"Really," she responded.

"Why are you running away, Emmy? You know I can catch you whenever I want."

"I would at least like to have the illusion I can get away."

I locked the door and looked at her. "You may as well forget all about that illusion."

I stalked toward her. She tried to move away again, but I caught her easily right in front of my desk. I pushed her against it. I put my hands flat on the surface on either side of her, trapping her. She swallowed audibly.

"You're in so much trouble," I told her again, my lips close to hers.

"I'd do it again if I was given the choice," she said. "That muffin bitch is lucky I didn't just kick her ass. Making her move out is easy."

I chuckled and pressed my erection against her. "You did all that for me?" I said.

"It was a lot of work," she admitted. "The owners didn't want to sell."

"I'll bet you dipped deeply into your money," I murmured as I inhaled the skin on her neck.

"Deep enough." She sighed with pleasure and tilted her head to give me better access.

My hands were on her thighs, hiking up her skirt. "How can I trust you not to dip into your money like that again, Emmy?"

"As long as there are no more Irises, I won't have a reason to," she said flatly.

"Touché, Mrs. Kessler."

"Iris and her old, dry vagina. Hitting that dry piece of ass would have been hazardous to your dick. Lord Jesus it's a fire," she said it like the infamous woman on YouTube.

I laughed as I rested my forehead on hers. "Do you mind not talking about Iris and her dry vagina? I'm trying to punish you for your actions. You're killing my hard-on."

She began to release the button and zipper on my pants as she looked up at me with a more somber expression.

"Are you really mad?" she asked quietly.

"I'm livid." I wasn't lying. I was pissed Emmy had spent probably a huge chunk of change on anything without discussing it with me. I'm the first to admit I can be very prideful. I'm the man, the husband, the father, and the head of my household and it is primarily my responsibility to care for my family on all levels, especially financially.

"I'm angry," I said after I felt her body slump, and she looked up at me with apologetic eyes. "But you did it to protect our family." I pushed a hand into her brown waves. "We are so lucky to have you, Emmy."

She smiled and drew me in for a soft, delicious kiss. I reached under her skirt and began to pull her panties down. She lifted her ass long enough for me to pull the fabric over her perfectly round cheeks. I pulled away from her mouth to remove the lacey scrap completely and then stepped between her open legs. I kissed her again.

"And," I added, smiling and speaking against her lips. "Imagining you walking into that shop, pissed off, protective and possessive and giving Iris her walking papers along with a piece of your mind is a major fucking turn on."

I kissed her without mercy, pouring all my love and desire for her into the kiss. Her sassy tongue challenged mine. Her saucy lips battled to dominate the kiss. Her smart-alecky mouth attempted to devour mine, but soon, she submitted and blissfully drowned in my kiss.

****

We walked into the house, singing a rock version of "The Wheels on the Bus." Lucas could really belt it out, but my air guitar solo was untouchable, and Kaitlyn's clapping blew other babies' clapping out of the water, because my kids are more awesome than other kids.

"Hello, wife," I said cheerfully and planted a wet and loud kiss on her cheek.

"Hello, husband and children," Emmy said, wiping away the moisture on her cheek.

"You don't wipe away the moisture when I—"

Emmy cut me off, placing her hand over my mouth. "Hey! There are children in the room."

"They don't know what I'm talking about," I said and wiggled my eyebrows suggestively at her.

Emmy rolled her eyes, but did nothing to hide the smile on her face before turning back to the dinner she was preparing.

"So, I'm Super Dad, and it's okay if you admit it out loud," I told her as I put a shopping bag on the table. "Not only did I take both kids out alone to the mall and the grocery store, but I didn't lose any of them or maim them. And I got all the groceries you put on the list and didn't give in to Lucas's breakdown in the checkout lane because he couldn't get candy."

Em turned back around and regarded me for a moment before looking at Lucas, who was busy running one of his cars over a kitchen chair.

"Lucas, baby, come here," Em said sweetly.

Lucas gave his car wings and made a 'vawooom' sound as he flew over to his mother. She smiled down at him and gently touched his face, swiping a finger under his bottom lip. She held the finger up for me to see. There was a dark smear on it. Em popped the finger in her mouth as she watched me through narrowed eyes.

"Chocolate," she said, putting her hand on her hip.

"I love you," I said, hoping that would sidetrack her. It didn't.

"You're such a sucker," she accused. "You give him everything he wants. Kaitlyn is going to have you wrapped around her finger."

I looked at my daughter and grinned.

"I'm already wrapped around her finger," I said and kissed her smiling face.

Em shook her head and started going through the grocery bag as she no doubt mentally checked off the items that had been on her list. She balled the bag up seeming satisfied.

"Good job, husband unit," she said smiling. "I'll let the chocolate incident slide this time. You may reclaim your Super Dad title."

"Oh, but there's more," I said dramatically as I took Kaitlyn out of her coat.

"Oh?" Em looked intrigued.

"Oh, yes, my dear, perfect wife." I reached into the diaper bag and produced an envelope. "I also stopped by the office to get secret mail."

"Secret mail?"

"Secret mail," I repeated. "I had it sent there so there'd be less of a chance of you getting to it before me."

"Getting to what exactly?" Emmy asked and crossed her arms.

"Why the secret mail, of course, my darling blossom."

She tried not to smile, but I could see it pulling on the edges of her pretty mouth.

She played along. "What is the secret mail, my handsome beau?"

"Why it is mail that is a great secret, my slightly dense beauty."

"You're killing me here."

I handed her the large envelope. She cocked an eyebrow at me. She seemed reluctant to open it.

"You may proceed, my luscious pumpkin."

"Your mood is downright giddy today," she murmured with a smile as she began to pull open the envelope.

"You make me giddy." I kissed the top of her head.

"Okay, let's see what this secret mail is." She breathed and reached into the envelope. She pulled out a folder. Her eyebrow raised again as she threw a glance at me. "A travel agency? This must be some kind of trick, because no one uses those anymore."

"Well, baby, you know I'm old fashioned. Open the folder."

Emmy laid the folder on the kitchen table and slowly opened it. I heard a light gasp. She glanced quickly at me before looking back to the contents of the folder.

"These are airline tickets," she whispered. "And villa reservations...for the Caribbean?" She looked up at me with wide eyes.

"Yes," I said quietly. "I thought it was about time we had our honeymoon—even though it's still a couple of months away. I know it's not even the most exotic place you have ever been, and you have been to more exciting places, but since we'll be leaving the kids in Louisiana with your parents, I thought we should be a little closer to home."

Emmy looked down at the tickets and the other traveling information. When she looked back up at me, she had tears in her eyes.

"Um," I said, feeling uneasy. I shifted Kaitlyn into my other arm. "I promise I'll take you anywhere else you'd like to go when the kids are older."

"This is...this is perfect, Luke." She smiled. "Anywhere you take me will be perfect as long as you're there."

She stood on her toes and kissed me slowly and sensually. If I didn't have one child in my arms and the other a couple of feet away, I would've done wicked things to her.

"There are children in the room, Mrs. Kessler," I admonished when she pulled away.

"The children will be napping soon, Mr. Kessler," she said in a sultry tone that made me almost drop the baby.

"Lucas, nap time!"

****

"I want to see you in this," I insisted to Emmy. I gave the hanger a shake for emphasis.

"I'm not wearing a bikini until my body is bikini ready," she said and shook her hanger for emphasis.

"Your body is more than ready for a bikini. In fact, I'd prefer no clothes at all on your body." I winked.

Emmy rolled her eyes. "You're the only person who would consider stuffing my muffin top into a bikini."

I possessively put my hand on her waist and firmly smoothed it over her hip and upper thigh before ending on her ass.

I leaned in close to her, my lips only centimeters from her lips, and said, "Every part of you is perfect, and I want you on display for my pleasure."

She shivered, touched her lips to mine for the briefest of seconds, and then she said in a soft, velvety voice, "I'm not wearing the bikini."

A grin slowly spread on my face. "So, you won't be wearing anything?"

She laughed softly. It sent fire up my spine and made my erection twitch in my jeans.

"I'll be wearing this tankini," she said flatly and then there was a hanger in my face.

Reluctantly, I hung the bikini back up on the rack. "You're really mean," I said with a pout.

Emmy laughed again, and to my surprise, reached past me and plucked the bikini off the rack.

"You're so cute when you pout. I'll buy both, okay?"

I grinned and kissed her. "Thank you."

"Cwacka!" Lucas shouted from the double stroller. I fished into the diaper bag and produced a couple of graham crackers for him. "Danku."

"You're welcome," I said, ruffling his hair.

"Don't forget, we're getting Diana a gift card so she can shop for her spring break clothes," Emmy said to me.

I nodded, acknowledging I'd heard her. We gifted Diana a trip to Miami Beach for spring break so she could join her friends and escape the brisk Chicago weather. As expected, she tried to reject the gift, but my wife had been very convincing.

We were at the mall, shopping for our honeymoon trip. When Emmy first opened the envelope, it felt like the trip was too far away, but before we knew it, weeks had flown by and we would be leaving in a few days.

I took off most of January. Emmy and I were married for almost a year already. Considering all we had gone through before getting married and then the struggles afterward, I wanted to give her and the kids my undivided attention for a little while. We'd drop the kids off with Emmy's parents and then fly to our honeymoon destination. After five days alone, the plan was to go back to Louisiana and spend a week with Emmy's family. If we weren't snowed out of Chicago by then, we would return home. I had some small projects to do around the house during my time off, and I was going to spend a lot of time with my kids and drool after my wife until she got tired of me. It'd be a great month. As long as Vivian didn't show up.

Vivian did something so utterly terrifying it still brings fear into my heart when I think about it. She convinced Iris to drop her case against Emmy and called it a no-strings-attached favor. I commanded Emmy not to take it, reminding her the beast bites when one least expects it, but my wife simply rolled her eyes and then had the nerve to make lunch plans with Vivian. If she got bit, I was not licking her wounds for her. Well. Maybe I'd lick her.

Emmy and Vivian formed an unlikely friendship. I often made remarks regarding Viv's evilness, but secretly, I really didn't mind the alliance. Vivian was a hardcore family woman after her divorce, taking on the smaller cases often so she wouldn't have to spend too much time away from her children. I appreciated that about her. She was more than capable of handling enormous, noteworthy cases, but she humbly took on only what would keep her schedule open for her family. She and Em had a lot in common. Emmy really appreciated Vivian's blunt honesty. She said she'd never have to worry about Vivian turning into an Iris because Vivian was so very straight forward, and it helped that we openly hated each other.

Two months after Emmy sneakily bought the building that housed Iris's muffin shop, renovations began in the building to accommodate Kessler and Keane. There were a few other smaller businesses inside the building, but they were mostly unaffected by our move. An accountant was asked to move his office to where Iris's shop had been, and he readily agreed. He got a bigger space for the same money and in a prime position for foot traffic. By the time I went back to work, the renovations would be nearly complete and we would be able to start moving everything over. I felt bad leaving Steve and the staff to pack up, but Steve reminded me he would soon be going away for several weeks himself and he wasn't going to feel bad about it.

"Luke?" a soft, feminine voice that wasn't Emmy's called my name, shaking me from my thoughts.

We were in the mall just after Christmas. We could've run into any number of people we knew—my own family, neighbors, clients, and friends. But she wasn't any of those people, though she used to be a friend.

I looked to my left and met Claire's eyes.

"Claire," I said coolly and took a moment to look at the child in her arms. Though the DNA results had ruled me out as the baby girl's father, I still had to look her over to make sure there were no identifying resemblances. There weren't. Red hair and green eyes.

"Hello," Emmy said in a friendly tone. She looked at Claire with a smile.

"Hi," Claire said, blushing. She looked down at the kids. "I heard you had another baby. She's gorgeous, and Lucas has gotten so big."

"What's your baby's name?" Emmy asked.

I tried not to groan. I still hadn't forgiven Claire for basically trying to trap me, and for screwing some other guy unprotected and not telling me about it. Emmy talked to her casually, and I didn't want to talk to her at all.

"Carrie," Claire answered, smiling adoringly at the girl for a moment before looking back at us. "You have a very nice family."

"Thank you," Emmy said, but I said nothing.

Claire looked at me, waiting for me to say something, but I had nothing to say.

"We were friends once upon a time," she said and then her eyes grew big as if she hadn't meant to say it out loud. She bit her lip and shook her head with a laugh. "Sorry. I really didn't mean to say that."

"Where's Carrie's father?" Emmy brazenly asked. I gawked at her. I couldn't believe she'd bring this up in the middle of the women's dresses with our kids and Claire's kid and every other shopper as an audience.

Claire's smile faltered and fell altogether. She looked at Emmy for a long thoughtful moment through eyes that looked like they'd seen hard times.

"He doesn't want to be a father," Claire answered above a whisper. She wouldn't look at me now.

"Does he help you at all?" I heard myself asking.

She still wouldn't look at me. She shook her head, took a deep breath, and stood up straight. "I can take care of her by myself. I don't need him or anyone else."

I knew Claire. Claire was trying to prove she was stronger than what she really felt. I could see it in her eyes.

Emmy looked at me and I looked back. I already knew what she wanted me to do and I didn't want to do it, but then I hated deadbeat fathers. I sighed deeply and turned my attention back to Claire.

"I can get him," I said and then held up a hand when she started to speak. "I know you said you don't need him. I know you make good money, but that doesn't mean he can shirk his responsibilities."

She looked at me and I could sense the regret she felt. "You would do that for me? Even after..." She faltered and looked at Emmy nervously.

"Even after the whole who's-the-daddy craziness?" Emmy asked her.

Stunned, Claire stared at her. "You know?"

"She's my wife," I said plainly. "She knows everything there is to know about me."

Emmy nodded in agreement.

I had told her about Claire shortly after I proposed to her. I'd felt so guilty for not telling her sooner, but Em soothed that guilt.

She didn't hold it against me because it happened before we were officially back together.

"Besides, I already knew," she'd said casually.

"What?" I'd stared at her disbelievingly. "How?"

"I was looking for something in your desk and found the paternity order," she'd shrugged. "I knew you'd tell me if that baby was yours, because you'd want to do the right thing for Claire and the baby. I wasn't sure if you'd tell me about it if the baby wasn't yours, but then it wouldn't matter, and it doesn't."

We had never spoken about it again, but now Claire stood before us and I pretty much sealed our fate. I'd have to not only talk about Claire again, but I'd have to see her again, repeatedly, until Carrie's father paid up.

Claire seemed to deflate before us, her shoulders sagged and she looked down at Carrie's stroller.

"I can't afford a big legal battle right now," she said and began to shift from foot to foot.

"What are you talking about?" I snorted. "You make great money at that marketing firm."

I didn't particularly want her money, but I was surprised to hear her say she couldn't afford something. Claire had made good money after clawing her way up through the company.

She looked up at me with a sigh. "They forced me to resign my position. I'm not even making half of what I made before."

"Why did they make you resign?" Emmy asked, just as puzzled as me.

"They were okay with me going out on maternity leave," she said and shifted Carrie to her other arm.

The little girl kept smiling and giggling whenever Lucas made his "Vwroom" sound with his cars. Admittedly, she was a very cute kid, though smaller than I expected. Maybe she wasn't as old as I thought. I started to do math in my head, but Claire's next words forced the numbers out of my head.

"Carrie was diagnosed with Cystic Fibrosis shortly after she was born," Claire said. "She's only one and we've spent a tremendous amount of time in the hospital since she was born. My superiors felt it was best I stepped down since I couldn't give them the eighty hours plus a week I used to give to them before Carrie was born," Claire said bitterly.

"They can't do that," Emmy said, and then looked at me. "Can they?"

I ran a hand through my hair. "Depends. Were you keeping up with your work?"

Claire nodded. "I worked right out of her hospital room. If I had to be in a meeting, my mom would go sit with her. It was a struggle, but I gave it more than my best. One of my coworker's had a son with leukemia. He spent a lot of time out of the office and they didn't make him step down."

"How are you paying Carrie's medical bills?" Emmy wondered. "And living day to day."

Claire sighed and a blush rose in her cheeks. "Carrie's bills are growing faster than I can pay them. Between the prescriptions and trying to make up for what I lost, my savings is depleting fast. I have medical insurance, but it's expensive and they are paying for less and less. I'm okay with basic needs, for now, but it's only a matter of time before I find myself standing in line at the county welfare office. The only reason I'm shopping at the mall is because my sister gave me a gift card."

Emmy scowled. "Sounds fucked up."

"Language," I scolded, shaking my head.

She shrugged and said, "Sorry, but it is."

"You should've come to me sooner," I said to Claire.

She gave me a look that said "Really? Should I have? Yeah, right." She didn't say what her eyes said. Even Emmy gave me a sideways look that said, "Yeah, right."

I looked back to Claire. I hadn't wanted to speak to her, but now that I had, I felt bad for her, and I felt bad she couldn't come to me. Another woman was in trouble and felt she couldn't come to me because I would be a jackass, which I probably would've been at first. I hated what Claire did, but what she was going through was beyond any kind of punishment anyone should ever receive.

"Okay, listen," I said. "I'm officially out of the office until the end of January, but I think you need to get started. I'm going to send you to Deluca."

"That scary woman you hated so much?" Claire asked incredulously.

"That scary woman is my friend," Emmy said proudly. "And this is a perfect case for her. She doesn't take any shit, especially from men. She'll legally beat the crap out of Carrie's dad and use your bosses' bodies to wipe up the mess."

I rolled my eyes. Emmy spoke with complete adoration for the heart eating bitch, but she was right. This was a perfect case for Vivian and it would keep the proper distance between me and Claire.

"That's all well and good," Claire said, eyeing Emmy wearily. "But I still don't have the money."

"We'll speak with her first," I said. "I'll have her call you either way."

She looked at me and then Emmy and back to me. Her eyes still flickering back and forth she said, "You don't have to do this. You don't owe me anything."

I didn't. I could've told her good luck and walked away, but like she had said a few minutes before, we used to be friends once. I didn't hate Claire. I didn't love Claire, but the circumstances with her daughter made me care.

"I know," I said with a slow nod. "But we used to be friends once."

She looked relieved that I said that. "Thank you," she said softly and then looked at Emmy. "Thank you both."

We exchanged a few more pleasantries before all the kids started to get restless. Emmy promised her Vivian would be in touch soon. The goodbyes were quick. Claire and Carrie started to walk one way and we started to walk another way. I felt a gentle hand on my elbow. As Em and the kids continued walking, I stopped and faced Claire.

"I just want you to know I wasn't trying to trap you," she said quietly, but her eyes screamed for me to understand. "I had some pretty strong feelings for you and I probably would've given up just about anything to be in her place." She nodded towards Emmy. "But I wasn't trying to trap you. I promise. I'm really happy for you, Luke."

I could feel her sincerity. The animosity I held toward her melted away.

"Thank you, Claire," I said sincerely and squeezed her hand. "Take care."

"You too." She grinned with relief and turned away.

I caught up to my family a moment later. Emmy looked up at me and smiled.

"You are an incredible human being, Luke Kessler," she said lovingly.

I grazed the back of my hand over her soft cheek. "You make me an incredible human being, Emmy."

For half a second, it was only the two of us in the entire world as we gazed into each other's eyes. Then the sounds of Lucas's whining and Kaitlyn's crying and the various noises of the mall brought us back to our reality, but it was a reality I was grateful to be in and there isn't anything or anyone in the world that could shake us from it.

Epilogue

Love (noun)

1. a profoundly tender, passionate affection for another person.

2. a feeling of warm personal attachment or deep affection, as for a parent, child, or friend.

3. sexual passion or desire.

4. a person toward whom love is felt; beloved person; sweetheart.

We are every definition of the word. I give and receive passionate affection. We have warm and personal attachments for our family. We are sexual passion and desire. She is my love and I am hers.

I repeatedly gave her the benefit of doubt, and she repeatedly forgave me for my own actions and words. She wasn't herself, but now she's more than herself. She's perfection in her new skin, after shedding the dead weight of the woman she was not. The woman I loved and have loved for some time fights her way through difficult circumstances, for her friends, and for her children and family. She fights for me, and most importantly, she fights for herself.

The woman I love has a strong mind and a strong soul. She has an abundance of confidence and knows she deserves respect, happiness, and monogamy, and I give her all that and more. Not just because I want to, but because she requires no less. She is faithful, devoted, loyal and true. She is not the most innocent person, but she's not cruel. She curses. She drinks. She flirts with her husband shamelessly, regardless of who's watching. This woman who grew from the ashes of the woman she used to be, is enduring, a weapon to those who dare trifle with those she loves, and a treasure to those fortunate enough to know her. She excites every part of me and she will never break my heart.

When you know in your bones, right down to the cellular level, that you are supposed to be with someone, you hold on to them with everything you have. When you know beyond a shadow of a doubt that someone is your soul mate, the one person in the universe you cannot be without, you fight for her. You knock down whoever gets in your way. You give her every reason to know her place with you. You will give anything and everything you have for her. You will die for her.

Emmy once told me I saved her, that I rescued her from her biggest enemy: herself.

"You picked up all of the pieces and put me back together again," she had said.

"If you're as cracked as your mother, I'll be putting you back together for the rest of our lives."

She punched me. I kissed her.

When my lips finally pulled away from hers, she bit that pretty bottom lip and placed her hand on my heart. Her eyebrows furrowed.

"I'm sorry I broke your heart," she whispered.

"It was a long time ago," I said dismissively.

"But I hurt you so badly." She looked up at me with tears pooled in her eyes.

"Emmy," I said gently, taking her hand in mine. "I was born to love you. I was made to be with you. That was one of many challenges we've had to overcome, and there'll be more, but we'll always face them together. As bad as that time was for us, it didn't ultimately keep us apart, and nothing and no one ever will. I will never stop fighting for you."

"But you already have me," she said, tilting her pretty head.

"If I stop fighting, I become complacent. If I become complacent, you could slip between my fingers, and I am unwilling to let that happen. You will never have to wonder if my heart is still in this. As long as I remain breathing and my heart continues to beat, I'll fight for you."

"I'll fight for you, too."

"You better, Mrs. Kessler." I said, smiling at her. "I am a fine specimen."

She smiled back at me and gently cupped my cheek in one hand. "Yes, you sure are, Mr. Kessler."

"And Em?"

"Yeah?"

"You saved me, too."

And she had. In ways neither of us will ever fully understand. I was incomplete before I knew her. I was broken after I did know her. Now, I am complete. Now, I'm whole again. We saved each other. We fought for each other and our lives together.

We are worth the fight.

The End